A HIGH-STAKES GAMBLE

Vince Petty was a snake. The owner of the Missouri Gunners was dangerous, he was imperturbable, he was brilliant. He was just what Angelina Moore wanted.

"You mentioned a trade on the phone," he said. "I know what you want. Now, what can you do for me?"

"I can save your football team," Angel said. "I can save Julian Lloyd's career."

"But his ACL and MCL are both torn. His kneecap is nicked. And then you have the fractured fibula. The doctors say he'll have to retire before he's played a single game. There goes my eighteen million dollars. Not to mention the whole season, down the tubes," Petty slammed his clenched fists against the desk.

Angel smiled up at him. "Genetics Life has the technology to heal Lloyd and get him back on the field. Of course, doing anything like this without notifying the government would be illegal. And I doubt the NFL would approve if they knew."

Petty gave one, quiet chuckle. "Go on."

"We have to do it quietly," Angel said. "What about Lloyd? Will he go along?"

Petty shook his head. "Not if he knows what it is. He would never go for genetic engineering."

"So you inform him you've found an alternative treatment," Angel said. "Make sure he doesn't know."

"That won't be a problem. When can you start?"

BOOK YOUR PLACE ON OUR WEBSITE AND MAKE THE READING CONNECTION!

We've created a customized website just for our very special readers, where you can get the inside scoop on everything that's going on with Zebra, Pinnacle and Kensington books.

When you come online, you'll have the exciting opportunity to:

- View covers of upcoming books
- Read sample chapters
- Learn about our future publishing schedule (listed by publication month *and author*)
- Find out when your favorite authors will be visiting a city near you
- Search for and order backlist books from our online catalog
- Check out author bios and background information
- Send e-mail to your favorite authors
- Meet the Kensington staff online
- Join us in weekly chats with authors, readers and other guests
- Get writing guidelines
- AND MUCH MORE!

Visit our website at
http://www.kensingtonbooks.com

11TH HOUR

BRADLEY WARSHAUER

PINNACLE BOOKS
Kensington Publishing Corp.
http://www.kensingtonbooks.com

PINNACLE BOOKS are published by

Kensington Publishing Corp.
850 Third Avenue
New York, NY 10022

All Kensington Titles, Imprints, and Distributed Lines are
available at special quantity discounts for bulk purchases for
sales promotion, premiums, fund-raising, and educational or
institutional use. Special book excerpts or customized
printings can also be created to fit specific needs. For details,
write or phone the office of the Kensington special sales
manager: Kensington Publishing Corp., 850 Third Avenue,
New York, NY 10022, attn: Special Sales Department,
Phone: 1-800-221-2647.

Pinnacle and the P logo Reg. U.S. Pat. & TM Off.

First Pinnacle Books Printing: September 2003

10 9 8 7 6 5 4 3 2 1

Printed in the United States of America

Dedicated to my family,
especially Mom and Dad
for all they've done for me.
Go Team Warshauer!

ACKNOWLEDGMENTS

I wish to acknowledge the staff at Kensington for their work on the manuscript, Neil Burstein for his legal help and faith in this story, all those from whom I got an occasional bit of advice, my Dad for actually setting this in motion by mentioning me that night with the editors . . . and most of all God, for this talent that has given me so much personal satisfaction for years. May it now pay off for the whole family. God willing!

Prologue

It was his dream. To be drafted to play the game he loved, and to be paid to play it, was what he had yearned for his entire life. And his dreams would come true in mere moments, on that stage, before fans and team representatives, and announced by the commissioner himself.

Off to the side of the stage was an almost private room where the predicted top half-dozen or so draft picks sat and waited for their cell phones to ring with the eagerly anticipated news. They were young men just out of college—indeed, some were only juniors and in some cases *sophomores*, who had left school when the possibility of a multimillion dollar contract was dangled in front of them, often by an agent hopeful to get a jump on his competition, in exchange for some professional football team's exploitation of their talents.

Julian Lloyd, however, had not only graduated from college, he had graduated with *honors* from the University of Southern California. His talents had made him a Heisman Trophy winner just a few months ago, the completion of his second straight two-thousand yard rushing season as the Trojans' primary offensive weapon.

Julian sat in an expensive leather chair, leaning forward, resting his elbows on his knees and shuffling around. He couldn't get comfortable, and was sweating despite the air-conditioning. He tugged on the collar of his gray tuxedo and sighed. He leaned back and scanned the room.

The moods of the other players were interesting to observe. On the end nearest the entrance to the main room was a big, solemn three-hundred fifty pound offensive lineman from Florida State who kept yawning. Across from him was a wide receiver from Alabama with wide eyes who looked downright scared. And next to *him* was a defensive end who was almost sleeping, with his head back and his eyes closed. Maybe he was just trying to stay calm, Julian thought, but if so, he was doing one heck of a good job.

A few minutes ago, another offensive lineman had been selected by New England. He'd given a few high-fives before lumbering from the room and engulfing the commissioner's hand in a mammoth grip while accepting his honorary jersey and flashing a big smile for the cameras.

Julian took a deep breath. Outside the room, just visible, was a big television screen displaying highlights from the previous season, and then highlights of the former collegians as their selections were announced. Right now the screen was showing the Cincinnati Bengals, who held the second pick. Some experts predicted that they would take him, despite having a solid starting halfback already. Others predicted a trade, while still others felt he would fall lower in the top half of the first round. Julian just wanted to get picked and go home.

He was leaning forward and sighing again when an insistent beeping emitted from his coat pocket. He almost jumped to his feet, but forced himself to remain calm and, with a quivering hand pulled his cell phone out and answered it. He took a quick glance around. The other men in the room were watching him, even the guy who had appeared to be asleep. Bracing himself, Julian said, "Hello?"

"Hello," came a cultured, mature voice. "Julian Lloyd?"

"Yes, sir," Julian said, his heart pounding.

"I'm Vince Petty, owner of the Missouri Gunners," the voice said. "I have good news."

The Gunners? Julian frowned. "Okay."

"We have just completed a trade with the Bengals," Petty said in a voice that almost sounded British, and that registered as a surprise, as the British were all soccer fans, weren't they?

"We've traded up and are going to select you. And I must admit, we traded somewhat heavily." A chuckle. "You were expensive, Julian. But we are ecstatic to have you. Welcome to the team."

Julian felt his mouth hang open. "Well, I . . . thank you, sir. Thank you."

"All right," Petty said. "We've just notified our people over there. They should be taking the announcement up to the commissioner now." A quick glance out into the main room confirmed this; a man was walking up the side steps of the stage, holding a card in his right hand.

"Wow," Julian said.

"Surprised, are you?" Petty said with a chuckle. "Don't worry." A pause. "Well, he's making the announcement. I had better let you go. Congratulations, Julian."

"Thank you, sir," Julian said again, and heard a click. He laughed, not knowing why, and stood up. He laughed again, and pinned the reason on extreme relief when he saw the commissioner walking across the stage.

Julian looked around the room. "I'm going to the Gunners!" he said, smiling, and received a round of cheers from the other would-be draftees. He looked at the stage again, just in time to see the commissioner stop by the microphone and glance at the card.

"The Cincinnati Bengals have traded the second selection in the draft to the Missouri Gunners," he said, reading from the card. "With that second selection, the Gunners choose runningback, from USC—" His next words were drowned out beneath a tsunami of applause from the assembled fans.

Part I
Draft Science

One

The sun filtered into the convention hall, bathing the participants of the first annual Genetic Engineering Awareness Conference in golden light.

He had the audience's complete attention. Five hundred pairs of eyes were transfixed to him, scrutinizing and cataloguing his every move as he stood, a stolid figure looking down at them from the dais. All of them were doctors, most of them physicians, but many were scientists and researchers who held an opposing view. They were the enemy, and they were here for no other reason than to find some parcel of information, some warning of his next move.

Dr. Eric Hendley let his words echo through the room, allowing the room to fall silent before he continued. The audience was watching in silence, motionless, an impressive feat considering they had been sitting in hard metal chairs for over two hours now, listening to this presentation or that, news of one breakthrough or another, one doctor's accomplishment at such-and-such a university. But Hendley knew why they were really here. They were here to listen to *him*, to hear what *he* had to say, and the first few minutes of his presentation had left them ready for more. The brown-haired, youngish-looking fifty-eight-year-old doctor paused for one extra moment, tantalizing his listeners.

"So," he said into the microphone, and that one word seemed to cause a tremor in the audience. "You've seen the side effects. You've seen the dangers inherent in altering the human genetic code. Now let us look at the supposed benefits—or, how those supposed benefits will be abused.

"Athletics, the supporters say, is but a single field in which their revered technology may be used. I agree. The world of athletic competition is a dog-eat-dog world in which only the best triumph. The supporters would use their revered technology to heal the injured, to cure the unfortunate athlete taken down by injury. In fact, that is what I do. I'm a sports doctor. I work with athletes as an orthopedic surgeon. I help them heal in the aftermath of injury.

"But many athletes, indeed, many of those with whom I have had the pleasure to work, would do anything—*anything*—to be the best. They take anabolic steroids, load their bodies with supplements, are always abreast of the next advance in technology that may allow them to gain an advantage. These people have no ethics. They have no morals. They have no sense of fair play or sportsmanship. They merely want to win."

Hendley paused, scanning his listeners. They were nodding and, in the case of many of the scientists, frowning and shifting in their chairs.

"Will these unscrupulous performers stop at healing a torn muscle or broken bone?" he continued. The obvious answer, mouthed by many in the audience, was something Hendley didn't need to say. "What happens when they turn to genetic enhancements to make them better athletes? I don't believe I need to tell you, but I will. These genetically mutated freaks will wreak havoc in their sport, dominating and concentrating the power and influence of their chosen profession onto a paltry few shoulders. This will force their competitors into a corner: Do they abandon the sport they love and have worked for their entire lives, or do they join the crowd, inject a harmless gene or two or three, and return to the medal podium?" He looked straight into the eyes of the nearest audience member. "What would *you* do? Again, the answer is obvious.

"When sports has become a freak show, a worldwide tent

of circus performers, what then? There will be no going back. Football will be no more than professional wrestling, completely scripted, as players become too big, too fast—and too dangerous. Baseball will die, absent of the drama of a record chase in a time when any single-A outfielder can hit sixty home runs.

"Unless something is done *now*"—he slammed his fist against the podium like a politician to accentuate the point— "the world of athletic competition that the people of the civilized world from Athens to New York, through history, have loved, will end. One of the most beloved aspects of human life will vanish."

Hendley sighed and let his eyes wander over the crowd. He was nearing the end of his warning tirade, and still every seat was filled, the aisles clear. He held back a smile and leaned forward on the podium. "And after sports falls victim to manipulation of the human genetic code, what then? The arts. Writing. Painting. Acting. Dancing." He rested an elbow on his speech notes, striking a casual but concerned pose.

"What will become of humanity, our future, unless we act?"

Another pause, to let the speech sink in, and then he stood straight, shuffling the papers on the podium in his hands. He looked ahead, staring frankly at his listeners, ready to give them the only option left to combat the evils of which he had just spoken. "Let me tell you about my nonprofit organization . . ."

Everything was dark. The table was shiny black, the carpet a heavy shade of blue, the walls made of polished wood panels. The people sitting around the table, four men and three women, all wore dark business suits. And all of them had brown or black hair and dark, drab eyes.

Dr. Nicholas Nagel wore a brown wool dinner jacket over a white shirt with gray pants, his dreary attire seeming to glow in comparison. He stood at the foot of the table, his briefcase lying open in front of him, filled with sheets of loose-leaf paper covered with scribbled handwritten notes.

"We can conclude," he said, "that genetic enhancement is the future. Cures for cancer, diabetes, Alzheimer's—real, viable treatments for osteoporosis and muscular dystrophy—these will come not from expensive or risky drugs, or from stem-cell research, but from within the afflicted person himself."

Nagel bit his lip, pushed his glasses up on his nose and closed the briefcase, bringing his presentation to an end. He tried to meet the gazes of the executives sitting around the table, but their dark, piercing eyes bore through him and he looked away, clearing his throat and waiting. Waiting. Finally, the heavyset, middle-aged man sitting at the head of the table shifted in his chair—not much of a reaction, but a reaction nonetheless, and Nagel looked his way.

"How much debt, did you say?" the man—something Austin, an energy tycoon, Nagel remembered—asked.

Nagel took in a deep breath. "Uh . . . about one-point-five million, I believe. Give or take," he added, chuckling nervously.

Austin glanced to his right at one of the women, frowned. "And your annual operating expenses . . . ?"

"Well—um." Nagel clicked open the briefcase and dug through the papers inside, pulling out a typed report covered with numbers. He scanned the pages. "Last year. We spent, oh . . . five-point-eight. Wait, that's just operating costs," he went on as Austin glanced at the man on his left, a bored expression on his face. "Total was—"

"Mr. Nagel," Austin said.

"Dr. Nagel," he muttered.

"Dr. Nagel," Austin went on without missing a beat. "You're asking for a research grant, correct?"

"Yes—that's what I said earlier, in the speech—" He let the paper slide back into the briefcase.

"Yes, you did," Austin said. "But in effect that research grant would be a subsidy for your operating expenses. Your business is one-point-five million dollars in debt, and you need help."

Nagel clenched his jaw. He looked down at the table. He gripped its side, his knuckles turning white.

The woman, Chloe Giles, leaned in. "Dr. Nagel," she said, "we understand your frustrations as fellow businesspeople. But you must understand our perspective. You're asking us to give you, with no possibility of return, a large sum of money to help your company pay off its debts. This money would also go toward supporting a cause that many of our investors tend to shy away from."

"It's just research," Nagel said.

"Controversial research," Austin corrected, stifling a yawn. "And besides, you aren't representing a university. You are the CEO of this company, Genetics . . . Genetics what, did you say?"

"Genetics Life," Nagel said, his stomach sinking. *Another dead end . . .*

"Right," Austin said. "We, as the board of a public corporation, cannot agree to subsidize another company. Just because you're a research company doesn't give you that extra right. If you made computer chips, this presentation would never have taken place."

"That's like . . . apples and oranges," Nagel said.

"Nevertheless," Giles said, "our decision has been made."

Nagel bit his lip. He shook his head, closed the briefcase and picked it up. "Well, I thank you for your time," he choked out, and walked from the room.

The Walker home, nestled in the New Orleans Garden District, was relatively quiet. The kids had control of the TV and Ryan and Vanessa were outside on the deck that overlooked their well-tended and, in Ryan's opinion, overly complicated garden. The house was over a hundred years old, as were most of the others in the neighborhood, and had what Vanessa liked to call "stunning" period architecture.

Their garden was a plot of lush vegetation surrounding a capacious fountain pool in which the kids kept goldfish the size of bass. The goldfish were swimming beneath the deck where it was shady, an attempt to hide from the humid, summer-like heat that was assailing this late April afternoon. Ryan was already starting to sweat as he leaned against the deck railing and lowered his eyes to avert his wife's gaze.

"I need an answer *now*," Vanessa said, crossing her arms over her chest. Her brown shoulder-length hair was hanging around her neck, sticking to her chocolate-colored skin in the humidity.

"It's only April," Ryan said. "I said I'd have a decision. I didn't say when. There's still a few weeks before the first minicamp."

"And you want us to go into football mode in the meantime," Vanessa breathed. Her voice always got quiet when she was frustrated or angry.

"Football mode?" Ryan asked, raising an eyebrow. "No, just normal. Normal life."

"That *is* normal life around this time. Everything goes around you and your football schedule. We aren't doing that this year, Ryan. You'll be on your own."

Ryan looked up, staring into her brown eyes. "I just don't know. I don't know yet. I can't make a decision."

Vanessa snorted out a laugh. "Yeah, that's the problem isn't it."

"Yet," he added. "I can't make one *yet*. Geez." He turned around and leaned forward over the rail, gazing into the pond.

"Right," Vanessa said with a sigh. "Ryan, do you really think you can do it? Do you really think you can go out and spend twenty weeks busting your butt? You're almost forty years old! You're gonna have to let it go one of these days, you know."

"I know," he said. "I know that. I just . . . can't decide now."

"You're stalling."

He didn't reply. He knew she was right; he *was* stalling, because he just didn't know what to do yet. Or maybe he did. Maybe he was just afraid to face it . . .

The sliding glass door opened, and six year-old Leslie stepped outside, holding the phone above her pigtailed head. "Daaad-ee!" she squeaked. "Somebody wants t'talk t'you."

Ryan turned around, gritting his teeth and avoiding eye contact with his wife as he stepped past her to retrieve the phone from his youngest daughter. "Thanks, baby," he said, and held it to his ear. "Walker," he said. He turned his back to Vanessa.

"Ryan," a familiar male voice said. "It's Gary. There's something I need to talk to you about."

What would Coach Harrell want with him on draft day? "Okay, Gary. What's up?"

"You haven't been watching?" Harrell asked, the pitch of his voice rising as if he was a little alarmed.

Ryan frowned; he could sense Vanessa's impatience and heard the deck creak as she shifted her weight from one foot to the other. "Uh, no, Gary. I haven't."

"Well, ah . . ." Harrell sounded uncomfortable. "I suppose it's a good thing I called. We just made our first-round pick about ten minutes ago."

"That's great," Ryan said. *Get to the point.*

Harrell sighed. "We took Falk, the kid from Notre Dame."

It felt like somebody had dropped a lead weight in Ryan's stomach. He gulped, and it was a moment before he could reply. "The—the linebacker? Inside linebacker?"

"Yeah, David Falk." Another sigh. "Look, Ryan, we're planning on starting him inside. We feel like he'll fit right in. He's a good kid."

"Ah . . . Gary . . ." Ryan bit his lip. What to say? "You aren't . . . uh . . . planning on going to the three-four, are you?"

The coach chuckled a little. "No, Ryan. We're not changing the scheme. We're just—well, we're replacing you in it." Finally, the point.

"So . . . you won't be needing me around, huh?" Ryan

asked, knowing how the question would sound to his wife, who was still standing behind him.

"Actually we will," Harrell said, his voice a little brighter. "You're still a key player. We need a veteran backup at the position, somebody to show the new kid the ropes. You fit the bill, Ryan. And you'll take time on special teams, if it works out that way." A laugh. "Hell, you're more important to the team now than ever before!"

Ryan nodded, rubbing his sweaty forehead with his free hand. "Okay, Gary. Thanks for the call."

"No problem. I'll see you at workouts then?"

"Yeah."

"All right. Bye."

Ryan hung up and turned to face Vanessa. She was standing with her arms crossed, her weight on one leg, tapping her foot. "What was that about?"

Ryan scratched at the back of his neck. His military-style crewcut was getting itchy. Humidity. Anxiety. He cleared his throat. "Gary called," he told her. "He . . . he said we drafted David Falk, from Notre Dame."

"The linebacker?" Vanessa asked. She smiled.

"Yeah, him. He's going to start." There, he'd said it. And the reaction was just what he'd expected.

"Great," she said, her smile broadening. "You've been replaced. Now you don't have to worry about feeling guilty."

"Actually it isn't that simple," Ryan said, a smile of his own clawing at his mouth. "Gary needs me to stick around, to help bring him in. Heck, I bet experience can beat out speed, even."

Vanessa closed her eyes and turned away, reaching for the door. "Well, that's your decision."

Ryan pursed his lips. He wasn't sure what to say. "Yeah. Yeah, that's it."

Vanessa nodded. "Okay. You're on your own with it this year." She turned to meet his gaze. "Don't expect support from us again. This is your decision, and you're going to do it alone."

"I understand," Ryan said.

She turned back to the door and pulled it open. "I hope you do," she said, and stepped inside, sliding the door closed behind her and leaving Ryan on the deck.

Alone.

Two

Genetics Life, Incorporated was converted from a small warehouse, between Highway 141 and a railroad line just outside St. Louis, Missouri. The warehouse had been spacious and versatile enough that, with the proper time, effort and money, it had been transformed into a static, sterile environment safe for medical experimentation. Inside, the warehouse was divided into five main sections—two laboratories, one fully-equipped operating room, one clean storage room where test animals were kept, and a dusty conference room where the company board was supposed to meet—with tributary hallways and corridors that led to individual offices and the small entrance lobby. Walking through the hallways, one could imagine being in a small hospital. The floor was hard gray carpet in the halls and white tile in the rooms, everything was brightly lit and the offices, though small, had a professional air about them. Each of them was supplied with a credenza and relatively up-to-date computer and each of them had internet access over a T1 line.

Nagel's office was a little larger than the others, though similarly furnished. It was colder than the rest of the building, though that was attributable to the central AC unit's location, just behind the room. His desk was cluttered with notes and pens and books, and the little trash bin beside it was overflowing with crumpled paper.

He sighed as he read over another income report. Genetics Life was compiling debt at an ever-increasing rate. More than 2.2 million total, an average of over $35,000 lost per month.

And Nagel could do nothing to stop it. The two months since his meeting with Austin and his board had produced nothing but more red ink.

He lay the report on top of a stack of clutter and ran his hands through his thinning brown hair. Nothing. There was nothing more he could do. All his attempts to find a research grant, or a sponsorship, or more investors—all those attempts had failed. The problem was . . . well, he didn't know exactly *what* the problem was. Genetics enhancement as a technology was being met with public skepticism, although no one questioned its commercial value. In fact, that might've been the problem, right there. It had so much commercial viability that too many companies had sought to exploit it in too short a time. There wasn't enough money to go around. Add that to the opposition coming from the green crowd, and the questioning nature of a public terrified of "GMOs" and a small corporation like GLI had as much of a chance as a duck swimming in a river full of piranhas.

GLI was a small association of some of the finest geneticists and doctors in America. That was something to take a bow for. Three years ago, Nagel had, over a period of eight months, sought after and hired four of the top scientists in the field. By making them equal partners and giving them what had been at the time an ample budget, supported by a diversified group of investors, they had combined their knowledge, matched and then overtaken the opposition. In three years, Genetics Life had developed no less than a five year lead over the nearest competitor. But when the investors pulled out, that budget had dwindled to almost nothing. Now they were floundering, almost dead in the water, and the sharks were circling.

Larger companies, huge industrial types that had managed to come up with a few key ideas to exploit the open market, were drooling over the tiny GLI's confidential research. Just this week Nagel had received three new offers from big genetic research corporations. One was a direct buyout while the other two were offers of partnership that would supply the larger company with all of the information, all of the techniques Nagel and his partners had discovered and perfected. GLI would, in turn, receive support and funding to keep the company operating. Not an inviting proposition, especially to Nagel's fellow researchers—

His door swung open. Nagel looked up in time to see Dr. Angelina Moore glide into his office without so much as a knock to announce her presence. The tanned, blond, thirty-year-old scientist smiled at him. "Hi, Nick."

"Hello, Angel."

Angel flopped into a chair across from him. Nagel just looked at her. Didn't she realize he had more important things to do than chitchat—

"The weekly income report," Angel said, as if she was reading his mind. "You wanted to talk to me about it?"

"I did?" Nick's brow furrowed. He didn't remember that . . . but hell, she was probably right. He'd been absentminded lately.

"Yes," Angel said, frowning. "You don't remember? I mean, I can come back if you're busy—"

"No, that's all right." Nagel picked up the report in question and handed it to her, then folded his hands on the desk in front of him. "That's it. You can take it. Is there anything else?"

She put the report back on the desk and leaned closer. "I see we haven't had any luck in the investors' department. Why is that?"

Something about the question . . . the way she said it . . . Nagel frowned. "Same old story. The bigwigs don't want to risk joining as investors, and don't feel comfortable with giving a research grant."

"What do you think the problem is?" Angel asked. She stared at him, her hands crossed on the desk in front of her. Watching. She wanted something.

"I don't know," Nagel said. "I guess—"

"They're looking for something in return," Angel said. "They aren't going to *give* away their money." Her lips twisted into a fiendish little half-smile. "You should know that."

"Well, what the hell do we have to give them?" Nagel demanded, his blood boiling. He clenched his fists. "You wanna sell out? I thought you were against that! I asked you about the idea and you—"

"No, Nick, I don't want to sell out," she soothed, in the way a mother might speak when trying to get a point across to a temperamental teenager.

"Then what?" he asked, her tone calming him down. He relaxed his hands and folded them again on the desk.

"I think you know," Angel said. She leaned in even closer, until her face was a foot from his. "I've brought it up before."

What was she getting at?

Nagel thought for a moment, trying to figure it out, just staring at her. Then it hit him. "No," he snapped. "Absolutely not." He backed away from her, straightening up in his chair.

"Don't blow off the idea," Angel said, sitting back. She reached for her hair and tied it up in a ponytail. "It might be our only chance." She shook her head, flinging her hair from side to side like a mare swinging its mane. "You know?"

"Yeah, well. It's illegal, Angel," Nagel said. "We don't have the proper approval to even run a gene-mod clinical trial on humans. Besides," he added, "name one potential subject. Name one person with both the will and the means."

She opened her mouth to reply, but he went on before she could speak. "See?" he said. "You can't. So just drop it. We'll have to find another way."

Angel nodded slowly. "I'm sorry, Nick. I'll drop it. You're right. We don't have the approval now and we'll probably never get it. Sorry."

Nagel's eyebrows shot up. "Thank you. Now, we just have to think for a while, consider all the options. You know? Something will present itself. In the meantime, we'll just hold on as long as we can."

They were silent for a moment, the only sound the hum of his computer's cooling fan and the distant rumble of the big air-conditioning unit.

"Are there any new options?" Angel asked. "Possible investors, open-minded corporations, something like that?"

Nagel laughed at the hopelessness of the situation. "I've been all over the Midwest," he said. "It would be nothing but repeats now."

Angel looked past him, tapping her nails on the desk. Then she turned her gaze back to him. "I may have some contacts," she said. "Do you think I should get in touch with them? Just for the heck of it. Maybe I'll poke around for a month or two. You never know," she added.

"Couldn't hurt anything," Nagel admitted. He felt a little uneasy with that idea . . . *oh, forget it!* he ordered himself. Screw it. What *could* she hurt? And maybe she could actually help—she had one thing he didn't, a pretty face. And maybe the bigwigs were just vain enough to take something like that into consideration. She was also much more persuasive than he, and younger, and probably smarter . . . Nick frowned. Why hadn't *he* thought of it?

"That's a yes?" Angel asked.

"Yes," Nagel said. "Go ahead. Sic 'em."

"All right," she said, standing up. "I'll get started. See you later, Nick." She turned for the door, but stopped, reached back and grabbed the income report. "Don't wanna forget this," she said, and left.

Nagel chuckled, allowing himself to feel some humor this time. "What have I unleashed?" he asked the world, and laughed.

The agent gave his counteroffer, and Geoffrey Marsh grimaced. Vince Petty, on the other hand, just smiled at the man and glanced at his general manager, his expression a dire warning to *pick up the pace!*

They were in Petty's office inside the Missouri Gunners training facility, sitting around his large black desk. Behind Petty's seat was a shelf filled with binders and books, information on potential signees, scouting reports on next year's rookies and even police background checks on current players. That was a sign of the times, Petty thought. The floor was covered with plush navy carpeting, the team logo imprinted in the center of the room like the presidential seal in the Oval Office. The walls were pristine white, with nary a scratch or smudge, and the temperature was well-regulated by a high-tech "Weather Control" unit that kept the heat and humidity to a minimum.

Marsh was sweating anyway, his white shirt collar soaked and his thick brown hair plastered to his head. His face was pale and flushed. Petty, twenty years older than the GM, with thin gray hair, a healthy complexion, and a cultured smile, just nodded to the agent.

"While Geoffrey considers that, why don't we talk about the base salary structure, Mr. Kovac?" Petty suggested.

"Okay," the agent said. He was a skinny little man with a mustache and black hair that was so covered with hair spray that it looked like plastic. He spoke with a New England accent that not even years of training in the art of haggling could erase. Assuming he *had* training, Petty thought. Sometimes "agents" were nothing of the sort, and the result was often an athlete with the contract from hell. Or heaven, if your perspective was that of the team involved. "I propose a base salary of five-point-one million this season that'll go up to five point eight incrementally in three years," Kovac continued. "Year five is an option year on your end. Pay him eight million even, or he walks as a UFA. Nothing outlandish, if you know what you're—"

Marsh held up a finger. "Ah . . . but with a ridiculous signing bonus like the one you mentioned a minute ago . . . I mean, his base salary would be five-point-one this year, but end up . . ." He stared at the ceiling for a moment, then looked back at Kovac ". . . counting as eight-point-eight million. That's a huge cap number."

"We can afford it," Petty whispered in a neutral tone. No need to fluster poor Geoffrey any more than he already was.

"I know we can afford it," Marsh said acidly, glancing at his boss. "But do you realize what will happen if for some reason we have to cut him? Or if he retires? All of that signing bonus will come back and hit us all at once. Do you know what his cap value will be *then?"*

"Geoffrey," Petty said in a warning tone.

"I'm sorry, Mr. Petty," Marsh said. "But we sent this guy a reasonable offer. Of course we're willing to look at a counteroffer, but *this is crazy!"* He turned to the agent. "Mr. Kovac, who do you think your client is? Superman? I know we traded a lot to get him, and I know he was the second overall selection, but that doesn't give you the right to an eighteen million dollar signing bonus!"

Kovac just sat there, his hands folded in his lap. "My client risked a lot to work the May minicamp," he breathed. "He wasn't under contract. If he had been injured, he would have received little compensation. But he wanted to get up here and work with the team. Now we want to get this thing done before the June minicamp starts. We've done you people a favor. Now you need to bend a little and work with us."

Marsh almost jumped out of his chair. "You're full of crap!" he said, his face turning red. "Every damn rookie in the league worked that camp! You think Lloyd is so special? Talk to the thirty-one other first rounders. They sure as hell aren't asking for any eighteen million dollar signing bonus. That money comes straight out of Mr. Petty's pocket—"

"Correct," Petty interrupted. Marsh shut up and sat back down, staring at his boss. "We are talking about my money, Geoffrey. Not yours. Not even the team's. Mine. I'm perfectly willing to front the cost necessary to get Julian signed early."

"But Mr. Petty—"

Petty held up his hand and turned to Kovac. "I want you to bring the papers to my office tomorrow morning. Be sure to contact Julian and have him come so we can get everything done then."

Kovac's mouth dropped a little, but a quick shake of his head erased his shocked expression. He held out his hand, and Petty shook it. "It's been a pleasure working with you, sir," the agent said.

"Likewise," Petty replied, and watched Kovac leave. He turned to Marsh as soon as the door clicked shut behind him.

The general manager's face was still red, and the veins in his neck were visible. He was panting as if he'd just run wind sprints with the team. "Do you know what you just did, Vince?" he demanded.

"Yes, I know what I just did," Petty said, raising his voice but not shouting. "I signed my first-round draft pick before any other team in the league. Julian Lloyd will be in camp, on time, and he will work with the team for the remainder of the offseason. He will not hold out, he will not alienate his teammates and the fans who support us, and he will give himself the head start he needs to be successful immediately."

"But Vince, for heaven's sake!" Marsh rasped. "What if something happens? It's bad enough we're mortgaging our future on one player, but if something goes wrong, that mortgage will be foreclosed! That signing bonus is a bomb waiting to go off. If Julian has to retire, or if we have to release him after signing the contract—for any reason—you're looking at us jumping ten million dollars over the cap right before the season. We'd never recover from that!"

"Let me worry about our necks, Geoffrey," Petty said. "I assure you, nothing will go wrong." Geoffrey was in self-preservation mode, Petty realized. It happened sometimes to front office personnel. Too many owners dropped the blame for their mistakes on their subordinates' shoulders these days for those subordinates not to feel uneasy with an owner's personal decision. "I will take all responsibility for anything that may go wrong," Petty assured him.

"But Vince—"

"It's done! Get hold of yourself, Geoffrey."

Marsh glared at him for a moment, then dropped his gaze. "Okay. As long as you take responsibility in the event that something happens . . ."

"Of course," Petty said.

Marsh took a deep breath. "Then I'll sign. But I still don't agree with it."

"That's your opinion, and you're entitled to it," Petty cooed. "Now, let's get back to work. We still have two draftees to sign, and I want their contracts completed within the next two weeks. I'll leave them to you. And Geoffrey," he added, "Nothing specific comes out of this meeting from our end. Do you understand?"

Marsh nodded. "Yes, Vince. I understand."

"Eighteen million dollars?" Julian asked, gaping at Kovac. They were sitting at the table in the kitchenette of his new apartment in St. Louis. It was a small but cozy place, with a living room, bedroom and bathroom besides the kitchenette. The rooms were always comfortable, and the large window beside the couch allowed the entire area to be lit by sunlight alone. And if what Kovac was telling him wasn't an outright lie, he had a feeling he'd be moving out of this place a lot sooner than he'd expected.

"Eighteen-point-five," Kovac said.

"And it's definite?" Julian asked, his head swimming. "It's real?"

"It's real," Kovac assured him. "We're signing the contract tomorrow. Be at the headquarters in the morning, first thing."

"I can't believe this," Julian said. "It's like a dream."

Kovac smiled and stood. "I know. Be there tomorrow." They shook hands, exchanged goodbyes, and the agent left. Julian strolled into the living room and sank into his sofa.

Eighteen-point-five million dollars.

For a black kid whose father had been murdered when he was just six years old, this could be nothing more than a dream.

Julian laughed. He felt giddy. Drunk with excitement and disbelief.

A dream.

He grabbed for his phone, dialed a number. Three rings, and then it was answered.

"Hello?" The gentle, feminine voice of a woman in her late fifties.

"Ma? This is Julian." He took a deep breath and held a hand over his face in amazement. "You're not going to believe this," he said.

He didn't either.

One of Humanity International Company's three modified Airbus A340 airliners soared high above the Atlantic, bound for New York from London. HUMINT CEO and president Lance Pollard sat in his private cabin in the rear of the plane, resting on the small leather couch that acted as his bed during these long trips.

The cabin, a small but elegant room, carpeted and furnished with a cooler and television and first-class caliber restroom, besides the couch, was but one part of the HUMINT jet's many comforts. The plane, like its two twins sitting in their hangar at Pollard's private airport outside San Diego, was a veritable Air Force One. Though smaller than its presidential cousin, the converted A340 was no less a technological wonder. All its seats were removed and separate rooms were built into the fuselage. In the small passenger cabin that remained, a space that had once encompassed thirty seats now held six reclining leather chairs complete with a built-in phone, radio CD player and miniature TV. One of the rooms acted as a commercial kitchen, where a crew of chefs prepared meals on demand. Pollard's cabin had internet access and a satellite phone system capable of putting him in contact with any of his vital personnel anywhere in the world. So he could run his company and eat a five star meal on the way home from a conference in London, all while flying 30,000 feet above the ocean.

Pollard, a fit, twice-divorced white man in his late forties, who happened to be a pioneer in the commercial exploitation of the human genome and a self-made billionaire, tapped a few keys on his laptop and made a high-speed satellite connection to the internet. He opened his VideoCall program and tapped in the correct code, then waited. If his people followed orders—which they always did—this wouldn't take long at all.

It didn't. His call was answered almost immediately, and the crystal-clear image of an ordinary-looking dark-haired woman appeared. "Dr. Pollard," she said in a deep, rich, 1920s stage-actress voice. It was a fortunate thing she didn't have the looks to match the voice, Pollard thought, or she'd probably be spending her time on Rodeo Drive instead of working for him.

"Yes," Pollard said, scratching the side of his nose. "You have the information I requested?"

"Yes I do," the woman said. "I've faxed it to headquarters. It'll be there when you arrive."

"Excellent," Pollard said, sitting up straighter on the couch. Good posture, his mother used to say, was a vital part of a positive first-impression. Surely she had the best posture of all the residents in that nursing home . . . "I know you did a good job," he complimented her.

"Of course I did," the woman said, smiling. Pollard covered up a grimace. His next words wouldn't be so well received.

"That's wonderful. Now the bad news. I want you to stay there a little longer," he said. "You can say your job offer fell through. I need continued information over the next few months and you're the only person in a position to get it."

To his surprise, the woman didn't react at all. She just looked at him, her face expressionless on the computer screen.

"Of course, if anyone begins to suspect something, you should get out," Pollard said. "I can't have you linking your-self to me. They won't exactly appreciate our spying on them."

"No, they won't," the woman admitted.

"I know you're ready to finish up," Pollard continued. "And you will. After this, you deserve a long trip down in the Bahamas or something. But for now, keep up the good work."

"I will," the woman said. "But I'd prefer Switzerland." Smiling, she cut off her connection.

Pollard shut down the laptop, closed it and set it aside. Then he stretched his arms over his head and lay back. Another two hours to JFK International in New York, and then a half hour layover while the plane refueled, followed by another long flight cross-country to HUMINT headquarters in San Diego. A long, tiring trip ahead. He yawned. Might as well get some sleep.

Switzerland. *Ha!*

He'd always liked the Bahamas.

Three

The weight room at New Orleans Saints Headquarters on Airline Drive in Metairie, Louisiana was well-stocked with equipment and brightly lit. It smelled of sweat, a by-product of hours and hours of men at work. Several players, men of varying shapes, sizes, races and temperaments, walked among the machinery and weight benches while others lay back lifting barbells or working this machine or that. Many were assisted by trainers, themselves assistants to the team Head Athletic Trainer, who now observed the activity from the doorway.

Most people in the real world would pay dearly to gain access to a place like this, but in the pro football world, it was the players themselves who were paid. They usually had contract incentives that guaranteed tens or even hundreds of thousands of dollars for working out on the prescribed off-season conditioning days, a sick role reversal that made entirely too much sense. To survive the twenty to twenty-four weeks of gladiatorial combat that encompassed professional football's preseason, regular season and postseason, the combatants had to be in the best physical shape possible. Even the apparently overweight three-hundred-pound linemen spent hours upon hours working out, and most could run forty yards in a scant five seconds, faster than most healthy 180-pound men.

Ryan's contract incentive for appearing at HQ today was a paltry $11,500. That sum had been determined the last time he'd extended and renegotiated his contract with the Saints, five years ago. Which was, not coincidentally, the year of his last Pro Bowl appearance. He hadn't thought about that money during his commute from the Garden District, though. Not that he didn't care—he did—but he had a new incentive for reaching and maintaining his optimum playing weight of 248 pounds, packed onto his six-foot-three form. That incentive was David Falk.

Ryan lay back on a weight bench, supporting a barbell across his chest. The 225-pound bench press, a standard measurement of strength in football. There was no trainer assisting him, no team official to log his repetitions. But he didn't need to log this. It was purely for himself. If he forgot his total in an hour, then so be it.

The first rep was easy. His ripped, bulging arms were accustomed to fifteen years of bench pressing, and this year was no different. Ryan breathed slowly, lifting slowly, concentrating on doing everything nice and slow. No need to hurry. Push against the weight, raise it high, and gently lower it. His arms were burning by the fifth rep, but he ignored the sensation and went on to do a sixth and seventh. Then the burning increased in intensity, flames within his arms. It was getting harder to breathe as his chest contracted when he raised and lowered the eighth repetition. With the ninth, he saw his biceps quivering, and on the tenth his chest muscles did likewise. Not good. Only ten reps . . .

He strained against the weight, struggling through the eleventh and twelfth. He could barely lift the thirteenth, and had to work hard to keep from dropping the bar when lowering it. A quick, deep breath to try and regain control, and then he *pushed* the weight up, as hard as he could . . . and lowered it again . . . fourteen. *One more,* he thought, blinking to keep sweat from dripping into his eyes. One more . . . lift . . . his arms rubbery, on fire, burning rubber . . . stop . . . lower . . . and . . . fifteen. Ryan got the barbells onto the rack and then just lay on the bench, breathing.

Fifteen reps in early June. Not very good for a veteran linebacker, he knew. There were rookie wide receivers at the scouting combine who could lift fifteen reps—or sixteen, seventeen, eighteen or nineteen.

But he had time. It just took him a little longer to get into real football shape these days. By training camp he'd be fine.

Breathing in his nose, out his mouth, one more controlled breath, he pulled himself up to a sitting position, then stood. He started to turn around—

"Hello, Ryan."

—and finished just as David Falk himself seemed to materialize in front of him.

"Uh . . . hi," Ryan said, managing not to grimace. This had to be the last person he felt like seeing right now. He took the time to scan the rookie. David Falk was taller than Ryan by a good two inches, and packed with even more muscle, but had a pale, blue-eyed All-American face that displayed a wholesome charm beneath a mound of blond hair. His appearance told his story: *Midwestern kid escapes farm with scholarship to Notre Dame. Leads third-best defense in country and helps the Irish return to the top ten in junior season. Wins multiple awards senior year and is drafted in the first round by the vaunted powerhouse of the . . . New Orleans Saints.*

"I don't want to keep you, but I did want to say hi before I got to work," Falk said cheerfully. "I've wanted to meet you for a long time."

"Oh," Ryan said. "Really."

Falk nodded, and swung a towel over his shoulder. "You bet. I've been watching you play since I was eight."

Bam! Ryan felt as though he'd been punched in the gut.

"That's great," he managed, unable to say much else. *Since I was eight,* he repeated mentally. *What the hell!* The kid obviously wasn't skilled on the proper way to compliment his elders, Ryan thought cynically. *Never put age in the picture!* Looking at the physical monster Falk was now didn't help much. Ryan could do little more than observe the sharp lines of the rookie's diamond-cut body beneath his workout clothes, and scratch his head in wonder.

Since I was eight.

"I'll get out of your hair," Falk said, walking toward a weight bench. "Looking forward to working with you, sir!"

Stymied and unable to move, Ryan just nodded. "Uh, right. Same here." He gulped, and decided most definitely *not* to relate this little incident to Vanessa when he got home.

No sir-ee.

Eighteen million dollars in the bank.

Julian walked into the Gunners training facility weight room, still not entirely believing that figure despite the fact that he'd signed the contract and then confirmed the presence of the money in his account.

What to spend it on? He could think of nothing. Nothing he really needed or wanted right now. He felt a little uncomfortable when thinking about that: *What should I spend $18 million on?* Two weeks ago, spending *eighteen dollars* was something he could only do with foresight.

And he couldn't forget the actual salary. Five million over sixteen weeks. More money there than he'd ever dreamed of, but suddenly it seemed like chump change.

His mother wasn't having that problem, though; she was already going through the upscale Chicago neighborhoods looking for a new house. Though Julian couldn't blame her. Lord knew she deserved it.

Okay, concentrate. He went to the nearest bench, checked the barbell's weight, then lay back and got ready to press 225. He lifted the weight off the rack, lowered it to his chest, and then breezed through five repetitions. His arms didn't begin to burn until the sixth, and his chest didn't hurt until the ninth. By fourteen, the weight was bearing down on him, getting harder to lift, but still nothing he couldn't handle. Focus on the weight, his muscles, the effort . . . he noticed someone approaching out of the corner of his eye, but didn't look.

"Lloyd! I see you're hittin' it early," the person said, the voice an affable male Texas drawl.

Julian didn't answer, still concentrating as he completed his sixteenth and seventeenth reps.

"Whew!" the man continued. "You got arms like a line-backer!"

Eighteen, and then he strained hard, forcing out his breath to complete the nineteenth and final rep. Julian breathed in and sat up, turning to face the man.

It was Rich Mitchum, the starting quarterback, a six-five, 220-pound lead-footed pocket passer with a cannon for a right arm. Mitchum had a towel draped around his neck and wore a tank top and team-logo workout shorts, but wasn't sweating. His blond hair was combed back, and his light green eyes were bright and cheery.

"Mitchum," Julian said, standing and extending his hand. They shook, and Julian smiled. "Nice to meet you."

"You too," Mitchum said, holding the ends of the towel and hanging his elbows. "You know, it's nice to see some rookie youngster zeal out of you," he smiled, "but you might wanna take it easy to start. The old man'll work you boys hard come minicamp."

Julian shrugged. "The last one wasn't that bad."

"I wasn't there," Mitchum said. "It was optional for us vets. When it's just the rooks, Coach goes easy on 'em. But when you got everybody together, like it's gonna be at the camp coming up . . . well, then it gets hairy. Ya know he was a Marine, huh?"

"I thought he was an Army Ranger," Julian said, grabbing a towel off of the rack beside the bench and wiping his face.

"Whatever," Mitchum said as if it made no difference. "But he runs the second minicamp like boot camp. And then just wait 'til *training* camp. Man! I'm talking two-a-days, *every* day, plus a three-a-day or two thrown in to keep it interesting. Get up at five and have a full-pads workout. Break for study the rest of the mornin' and then you got another practice at noon. Study again—and the studying's brutal for the rooks—

and then a no-pads walk-through. You ready for an average day at Camp Jake Davis?"

Julian grinned and slapped a hand on Mitchum's shoulder. "More than ready," he said.

Mitchum laughed. "Oh, don't forget about the hazing," he said. Julian frowned. "Naw, don't worry. Ain't that bad. Can you sing or dance?"

"Well . . . I can sing, actually. But I can't dance," Julian said, scratching his head. "Why?"

"That's great!" Mitchum said, as if he hadn't heard the question. "I'll tell the guys you'll be dancin' at the show." Mitchum offered his hand again and Julian shook it. "See ya later, Julian," he said, and walked past him to an upper-body weight machine.

"What show?" Julian asked the air, frowning and moving on to the next machine.

When Ryan stepped onto the sidewalk leading to the front door of his home, the mid-June sun was nearing the horizon, disappearing behind a line of trees to the west. The air was still hot and muggy in the golden twilight glow, but he didn't really notice as he opened the door and went inside.

The house was almost quiet. He could hear one of the kids playing a video game in the den, ahead and to the left, but other than that the only sound was that of his own footfalls against the wood floor. Ryan closed the door and went right, to the dining room, and through it to the kitchen.

Vanessa was indeed there, as he'd expected. She was standing at the counter, tossing a salad. She glanced up at him, but then went back to work. Ryan walked over to her.

"Hey, babe," he said, leaning over for a quick kiss.

She gave him one, but pulled back. "You have something to say?" she asked. She didn't sound angry, but was most definitely not happy.

And he was expecting that, too.

"Yes," Ryan said, pulling off his light workout jacket and folding it over his arm. "Yes, I do. I'm sorry."

Vanessa stopped tossing, set the spoons aside and picked up a bottle of dressing next to the bowl. She poured a quarter of the bottle into the salad before answering. "I'm glad. But don't tell me," she said. "Tell Dylan."

Ryan nodded. "Okay." He took a breath, bracing himself. "He's in his room?"

Vanessa nodded.

Ryan turned, backtracking through the dining room to the foyer and then thumping up the stairs, turning left and stopping at a closed white door. He tapped the door with his knuckles and waited.

"Come in," Dylan called from inside. Ryan opened the door and went in.

Dylan Walker was fourteen, and looked just like his father, or so Ryan liked to think. He was a light-complexioned African-American—much lighter in skin tone than Vanessa—with his Dad's military crewcut and penchant for athletics. Dylan preferred baseball, however, as his room's decoration attested. Posters of Sammy Sosa, Barry Bonds and that Ichiro guy lined the beige-painted walls. But the center of attention was an autographed photo of Mark McGuire from 1998 that Ryan had finagled from a former Gunners player who'd spent some time with the Saints and had a friend on the Cardinals baseball team.

Dylan was reclining on his bed, reading a book. A peek at the cover identified it as some baseball hitting manual, written by some genius coach or other. Ryan stepped deeper into his son's abode. "How you doing, Dyl?" he asked. He noticed he was still carrying his jacket. He tossed it onto the homework desk to his right.

"I'm good," Dylan said, looking over the book. "Real good."

"Really?" Ryan asked. "Or are you just messing with me?"

Dylan closed the book and grinned. "I'm messing with ya."

"Figured that," Ryan said, returning the smile. "Look, son,

I'm real sorry about missing the game today. You know I wanted to be there."

"I know, Dad," Dylan said. He opened the book again. "But baseball's not your thing, anyway. It's no big deal."

"No, that's not it," Ryan said. "I just had to get into film study with Coach . . . I mean, you know how it is. But I should've been there. It isn't every day you're in a city all-star game."

"Yeah," Dylan said. "Well, there's always next year, huh?"

"And next year will be different," Ryan said. "I promise."

Dylan's eyes went to the book, and he sighed. "Yeah, Dad. I know."

Ryan nodded, not liking his son's apathetic tone . . . but what could he do? He grabbed his jacket and backed out of the room. "I'll call you down for dinner," he said, awaiting Dylan's delayed, "Okay," and then he closed the door and headed downstairs to greet his daughters.

Angel's office was smaller but neater than Nagel's and, due to its more confined location in one of the corners of the building, was far more quiet. A narrow corridor connected it to the rest of the small GLI complex, a corridor that could be avoided by Angel's coworkers on the rare instances they were required to pass by the area. The office itself was furnished the same as Nagel's, with a credenza/desk and a file cabinet lined against the back right corner the largest objects in the room.

Angel sat behind her desk scanning a list she'd compiled of names and phone numbers, her shoulder-length dirty-blond hair hanging around her head. Possible investors and patients were her main interests. She went though the names one-by-one, calling the listed numbers and asking if that person's group or this person's company was interested in entering a partnership with or providing investors to a small medical research corporation like Genetics Life. Unfortunately, the first part of the company's title usually scared people off as soon as it was mentioned, and it didn't seem to matter what the person's political leanings were. Those left of the middle asked about possible harm to the environment while those right of the middle warned about the evils of human cloning.

Working through the first three quarters of the list was a continuing exercise in tedium. The last quarter was even worse. Angel had singled out a few people, most of them patients with only months to live that she thought might consent to join a testing trial. But most of these people, it seemed, already had undergone some trial or another, and as a result knew what questions to ask. And Angel couldn't supply them with the answer to one in particular: *How long have you had FDA approval?*

She crossed another name off the list and tossed it aside, holding her chin in her hands. She hadn't spent seven years in college and graduate school earning a doctorate in physiology and human genetics—and then spending a few more working at the Genome Sequencing Center at Washington University in St. Louis—to spend her time begging for money.

Nicholas Nagel. It was his fault, Angel thought. His responsibility. As a researcher he was brilliant. But as the chief executive of a company—a company that *should* have been thriving, by all rights—he was downright incompetent.

So, now it was up to her to clean up this mess and save the company.

Just the way she wanted it to be.

Angel smiled, leaning back in her chair.

The only way Nagel could be removed from his executive position was a majority vote in a meeting of the board. But that board was made up of researchers now. There were no real outside investors with whom she could safely bargain with or lobby. And she couldn't afford to have Nagel know she was working for his removal. He had the power to fire her without a second thought if he felt threatened.

First things first. The company needed to be saved, and to

do that it needed its debts paid off, either through a research grant of some sort or a rapid influx of new investors. Then, and only then, would it be worth it to get Nagel demoted or removed. Then a new, business-savvy CEO would replace him and Genetics Life, Incorporated, a small company stocked with brilliant scientists, would grow into a remunerative member of a burgeoning industry.

But first things first. Angel grabbed the list again, read the next name on it and picked up her phone.

Four

The shrill blast of the coach's whistle pierced the morning air, signaling the end of warmups and stretching. Forty-three men, every current offensive player on the Missouri Gunners roster, jumped to their feet and waited for the next instruction.

Julian scanned the scene as he stood. The sun was rising over the trees and fence separating the highway from the practice facility, slowly burning off the morning mist and warming the mild air. The coaches, wearing caps with the team logo and gray shirts and shorts, walked among the players. On the other field, across the facility from here, the defensive and special teams players were just finishing their own warmups.

The whistle blew again, bringing Julian's attention to its source: Jacob Davis, coach of the Missouri Gunners. Davis was an imposing former Army Ranger turned tight end turned coach, with graying, jet-black hair and intense blue eyes. He stood before his offense, holding a clipboard. "All right," he shouted. "Passing drills. Let's go! From the thirty."

The four quarterbacks currently on the team jogged to the thirty-yard line, followed by the wide receivers and tight ends. Like Julian and the rest of his teammates, they wore just a light jersey with "shells" on underneath and the bare minimum of pads under their pants, over their thighs. The only complete protection they wore was the helmet for the upcoming "minimum contact" exercise that was, in reality, a full-tackling, almost scrimmage-like environment in Jacob Davis's ultra-realistic June minicamp.

"The rest of you take a knee," Davis said, following his receivers while checking something off on his clipboard.

Julian watched them for a while, the quarterbacks dropping back and throwing to the receivers as they ran their routes. The receivers caught most of the balls; each pass looked perfect. That meant very little however, as Julian had learned over the past few weeks. There wasn't as much variance in talent in the pros as there had been in college, and in early training camp practices all the players could look almost the same.

The passing drill went on for a few more minutes. When it ended, the coaches called the starting defensive team over to the field.

"Minimum contact!" Davis ordered, checking off something else.

Julian followed his teammates to the thirty-yard line. Rich Mitchum brought them a few yards back, forming them into a huddle. "All right," he said. "These aren't scripted, fellas, remember that. Ace right fifty." Most teams scripted their plays beforehand, running them in the order in which they were arranged. That had been the system the coaches used back at USC. But it seemed like Davis liked to develop his team's ability to react to spontaneity. He didn't script his practices, not even these actual scrimmage-like full-contact deals.

Julian followed his teammates to the line. Mitchum crouched behind the center, and Julian dropped into his stance a few yards behind. "Set! Hut, hut!"

Julian dashed forward, then cut off the right side and darted downfield, looking over his shoulder for the pass. It didn't come his way. Instead, Mitchum launched a floater that fell incomplete fifty yards downfield, just ahead of the intended receiver.

"Again!" Davis yelled.

They huddled up.

Gonzalo Perez stood behind Davis, awaiting his chance. Perez was an undrafted rookie free agent, a guy who'd been brought in to be a tackling dummy for the drafted rookies and veterans. Every year, dozens of these players were signed by each team. Some got lucky and actually made the final roster. Most didn't, and many never strapped on a football helmet again. They all had shortcomings in talent that made the jump from college to pro too hard, or some attitude or personality problem that the scouts shied away from.

It wasn't fair, Perez thought. He had been a star defensive end in college. Fast and agile for his position, he'd wreaked havoc on Division IAA offenses. But there was a reason he was a Division IAA player and not a major college Division I student-athlete; he was undersized. At 240 pounds he was physically better suited to playing outside linebacker in the NFL. But then his "attitude" and "lack of football smarts" came into play. Those were the terms the few scouts he'd met had jotted down on their notepads after interviewing him at his school's pro day.

Perez was determined to make an impression, though. If he could just get a shot, he'd show them.

He wasn't expecting that shot to come so soon.

Davis turned to him, staring at his clipboard. "We're putting in some of the rookies," he said. "Get in there next play."

"Hut!"

Mitchum tossed the ball to Julian as he ran left. He tucked it in, lowered his shoulders and took off straight down the field, dodging a defender and finding his way into the open. The whistle blew.

"Again!" Julian heard Coach Davis exclaim.

Perez lined up, feeling his adrenaline rush. His first real work on a professional football team! "Bring it on!" he screamed as he dropped into his stance across from the offensive tackle. He turned his head to watch the ball, trying to ignore the signals that Mitchum was calling. The ball flashed back into his hands.

Perez ran forward, hitting the tackle shoulder to shoulder and whirling around with impressive speed. He saw a blur shoot past out of the corner of his eye, recognized it as Julian Lloyd and started chasing it. Then the whistle blew.

"Stay in your lane, Perez!" Davis yelled from the sideline.

They lined up again. Mitchum called his signals, the center snapped the ball and once again he flipped it out to Lloyd, running left. Perez used his spin move, but this time stayed in the hole, trying to maintain the line. He caught a glimpse of Lloyd coming straight at him, opened his arms wide to wrap him up and threw his body at the rookie half-back. A collision, and Perez felt himself being thrown down hard. *The guy had run him over!* By the time Perez rolled onto his stomach and got back to his feet, Lloyd trotted back to the huddle and laughed at something one of coaches said to him.

"Watch it!" Perez screamed in Lloyd's general direction, and grew even more angry when the runningback just glanced at him. Infuriated, he walked back to his place and stood there with clenched fists.

Julian wore a smirk as he stood in the huddle. "Give it to me again, same lane," he said. "That guy's got no chance. I guarantee I'll break through him again."

Mitchum nodded, a smile visible beneath his face mask. He called the play: "Twenty-four veer left, single basic, on two."

The offense came back to the line. Perez took an extra moment to scan it before falling into his three-point stance. Julian Lloyd was the lone 'back, with all other players in the same lineup as before. *It's the same play*, Perez thought.

"Hut! Hut!"

Instead of surging forward into the tackle, Perez took a step back and moved to fill the hole he knew that Lloyd would run through.

He was too late. The Heisman trophy winner had already dashed through the opening and was squeezing past Perez, who made a desperate lunge for him. He managed to grab a handful of jersey, but the pure momentum of his target jerked him right off his feet. He fell on his stomach, and watched Lloyd evade the secondary, which made only a half-hearted attempt to catch him.

Perez watched Lloyd flip the ball to a coach and jog to the huddle. He pounded the ground and jumped up, pointing threateningly. "Enough of this crap! You're mine!" And again, Lloyd just shrugged and returned to his huddle.

"We got a madman," Mitchum laughed. "Always happens to those fellas. They know they got no shot at making the team, and they figure it's because the guy ahead of them's making more dough. Never occurs to 'em that it's because that guy is better."

Julian nodded. The guy had tried to chew him out twice now . . . but that was all part of the game, wasn't it? He doubted the "madman," as Mitchum called him, had received an eighteen-point-five million dollar signing bonus, so Julian understood his anger. But heck, this was football, and it was supposed to be fun. It always was for him. He half-grinned. "Let me have it again," he said.

Mitchum leaned forward, hands on his knees. "Twenty-five toss left, single basic, on one." They returned to the line. Mitchum called the signals, took the snap and tossed the ball to Julian, who sidestepped a diving effort by one of the defensive linemen and blasted off for the hole past the left tackle. "Madman" pushed away from his blocker, running hard to meet him. Julian slipped the ball over to his left arm, raised his right to ward off the defender, but the guy went low. Julian planted his right leg to push off and avoid the tackle attempt, but the guy was moving too fast, and he slammed right into his knee, and suddenly Julian was lying on his back.

For a moment he lay there, stunned. He didn't remember going down. He just lay there for a few seconds, trying to catch his breath. The world above him was spinning, and he felt a wave of embarrassment wash over him.

He didn't feel the pain until he tried to get up.

Dr. Eric Hendley's primary office was inside the St. Louis University Hospital. A surgeon specializing in bone and joint diseases and injuries, Hendley drew heavy interest from the surrounding athletic programs, including the Missouri Gunners, who used his skills to fix broken players injured beyond the abilities of the team physicians. His status as an opponent of genetic athlete-enhancement—the new steroid—had almost given him celebrity status, an added benefit to the teams that came to him. They could claim his support when the international governing bodies or powerful leagues and conferences came snooping for illegal blood doping or modifications. *If Hendley's behind us, we've got no problem!* While not completely accurate, those statements carried a lot of weight with the authorities, and could often end an investigation before it got started.

Hendley was sitting behind his desk sipping a cup of coffee when the phone rang. The desk was metal, but shaded brown and black to look like wood. He had no computer, depending on his technicians and secretary to keep the electronic files in order, but did keep a cabinet full of paper patients' files. The walls around him were covered with charts of bones and joints, which were for show when he met with possible patients, as were the books on the waist-level cart beside the desk. He used the X-ray board on the wall, however, all the time.

Setting down his mug, Hendley picked up the phone and

brought it to his ear while wiping his mouth with a napkin. "Dr. Hendley," he said.

"Hello, doctor," a cheerful female voice greeted him. His receptionist, Fran. "A new patient is coming in. I think you'll want to take him immediately."

Hendley frowned. No patients were scheduled for . . . he didn't know, exactly, but he hadn't been expecting anyone *now.* "I didn't think we had any patients for a while."

"New patient," Fran said. "He's a football player. Just injured this morning in practice, so they tell me."

Uh-oh. "From the Gunners?" Hendley asked.

"Yes," Fran replied.

"X rays?"

"Kimberly's bringing them now."

There was a knock at the door. Hendley looked up. "That's her now," he said. "Thanks, Fran." He hung up. "Come in," he called, standing and stepping over to the X-ray board.

The door swung open and one of the nurses, Kimberly Ehrett, stepped inside holding a large yellow envelope in her right hand. "Doctor," she said, and handed it to him.

"Thanks," Hendley said. He waited until the door closed behind her before opening the envelope and extracted the pictures. There were three of them. He stuck them all on the board, then flicked on the light. His eyes narrowed.

It took the accomplished doctor of twenty-one years, a veteran of thousands upon thousands of orthopedic surgeries, almost ten seconds to realize that he was looking at an X-ray scan of a human knee.

What was left of it.

Hendley strode into the hospital room down the hall from his main office. He went in and closed the door behind him. Three men dressed in gray shirts and shorts and wearing Gunners team caps were standing inside. The injured football player, a handsome young black man with a strong build and short dark hair lay on the bed under sedation. His right knee was wrapped and swollen to almost twice its normal size.

It looked almost as bad from across a hospital room as it did in the X rays.

Hendley stepped closer to the three men, returning their nervous stares. He recognized the shortest one, a tanned white man with a short dark brown beard and a swelling waistline. They called him Skip on casual occasions, but this wasn't one. "Dr. Lockett," he said, nodding to the other man. "Come with me, please."

Skip Lockett stepped away from his companions, and Hendley placed a hand on his shoulder as they went outside the room to the carpeted hallway. He closed the door behind them.

"Did you study those X rays carefully?" Hendley asked, his voice just above a whisper.

Lockett nodded. "Yes I did," he answered in a similar tone. "It's bad."

"Extremely," Hendley agreed. "Anterior cruciate is torn, lateral meniscus is crushed, the medial is slightly ripped and he's got a cracked fibula. There appears to be some damage to the patella as well, and there's no telling what condition the nerves are in. I'm going to have to go in and find out. I want to schedule an orthoscopic surgery as quickly as possible, preferably while he's still under this current anaesthetic." He shook his head, rubbing his brow. "It's like four major injuries combined. One of the worst I've seen in years."

Lockett braced himself, pulling his form up, like he was preparing for a collision between speeding trains. Hendley already knew what he was going to say.

"The prospects for a full recovery . . ."

Hendley shook his head. "What prospects?"

Coach Gary Harrell met Ryan as he entered the training facility, fresh off the field from working seven-on-seven drills. He held his helmet under his arm, but wore no other pads under his jersey and workout shorts. It was all non-contact at this minicamp. Harrell, a lanky former defensive back in his late forties with dull brown hair and a rugged, wrinkled face, ran scripted practices that avoided full contact this time of the year. Not until several days into the July full-scale training camp did he begin actual hitting and scrimmaging.

"Talk a minute?" Harrell asked when Ryan stepped inside, alone.

"Sure," Ryan said, letting the tinted glass door swing shut behind him. "What's up?"

The hall was dark. Dark and quiet, like a high school hallway in the middle of the night. He leaned against the wall and tapped his foot on the hard white ceramic floor.

"The front office is up," Harrell said, his mouth glued into an unhappy scowl. Whatever he had to say, he wasn't excited about saying it. "I wanted to give you a heads-up on something they're going to ask you to do. Probably this week."

"Uh-huh . . ." Ryan murmured, trying to get more out of him. He crossed his arms and shifted his weight, bending his leg and placing his right foot on the wall.

"They're going to ask you to take a cut," Harrell sighed.

Ryan froze. "A cut? What do you . . . ?"

"I mean a cut in pay, a salary reduction," the coach said, making eye contact with his player. "Since Falk is the starter now, and since he's going to make starter's money, you're just . . ." His voice trailed off and he dropped his head.

"Just what?" Ryan prodded, not so sure he wanted to know.

"You just aren't worth the money you're making," Harrell said. "At least not in their eyes. They want you to agree to cut your salary to vet minimum."

With Ryan's years of experience, that meant $750,000. Nothing to sneeze at, but less than half of his current contract, which expired next season.

Ryan let out a deep breath. "And if I don't agree?"

"Dammit, Ryan, this is what I was worried about!" Harrell said, desperation tinging his voice. He dropped to a whisper: "If you don't agree, they'll release you during camp."

Ryan bit his lip. "Look, Gary, it isn't the money. It's the idea that . . ." he faltered, then regained his nerve. "It's the idea that I'm all of a sudden . . . you know . . ."

"Expendable," Harrell muttered.

"Right," Ryan said. "What was all that talk about how I'm still important to the team, and all that?"

"You are," Harrell said, stressing the second word. He removed his cap and ran a hand over his head, then replaced it. "Just . . . just make the right choice, okay, Ryan?" The coach squeezed Ryan's shoulder, an expression of a long friendship, and then turned and made his way back outside onto the practice field.

Ryan groaned out loud, turned around and slammed his fist into the wall. His hand throbbed. *Make the right choice.* Yeah, sure. As if he *had* a choice. Helping David Falk learn the nuances of professional football wasn't going to be an enjoyable task. Friggin' college kid . . .

Ryan waited for a moment, calming himself with a few deep breaths, then pushed the door open and went outside into the blistering sunlight.

Petty stared through Randal Lockett. Around them, the temperature of the owner's office seemed to plummet, and the team doctor braced himself for an outburst.

It didn't come. Petty just breathed, and Lockett could almost see the older man's mind working behind those steely gray eyes. He focused on Lockett, who met his gaze.

"This could be a disaster," Petty said and, to Lockett's mind, understating the reality by a huge degree. "We only signed the contract two weeks ago."

Against Geoffrey's better judgement, but Lockett couldn't bring himself to say that aloud. He was angry and worried, but not suicidal. Yet.

"The damage . . ." Petty went on. "How serious is it?"

"Sir, I've already gone over this," Lockett said, but went on. "His ACL and MCL are both torn. *Both*. At the same time.

I've never heard of that happening in the same leg at the same time."

Petty folded his hands in front of him, his expression going blank. "Nor have I."

"But that's only the beginning," Lockett continued. "His patella tendon has a slight tear and the kneecap itself is nicked. And then you have the fractured fibula. It's only slight, but on top of the rest it's bad enough. We don't know the rest. The surgeon was about to go in to get a complete diagnosis when I left."

"I need to know what will happen," Petty said. "Tell me what will happen."

Lockett shook his head. Another repeat. Vince Petty seemed to be in shock, or at least as close to shock as he could get. "My opinion?" Lockett said. "My opinion—and Dr. Hendley at the hospital agrees—is that Julian Lloyd will never play football again. There's simply too much damage. Oh, he could *try*," Lockett added as Petty opened his mouth. "But not until next season, or more likely the season after. By then he'll have been out of football for two full seasons. And don't forget he's *never* played an NFL game."

"But . . ." Petty interjected.

"But that's the best-case scenario," Lockett went on. He was on a roll, his frustrations spilling out in a cascade of calm medical prognoses. "Most likely he'll need a total knee replacement, and with the damage he's sustained not even *that* will return him to form. Think of it as a Bo Jackson thing."

"But that was different entirely," Petty said, breaking out of his reverie. "The blood flow—the hip—was the reason he couldn't come back."

Lockett laughed in derision. "Vince, don't try to act like a doctor. Yeah, the blood flow problem was part of his injury, but the main thing was the simple fact that man can't improve on God. He had an artificial hip, just like Julian will have an artificial knee. I'm going to recommend—"

Petty slammed his clenched fists against his desk. "Your recommendation makes no difference!" he exclaimed. "We will wait for the official word from Dr. Hendley and then proceed from there."

Lockett felt his face go red, warm. He jabbed a finger in the air. "Vince, be realistic! We're talking about a running back, here! In most other positions he might be able to overcome this in a year or two and get back on the field. But a running back—especially a running back of his style—simply can't. So I'm going to recommend—" Petty looked as though he were trying to interrupt again, but Lockett held up his hand to stop him. "I'm going to recommend that Julian retire. There's no point in him coming here to work and prepare for something he's never going to attain."

"That is unacceptable," Petty said, in control of his emotions again. "It's out of the question. He *cannot* retire. We'll place him on IR."

"For what?" Lockett demanded. "The only purpose that could serve is to save face. Well I've got news for you, Mr. Petty; it's too late for *that* now! As soon as this hits the wire you're going to look *exactly* like the *stupid* son of a bitch you *are!*" Lockett closed his mouth, gritting his teeth. That last sentence had slipped out; he hadn't meant to say it . . . but it was too late for regrets now. He sat, eyes downcast.

Petty pushed away from his desk and stood. "Randal, I want you to leave," he said. Lockett stood, preparing himself for what he knew was to come next.

"I want you to leave permanently," Petty continued. "Pack your belongings. I'm afraid your services are no longer required."

You're fired.

"No," Lockett said. "I quit." And he turned on his heel and exited the room, slamming the door behind him.

Five

The white lab rat, officially designated R22 but known around the GLI facility as "Arnold," ran to the near end of his clear plastic cage when Angel opened the top with a rubber-gloved hand. Beside her, Paul Franklin, a short, overweight man wearing a full doctor's regalia—white coat and all—reached into Arnold's confinement, secured the rat and slipped a small weight belt around his midsection. The weight was twice as heavy as the rat itself, but when Franklin released the animal, it moved with ease around its cage, stopping to drink from its water bottle as if the belt didn't exist.

Yawn. *What did he expect?* Angel wondered. They knew their technique worked. This entire observation process was little more than a necessary formality. She brushed a strand of blond hair out of her face.

"Subject appears to have completely adjusted," Franklin said into a tape recorder. "Commencing second test phase," he continued, and Angel rolled her eyes. Franklin picked up Arnold the rat and set him down beside the cage. He placed a small ladder next to it—the only way R22 could return to his home and food.

The rat hopped onto the ladder, climbed up and over the edge and then leaped into the cage, landing like a feather.

"The added one point seven eight pounds has no percepti-ble effect," Franklin observed into his recorder. Angel wanted to agree: *You don't say?* But decided against it. Never inter-rupt Dr. Paul Franklin at work, no matter how ridiculous he looked, because in doing so you made an enemy for life.

"Phase two testing complete," Franklin said. "Will enter phase three tomorrow. End recording." He clicked off the recorder and slipped it into his coat pocket.

"Well," he said. "That went well."

Angel closed the cage. "Yeah."

"R22 really is turning into the Terminator," Franklin continued. "Good name you came up with. 'Arnold.' Clever."

"Yeah," Angel said again. She really should be working on those potential investors. The rats were a moot point without money to buy them feed. She grimaced; so were the scientists, she realized.

"What old Petty wouldn't do for the kid to be like that rat . . ." Franklin said, as if oblivious to Angel's presence.

"What kid?" Angel asked, staring in the direction of the doorway. There were a few more names on the "investors" side of her list. Law firms and such. Long shots, all of them, but calling any of them would be a better waste of time than *this*. And maybe it would end up not being a waste at all with a little luck.

"Julian Lloyd, Gunners runningback," Franklin said, his voice dripping with contempt. "Geez, Angel, don't you ever read the papers?"

"I usually skip the sports," Angel shot back, frustrated. "Look, Joel, I have to go . . ."

"I mean, it was front-page news this morning," Franklin continued. "I can't believe you missed it."

She said, "Missed what, Paul?" just to get it over with.

"Lloyd!" Franklin said. "Julian Lloyd tore up his knee in practice yesterday. They're checking out the options. But right now it looks bad."

"That's great," Angel said, making her way toward the door.

"Actually it's not," Franklin said, glaring at her. "I was just wondering what Vince Petty would pay to have Lloyd cured. He bet the whole deal on the kid. Now they're up a cree—"

"Wait a second," Angel interjected, freezing in her tracks. "Who? Vince who?"

"Petty. He owns the team. Had poor Marsh trade half the

draft and two players to the Bengals for Lloyd in April. You realize what's gonna happen if the kid retires? That was a helluva bonus he signed for . . ."

"Petty," Angel murmured, trying to filter out Franklin's continued comments. Petty . . . the name was familiar, agonizingly so. Where had she heard it? *Recently,* she thought. She'd heard it recently, in the last few days.

Her list. Law firms. Something about law firms. What were some of the big firms she was planning on contacting? Smith and Daniels . . . Reardon and Jordan . . . Kyle, Jacobs and Landon . . . Johansson, Harris and—

"Petty," Angel said again, aloud. Franklin stopped talking and looked at her, scratching his head. "Vincent Petty," Angel explained. "He's got a big law firm in the city, right? Didn't he make a couple hundred million in those tobacco lawsuits a few years ago?"

Franklin shrugged. "I guess. He doesn't really run the firm anymore. Concentrates on football now."

Angel whirled around and made her way for the door. "Where you going?" Franklin shouted after her.

"I have some calls to make," she said over her shoulder. She walked down the hall, pulling off her gloves as she went. She passed a few fellow researchers as she came down the corridor, and some of them looked up from their papers or folders or clipboards to say hello, but Angel ignored them and slipped inside her office.

She searched through the papers on her desk, digging around and tossing some of them aside until she found the one she was looking for. LAW FIRMS—*potential investors???* she had scrawled across the top of the page. She scanned the list and found the phone number for the firm in question. She picked up her phone and dialed.

Two rings, then: "Good afternoon." A pleasant female voice. "Law firm of Johansson, Harris and Petty. You've reached Mr. Petty's office. How may I direct your call?"

"I'd like to talk with Mr. Petty," Angel said, forcing herself not to hurry. "I'm a client."

"Name please?"

"Ah—Angelina Moore. He may not know me," Angel said. "I actually represent a possible client of his, Genetics Life, Incorporated, in Valley Park."

"Mr. Petty takes all business calls at his team headquarters. We can forward your call, but there is a small surcharge."

"Fine," Angel said.

"Very well. Thank you." A click, and then the phone began to ring again. Once, twice, three times—

"Missouri Gunners Training Facility, Mr. Petty's office." Another pleasant female voice, almost a clone of the first. "Can I help you?"

"Yes," Angel said, forcing her voice to be cool and professional now. "I represent a possible client of his, Genetics Life in Valley Park. I need to speak with Mr. Petty. It's important." She would have twisted the phone cord around her fingers, but this was the 21st century and there *was* no phone cord to twist. She held her free hand flat, palm-down, on the desk.

"I believe Mr. Petty is free at the moment," the voice said. "Please make your call brief."

"It will be," Angel said.

"Please hold."

Click. Then: "Hello. Petty speaking." A quiet voice with an almost British accent that couldn't have been authentic.

"Mr. Petty, my name is Angelina Moore," she said, hoping her voice wasn't shaking as her hand was. "I need to talk to you about Julian Lloyd."

Several seconds of silence went by. "What about him?" Petty asked, his tone changing somewhat, becoming even colder.

"I'm with a company called Genetics Life," she said, dropping any pretense of a background in law. "You might've heard of us. As a matter of fact, we probably made a presentation to you recently."

"I don't remember any presentation," Petty said.

"Or maybe not," Angel said. "But that's beside the point. Um. The reason I'm calling is to tell you that I know a quick and painless way to heal Julian Lloyd's injury. It's not exactly . . . uh . . . conventional . . . but I assure you it is highly effective and—"

"I think I do remember," Petty interrupted. "Yes, I do. It was a man. Glasses, worn-out suit—a doctor, I believe. He wanted money but offered nothing in return."

"Yes," Angel said. "But now I'm offering you something in return. No, I'm offering to do you a huge favor in return for another, smaller favor. I'm offering a trade."

Another moment of silence. "I want you to come over here today," Petty said. "We'll talk about this in greater detail. I'd rather not discuss it over the phone. 'Not conventional' means illegal, does it not?"

Angel's heart skipped a beat. "Mr. Petty—"

"No, don't worry," he said. "There is no problem. Come at three and we'll talk. Just give your name to the office and they will let you in. I'll be expecting you," he added, and before Angel could thank him or even open her mouth to speak, he hung up.

Angel hung up her own phone, stretched her arms over her head and sighed, breathing deeply to slow her racing heart.

Time to get to work.

Julian had never felt this alone. He lay by himself in the hospital room wearing a medical gown that, thank God, went below his heavily bandaged, numbed knee. The lights were on, but the television was off. All he wanted to do was think. Think of what might have been, should have been, if only he hadn't been in that place at that time.

It was amazing how one moment could change your life. Julian had spent long hours just thinking *what if?* What if Mitchum had chosen a different play? What if Julian had just run through Perez, instead of trying to dodge him? What if Perez hadn't dove at Julian's legs? What if . . .

But he stopped himself. Thinking *what if* was a useless waste of energy. What mattered was that it had happened. His football career was over before it had ever really begun; despite the confidence and bravado—false bravado—he was hearing from the well-wishers from the team, deep down he knew the truth, and he felt like a complete failure. All his goals were impossible now, he'd never run for one thousand yards and score twenty touchdowns in his rookie season. He wouldn't set a rookie rushing record. He would never live up to the Heisman hype. But he *would* go down in history as one of the all-time biggest busts in pro football history. And in its own sadistic way, that was something.

The funny thing was, all through college he had never so much as sprained an ankle. Three years of getting the ball on almost 50 percent of his team's plays, three years of being the center of the opposition's attention, three years of being hit more often and harder than any of his teammates, and the worst injury he had suffered was a nasty bruise on his forearm. God had a wry sense of humor.

Julian heard a soft knock at the door. He turned his head that way, looking sideways. "Come in."

A tiny black woman, just over five feet tall, ambled inside. She was youthful in appearance despite her gray hair. She stood beside him, looked down at Julian and shook her head. "You gotta learn when to jump, boy," she said.

"Hello to you too, Ma," Julian said.

Jacklyn Lloyd smiled. "How are you?"

"Okay," he whispered. He knew he didn't, and he couldn't fool his mother. In her fifty-six years of life, she'd experienced pretty much everything. Julian, the youngest child in his family by four years, had seen the results of that experience even more than his three siblings.

"You don't look okay," Jacklyn said. "You look pretty bad, actually."

"Thanks a lot."

"Oh, come on, Julian. I know you're feeling pretty bad, but you know what I say. No matter how bad you feel . . ."

"You can always smile. I know." Julian forced a smile. "I don't know what I'm going to do, Ma," he said, then went on before she could reply, opening up. "Nothing like this has ever happened to me. Everything seems impossible." He felt his eyes misting and blinked away the moisture. "I just . . . don't know what to do. Without football I mean. It's been part of my life since . . ."

"Life changes direction all the time, Julian," his mother said. "Maybe it just wasn't meant to be."

Julian cracked a real smile, but it was a smile of scorn. "I guess not. Maybe God enjoys playing pranks on people."

Jacklyn's face became stern, her voice took on an edge. "Don't talk that way, boy. It isn't right. And it isn't true. You know the old saying, closin' the door, openin' the window, you know?"

Julian shook his head and stared at the ceiling. "My window was open. I had everything going for me, and I ruined it."

"How did *you* ruin it?"

He closed his eyes. "Ma, I was taunting the guy. He was a tackling dummy. He wasn't good enough to make the team, and I knew it. I was better than him, and I knew it. I told Mitchum to give me the ball again and again, and I kept running right at him. He got frustrated, and decided to get even. He dove at my leg. And then I had the nerve to be embarrassed. Some nobody tackled me." Julian took a deep breath and opened his eyes, turning his head to look at his mom. "And you know something? I didn't feel a thing until I tried to stand up."

"Ain't that always the way?"

Julian shrugged. "They showed it on the news last night, Ma. You should've *seen* it. My leg bent completely back and sideways at the same time. It was sick, like it was flying off. I can't believe I didn't feel anything. I mean, I was dizzy, like I was getting an upset stomach, but that was it. The doctor said that it was caused by the trauma." He ran through the words, jumbling many of them together. He was rambling.

"Quiet down," Jacklyn said. "Why don't you get some rest?"

"I've been resting ever since," Julian said. "I'm tired of sleeping." He stopped, allowed a half-smile and laughed. "That was good."

Jacklyn grinned. "Imagine *you* puttin' your foot in your mouth."

Julian's smile widened. "Yeah." He sighed. An earnest expression came over his face, masking the worry he felt. "You think it'll be okay, Ma?"

"It'll be fine. You're always gonna have that eighteen million dollars to fall back on, eh?"

He laughed again. "I don't know if I should be happy or guilty over that."

Jacklyn shook her head, clucking. "You know how them contract negotiations work, don't you? Your agent tries to screw *them,* they try to screw *you,* and you usually end up somewhere in the middle. This time they didn't try an' get to the middle, so it's their fault, not yours." She smiled. "I sure don't mind."

"But I get the benefits," Julian said.

"The Gunners took a risk when they signed you," Jacklyn said. "They knew injuries happen. They jus' bet that you wouldn't get hurt, and they lost that bet."

"I just feel like I let them down."

"You didn't let them down. Accidents happen. It wasn't your fault."

Julian nodded and sighed, shifting in the bed as much as his bandaged, immobilized leg let him. "I guess you're right."

"I usually am."

"You are. What is it about mothers that gives them the ability to be right all the time?"

"Trade secret."

He laughed. "I'm glad you came, Ma. I know you hate to fly."

She shrugged. "Yeah, well. You know."

"The guys heard?" he asked, referring to his two brothers and sister.

Jacklyn nodded. "They couldn't come. Annie had the kids,

Blaine couldn't get away from work, Derrick . . . well, he's busy, too."

Couldn't get away from work. Julian frowned, feeling guilty again. "Blaine's working two jobs so his family can go grocery shopping more than once a month and I'm lying in bed making millions. I can't help but feel bad about that."

Jacklyn grinned. "He asked when the first check's coming in. Wants to know when he can retire."

Julian returned the grin. He felt a little better knowing that at least he would be able to share the cash. There was no way on God's green earth he would be able to use all that money in one lifetime. He'd be able to make his entire family comfortable, and he knew as well as anyone how much they deserved it. But still . . . "I won't be able to stand not doing anything and still making money." Jacklyn's lifelong example of hard work had burned that principle in him. She'd even convinced him to vote Republican.

"Geez, honey, get a job!" she said. "Be a scout or a coach, or whatever else they got. Go back to USC and join the football staff. Like I said, there are always going to be windows. You just gotta take advantage of them. Now, get some rest. You look tired."

"I am," Julian admitted.

Jacklyn leaned over and kissed him on the forehead. "See you later," she whispered and left, closing the door behind her.

The air was dry but warm, the sun still high when Angel stepped inside the Gunners team training facility. She was glad she wasn't wearing a hot business suit. GLI was an informal place, and the fact that the researchers spent hours wearing hospital scrubs and various accessories over their clothes kept company fashion to a casual minimum. Angel just wore jeans, a beige turtleneck sleeveless sweater and gray sunglasses.

She pulled off the sunglasses when the doors swished closed

behind her. She was standing in a hallway that went forward for a few dozen feet and then split left and right, the walls decorated with framed pictures of football players in action.

The office. That was all Petty had said.

Where was the "office"?

Angel walked forward to the hallway intersection, looked both ways and caught sight of someone walking toward her from the right. She turned as the man, a skinny guy dressed in a suit, went by.

"Excuse me," she said, stopping him and looking up, making eye contact. *That* was something she'd worked a long time on. She wasn't tall, only five-two, and maintaining a constant eye contact that made people uncomfortable—an ideal goal in certain situations—was often difficult. Luckily this wasn't so important a task that such a goal was crucial. "Where can I find Mr. Petty's office?"

The man pointed back the way he'd come. "Down that way, third door on the right," he said.

"Thanks." Angel smiled up at him. He nodded, smiled back, and continued strolling across the hall. Angel went straight to the third door—they were all plain and unmarked (*How did they navigate around here?*)—and knocked. No answer. She tried the handle and found that the door wasn't locked, so she opened it and stepped inside.

The room resembled a small doctor's waiting area. A fortyish woman sat behind a desk beside another door, tapping keys on a computer. Angel strode to the desk and the woman looked up. "Can I help you?" It was the same woman she'd talked to on the phone earlier.

"I'm here to see Mr. Petty," Angel said. She gave her name. The woman picked up her phone and pushed a button, said something into it and then hung up. "Go right in," she said with a smile.

Angel smiled back, just to be nice and leave a good impression, and went to the door.

* * *

Angelina Moore came inside and closed the door behind her, and Petty rose from his chair to greet her. He extended his hand over the desk. "Dr. Moore, it's nice to meet you," he said as she took his hand. "Please—" he motioned to the chair across the desk from him—"have a seat." He sat down. "Would you like something to drink?"

"No, thanks," she said, sitting down. She was attractive, with dirty blond hair, light brown eyes and a tanned, trim athletic body. Petty recognized the type. She obviously took great care in keeping herself fit. Her beauty was a weapon, he realized, and he had no doubt that she could use it to deadly effect.

He leaned forward, resting his arms on his desk. "Well, Dr. Moore. Let's hear it."

Vince Petty was a snake, Angel thought. Cultured and well-groomed, with that fake British accent that he did so well it probably sounded real to most people. There was a malevolent intelligence behind his gray eyes, and Angel realized with complete certainty that *he was the one!* His reputation was of a man who had often skirted the law, or bent it to fill his needs. But like the crooked career politician who kept getting reelected, none of his enemies could pin any one incident on him with enough force to make it stick. Hence, he still held a law license despite three hearings in the last fifteen years with the state bar association, any one of which could have revoked it permanently and kept him from ever becoming successful enough to purchase a $600 million professional football team. Angel had indeed done her research on him in the past few hours, taking in as much as she could in hurried internet searches. He was dangerous, he was imperturbable, he was brilliant.

He was perfect.

"First of all," Angel said, sitting erect in the leather chair, "I need to ask you why the unconventional nature of what I'm about to propose doesn't bother you."

"You're my only option," Petty said.

Angel held back her surprise. "What do you mean?"

"I mean I've gone over the material your Dr. Nagel gave my partners when he met with them in May. I believe we were his second failed attempt at receiving assistance in a matter of weeks. From executives to lawyers." Petty shook his head. "He was desperate, wasn't he?"

"He still is," Angel said.

"That is perfectly understandable," Petty said. "Now, from the information he left, I understand that you have a considerable lead over your competitors in the biotech industry. Five years?"

"That's our estimate, yes." This wasn't going to be hard at all, she thought. Petty had already done most of the work for her. She guessed he'd obtained a copy of the material Nick gave all those he met with when discussing funding for GLI and reviewed it in the hours between their call and this meeting.

"If you don't mind my asking," Petty said, his face showing skepticism. "How did you develop that lead? Your company is extremely small. According to the information I have, your annual operating budget is only eight figures. Some of the other genetic research companies operate in the billions of dollars."

Angel smiled. "Money isn't everything in scientific research, Mr. Petty," she said. "The media might make it seem like that, but it isn't true. You need brilliant people. People developed that five-year lead. When Dr. Nagel brought a few disgruntled geniuses together from universities and larger companies—"

"You included?" Petty interrupted.

Angel nodded. "Yes, me included. The information was basically all there. It was in the minds of the people he hired. I'll give him credit for that; he put us together like the pieces of a puzzle. We each specialized in a particular area, and when we were put together we progressed more in three years than the billion-dollar monsters advance in ten. Does that answer your question?"

Petty nodded, the skepticism disappearing from his face. She could tell he believed her. Either that or he was a great actor, which was possible. "Yes, it does. But apparently something is wrong, considering the debt you've been accumulating. What, over two million in three months?"

"Our investors pulled out early this year," Angel said. "It's hard for a small advanced technology company to operate without investors." She let her eyes drop and lowered her voice a little. "And Nick isn't exactly a genius when it comes to exploiting his research." Angel smiled. "He couldn't sell cold lemonade from a sidewalk if it was a hundred degrees in the middle of a twenty-mile marathon."

"Do you have any idea why they pulled out?"

Angel looked back up at him. "War," she said. "There's a war in the industry, and with us it's like the Marines invading Vatican City. We don't have the ammo to fight back." By this she meant money, and the promise for profit. The investors had been lured away by those things, reeled in by one of the rival monster corporations.

Petty nodded in apparent understanding. "You mentioned a trade on the phone. I know what *you* want. Now what can you do for me?"

"I can save your football team," Angel said, staring into his eyes. He met her gaze without flinching. "I can save Julian Lloyd's career."

For a moment it seemed as though Petty was going to argue over the fact that Lloyd's career needed saving at all. He hesitated, but didn't break eye contact. "How?" he asked.

"I think I have two associates who might be willing to help me," Angel said. "We'd bring him in, run some tests, get a reading on his genetic makeup and then do the operation. And that'll be nothing, a few injections and we're done. Of course, Dr. Nagel would never approve. Technically, doing anything to Lloyd without notifying the government would be illegal. And I doubt the NFL would approve if they knew."

Petty gave one, quiet chuckle. "They would probably suspend him and enter him into the substance abuse program."

"So we have to do it quietly," Angel said. "What about Lloyd? Would he go along?"

Petty shook his head. "If he knows exactly what it is, then absolutely not. He's a very intelligent person. Somewhat naive and overly trusting, I think, but intelligent."

"So you inform him that you've found an alternative treatment," Angel said. "Make sure he doesn't know."

Petty nodded. "I don't think that will be a problem. Now, this treatment you're suggesting . . . how long before it would take effect?"

"It'll start working immediately," Angel said. "We inject him with the new genes, his body accepts them and then they start pumping out hormones like crazy. I don't know exactly how bad the damage is, but I'd guess he would be ready to play by the football season. When is it, September?"

"Yes," Petty said. "That would work wonderfully." He leaned back, displaying a sudden comfort with the situation that Angel wondered if he really felt. As she thought that, she realized with no small surprise that she, too, felt relaxed. It was going to work. It was *really* going to work. "And finally, what compensation are you looking for?"

"A research grant," Angel said. "You can call it a research grant. Mark it down as charity. Tax-deductible and all that."

"How much?"

Angel closed her eyes, picturing that income report she'd gone over . . . "Two-point-five million would be great," she said. "We'd be able to pay off our debts." *With a little left over.*

Petty didn't flinch. "Agreed. One million before the operation and the balance after its completion."

Angel hesitated, considering that for a moment, but then nodded. "Okay. I'll get in touch with you when I'm ready. I need to approach my two colleagues with the idea."

Petty leaned forward again, arms on the desk. "Do *not* mention my name until after they agree."

Angel almost laughed. Football freak that he was, Paul Franklin would know right away where the proposed research grant was going to come from. But Petty didn't need to know that. "Of course I won't," she said, as if the very idea of talking about him was idiotic.

"Good," he said, standing up. Then he held out his hand. "It's been pleasant doing business with you, Dr. Moore."

"Yes it has," Angel said, standing and shaking his hand. "Thank you."

"Thank *you*," Petty said. He reached into his desk drawer and pulled out a business card. He handed it to her. "My private number," he said. "Use it when you need to reach me. Never use the outside line."

Angel nodded. "Thank you."

"Don't disappoint me, Doctor," he warned, fingertips on the desk. He nodded a dismissal.

Angel couldn't hold back a little half-smile. "Goodbye, Mr. Petty," she said.

He returned the smile as he returned to his seat. "Please, call me Vince."

Six

Film study was almost as vital to the success of an individual football player as the endless hours of conditioning and practicing. Ryan sat alone in the dim film room, sitting on a metal folding chair a few feet in front of a twenty-five-inch television set. Behind him were a couple dozen other chairs, enough for a starting defensive unit to sit with one or more of the assistant coaches.

The purpose of game film was to discover just what you were doing wrong, and doing right, and then to improve on your failings. But as Ryan watched play after play of just one game from the end of last season, he realized with a sinking feeling that he wouldn't be able to improve on his failings. Because they weren't mental mistakes. He just wasn't fast enough to run down the halfback who slipped around the tackle and darted into the secondary for a big gain. He couldn't stay with the receiver-like tight end who caught a pass down the seam of the field and carried the two safeties forward for ten yards. And he wasn't able to make the stop when the fullback barreled his way up the gut on fourth and one, gaining two yards when he'd simply slammed into Ryan and carried him over the first down marker. These weren't simple mental errors that he could work on and fix. They were problems caused by his lack of athleticism, his lack of speed and strength when compared to the other players on the field. He was way past his prime, and the proof was given in stark manifest in the video before him. Ryan couldn't blame the front office for demanding that he take a pay cut. David Falk had talent and speed, and *he* was the defensive leader now.

And that thought made Ryan feel sick. He should've listened to his wife . . .

A part of him said it wasn't too late, that he should go and turn in his retirement now, before training camp started. After all, many players hung up their cleats rather late in the off-season. He wouldn't be the only one. But another, stronger part of him wouldn't allow this. He'd started something, started this season, and he now he had to finish it.

The door to the room opened, bathing it in light for a few seconds. Ryan turned to see Falk walk inside and toward him, pulling up a chair and sitting beside him. "Mind if I sit here?" the rookie asked.

Ryan shook his head, concentrating on the film, which wasn't much easier than making eye contact with Falk. On the screen, the center exploded out of his stance and hit Ryan in the chest, knocking him backwards and allowing the halfback to burst unhindered up the middle of the field. Ryan grimaced.

"Film from last season?" Falk asked, watching with Ryan, his elbows resting on his legs, arms hanging.

Ryan nodded. "Yeah," he said, glancing sidelong at the rookie.

"That's great. I was kind of hoping you'd give me a hand with some film study," Falk said, still watching the screen. "Maybe we could go over my college tapes sometime. You could tell me what I need to do. The coaches, they do a good job, but it's different hearing it from a player." Falk smiled as he observed the tape. "Especially hearing it from you," he said.

Ryan looked at the kid, brow furrowed in thought. "What do you mean?"

Falk shrugged. "You were . . . I dunno. You were like my idol growing up. Five straight Pro Bowls and all that. I never thought we'd be playing on the same team, I mean, I figured you'd be retired by the time I got drafted." He frowned, as if he realized that last comment wasn't the best thing to say.

And it wasn't. Ryan bit his lower lip. "Why would you think that?" he snapped, managing to hold back most of the sudden anger he felt. Anger that surprised even *him*.

Falk looked at him, earnest blue eyes staring at him. "Look, I know how you must feel. Like I came in and stole the job." Ryan opened his mouth to protest, but Falk went on. "Come on, admit it. We're on the same team."

Ryan felt his anger and frustration recede. He smiled. "Yeah, I guess I did feel that way."

"Well, I understand," Falk said, nodding his head in appreciation. "I actually felt pretty bad when Coach Harrell told me I'd be starting." His expression went dead serious. "But you have to understand something too. I'm here to play the game the best I can. I want to help this team win. I don't plan on just rolling over and playing dead so you can have the starting spot back."

Ryan smiled, feeling a hint of embarrassment at his earlier anger. The kid wasn't so bad. "I wouldn't want that."

"Great," Falk breathed in a sigh of relief. "Anyway. I'm hoping we can get to know each other a little, you know, maybe become friends."

He had that All-American quality about him that just *made* you like him, Ryan thought. Professional sports could use a few more like him.

"I think that's something we can handle," Ryan said, reaching for the VCR and turning off the tape. Then he shut off the television and stood. "It's nice to talk to you, David."

Falk stood, and they began to walk down the aisle toward the door. "You have no idea how thrilled I am," he said.

"Just wait for the work," Ryan said, chuckling. "Competition gets a little stiff, especially in camp."

Falk shrugged. "I'm always open to a little friendly competition." He opened the door and stepped aside to let Ryan out first. "Age before beauty."

Ryan laughed. "Thanks." They stepped out into the tiled hallway. "But let me tell you something; the competition is almost never *friendly*. You have to be ready to kick a guy when

he's down in camp and then pick him up during the season.
You want your first advice from the old wise man? Get your
contract signed and get your butt into camp. Rookies hold out
all the time, and it hurts 'em, bad, usually."

"I'll remember that," Falk said.

"Yeah," Ryan said. "Just make sure your agent knows."

"I will. It's just a shame all of us can't negotiate with the
Gunners."

They both laughed, and headed for the tinted glass doorway at the end of the hall.

The HUMINT central complex east of San Diego, California was a collection of glass and metal buildings that
looked as advanced as the information and technology inside.
The three main buildings, octagonal in shape when seen from
overhead, were connected to each other via enclosed walk-
ways stretching out from the fifth story of each. Building
Three held the mundane systems, generators, air-conditioning plants, kitchens, backup computers and more of the like.
Menial systems whose operation was below the level of the
proud researchers who performed their experiments in Building Two. Building One, though identical to the others from
the exterior, was more luxurious in its refinement in the interior. The walls were sound-insulated, the floors covered in
white carpet. The offices were appointed with almost every
amenity a scientist or executive could wish for.

Lance Pollard's spacious office more closely resembled an
apartment, and it made even the appointments on the three
company aircraft look like steerage on the *Titanic*—after it
had sunk. Though the main area just inside the door was that
surrounding his presidential-style antique oak desk, just to
the right of the doorway was a short hall that led to a private
conference room, bedroom, living area and a well-stocked
wine cellar from Pollard's own vineyards in Napa Valley. And
the front office, just through the doorway from his desk, was
equally impressive. Three secretaries manned the phones and

managed the files. They were each given seniority over almost anyone in the company. Pollard had chosen the two women and one man purely because of their personalities. They were authoritative and demanding of any visitor or caller. If you messed with Mr. Pollard, you were messing with each of them as well, and they could make your stay a living hell. But if Pollard's wish was to impress, they were equally adept at making one feel at home. It was just a part of the business, and a critical one at that.

And the competitors wondered why they couldn't survive. You couldn't be too nice in the corporate world, Pollard thought. It was no place for the weak of heart. One needed a certain degree of ruthlessness to survive, and only those with the will to do whatever was necessary at any given time could *thrive*. And Lance Pollard had thrived beyond anyone's expectations except his own.

He wasn't a scientist—he just hired them and paid them. But he was an opportunist who had been looking for a market to dominate. The biotech industry, exploding on the heels of the Human Genome Project and the successful cloning of mammals in the mid to late nineties, had been that market. A businessman who had been successful in more conventional enterprises—a millionaire already—he'd launched HUMINT six years ago, assembling a cast of researchers with reputations he could appreciate; unscrupulous and willing to do whatever it took.

That approach made HUMINT unpopular among its competitors, but Pollard's ability to exploit his researchers' discoveries made that fact moot. While they were struggling to stay afloat, Humanity International was raking in billions in profit. Many of the smaller, more conservative companies had either sought out a separate niche—Pollard considered that tactic was finding a hole to hide in—or capitulated through a buyout. None of them could match the influence and funding HUMINT had at its disposal, and Pollard's company was second to none in America in the field of genetic engineering of the human genome.

Except one.

Genetics Life had been around for only a few years, but somehow—through amazing luck, he figured—that tiny insect of a corporation had developed a huge lead in technology. Their secrets were carefully guarded and easy to keep, an advantage of being so small, but Pollard's people felt they had an idea of what some of them were. They believed GLI could control their manipulation of the genome. While other companies struggled to stop a new gene from producing muscle growth hormones, for example, when the desired objectives were made, GLI could stop it at will. Or so the theory was. No one outside of that company's walls knew for certain, and Dr. Nicholas Nagel wasn't telling.

At least he hadn't yet. Pollard was certain Nagel was nearing bankruptcy. The poor doctor's investors now sat on Lance Pollard's board, lured away with promises of rapid development and huge profits. As of now, only the second of those goals had been met.

The first wouldn't take much longer to reach if everything went as planned.

Pollard stood in the living area of his vast office space, holding his cell phone to his ear. He was wearing comfortable, informal clothing—khaki shorts and a T-shirt—as he had no planned meetings for several hours. And there was a closet beside the door to his right full of black and gray suits, if he needed to change into something more befitting a multi-billionaire.

"No, dammit!" he snapped into the phone. The man on the other end started to say something, but Pollard cut him off. "Look, you get that offer to him, I don't care what it takes."

"How much are you willing to put out for this stuff, though?"

"This 'stuff' is the research we need," Pollard explained, forcing himself to remain calm. He walked over to his white leather sofa and sat down, still holding the phone to his ear. "I've already worked too hard on this thing. I don't care *how* much you think it'll take. You make him an offer he can't refuse. Got it?"

"They're about two million in debt," the man said. "Maybe I can convince him—"

"No, Ned," Pollard said. He leaned forward on the sofa, rubbing his forehead with his left hand. "You said it yourself. It's going to take a lot more than two mil to get that top secret research crap out of him. Offer him eight to start. If that's no good, go ten. My point is, whatever we spend on this thing we'll make up. I promise you we'll break even."

"I just don't see why this is so important," Ned muttered, static cutting though his voice for a moment. "I mean, we're bringing in—"

"This isn't a matter of the bottom line, at least not right now," Pollard growled. He reclined on the sofa, pulling his shoeless feet up. "But it will be in a few years, and I want the jump-start. And I want it now, before GLI goes down the tubes and the race starts."

"We'd win that race," Ned pointed out.

"Your confidence is reassuring," Pollard muttered. "But I'm not taking that chance when it's unnecessary. Just do what I said. Make the offer and be ready to negotiate. It isn't going to be easy, but when the dollar signs go off in his head, Nagel is just like the rest of them."

Ned sighed. "Okay, boss. I'll make an appointment with him."

"Good. And Ned, do it from your cell and not with the hotel phone, for heaven's sake."

"Right. Bye."

"Bye." Pollard turned his phone off and tossed it aside.

Good help was *so* hard to find . . .

Seven

Nagel was sitting at his desk writing a handwritten report on a recently completed experiment involving rat R22B—one of Arnold's sired newborn pups—scribbling, the fine-tip pen scratching against the paper, when his phone rang. He continued writing until it rang a second time, then dropped the pen and answered it, swearing quietly. What he wouldn't give to be able to pay someone to answer his calls . . .

"Genetics Life, Incorporated, Dr. Nagel speaking," he said.

"Dr. Nagel," said a somewhat high-pitched male voice, "My name is Ned Easley. I'm with the Humanity International Company. I'd like to see if we can make an appointment at your building so we can talk about a possible deal we'd like to make with you."

"What kind of deal?" Nagel asked, perking up.

"It'd definitely take care of your debts," Easley said. "What time can I meet you?"

Nagel checked the time in the bottom right-hand corner of his computer monitor: 11:38 A.M. "Is twelve-thirty good?" he asked.

"Wonderful," Easley said.

"Good. Meet me in our conference room. Just walk in and follow the signs."

"I'll be there," the man said, and hung up.

"You're screwing with me," Franklin said, his jaw dropping. Beside him, Dr. Jody Kicheski, a tall, angular woman with pale skin and hair so light blond it looked white, just stood with her arms crossed.

Angel was standing behind the desk in her office. She'd just told her two fellow researchers of the possibility of working on Julian Lloyd, and Franklin put two and two together.

"So old man Petty is gonna pay two million bucks for us to patch up Julian," he said. "I'm game. Let's do it."

"Have you considered the fact that it isn't legal?" Jody said, stabbing at Angel with a glare.

"We'll go to the government," Franklin said. "High profile case like Lloyd would get us approval, no prob—"

"We can't do that," Angel interrupted, folding her hands in front of her. "Do you actually think the NFL would let him play if it knew? The world isn't ready for genetic enhancement in athletes yet, Paul. We can't let anybody know."

"Oh," Franklin muttered, his face dropping. "That's different, then. I don't know about it, I mean, it's . . ."

"Illegal," Jody Kicheski repeated. "I'll have nothing to do with it, Angel. Sorry. And if you try it alone, I will . . ."

"What?" Angel demanded. "You'll tell Nick? We built this company, too, Jody. We should have a say in how it's run, don't you think? And right now we don't. What, you wanna sit back and work with the rats while GLI goes down the drain? I don't, and I won't. We have an opportunity here, and to hell with it all if we don't take it. Nick has absolutely no idea how to run a successful corporation. With the proper leadership—"

"What's that? You?" Jody said.

Angel's eyes narrowed. "Why not all of us? That's how it was supposed to work in the beginning, wasn't it?"

"Yeah," Franklin said. "Yeah, it was."

Jody shook her head. "No—I mean, yes, it was. But Nick's doing his best. He's working on the problem."

"He's been working on the problem since January," Angel said, sitting halfway on her desk. "Has it helped? No. And I'm not planning on waiting for bankruptcy court. If you—"

A loud knock at the door interrupted her. Angel stood up straight. "Open that for me, Paul."

He did, and he and Jody stepped back to allow Angel to see her visitor. Nagel stood there, gasping for air. "Ah, good," he breathed, his eyes scanning the three of them. "You're all here. Come with me. I think we've got a taker."

"What?" Angel asked, a wave of surprise washing over her.

"Come on," Nagel said, pointing down the hall. "Let's get the conference room set up."

Thirty minutes later, the table and chairs were dusted, a can of Lysol was sprayed to freshen up the stale air, the lights were on and the GLI conference room, empty since February, was back in business.

Nagel sat at the head of the table, Angel, Kicheski and Franklin next to him, side-by-side. The visitor came in a few moments after they had sat down, carrying a small briefcase. He was an average man; average height, average weight, brown hair, dull eyes. He wore an expensive-looking tailored suit, though, and a quick glance at Nick confirmed that he was impressed. Angel tried not to cringe, realizing how unprofessional she and the others looked in comparison. Denim and khakis weren't exactly high-fashion. But the man didn't seem to notice.

He took his place across from Angel and set his briefcase on the table. "Thanks for meeting with me on so little notice," he said, looking at Nagel. Nick stood and shook the man's hand. "Angel, Jody, Paul, this is Mr. Ned Easley. He's with . . ." Nagel looked at Easley.

"Humanity International," Easley said, smiling and offering his hand to Franklin, Jody and then Angel. He tried to linger a few extra seconds on her, obviously attracted, but Angel cleared her throat and dropped his hand. *Great.* HUMINT, she realized. Nagel obviously didn't know much about *them,* because if he did, he would've been on an extremely high moral horse.

"Well, I'll be quick," Easley said, taking his seat. "My company has instructed me to offer you an eight million dol-

lar grant, in exchange for some limited access to your research files. A simple trade, Dr. Nagel."

Nagel went pale. "Ah . . . we have a policy we agreed on . . .
we don't . . ."

"We are, of course, willing to negotiate," Easley said, opening his briefcase and pulling out a sheet of paper. "Our
earnings report from last month." He gave it to Nagel, who
looked it over and then went even whiter.

"Perhaps with the proper compensation," he said, blinking
his eyes as if the light in the room was too bright for him.

Angel glanced at Jody out of the corner of her eye. Dr.
Kicheski's face was flushing red, and she sat stiff in her chair.

"Could you give me an idea of proper compensation?"
Easley asked.

"Well, actually . . ." Nagel looked like he was in shock.
"Eight million would easily pay off our debts and . . . ah . . ."
He seemed to brace himself. "Twelve million. Twelve million
would work fine."

"Done," Easley said.

It happened so fast that Angel didn't have a chance to in-
terject with a comment. She bit her lip and kept quiet. Jody,
on the other hand . . .

"Wait a minute!" Kicheski said. "Nick, this goes against
our agreement. We'd never allow outside access to our research. We agreed on that!" She glanced at Franklin and
Angel as if to rally support, but the two of them remained
silent. Angel just watched. This would be interesting . . .

"Jody, just hold on," Nagel said, waving a hand at her. "Uh,
Mr. Easley—"

"Hold on my *ass!*" Jody shouted. "You're breaking an
agreement made between all of us, Nick, and you *can't do
that!* You can't!"

"Jody, shut up!" Nagel snapped, and looked back at Easley.
"Mr. Easley, I apologize. I'll work this out and get back to you
within the next week. But consider the deal done."

Easley nodded. He looked happy with himself as he ambled
from the room.

"Jody," Nagel said, looking at her. "What—"

"Just shove it," Jody said, getting to her feet and storming from the room. She stopped outside the door and spun around. "Angel, I need to talk to you." Then she disappeared down the corridor.

Nagel looked at Angel, his mouth open. "About what?"

"Nothing," she replied, shaking her head. "I'll calm her down."

Nagel nodded. "Okay. Look, Angel, Paul, I can't turn down an offer like that . . . you understand?"

"I guess you just don't have a choice, do you, Nick?" Angel asked as she stood.

"No, I don't. I don't want to give another company access to our data, either, but in this case we're desperate. If I had another option, I'd take it."

"Yeah." Angel stepped toward the door. "Hold off a couple days, though, before you accept that guy's offer," she said. "I'm working on a last-ditch shot with somebody right now. If it works, we'll get a big enough grant to pay off our debts without giving up any research."

"Angel—"

"It's just a couple days," she said, touching his arm. "It won't make a difference. This Easley guy will still be there. Okay?"

Nagel hesitated. "Okay. Make it fast, Angel. This might be our last chance."

You have no idea, she thought as she left the room.

Nagel sighed. "What do you think, Paul?"

Franklin shook his head. "I think I'm gonna get back into football."

"It's the offseason," Nagel pointed out.

"I'm a big fan," Franklin said, stood and followed Angel's path out the door.

* * *

"Go for it," Jody said, on the verge of tears, back in Angel's office. Her face was still red, her eyes watery. "I can't believe him. He agrees to something like that so quickly—I mean, I thought he was a scientist first, executive second, but in there it was all about money. So much for the glories of science and all that crap he spewed when he talked me into this joke of a company. So go for it, Angel. We can't let him do this."

Angel nodded. "Desperate times, huh?"

"Yeah." Jody turned without another word and left.

That had been *too* perfect. No way she'd have been able to convince both Jody and Franklin to help her until Nick's little stunt.

Angel laughed to herself. Nicholas Nagel had just put the first nail in his own coffin.

"Vince?" she asked over the phone an hour later. She was still smiling over the events of the afternoon. *Too perfect,* she thought. Just too perfect.

"Yes, Angelina," Petty's suave voice came. "You have good news?"

"The best," Angel said, kicking off her slip-on shoes and putting her feet up on her desk. "It went beautifully. Now you need to tell your football player. Remember, don't let him find out—"

"I understand. He won't know a thing we don't want him to," Petty assured her. "One last question, however. How do you expect to explain your sudden millions to your Dr. Nagel? I imagine he will be suspicious."

"Actually," Angel said, "I already have a plan for that . . ."

With the sudden, unfortunate resignation of Gunners team physician Randal Lockett, his assistant, Dr. Stanley Rice, was promoted to take his place.

At least, that was the gist of the press release the team issued on Petty's orders. He called Rice into his office a few minutes after hanging up with Angelina. The forty-something man had dark hair and a nose that seemed to have been broken several times. Rice had once been a boxer, Petty knew, in college before medical school, and still had the wiry build of a trim middleweight.

"Vince," Rice said in greeting as he came in. "What's going on?"

Petty stood behind his desk even when Rice sat. The doctor had to look up at him, and that was the way he wanted it. "It's about Julian," he said. "I have been making some inquiries, exploring alternative treatments and the like. I've discovered an interesting clinic right out in Valley Park. They have some of the best doctors in the world there . . . it's expensive, but money isn't an object in this case. I'd like to take Julian in for treatment."

"That isn't necessary," Rice said. "Dr. Hendley has an excellent reputation. We've sent players out to him for years now."

"Never one with an injury so serious, however," Petty said. Now he did sit, making level eye contact. "The doctor I spoke to . . . I described the injury, and she said she believes that with their treatment he can be back on the field before the start of the season."

"That's impossible," Rice said. There was no uncertainty in his voice at all.

"Not with this treatment," Petty said.

Rice laughed, leaning forward. "What are you talking about, Vince? Genetic enhancement?" He laughed harder.

Petty just stared at him until he stopped laughing. The doctor's face went dark. "Is it?"

Petty didn't answer. He remained motionless. There was no way to convince Rice otherwise now, he knew.

"It is," the doctor breathed. "Vince . . ."

"It's a viable treatment," Petty said. "I am not talking about some kind of cheating, making him stronger or faster. I'm talking about curing him of an injury so he can continue his football career."

"FDA approval?" Rice asked.

Petty waved a hand dismissively. "Please, Stanley. That was the first thing I investigated. Of course."

Rice looked away, eyes unfocused as if contemplating what he'd heard. Then he looked back at Petty. "Then I'll give my consent," he said. "Should I inform Julian?"

"Certainly," Petty said. "I'll make the necessary arrangements with Dr. Hendley at the hospital. When can Julian go home?"

"Well, Hendley's already gone in and put things back together," Rice said. "He was debating whether or not the damage is severe enough to warrant an artificial knee." He shrugged. "He can go home tomorrow, most likely, as long as he has twenty-four-hour care. He won't be very mobile. He'll need crutches, at the very least."

"Excellent. Stanley, you go to the hospital and inform Julian. Explain everything to him. As for care, I believe his mother is in town to handle that anyway, or so he told me over the phone. Oh, Stanley, one more thing." The doctor was standing, about to turn and head for the door. "Don't mention anything about genetics," Petty said. "You may frighten him."

Rice froze, placing his hands on his hips. "Vince, he's not a child. He deserves to know what's going to happen to his body."

Petty's eyes narrowed, a warning expression. "Refer to it as a medical breakthrough. Do *not* mention genetic enhancement specifically, Stanley."

Rice sighed. "All right, Vince. A medical breakthrough. New technology. The mother will want to know, too."

"Then tell her," Petty said, wondering if he should handle this himself. No, he decided. Julian would be more likely to trust the information coming from a physician. Especially a physician who really didn't know any better. "Just no genetics. Do you understand?"

Rice nodded. "Yes, Vince. I'll be going."

"Goodbye," Petty said, and watched the doctor leave.

* * *

In Julian's hospital room, Rice explained everything as Petty had explained to him—except, of course, for the genetics. He didn't know why Vince had asked him to leave that aspect out of it, but it wasn't his place to question his superior.

"Is that even . . . I mean, is it possible?" Julian said, his voice quivering. He was sitting up in bed, the television on but the sound muted.

"It is," Rice said. "Believe me. I've heard a little about the treatment they're talking about. It's new, and isn't available most places. You're just lucky it's here."

"September?" Julian went on, shaking his head in disbelief.

"Yes. In time for the season."

"I . . . I don't believe it," the football player breathed, laying his head back. "I just don't believe it."

"It's the truth," Rice said. "So don't listen to the media reports, Julian. Your career is far from over."

"Yeah," Julian said, picking his head up and smiling. A big, wide smile showing his straight white teeth. "Wow. I mean, no doctors actually came out and said it was over, but Dr. Hendley seemed pessimistic, and the media and all . . . I just figured it was. Like that was it, no way back."

"Well it isn't," Rice said. "Mr. Petty is clearing your release with Dr. Hendley. There's really not all that much more he was planning to do anyway. You'll go home tomorrow, and we'll be setting up a visit with the clinic's doctors to talk it over sometime this week."

"Wow," Julian repeated, still smiling. "Ah . . . do you mind if I make a phone call?"

"Not at all."

Julian reached for the phone attached to the bed rail, dialed a number and held it to his ear. "Ma?" he said after a moment. "Yeah, it's me. Look, Ma, I hope you're sitting down, because I got some really good news . . ."

"Wait a minute," Nagel said, freezing in mid-movement. He and Angel had been walking from Lab 1 in the direction of his office when she'd dropped the bomb on him. The Johansson, Harris and Petty law firm wanted to give Genetics Life, Inc. a research grant of two and a half million dollars. "You mean they definitely want to?"

Angel nodded, stopping beside him. "Yes. Definitely. The first million is already on the way into the primary account." Which was the complete truth. Petty had informed her of the fact after his success in convincing Julian to undergo "advanced" treatment yesterday. He'd called to get the information he needed for an electronic transfer. It was probably already there.

"And the rest?"

"They want to meet you again and talk it over," Angel said. "One more time before they commit the rest of the money. But it's a pretty safe bet they're already convinced."

Nagel sighed and leaned his body against the wall. "Just like that. And we don't need to give away research data. I guess I owe Jody an apology."

"That might be nice," Angel said.

He stood straight again. "So when do they want to see me?"

"Day after tomorrow," Angel said. "Noon."

"Great. This is wonderful. A weight off my shoulders." He laughed. "It's funny too. Those guys were even less interested than whatshisname Austin and his people."

"Wow," Angel said, trying to sound sincere in her amazement. "I guess they had a serious change of heart. Who would've thought."

"Makes you want to believe in miracles," Nagel said. He was beaming. "There's no other way to explain it, is there?"

Angel shook her head. "None that I can think of, Nick."

Petty called her a while later to give her directions to Lloyd's apartment. The football player wanted to talk to her, or at least have her explain the procedure to him and his mom. The visit was vital, he told her. If she screwed up and aroused the suspicions of either the mother or her son, the whole deal would fall through. "He might be naive," Petty told her, "but he isn't stupid."

It was a twenty-minute drive from GLI to the apartment building in which Lloyd lived. Angel told Nagel she was going for lunch, then drove straight there.

It was a normal apartment building, twenty or so stories high and painted a weather-beaten whitish pink. Angel went to the front, buzzed the specified room, identified herself to the voice that answered and went inside to the elevator.

A few moments later she was standing at the door to the apartment. She knocked and waited, her hands at her sides. She heard footsteps coming, and then heard the door being unlocked, and then it was opened to reveal a small black woman with gray hair. "Can I help you, miss?" she asked, looking Angel over.

"I'm Dr. Moore," Angel said, giving the woman a pleasant smile. "I'm here to speak with you and Julian about . . ."

"Oh, yeah, come on in!" the woman said, stepping back to let her in. "My name's Jacklyn," she continued. "I'm Julian's mom."

"Nice to meet you," Angel said, stepping inside. The apartment was small but comfortable-looking, with a kitchenette and den with a sofa, coffee table and television, and a door to her right. Lloyd was laying on the sofa, a white knitted cover up to his chest. He was *built,* with dark hair. At first Angel thought he was sleeping, but his mother called his name and his eyes snapped open. They were keen, intelligent, set in a handsome face that was covered with stubble.

"Hi, Julian," Angel said, walking toward the sofa, Jacklyn Lloyd in tow.

He was surprised when he saw her come in. He'd been expecting a man. The fact that the doctor was a woman didn't bother him, though, as much as her age. She couldn't have been all that much older than he. Thirty at the most, and that was only eight years. Becoming a doctor took a long time after normal college ended at twenty-one or twenty-two, so that meant she couldn't have been one for long. Really, he thought as she came into the den, it didn't so much *bother* him as *surprise* him. She looked professional enough, wearing a khaki blouse and knee-length skirt. Her hair was brownish-blond and pulled up in a bun, her face a soft oval with unblemished olive skin. He felt more comfortable when she smiled, flashing a bright set of perfect teeth.

"Hi," Julian said, pulling himself up to a sitting position, or as close as he could get. His knee was throbbing as the effects of his latest dose of medication wore off, but he tried to ignore it. "I'm sorry. I don't know your name . . ."

"Angelina Moore. Call me Angel." She stopped at the foot of the sofa, and his mom came around to his head, across from her.

"Angel. It's Dr. Moore, right?" Julian asked.

"Yes," she said. "So, what would you like to know about us, Julian?"

"Well, Dr. Rice has already explained a lot," Julian said. "He's the new team physician," he explained. "He told me it was new, advanced, and very rare, and that I'm lucky to have access to it here."

"Well, he's right about that," Angel said. "The only reason it's here at all is because a few brilliant people joined our company from around the country. It's barely through the FDA approval process. You'll probably be one of the first it's used on since."

"What exactly will you do?" Jacklyn asked, resting her hands on Julian's shoulders.

"The treatment itself is simple. We just give you a series of injections. The work comes in afterwards. You *will* need to train and work hard at rehab to get back on the field by September. The treatment alone won't do it."

He nodded, chewing at the inside of his lip. Angel—Dr. Moore—seemed sincere. She wasn't rushing her words, and her explanations meshed with those Dr. Rice had given to him.

This was for real.

"When should we come in for the treatment?" Jacklyn asked.

"We're open the day after tomorrow," Dr. Moore said. "Noon would be perfect. You can make it?"

Julian nodded. "We'll be there," he said, smiling and feeling moisture in his eyes. Tears of relief and happiness.

It was *for real!*

"Two days," Jody echoed, her eyes staring off into space.

They were standing just inside Angel's office, the door closed to keep prying eyes and ears away.

"What about Nick?" Franklin asked, standing behind Angel next to her desk. Angel glanced at him. He was looking at her computer, fiddling with the mouse. It was quite obvious that neither he nor Kicheski were comfortable with the situation.

But they'd get over it.

"Nick's got a meeting with Petty's law firm the same time we'll be working on Lloyd," Angel said, grinning as she went over her handiwork. "It'll explain where the money comes from *and* get him out of the way."

"Clever," Franklin muttered, not looking up.

Angel turned back to Jody. The taller woman was standing still, eyes unfocused. She turned her gaze to Angel. "There are risks," she said. "It might not go smoothly. I mean, we've never done it to a person before. His body could reject the genes, or his immune system might think they're a virus, or it could affect his neuro-function—"

"Stop it," Angel said, touching Jody's arm.

Jody's eyes flashed anger. "I won't do it unless you tell him about the risks."

"Okay," Angel said. "Don't worry. I'll call him when you guys leave."

"Nothing's gonna go wrong," Franklin said, looking up

from the computer. "This is Julian Lloyd we're talking about. You think I'm gonna let somethin' happen to *him?*"

"That's the spirit," Angel said, smiling at the chubby scientist. She stood between them, a uniting influence. They had to be a team, or the whole thing would fall apart. And she wasn't going to let that happen.

No matter what it took.

A few moments later she was typing up a routine report on "Arnold's" progress. It took only ten minutes to complete, and then she got up to bring it to Nagel, who had been much more cheerful in recent days. During those ten minutes, she only made one call . . .

. . . to make sure the Chinese restaurant down the road was open tonight. She felt like eating mandarin chicken.

Eight

Coach Gary Harrell stood in front of the eighty-nine men that currently made up the New Orleans Saints. The June minicamp—the last offseason hurrah before training camp and the preseason that led to the twenty week run to the Super Bowl—had been underway for a few days now. The players sat in folding chairs, conversing with the guys next to them, waiting for their boss to start the meeting. Harrell let them wait for a few seconds more, then began.

"Okay, boys, listen up," he said into the microphone attached to the podium at which he stood. His voice echoed, an effect amplified by the mike. "You guys have a treat this morning. A full pads workout, eleven on eleven, scrimmage style. I know what you're thinking. The old man has lost his marbles. Not so. Not yet." He drew a little laughter. "We're gonna do this one time this morning, one time before camp, just to get you into the real swing of football. The first team offense will play against the second team defense. Then we'll swap, the second team offense playing the first team defense. I'll call the plays myself. I don't want you guys to go and make stuff up as you go. This isn't a game. No audibles, quarterbacks. No adjustments at the line, linebackers." He scanned the players as he mentioned their positions. "All you need to do is look at the Gunners to find out what happens when a practice turns into a game."

Gary Harrell and Jacob Davis had conflicting practice styles. Harrell scripted each scrimmage. Davis let the quarterbacks call the plays. Davis said that Harrell's more common style slowed the development of younger players. Harrell said Davis's style resulted in unnecessary friction between team members and too many injuries caused by adrenaline-pumped youngsters. Right now Harrell was winning the debate, he thought, for obvious reasons.

"I want this to go quick and smooth," the coach said. "No playing or dancing around. Save that for the season. We're here right now to work, not play. You don't *play* football in training camp. If I catch any of you having *fun,* you're running wind sprints 'til your body falls off your legs." He looked over his men, satisfied with the cold, professional expressions on their faces.

"And," he added as if talking to a buddy alone in a dark corner, leaning forward against the podium, "whichever defensive unit allows the most touchdowns has to buy cold ones for the rest of the team."

A general cheer went up among the players; they clapped, hollered and patted each other on the backs, ready for the challenge. A few guys got into minor arguments; boasting displays of male bravado were prevalent.

Harrell hoped they were this motivated in September.

Ryan and Falk jogged onto the field together after leaving the locker room where the team had just gotten into their pads and uniforms. It was hot and humid as the sun climbed toward its eleven o'clock position, and he was starting to sweat beneath the pads.

"Get ready to pay up, Junior," Ryan said, slapping the younger man hard on the shoulder pad.

Falk put on his helmet and raised his eyebrows beneath the face mask. "Pay for what? I'll be too busy drinking that beer."

Ryan laughed and ran to meet up with the rest of the second team defense. They formed a huddle near the thirty-five-yard line. He looked to the sideline in time to see Harrell watching him, a hand covering his mouth. There was a crackle in Ryan's helmet, and then the coach's voice came over. "Normal. Dive basic."

Ryan repeated the scheme and the defense went to the line.

As the middle linebacker, Ryan's first job was to stuff the run, to keep the running back from breaking a big gain up the middle. The offense lined up, and he observed the halfback. The quarterback, Ethan Daniels, was a little short for the position at just over six feet, but had a decent arm and the ability to run in the open field. Daniels began calling signals, and Ryan felt rather than saw the four big defensive linemen in front of him tense up.

Daniels shouted, "Set hut!" and the center snapped the ball back to him. The offensive line surged forward, and the center assisted in a double-team on one of the defensive tackles. *Run, up the middle!* Ryan's mind told him, and he jumped into position, waiting . . . *waiting* . . . and with a collision of plastic-clad bodies, Ryan wrapped the halfback up and brought him down, getting carried a couple yards backwards by the pure speed and mass of his target.

Ryan got back to his feet, helped the running back stand, and walked back to the huddle. The ball was being spotted at the twenty-three. A gain of three yards.

The opposing sides lined up again. Daniels took the snap, faked a handoff to the halfback and rolled out to his right, planting his foot and firing a pass down the sideline that was pulled in by one of the wide receivers, who let his momentum carry him out of bounds. An all too easy twenty-yard gain.

Ryan led the defense into the huddle again. "They'll use that bootleg again on this drive," he said. His teammates agreed. Ryan relayed Harrell's play, and they returned to the line.

"Hut!"

Daniels handed off to the halfback again, and once again he ran straight up the middle. This time, instead of double-teaming a tackle, the center darted forward and hit Ryan, knocking him off balance and allowing the halfback to squeeze past, running free into the secondary before being tackled at the fifty by the strong safety.

"Let's go defense!" one of the assistant coaches shouted from the sideline.

Huddle, break, line up.

"Hut, hut!"

Ethan Daniels dropped back deep into the pocket, waiting a couple seconds and then stepping up, letting fly with a deep pass that carried fifty yards in the air. As it came down, both the intended receiver and the cornerback covering him leaped, trying to snag it. A brief scuffle, and the corner came down with it for the interception.

Gotcha, Ryan thought. One drive down, two to go.

They lined up at the twenty-yard line, opposite the one they'd started on. The sides called their plays and settled into formation. Daniels called for the ball and again dropped back deep, but this time he handed the ball off to the halfback. Ryan saw it coming, and slipped into the backfield, hitting the runner square in the chest with his shoulder and driving him into the ground. He heard both cheers and jeers coming from the sideline as he returned to the defensive huddle to receive some congratulations and relay the next set of signals.

They were less fortunate on the next play. Daniels launched an almost lazy deep pass, hitting his receiver in stride as he sprinted down the field behind the defense, untouched into the end zone. One score.

The first play of the next drive was a similar pass, but the cornerback in coverage managed to bat the ball away. The next play was a handoff. The halfback ran behind the left guard, breaking an arm tackle by one of the defensive linemen. He managed to get to the sideline, running in the open field. Ryan had an angle on him and closed in, almost getting outdistanced but managing to grab the collar of the running-back's jersey. He dragged him down from behind and fell to the grass beside him. But not before he'd gained a hefty forty yards.

Another huddle, another journey to the line and another call of "Hut!"

Handoff to the halfback running straight up the middle,

slamming into Ryan and knocking him back. Ryan held on to the back's legs until help arrived in the form of a safety and defensive lineman.

A short break, huddle, line up.

"Set hut! Hut!"

A pass over the middle, gaining eight yards and a first down.

The next play was a similar pass over the middle, but much longer, and the receiver caught it, bowling his way down to the goal line, falling just short of a score.

Ryan gathered his teammates together in the huddle. "This is absolutely pitiful, people," he said before relaying Harrell's signals. "They're moving down the field like we're not even there. I don't want to see any of you letting them in the end zone, you got that?" He heaved a breath.

His teammates nodded in agreement.

"Then let's go," Ryan said.

They lined up in a goal line defense, with almost everyone up close to the line of scrimmage anticipating a run up the gut. Ryan stared at the ball, awaiting the snap. When it came he turned his attention to the halfback, saw him take the handoff, run forward and leap over a pile of blockers and defenders. Ryan moved to intercept him. They slammed into each other, and Ryan felt himself fall backwards along with the halfback, both of them landing in the end zone. Touchdown.

Ryan stood on the sideline now, watching as the second team offense and first team defense took the field. Led by David Falk at middle linebacker, the starting defense was a talented group. The defensive line was strong, the secondary fast and physical, the linebackers smart. A week ago Ryan would have considered Falk the weak point in that lineup, but after their conversation the other day and subsequent talks since, he had been forced to admit that he was wrong. Falk was a natural at his position. He had uncanny field awareness, the ability to react to something as it happened instead of waiting for it to finish. Combined with his considerable natural athleticism, Ryan felt that David Falk would be a Pro Bowl starter within the next season or two.

Falk made the first play. The backup quarterback handed off. The running back tried to get outside the left tackle, but Falk was right there on top of him. On the next play, the quarterback attempted a pass over the middle of the field but someone tipped the ball at the line of scrimmage and Falk snatched it out of the air.

It was a mismatch. The Saints starting defense was one of the league's best, and the backup offense was just that; a group of backups. But the utter domination shocked Ryan. He stood on the sideline holding his helmet under his arm, just shaking his head.

The next play was a run up the middle, a big mistake. Falk knocked the halfback backwards and stood over him. Next the offense tried a short screen pass that was smothered, a pitch off the end that the strongside linebacker sniffed out and stopped, and a deep pass to the left sideline that hit the ground and bounced away. Turnover on downs.

The offense had one drive left, but the contest was already won. The starting defense had displayed its obvious supremacy, and the backups could do nothing but protest as they gave up the cash for the beer. Ryan felt a strange combination of embarrassment and pride. Embarrassment in his performance, pride in his team. For the first time since draft day in April, Ryan Walker felt like he belonged again.

David Falk might have been the starter, and a future superstar, but he wouldn't get there without help.

And supplying that help was now the only reason for Ryan's continued existence in the pro football world.

They walked into the living room of Ryan's home after practice. The sun was setting but the house was lit. Vanessa was in the kitchen. Ryan brought Falk there to introduce him to her. She was on the phone when they strode over, but she hung up as they neared.

"Hey, babe," Ryan said, leaning down for a quick kiss. He motioned at Falk. "David Falk. I invited him over to look at a game tape." He turned to the rookie. "David, my wife Vanessa."

"Nice to meet you," Falk said.

"Same here," Vanessa said with a smile. "You're gonna be here for a while? I just ordered pizza. There should be enough for everyone."

"Ah . . . I don't want to get in the way . . ."

"It's no problem," Ryan said. He looked at his wife. "We'll get started, okay?"

"Sure," she said. "I'm getting the table ready. Kids are upstairs."

"All right." Ryan led Falk back into the living room and slipped one of the tapes into the VCR. The TV was set to ESPN, and the sportscaster on the screen was talking about Julian Lloyd's injury. Ryan caught a fragment of a sentence—*not as serious as originally thought*—before the tape went on. They both sat on the couch and watched the first play of last season's Notre Dame/Nebraska matchup.

Ten minutes into the tape, the kids tramped downstairs. The girls gave quiet, bored hellos and then went back upstairs. Dylan was about to do the same when Falk stopped him.

"Your dad tells me you're into baseball," he said, resting his elbows on his knees.

Dylan stopped, turning to Falk with a smile. "Yeah, big time. I just was in the city all-star game." He sat in the easy chair beside the couch. "You like baseball? Dad can't stand it."

Ryan was leaning back watching the tape. He held up a finger. "I can handle going to the games," he said. "It's fun."

Dylan leaned closer to Falk. "He thinks an error and an ERA are the same thing."

Ryan laughed. "Isn't it?"

"Not exactly," Falk said. He was paying more attention to Dylan than to the television. Ryan smiled. "I played center-field all through high school," Falk went on. "Couldn't hit, though. Coach said I should play football, and there you go."

"What was your average?"

"Two-forty," Falk said. "Not good in high school. Yours?"

"Four-fifteen," Ryan muttered, holding back his smile. "See, Dyl? I remembered."

"Amen," Dylan said. He pulled his socked feet up onto the chair. "Twenty homers. I play shortstop and third base. Started at shortstop at the all-star game."

"Play anything else?" Falk asked.

Dylan shook his head. "Nope. Baseball's my thing."

"Cool. I used to like baseball more than football, to be honest."

"Really?"

Falk nodded. "You bet."

Vanessa interrupted them, calling from the kitchen: "Pizza's here!"

"He seems like a good guy," Vanessa said, lying beside Ryan in bed later that night. Their bedroom was big, and Vanessa kept it decorated and off-limits to the kids. All of her grandmother's old . . . *stuff* was in here. It looked beautiful to the visitor, but cluttered to Ryan. The carpet was beige, the walls white, and the king-sized bed was raised to stomach-level.

"He is," Ryan said, sliding under the covers.

"Surprised you, huh?" she asked, watching his face.

"Yeah," Ryan admitted, meeting her stare. "He did. He sure did. I was almost hoping for some stuck-up screwball, but he's down-to-earth. Good kid."

Vanessa sighed, looking up at the ceiling. "You know, Ryan . . . well. It must've been hard for you. To step back and let him take over. And then to help him like you're doing . . ."

"For the team," Ryan said. "For the team."

"But it's a good thing," Vanessa said. "It really is. I—I still wish you'd decided not to go back, but I'm kinda glad you did."

A warm feeling overtook him. He gave her a little half-smile and turned on his side to better see her. "You mean it or are you just messing with me?"

"I mean it."

Ryan sighed, rolling onto his back. "Thanks, hon. It means a lot to me."

"Yeah . . ." her voice trailed off. She reached over onto her nightstand and turned off her lamp. Ryan did the same on his side. "Yeah," she said aloud. "But I'm still not carpooling twenty screaming toddlers to football games for the other wives!" she said. She chuckled. "Goodnight, Ryan."

She meant that, even though she'd said it in jest, Ryan knew. But she also meant what she'd said before, and that really did mean more to him than anything else she could have done.

Ryan reached under the covers for her hand, found it and gave it a squeeze. "Goodnight, honey."

Nine

The sun was trekking across a cloudless blue summer sky, heating the noonday air to almost ninety degrees and forcing most sensible people inside their homes or businesses, even high up the Mississippi River in St. Louis, Missouri. Nick Nagel, on the other hand, dressed in his best suit, was on his way out the Genetics Life door when he turned to Angel. He'd been squeezing information out of her—What had the lawyers said when she'd talked to them? Which one seemed to be in charge? How interested were they, really?—and she could only answer his questions while at the same time working to get him out of the building before it was too late.

"Wish me luck," he said, drawing himself up and opening the door.

"I think everyone did," Angel said. Outside in the parking lot she could see several of the dozen or so employee cars beginning to pull out, their owners heading out to get lunch. Angel had convinced Nagel to give everyone an extra hour on their break—the rats could wait, she had said, and they could all use the small congratulatory rest—just to be on the safe side.

"Yeah, they did," Nagel said. "I'll see you later, Angel. This is it!" He went outside and Angel closed the door behind him. She turned away and took a deep breath. The building was empty now, except for her, Paul Franklin and Jody Kicheski. And they could do nothing but wait for Lloyd to show up.

Franklin and Jody were waiting in her office. Angel went back there to join them. She sat down on the edge of her desk, gripping it with her fingers. Franklin was sitting in her chair, and Jody stood like a statue beside the open door.

"What if he doesn't show?" Franklin asked, sounding worried. "I mean, it's after twelve already."

"He's coming," Angel said. "I called this morning to confirm."

"Well, what if his mother got in an accident or something?" Franklin continued, rambling on. "You said she was an old lady. Maybe she shouldn't be driving around town with him."

"She isn't that old, Paul. Calm down, will you?" Angel started tapping her foot on the ground, sitting there with her shoulders hunched a bit.

The injections weren't going to take very long. Maybe twenty minutes. But if someone came back from lunch early and walked in while Lloyd and his mother were still here then there would be a *lot* of explaining to do. And with two ignorant, innocent-minded people in the room, it would get nasty quickly.

Positive, Angel. Think positive.

Nagel wouldn't be back for a few hours. The drive alone, there and back, would take forty minutes. Petty's firm partners would keep him maybe two hours. So Nick wasn't the problem. The technicians and junior research partners, ten in all, were. With their normal thirty-minute lunch break extended to an hour and a half today, by all rights they should be gone at least two-thirds of that time. That would give them plenty of time to get Lloyd in, injected, and then back out.

Plenty of time.

But if Lloyd was late . . .

"It's twelve fifteen," Franklin said. "Something happened. They canceled, or maybe they got stuck in traffic. Something."

Angel frowned, trying not to look at Franklin or legitimize his concerns with a reply. She glanced at Jody. The tall woman was still standing there, motionless, her eyes half-closed as if in deep thought.

Angel looked down at the floor, trying to keep her own

nervousness from showing. She shifted on the desk, almost telling Franklin to get out of her chair, but she decided not to bother him. As anxious as he looked, he would blow up on her given the slightest provocation.

She was starting to feel clammy, her skin damp. It was getting hot in here. She stood up, stepping out into the hall to lower the thermostat, but she heard something down the corridor . . . yes, the front door closed! She whirled around. "They're here," she said, and headed down the hall to the lobby/waiting room.

They were indeed. Lloyd was standing with crutches and his mom, Jacklyn, was looking around as if to find someone to ask where to go. "Hello, Julian, Mrs. Lloyd," Angel said, getting their attention. "Glad you made it."

"So am I," Jacklyn said. Lloyd didn't say anything. He looked a little uneasy.

"You can follow me," Angel said, leading them back down the corridor. "The rest of the staff is out at lunch. It'll just be Dr. Franklin, Dr. Kicheski and me."

"That's all you need?" Lloyd asked from behind her.

Angel glanced back at him as she walked. "It's a very simple procedure. Like I said before, *you're* going to do the main work. We'll just be helping you along."

He nodded, exchanging a hopeful/worried look with his mom. Angel looked back ahead, took a left turn down another hallway and then a right into the operating room. Franklin and Kicheski were already there, both of them wearing their doctors' garb and surgical gloves and masks. Angel went to the corner and slipped her own gloves and mask on, then motioned for Julian to sit on the operating table.

"Just sit there and lie back," she said, her breath feeling hot against her face in the paper mask. "Dr. Kicheski, get the syringes."

Jody complied, bringing a tray with several small shots filled with yellowish liquid. The liquid itself was just a decontaminant. The important stuff was too small to see; individual, modified viruses, stripped of their disease-making abilities and "redesigned" to implant modified genes into Julian Lloyd's genome, genes that would instruct his body to let loose with a barrage of hormones capable of rebuilding his mangled knee structure with ten times the effectiveness and in less than a fifth of the normal time than the human body alone was capable of. Of course, the effects would alter the rest of his body too. He'd get bigger and stronger and faster the more he worked, but that would be corrected in a month or so when they deactivated the genes, allowing his body to return to its pre-injury norm.

Angel picked up the first syringe from the tray Jody was holding, and held it over Julian's tense body. "It's okay," she said, her voice sounding a little muffled to her own ears. "Just relax."

"I'll try," Lloyd said. "I've just never done something like this, that's all."

Neither have I, Angel thought, and lowered the syringe toward him.

"This has been a much more enjoyable meeting than the last one," Nagel said with a smile as he sat around the table with Gregory Johansson, Melinda Harris and Vincent Petty of the Johansson, Harris & Petty law firm. The room was different from most of those in which he had these meetings. The walls were painted white, the floor made of white ceramic, the overhead lights bright, decorated like chandeliers. Johansson and Harris looked as though they could have been twins. Middle-aged, both had graying dark hair and almost black eyes contrasting with sickly pale skin. Petty, on the other hand, looked fit and healthy for his age, with intelligent eyes and a cultured voice.

"Yes, it has," Petty said. He'd done most of the talking. His two partners had looked a little confused for the majority of the time, and more than a little bored now. But Petty seemed excited and eager to talk. "Your Dr. Moore is a delightful person. She did an excellent job of selling your company and work to me."

"Yes, she has done a good job," Nagel said, and meant it. "Well, I assume you already have our account information . . ."

"Yes," Petty said. "Dr. Moore supplied us with it. Thank you for coming personally, Dr. Nagel. I know you are a busy man, and I appreciate your taking time away from work to iron out the details."

"The pleasure is mine," Nagel said, and he meant that too. He stood and shook hands with Petty and nodded a goodbye to the two partners. "Thank you so much."

"You're welcome. Anything for the pursuit of medical science, Doctor."

Nagel made his departure from the firm, which occupied most of the twentieth story of a downtown St. Louis office building, rode the elevator down to street level and walked toward his car in the parking garage. The streets were almost empty, with only a few people in suits shuffling in and out between the buildings.

Nagel reached his Saturn, opened the door, but before he got in he dug his cell phone out from his jacket pocket and dialed Ned Easley's number off the business card the man had left him.

"What?" Pollard demanded, jumping to his feet and pacing the floor of his office living area. "What the hell are you talking about?"

"It's what I said, Mr. Pollard," Easley told him. The man's voice sounded nervous, shaken, but Pollard didn't let that distract him from his own anger.

"That's *impossible!*" he shouted into the phone. "There's *no way* Nagel could have dug up funding that quickly. And from where?"

"Some law firm."

"Law firm!" Easley clenched the phone in his hand, not caring if he broke it. "Something smells bad in this deal, Ned. Something stinks. You stay in St. Louis and find out what's going on. I want to know the partners in that firm, their backgrounds, what they make, their family lives, who their friends are, what kinds of pets they have, what they eat, where they shop. Get their frigging shoe sizes if that's what it takes! And while you're at it, run a check on Nagel's people. That fat guy, Franklin, I already know a little about him. He worked at San Diego State eight or nine years ago. But the others, find out everything. Got it?"

"I'll do my best." Easley didn't sound very confident.

"Dammit! I don't want your *best,* Ned! Get it *done!* I'd put Jeanette on it but she's already working a job. You're the only person I have available for GLI, Ned. *Do it!"*

"Okay, okay, I'll do it," Easley said. "I'll report back later, Mr. Pollard."

"Yeah, stay in touch, Ned," Pollard said, turning the phone off and falling onto his sofa.

He swore under his breath. What the hell was going on?

Lloyd hobbled his way out the door, Jacklyn walking behind him. Angel stopped his mother and handed her a slip of typed paper with her number on it. Her direct office number. She couldn't have them calling and getting Nick, could she?

"If you have *any* questions," Angel said. "Call me. How long will you be in town?"

"Until he's on his feet," Jacklyn said. She chuckled. "I guess you can tell me how long that's gonna be."

"Not long," Angel smiled.

Jacklyn returned the gesture. "Thanks, Dr. Moore. We really appreciate it."

"Just happy to help," Angel said, and watched them leave.

Nagel wore a big smile when he came into the laboratory. His eyes were bright and cheery and he looked well-rested. He walked toward Angel, who stood beside Franklin as he observed Arnold the rat's behavior, digging a notepad out of the pocket of his lab coat.

"You look happy," Angel noted, glancing up at him.

"I'm thrilled," Nagel said, stopping beside her and watching Franklin as he handled the rat. "How is this going?"

"Fine," Angel said.

"His strength is at four-hundred-ten percent," Franklin said. "Dexterity has improved. Agility has actually gotten better with the new muscle growth, and he's quicker and more alert than ever." Franklin glanced at Angel with a little frown. "He'd be a Pro Bowl running back in the Rodent Football League."

"Great," Nagel said. "Well. We don't need to hold back anymore. Thanks to Angel's hard work and Mr. Petty's generosity, we're back in business." He sighed, and smiled at her. "How does it feel to be working for a debt-free company?"

"I love it," Angel said. *You want me to bake you some cookies?* Running in the black was normal. Red ink was bad. It meant you were failing. To be a success, of course you needed to make a profit. Nick Nagel, biologist, was clueless. Angel managed not to let her feelings show. Nagel wouldn't understand them at a time like this.

No. More likely, she corrected, he wouldn't even notice.

Ten

The capacity of a human being to lie to himself was astounding. Vincent Petty had always struck Hendley as a calm, calculating realist. But the depth of his disbelief and his refusal to listen to the medical analysis given to him and his employees shattered that image. He was nothing if not a frantic eccentric now, ignoring Hendley and running around for a "second opinion" while pulling Julian out of the hospital at the earliest possible date. Never mind that the man couldn't walk. Never mind that his knee, although Hendley had worked long and hard in patching it back together, was still in shambles. Petty wanted a second opinion, and when the second opinion agreed with the first, he'd seek a third and a fourth, and so on, until the fans screamed for him to do something and started to cancel their season tickets.

Not that Hendley didn't care—as a football fan, he did, and it was a tragedy what had happened to Lloyd—but *he* was a realist. As a doctor, he *had* to be. He had to have the ability to tell an injured athlete the truth about his or her condition. Eric Hendley, doctor, couldn't in good conscience tell a football player that there was hope when there was none.

Well, the most optimistic opinion Vincent Petty was going to get would be a *possible* return to football in eighteen or twenty-four months. Lloyd wouldn't be able to run for almost a year. And his speed, power and explosiveness would never return. But in theory he would be healthy enough to make an attempt . . .

Although he'd fail. Hendley had seen thousands of sports injuries, hundreds and hundreds of athletes in dozens of sports from football to figure skating. Running backs in professional football didn't just jump back into the game after blowing out a knee. There were always residual effects. Even the 'backs who did return were rarely the players they had once been. Even if his athletic abilities did come back, a player's confidence in those abilities often did not. He felt an underlying fear, festering just below the surface, of getting hurt again. Three hundred pound linemen and linebackers that hit like eighteen-wheelers made sure of that. And one couldn't discount the psychological warfare that occurred during your average football contest. Opposing players would never let him forget, and for a naive rookie fresh out of the somewhat less savage world of college football, that aspect alone could make a successful return impossible.

But that was all for the average blown-out knee. Julian Lloyd's injury wasn't average.

Hendley sat at his desk just behind the quiet front office. It was early yet, just after seven. The first patient wasn't due to arrive for a half hour. Fran and the rest of the staff always had the records in order, so he had plenty of time to drink a cup of coffee and go over the morning newspaper.

He flipped through the front page news section of the *Post-Dispatch*. More and more of the norm in today's world . . . the environmentalists were concerned over the Republican administration's perceived lack of "tenderness" toward the natural world. Tenderness. They'd actually used that word in the headline. Hendley shook his head and sipped his coffee. He turned to the sports section—

And almost choked.

In bold headlines, right there on the page in front of him, was written:

CONFUSION IN THE CAMP
Petty: Lloyd's injury not as serious as reported

What the hell was *this?*

Hendley set down his mug and held the paper in both hands, studying the article. Lloyd's injury, it said, originally reported as being season- and possibly career-ending, was in fact much less serious than first thought. And that came from—who else?—Vincent Petty himself. Hendley was glad to see his own skepticism and disbelief voiced in the article. Sportswriters tended to dislike sports franchise owners as soon as the owner was in that position for more than three or four years. Owners were all greedy, self-centered megalomaniacs. All of them. Unless they were moving a team to your city, of course, in which case they received a new three-year honeymoon as the benevolent philanthropists they thought they were. And then they were greedy monsters again.

Hendley knew better from his own dealings with sports team owners. Most of them wanted to win as much as the fans did, bless their ignorant hearts. But some did match the media-supplied stereotype, and from reading this story, it was apparent that Vincent Petty did.

There was no way Julian Lloyd could be ready in . . . in what, three months? The season started in September. Three months.

No way.

So what was Petty hoping to accomplish? Didn't he realize that the hopes of the fans would rise and then be dashed in only a matter of months? And didn't he know what would happen as a result? His ticket sales would hit the basement. His bond of trust—what little of it existed between fans and owners—would be shattered. Gunners fans throughout the region would demand Vincent Petty's head on a platter, and being the businessman he was, Petty *had* to know that. Right?

Hendley shivered, folding the newspaper on his desk. Of course he did. He knew it. So there were only three options that Hendley could see. One, Petty was insane. Not likely. Two, Hendley himself had been wrong about the injury. But that was impossible. Anybody with the ability to see could check out that X ray and observe the damage. You didn't even need a trained eye, it was so striking. Three, Petty had uncovered a new form of treatment. The only option left. It had to be true.

But Hendley prided himself on keeping abreast of the new technologies in his particular medical field. To be one of the best, he had no other choice. There was nothing on the horizon that could heal someone with such a serious injury in ninety days. Julian Lloyd would be lucky to walk without crutches in three months. There was no new, groundbreaking treatment.

Unless . . .

The ensuing thought caused Hendley to jump up like a spring and all but run to the front office, his white doctor's coat trailing behind like the contrail of a jet fighter.

Only one person sat in the front office, a small, petite woman sitting at a computer. She had short dark hair and big, black thick-frame glasses. Her shoulders were hunched as she typed, and she didn't seem to notice Hendley approach.

"Fran," Hendley said, keeping his voice steady. He thanked all the speeches and speech rehearsals for helping him develop that ability. His nerves were tingling, his hands shaking, but his voice was steady and calm, the way he thought a doctor's voice should be.

The petite woman stopped typing and looked up. "Yes, Dr. Hendley?" Her voice was quiet and unassertive, with little in the way of distinguishing qualities. It matched her appearance.

"I need you to find out what's going on behind the scenes with Julian Lloyd," Hendley said. "Did you read the paper this morning?" he asked when he saw her blank expression. She shook her head. "That's fine," Hendley went on. "It reported that Lloyd's injury isn't as serious as originally thought."

"But I saw those X rays . . ." Fran said.

"Exactly." Hendley leaned closer to her as one of the technicians made a morning sweep through the waiting room to check for any trash the janitor might have missed the night before. "He's hurt badly. So this story makes no sense whatsoever, unless they have a new treatment. But if there *is* a new treatment, I would know about it. So that can only mean one thing."

"I see," Fran said. And that said everything, in her quiet mousy way.

"So you'll research it for me? Find out whatever you can." He stood erect, but kept his voice low. "I'll pay you overtime for any extra hours you need to work."

Fran nodded. "I'll get started."

"Thanks," Hendley said. He stepped back and was about to turn away from her when another thought occurred to him. "Fran, get me Dan Newman on the line." Newman was the business head of APEX, American Physicians united against genetic EXperiments, Hendley's organization. He was a certified accountant, not a physician. But Hendley wasn't about to try to run the business side of his operation alone. And he wasn't about to put another doctor in charge, not when he had a real, concerned, successful businessperson to do the work. "I need to talk to him," Hendley said.

Fran picked up her phone and started punching in a number. "Yes, Doctor."

"I hope I'm wrong about this," Hendley said, but Fran was already working again and didn't reply.

Jeanette Dean was wearing those big, ugly glasses and speaking in a quiet, shy tone when she contacted Pollard on VideoCall and reported on the latest developments. The HUMINT CEO recognized the partial disguise as part of her "Fran" identity, which she had assumed about fourteen months ago when Pollard had needed someone on the inside of APEX, someone who could keep him up-to-date on Eric Hendley. That man was dangerous, Pollard knew. If Hendley and his fellow APEX members got their way, Humanity International would become a stagnant company in a stagnant industry. A complete ban on human genetic engineering in athletes . . . tight restrictions on genetic engineering in humans, period . . . not to mention the normal restrictions on human cloning and the like . . .

In effect they wanted to tie the hands of an industry and in the process wipe out the entire next phase of medicinal evolution. And another round of multiple billions for the company best able to capitalize on that evolution. Which would be HUMINT, regardless, Pollard thought. But things would be so much easier if Genetics Life would stop being so *difficult!*

"Are they nuts?" Pollard said, shaking his head and sipping his cappuccino. "Nagel must be out of his mind!"

"I doubt Nagel has anything to do with it," Fran said, her voice rising in decibel and falling in tone as she morphed back into Jeanette.

"What makes you say that?" Pollard asked. He wasn't completely awake. He'd come to the office early today, and now he was regretting that decision. "It's his company."

"Call it experience," Jeanette said. "For now, though, I'd rather not say."

"Fair enough," Pollard said. It didn't matter, anyway. Jeanette Dean was always accurate. She was a legitimate weapon. How fortunate had he been to grab her straight out of school? A better question would be to ask how stupid the rival companies were to shun her over one little incident, one little *thing* that had happened while she'd been earning her doctorate. In fact, it was that little incident that had caught Pollard's attention in the first place. She was the type of person he'd needed at the time to reach the top and still needed to remain there.

"Hendley wants information," Jeanette said. "How far should I go?"

"That depends on what you could give him. Anything that could damage GLI?" They couldn't afford to let anything happen to Genetics Life, at least not yet. If the government found out about what they might have done to that football player it would pounce on them. And Pollard could kiss any chance of acquiring that research goodbye.

"If I can prove Hendley's theory on this Julian Lloyd thing, yeah, definitely," Jeanette said. "That's enough by itself to throw the researchers involved in prison. And they'd have some major problems trying to keep from getting their hardware confiscated."

"We can't have that," Pollard said. "Sit on it, Jeanette. Find something superficial, or make excuses. I'll leave it up to you to figure out the details. Just don't let it get out of hand." He rubbed his eyes and took another sip from his cappuccino.

"It won't."

"Good," he said, swallowing. "Be careful, *Fran.*" For his sake, not hers. She knew that, Pollard realized, but didn't care.

"I will." Her image vanished, her expression remaining bland as it disappeared.

It made all too much sense, Pollard thought, groaning; he was so tired. The sudden "research grant" from Vincent Petty's law firm . . . a guy like Petty didn't give away money for no reason. And the best reason in the world for him to spend money these days was Julian Lloyd. Petty, like Pollard, had skirted the law before. They both knew what it felt like to come close to the edge. Both of them, Pollard knew, had much to lose. But Petty felt he couldn't survive professionally if Julian Lloyd didn't produce. If Petty got caught, Pollard figured, he'd get off on some legal technicality or manage to hold out on appeal until he reached his deathbed.

All Petty's money had bought GLI was time. That was all, more time. Nagel, with his executive ignorance, was still in charge of the company. He still had no principle investors. He still couldn't produce a sellable product, running a biotech company like a pure research institute. It just didn't work. Sooner or later he'd be back in the red and would be as desperate as he'd been just a few days ago, if not more. The problem was, with that time came opportunities. Pollard couldn't just buy out every potential investor that came Nagel's way. Eventually a few would slip through the cracks and GLI would get the financial support it needed.

So the question was: Would the money Petty had given them for this Lloyd thing keep them going long enough?

Not if I can help it.

And he would help it. It was just a matter of time. He had Easley in position to keep an eye on things, too.

Easley.

Why hadn't Easley seen this coming? That fool had been closer to this whole deal than anyone else in HUMINT. Anyone else *anywhere,* outside of GLI! Why hadn't he known?

Pollard picked up his phone and dialed out to get Ned Easley.

Geoffrey Marsh slapped the sports section on Petty's desk and stood in front of him with his arms crossed, his face red. "What the hell is going on here?" he demanded, his voice hoarse. He'd been under as much stress as Petty had, the owner thought, and poor Geoffrey didn't handle stress well. At least not real-world stress.

"I was under the impression that I had already explained it," Petty said, looking up from his weekly status report on the business side of the team.

"No, you explained some new treatment we were trying. Stanley told me as well. I'm talking about *this!*" He stabbed the headline with a finger. "I'd like to know what the hell you're trying to do."

Petty looked at Marsh, locking onto the general manager's eyes. Eye contact, a soothing, gentle expression. "It's part of the game, Geoffrey. You know that. There are some cases in which a little manipulation of the media is necessary to the success of the team."

"So you lied," Marsh growled. "You called up the paper and fed them a load of crap."

Petty took a deep breath, folding his hands in front of him. "Geoffrey, I gave them the information they needed, the information *we* needed to give them. When Julian returns to the field—"

"If he returns," Marsh interrupted, and Petty's eyes flashed with anger.

He blinked it away. "When Julian returns to the field, they won't be surprised," Petty continued.

"Why not tell the truth?" Marsh said. "Where would the problem be with telling the truth for once?"

"Come now, Geoffrey. Are you going to sit there and tell me that you have never manipulated the media? The trades you've worked, the free agents you've signed, the players you've drafted . . . all of that without a little manipulation? It isn't possible, Geoffrey, and you know it. Misinformation is an absolute necessity."

"I don't understand your reasoning," Marsh said, the redness fading from his cheeks, replaced with a pale, dejected frown. "If this treatment is going to help him as much as you say, why not go public with it? It's good news. Isn't it?"

"Extremely good news," Petty said, then looked away as if in humble subjection. A necessary expression of feelings that weren't there. He looked back at Marsh. "Geoffrey, I'll tell you the truth," he said. "The doctors who performed the operation on Julian do not want press coverage at this time. It would be detrimental to the future of their company, for technical reasons. Perhaps one day," he added, raising a hand to ward off the GM's questions, "but that day is not today." Petty held back a smile. The fact that most of what he'd said wasn't entirely untrue was not lost on him.

"I still don't understand," Marsh had to say. *Why won't he just cooperate?* Petty thought. "I'd think they would *want* good press. That would make sense, wouldn't it?"

"In their case, no," Petty said, shifting in his chair.

"But—"

"Let me say it another way," Petty said with an edge. "If you leak any information on the specifics of Julian's case, you will be allowed to seek a new position with another team. Do you understand *that?*"

Silence. Then, "Yes, Vince."

"Good." Petty motioned at the door. "We can talk more later, Geoffrey." He placed a hand on the report on the desk. "Right now I have work to do."

* * *

Something was different.

Julian awoke the morning after the treatment expecting a flood of pain to wash through his body from his right leg. Every morning since the injury had been the same. Pain, throbbing, aching, burning pain. The drugs always wore off during the night, leaving him no insulation from his injury and precipitating a miserable, crutch-assisted stagger into the kitchen for a mom-administered dose of Tylenol.

But this morning, something was different.

His room was dark; the curtains were drawn, and only a dim line of light streaked in under the door that led to the living area. Julian started to work his upper body to a sitting position so he could find his crutches, and again he gritted his teeth in anticipation of pain.

None came.

Oh, it still hurt. It wasn't comfortable, that was for sure, and it didn't feel normal. But it just wasn't throbbing, swelling. It didn't have that migraine-headache feel.

Dr. Moore hadn't been kidding, Julian thought. He'd make sure to remember her and Mr. Petty and Dr. Rice in his morning prayers. He owed them a lot.

He shivered. It felt a little cold in here. Or maybe it was something else, something psychological. He couldn't tell because everything was already going so right.

The cold feeling, a frigid chill, stayed with him for a moment, just long enough for him to wonder about it and ponder it, and then it vanished. Maybe he should ask Dr. Rice about it when he reported back to the training facility for classroom work next week, he thought. Yes, he should. He made a mental note to do so.

And a couple seconds later, he forgot about it.

Part Two
Whatever It Takes

Eleven

The sun scaled the horizon, casting a golden radiance over the dew-covered grass practice field at the Missouri Gunners training facility. The dew glittered like a million diamonds, evaporating as the temperature rose.

Wearing workout shorts with a team logo, the word "Gunners" spelled out on a black helmet, and a light T-shirt, Julian sat on the grass amid his similarly-clad teammates and went through a fifteen-minute stretching routine. His leg felt normal. No pain. If the large faded scar on the outside edge of his kneecap hadn't been there, one wouldn't have known the injury had ever happened.

Well, his leg didn't feel *completely* normal, he thought. Something still wasn't right. His movements felt a little rusty, and he wasn't as fast in the agility tests as he'd been three months ago. But that would come. He'd had a few conversations with Dr. Moore over the last few weeks, and she had assured him of that fact. How could he even *expect* to be back to normal in less than ninety days?

How could he? Especially when his mind still told him he should be hobbling about on crutches and not preparing to run through drills with a professional football team. In time he would return to normal. Just a little more time. If he had to miss a few games, that was okay.

Except it wasn't. Julian wanted to get on the field. He was getting paid millions, and he needed to do something to earn that money, if only to salve his own conscience. Julian chuckled. His mother still said he was stupid for feeling bad. She called from Chicago almost every day—from her new home on Lake Shore Drive—and their conversations invariably came around to that subject.

The practice field seemed a little empty. Julian had watched all of training camp and the preseason from the sidelines, learning as he observed, and feeling bad about it the entire time. So he hadn't really *felt* the post-camp roster reductions. Guys just disappeared, stopped showing up. At least it seemed that way. Jacob Davis liked to let his camp bodies go without much fuss to avoid teasing the young players with false hopes. At its peak, the roster had numbered ninety-one. Now it was a trim fifty-three, plus five practice squad members who were free to sign with another team if they so desired—and if another team showed interest.

The stretching went by uneventfully. It felt good to be out here in the sunlight, working out with the team again. When the last exercise was completed, Davis blew a whistle and shouted in a commanding tone, "On your feet! Passing drills! Skill positions at the goal line with Coach Finley!"

The skill positions were the ball handlers, the quarterbacks, running backs and wide receivers. Together, they formed a group of seventeen men, three quarterbacks, three halfbacks, two fullbacks, three tight ends and six wide receivers. Rich Mitchum was already standing with the quarterbacks coach, Elijah Finley, at the goal line. Ahead of them, the field cleared of players, coaches and equipment. Mitchum would be throwing with the sun to his back, but that meant his receivers would be looking straight into it when they turned around. Which could cause difficulties when Mitchum unleashed a twenty-yard curl that *whooshed* audibly through the air and zipped on a flat trajectory into the receiver's not-so-ready chest. An unprotected chest on a practice like today's, with no pads. And that was painful, the pointed end of a football slamming into your chest; painful when the big kid on the playground threw it. It was downright agonizing when fired by the cannon arm of one of professional football's strongest-armed passers.

Julian lined up first in the small crowd of running backs. They would run their routes after the wide receivers and tight ends. Julian stood, watching the speedy wideouts dash across the field, cutting right on the grass, reaching out and snagging Mitchum's passes with their hands, bringing the ball in on the run. Perfect technique that was important but impossible to master. Catching the ball on the practice field in shorts was one thing. Catching it while running full-speed over the middle of a football field during a game, with a speeding tank of a defensive back on a collision course with you . . . that was a different animal.

The tight ends ran shorter routes than their smaller companions, but they were much slower and more plodding. Mitchum seemed to take more time as he dropped back and flicked his wrist, sending the ball skimming the air over fifteen yards to his target. The tall quarterback was almost lazy in his movements, as if it was the easiest thing in the world to throw a football forty yards down a field to hit a moving target, while managing to keep the ball on a straight line in the air. No arc in its flight whatsoever.

His technique was picture-perfect. Mitchum dropped back, light-footed despite his self-deprecatory humor to the contrary, planted his rear foot, brought his arm back behind his ear and then exploded from the elbow, snapping his wrist and stepping through, shifting his weight onto his front foot. Textbook Johnny Unitas stuff. A coach's dream.

The last tight end was more of a blocking specialist. The 270-pound man stomped through his route and caught the ball with his body, clutching it against his chest. Not good technique, but that was why he was a *third-string* tight end.

"Julian."

He stepped forward in response to the assistant coach's call. He lined up next to Mitchum, about five yards down, and leaned into a wide receiver's stance.

"Okay, just run a little fifteen yard out," Mitchum said. "We ain't tryin' too hard today."

Julian nodded, pumping his fists. Mitchum called, "Hut,"

and Julian pushed forward, accelerating straight, then planting his left foot and cutting to the right, reaching for the pass—

It skimmed past his hands, skipping across the ground before another assistant chased it down.

"Lookin' a little rusty," Mitchum said, taking another ball from the QB coach.

"I feel a little rusty," Julian said, returning to the line and dropping back into the stance.

"You were slow off the start," Coach Finley said. "And try to keep the cut crisp. You rounded it off."

"I know, I felt it," Julian said. Rounding off routes weren't often a problem for a 225-pound running back. But with his speed and hands, he could be a veritable receiver out of the backfield. The coaches at USC had liked to line him up in the slot on third downs, and he could beat linebackers and even safeties one-on-one.

That last route wouldn't have beaten anybody, though. Julian sighed, focusing ahead. Just calm down and do it.

"Try cutting the other way," Mitchum said. "Ready?" Mitchum asked, holding the ball in one hand. Julian nodded, still looking ahead. "All right. Hut!"

He pushed off harder this time, running as fast as possible straight down the field for fifteen yards and then planting his right foot—

He slipped.

His right leg collapsed beneath him and he fell face-first onto the ground, skidding to a stop. For a second that seemed to take forever, Julian lay there, wondering what would happen when he moved. He hadn't felt the injury until he'd moved . . . hadn't felt it until he'd moved, and now he didn't think he could move for fear of it happening again.

He had to move. Gathering his courage about him, he set his palms on the ground and pushed himself up to his feet. No pain. He was okay. He was fine, thank God. He looked down at his knee, staring at it as he returned to the line.

"You all right?" Mitchum asked, holding a new ball at his hip.

Julian looked up. "Yeah, I'm good. Just slipped on the grass. I, uh—I guess I'll have to get used to it again."

"You're sure?" Finley said.

Julian nodded. "Yeah, I'm sure. Um, let me take a break. I'll go again the next go-round, all right?"

Finley nodded in understanding. "No problem. Jimmy!" He turned to the smaller backup running back. "You're up."

Julian walked a few yards away, back out of the way where no one would notice him until the next exercise. He watched, keeping quiet as his backup and then the big, slow fullbacks all ran perfect routes and made perfect catches. And he sighed again. It was insanity to be so disappointed after an injury like the one he'd suffered, but still . . .

"Julian."

He turned, and saw Jacob Davis walking toward him, wearing a Gunners cap, a gray sweatshirt and khaki shorts and a whistle around his neck. His dark sunglasses and graying black hair gave him the appearance of a grizzled old fighter pilot turned football coach, but Davis probably would've taken exception to that description, old Army man as he was.

"Yeah, Coach?" Julian said, hands on his hips.

"You all right?" Davis asked, looking concerned, even though his eyes were hidden behind the glasses.

"Yeah, fine." The snappiness of his reply surprised him. Julian stared at the ground.

"I saw what happened."

Julian looked up at him, not sure what to say.

"You slip, or what?"

Julian moved closer to him. "My knee just buckled," he said, just loud enough for the coach to hear. "I'm a little worried about it."

"Well," Davis said, and he smiled. "Don't be worried. After what you went through, a little slip every now and then is normal. I'd be worried if you didn't screw up."

Julian smiled back. "Trying to make me feel better, huh Coach?"

"Is it working?"

"Yeah, I guess it is." Julian took a deep breath. "So, I worry too much."

Davis crossed his arms over his chest, placing his weight on one foot. "That's one thing the scouts had against you from your interviews at the Combine. They marked it as a negative that you worry and that you're hard on yourself." He shrugged. "I didn't know why at first. But you know, it really can hurt you. Knowing you need to improve is one thing. But placing unrealistic expectations on yourself doesn't help you, either."

"I just want to be there, Coach," Julian said, looking away again. "To help the team."

Davis shrugged again, nonchalant. "What? You don't think Jimmy over there can handle it?"

Julian shook his head. "No, it's not that. It's just that I'm getting paid to play football, and I haven't done that yet."

"What's Jimmy getting paid for, making cotton candy?" Davis asked, an eyebrow raised.

Julian laughed. "I see what you mean."

"Good. Because I'm not putting you on the field until you're ready, until you're comfortable. If you're playing while you aren't comfortable, you'll end up hurt again. And we don't want that."

"No," Julian agreed.

"So take your time," Davis said, turning around. "There's plenty of time for you to get on the field yet." He held the whistle to his mouth and blew it. "All right!" he shouted. "Line drills! Four-man sleds! Let's *move,* people!"

"Take my time," Julian said to himself, and frowned. He understood that. It was necessary for his optimum athletic performance. He wouldn't help the team if he rushed his recovery and tried to come back too soon. He'd end up hurt again. So he had to take his time.

He just hoped he didn't have to take too much time.

* * *

Petty was watching the practice session from the sideline when Davis came over to him.

"I need to talk to you, Vince," the coach whispered, standing close beside Petty.

Petty turned his head to him. Something about the tone of his voice . . . "Go ahead, Jacob."

"It's about Julian," Davis said. "He isn't going to be ready for the game Sunday."

Petty froze, staring at the taller coach. He turned his back to the practice and looked up into the man's eyes. "What do you mean?"

"He either doesn't have the confidence to play, or he isn't physically ready yet," Davis said. "He's just not the same player he was before the injury. He's going to need more time."

Angelina Moore had told Petty that Julian would be ready for the opening game. She'd told Lloyd that it would likely take a little more time, but that was at Petty's request. It sounded more natural. But he should be ready by now, she'd said . . .

Petty closed his eyes, keeping himself cool-headed. "Don't put him at risk," he told Davis. "I'll talk to the doctors and find out what their opinion is."

"Okay." Davis moved off, putting the whistle to his mouth again and bringing this latest exercise to a close.

Petty went straight to his office and grabbed his telephone, punching in Angelina Moore's direct number.

Angel was just finishing up a test on a rhesus monkey they called Cleo, leaving the laboratory and stripping off her gloves when her cell phone beeped at her from inside her shirt pocket. She pulled off her blue frock and grabbed the phone.

"Angelina Moore speaking. Who's calling?"

"Vince," she heard Petty's voice. He sounded a little frustrated, and that was most definitely out of the ordinary considering his usual monotone. "I need to talk to you, Angel."

Angel scanned the room around her. She was alone, but had no idea how long that would last. Not long, she figured. Jody would be finishing up with the monkey now and heading into the room to change. "Give me a minute to get to my office," Angel said.

"No, I need to talk to you in person. We have some things to discuss."

Angel frowned. "I guess I can come over on my lunch break. What's wrong?"

"That is what I hope to discover," Petty said. The phone clicked as he hung up.

She stepped inside his office twenty minutes later to find out. It was hot outside as a late summer heat wave rolled over the Midwest. Hot and humid. Her blouse's short sleeves were sticking to her arms, and her face was damp with sweat. The air conditioning in the office felt great, as the perspiration evaporated off her body.

Petty was sitting behind his desk, as usual, looking calm and suave in his gray suit. His elbows were on the desktop, hands folded as though he were praying.

"Okay, Vince, I'm here," Angel said, taking a seat across from him. "What's up?"

His folded hands moved to the desk as he sat up straight, his eyes boring into her. She met his gaze, sending a message of her own. He should have known by now that all those little psychological manipulations had no effect on her. Although she'd had to come to grips with that same fact; her little efforts didn't affect him, either.

"Julian won't be ready for Sunday," Petty said. "He has not been doing well at practice. His knee is still bothering him."

Angel shrugged. "He needs more time."

Petty slammed a fist into the desk, a sudden outburst that caused even Angel to flinch. "I don't want to hear that crap!"

he shouted. "You did *not* tell *me* that! You said he would be ready."

She had, two weeks ago. She'd also told Lloyd he would need a little more time before feeling totally normal again, at Petty's behest.

"Maybe I was wrong," she tried.

"I think you definitely were wrong," Petty said, his voice lowering. "Now, tell me what the problem is."

Angel shook her head, leaning forward. "I don't even know if there *is* a problem," she said. "This could be entirely mental on his part." Or *yours,* she added silently. "I guess we'll have to take a look at him. If it'll make you feel better."

"Wouldn't it," Petty said, his voice cloaked in sarcasm. "Shall I tell him to stop by tomorrow?"

"No," Angel said, shaking her head. "No way. Tell him I'll come to his apartment tomorrow afternoon, after four. Dr. Kicheski and I. We'll check him out. All right?"

Petty nodded. "Very well." A slight head tilt, toward the door, signaled her dismissal. Angel hesitated, just to challenge his authority, and then got up to leave when he displayed the first signs of annoyance.

That was a part of the game.

Jody sat fidgeting and shifting in her seat, as Angel drove into town, heading for Lloyd's apartment. Angel glanced at her, finally becoming tired of the constant anxiety radiating outward from the other woman.

"Jody? That seat bothering you or something?" Angel asked, looking at her as long as she could keep her eyes off the road.

"No," Kicheski said.

"Then calm down, will you!" Angel looked back at the road.

"I can't," Jody said, her voice just above a whisper. "This entire thing is bothering me."

"Why?" Angel asked, annoyed. She had to cure the other scientist of this, or she would end up blowing their cover.

"He should be normal by now," Jody said. "I know we haven't actually run clinical trials, but the way we put our technology together—I mean, it was all proven stuff that we just combined. It should have worked."

"It is working," Angel muttered, shaking her head.

"It's taking too long," Jody said. Her arms were stiff, her hands palms-down on the seat beside her. She shifted in the seat again, and glanced at Angel. "I think I know what we're going to find out."

"What are we going to find out?" Angel asked, her voice weary. Jody was becoming a wreck, a paranoid wreck. Maybe she should have left her out of the whole thing—no, she needed Jody's medical background. Kicheski was the only member of the GLI staff who had once practiced medicine. She'd been a physician with the infectious disease department at Johns Hopkins, specializing in viruses, for five years before going back to school and getting a degree in biology to pursue a career in research. Nagel had discovered her a few years later.

"Nerve conduction time," Jody said. "It's possible his nerve conduction time has been increased as a result of the damage. He had some damaged nerve tissue."

"So his reactions are slowed," Angel said.

"That's my guess." Jody sighed. "He'll never be back to normal, if it's true."

Angel bit her lip. Even if Jody was right in her thinking, she was wrong in that last conclusion. Julian Lloyd would be back to normal. She would make sure of it. There were other ways to genetically modify a human being. Forty thousand genes made for a lot of options.

Lloyd was pleasant enough, though he wore a concerned expression during their meeting with him. They took small blood samples from three different areas of his body, including the right knee. Jody ran some reflex tests, then frowned. Lloyd frowned, too, but Angel smiled at him to allay his fears. *Nothing to worry about.*

They went back to the GLI building, empty at this early evening hour. Crickets chirped in the woods behind the old warehouse as the sky turned purple and red, a brilliant sunset in the west.

Jody hurried through some tests on the blood samples, and an hour later came to Angel in one of the labs with the results.

She held out a sheet of paper covered with numbers and readouts. "Well, we do have good news," she said. "The modification has acclimated to his genome, and his body is still working overtime."

"That's good," Angel said. "See, I told you there was nothing to—"

"But there's bad news, too," Jody interrupted. "I was right about the nerve conduction time. It's high. He won't ever feel normal."

Angel hesitated. So it was true. She would have to tell Petty, of course. He would demand to know everything they had discovered. And he would want to know all of his options, all of the possible treatments for Julian Lloyd.

There was one, at least.

Angel explained that idea to Jody, who gaped when she finished, her already pale skin going even whiter. "You're crazy," Jody said. "That's nuts."

"You got a better idea?" Angel asked, her eyebrows raised as if she was open to any suggestions. Which she was. But she knew none were forthcoming.

"Yes, I do," Jody said. "Just let it go. We can't do anything more for him."

"I just told you what we can do for him."

Jody took a step back and held her hand in front of Angel's face. "No. It's experimental. We'd be playing with something we haven't tested in humans—"

"No one has," Angel corrected. "But it's worked in primates. I had a rhesus the other day, Jody. Clumsy and slow to react. After just a couple days she's already alert and quick. It'll work for a person."

"But Angel, we'd be playing with the brain, the mind." Jody shook her head. "There's too much of a risk."

Angel looked up at the taller woman, nailing her with eye contact. It worked, yet again; Jody looked away, chewing at the inside of her mouth. She wouldn't be able to hold up much longer, Angel thought. Good. "Jody, we have the ability to do things other companies just dream about. This is one of those things. It'll work, Jody. We just have to be bold enough to try."

"The meek shall inherit the Earth," Jody mouthed, the words almost inaudible.

Angel closed the distance between them, eyes still locked. "Sometimes you need to take a risk, Jody."

"Angel, I don't know—"

Angel stepped back, opening her arms to encompass the room. "You see all of this, Jody? All of this we built? It isn't going to be here forever. Nick's clueless, as usual. We still aren't making a profit. Enough of a profit to stay in operation," she added at Jody's dirty look: *Profit!* "What if I can buy us more time? A few more months and we'll be able to put together a board of investors, and we'll have a real income again. A few more months. And this treatment could buy us those months." Jody blinked. There was moisture in her eyes, Angel saw. The woman was on the verge of tears. Obviously she wasn't looking forward to doing what had to be done. She was almost crying.

Victory.

"But Paul . . ."

Angel put on a gentle smile, and placed a hand on Jody's shoulder. A connection, a display of sincerity. "Paul will be with us. You know that."

"Yeah, I know . . ." her voice was coarse and quiet, a defeated whisper. "Okay, Angel. I'll—I'll help you."

"That's the right decision," Angel said. "You won't regret

it." She stepped past her colleague and went through the door. Sometimes you just had to do whatever it took.

She explained the problem to Petty over the phone when she returned to her office, and then told him the solution. He was skeptical.

"I wonder why you didn't bring up this possibility before," Petty said.

"We didn't see it coming," Angel told him. "But it shouldn't be a problem. It's correctable."

"With this technique," Petty said. "Is it as safe as the first procedure?"

"Absolutely," Angel said. "Don't worry about a thing."

A slight hesitation, then: "I'll inform Julian that you're going to bring him in for a follow-up treatment. In fact, I'll have Dr. Rice inform him. That will be more routine."

"Okay, that should work fine." Angel looked down at the notebook on her desk, flipping through it to find the remainder of her week's schedule. "I'll pack up the material and meet Julian at his apartment again on . . . Thursday. After we get off. Will that work?"

"It will work," Petty said. "But will it have him ready by Sunday?"

"It should," Angel said. But the truth was, she had no idea. "Now, Vince, we need to talk about the payment . . ."

The second set of injections went well. Franklin hit it off with Julian, discussing football for the entire duration of their visit. Jody gave him the shots, and even she seemed a little more cheery. Angel just smiled and added the occasional necessary comment, trying to project a calming presence.

But back in Angel's car, as they returned to GLI, Dr. Kicheski shook her head and sighed, staring into the setting sun.

"You have no idea what we've done, Angel," she said.

Angel kept her eyes on the road and allowed a smile. "Yeah I do. We just put a million dollars in the bank."

"Is that all that matters?" Jody asked.

Angel glanced at her, the world tinted dark blue through her sunglasses. "Sometimes it is," she said. She looked back at the road. "Sometimes it is."

Twelve

Through most of his life, Julian was a morning person. Getting up early had never been a problem for him. Today, though, he slept straight through the alarm, which blared in vain at him for half an hour before turning itself off, as if sensing the futility of its endeavor. Julian didn't wake up until after nine. Check-in time for the day's practice was eleven, and the fact that he had only two—instead of what he had expected to be five—hours to prepare sent a shock up his spine.

He rolled out of bed onto his feet, hurrying through his morning hygiene. Then he made his way to the living area, pulling on a pair of workout shorts and slipping on his shoes as he went. As he turned on the light in the kitchenette, he lamented the fact that his mother wasn't here with breakfast ready.

Julian went to the cupboard, took out a big plastic container and brought it to the counter top, setting it down next to his blender. He opened the protein shake mix, dumped a couple scoops of it into the blender and filled it with water.

After using the blender to mix the stuff, he poured it into a thermos and made his way downstairs to the parking lot, sipping it while he tried not to flinch; it tasted like wet sand.

He gulped the rest of it down when he reached his car, trying hard not to taste it. Then he opened the door and tossed the thermos on the back seat.

If he wasn't two hours early, then in his opinion, he was late.

* * *

Davis met him outside the main building as they both walked up to the entrance.

"You look tired," he commented as he pulled the door open. He motioned for Julian to walk in, then followed his player.

"I am, a little," Julian said, understating his feelings; in reality he was exhausted, like he'd been awake the entire night.

"You up to practice?" Davis asked.

Julian looked at him, nodded. "Yes, sir, I am. I'll wake up." Why did Davis act more like a player than a coach around him?

"The reason I ask," Davis said, "is because I'm going to have to make a decision on whether or not to keep you active for Sunday, and I have to base my decision on your performance today."

"I'm up to it, Coach," Julian said, and he meant it. Or at least he hoped he did. He was too tired to be sure. "What's first?"

"I'm going to map out the practice with the assistants," Davis said. "Privately. You can study film, work out, do your own thing. Whatever it is you do for two hours before every practice."

Julian smiled. "I think I'll warm up."

"Don't work too hard," Davis said, not able to hide the concern that Julian knew he felt.

"Don't worry about me," Julian said. "I'm fine. Gotta work."

"I like to hear that from my players," Davis said. "But in your—" He stopped, shaking his head.

"Don't stop. I want to know how you feel." Julian felt awkward, saying something like that to his coach. During most of his football life coaches had been almost divine figures that one looked to for direction and discipline. But thus far, in the professional ranks, where most coaches were former players themselves, the head men were much more accessible. Often they were friends and confidants. Another shock for a rookie to endure.

"But in your case," Davis continued, "considering that certain people have placed a huge value on you—I can't afford to let something happen to you."

"You mean I'm a selling point." Julian smiled, but without humor. He was the franchise marketing plan. He was supposed to sell the tickets with his mere presence. He knew that, but it wasn't something he liked to think about.

Davis fidgeted, shifting his weight back and forth between his feet. "You could say that, I guess."

"I know, Coach. Do you know how many times I've been stopped in the street by people asking if I'm ready to earn my money?"

Davis nodded. "I can imagine. It's the nature of the business these days. Well . . ." He reached for the door handle. "Go do your thing. I've got work."

Julian nodded, watched Davis enter the meeting room, and made his way toward the workout room.

At first he did no better than before, but he improved as the day wore on. When his teammates stood sucking air, their hands on their hips, Julian felt like running some more. Coach Davis nodded in satisfaction as he watched the afternoon workout, and approached Julian as the rookie wiped sweat from his face with a towel after a set of wind sprints.

"Feeling better I see," he said.

Julian nodded. "I'm feeling *much* better, Coach. My whole body. I'm not even tired."

"And the knee?"

Julian flexed his right leg, swinging it like a pendulum a couple times. "It's getting there. Doesn't feel normal yet. It's . . . I don't know . . . *weak,* I guess. Which really bothers me. All I've done is work out for the last month."

"You'll get there." Davis patted Julian on the shoulder. "How do you feel for Sunday?"

Julian smiled, taking a deep breath of humid morning air. "I think I'm good to go."

After the first offensive practice, with an hour of free time to burn, he went to the weight room. He was the only person in there, sitting by himself among the weights and plethora of exercise apparatuses. The room was cool, but humid, and that was somehow more uncomfortable than the heat outside.

He was concerned with his leg; he did a few bench and military presses, bicep curls and the like, but mainly he worked his lower body.

After a set of squats, Julian replaced the barbells and moved over to the lower-body machine, sitting and strapping in his right leg. He raised his leg, then lowered it. He repeated the motion seven times, then stopped and increased the resistence.

Julian did a couple sets, until he began to tire. He felt a slight burn, but nothing incapacitating. He stopped again, waited a couple minutes and added more weight. He did another set.

I'm obsessed, he thought.

He continued, alone, for another twenty minutes.

Ryan walked down the hall toward the tinted glass doors leading to the practice fields. The hall was empty; most of the players, coaches and staff were outside going over a walk-through of the gameplan for the upcoming opener against San Francisco. Ryan had been held up while going over some practice tape with the defensive quality-control coordinator— a complicated title for a man who was in reality a simple aide to the defensive coordinator.

Ahead, on the right, the door to Gary Harrell's office was open and the light was on. That was odd. Harrell was usually an on-the-field coach—he liked to be out on the practice field before his players. Ryan paused just before the door and peeked inside. Harrell was standing before his desk, a phone pressed to his ear, his back to Ryan. He was shifting from foot to foot, and held his Saints cap in his left hand at his side.

"And I'm telling you we need to keep Gordon activated. We need that extra corner," Harrell said into the phone. Gordon was a backup cornerback, a second-year guy who had spent the off-season gaining experience in the NFL-affiliated European league. "No, the coverage teams will be fine," Harrell continued. "And it's just for this week." A pause. "Well, it's my call, and I'm making it. We'll talk about it tomorrow . . . Yeah. Yeah, get over that crud, we're gonna need you at a hundred percent Sunday. Yeah. Bye." He turned off the phone, slid it into his pocket, put on his cap and turned around. Ryan jerked back and then walked forward, trying to look casual.

He passed the office just as Harrell came out. The coach stopped and looked at him. "Ryan. You've been listening in on me?"

Ryan tried not to grimace. "I was passing by. I heard some. A little. Why?"

Harrell shrugged. "No particular reason." He started toward the doors. Ryan came into step beside him. "I was just talking to Sam." He meant the special teams coach, Sam Walden, who was home with a nasty summer cold.

"About?"

Harrell sighed, but went on without hesitation. "Sam's a little worried about how his kick coverages will be able to handle that speedy kid the Niners have . . . without you in them."

Ryan almost stopped in his tracks, but forced his legs to keep moving. He locked his eyes onto Harrell's impassive face. "Wait a minute. You're deactivating me?"

"Just for a week," Harrell said, stopping as they reached the door. "We need an extra DB, not an extra linebacker."

"So naturally you picked me," Ryan said, frowning. He hadn't been deactivated since his rookie season. And as a fifth round draft pick that year, he had expected to be inactive as he learned to play in the NFL. Well, there had been his little brushes with injuries—dislocated shoulder, broken ankle, a few others—but he had played around ninety percent of the possible time for the last fourteen years. An amazing statistic, if he could say so himself. And now to be put on the bench—not only on the bench, but on the bench in street clothes—just because the team needed to dress an extra defensive back . . .

Swallow your pride. "Just this one game, Gary?" Ryan asked.

Harrell nodded. "Yes." He pushed the door open. "Most likely," he added as he stepped outside.

Ryan waited a moment, then followed.

Subject P-Rh4 was the female rhesus monkey named Cleo. Cleo was the closest thing to a human being that had undergone the same treatment as Julian Lloyd's second series of injections, and that fact bothered Jody Kicheski immensely. The technology was advanced, of course. Advanced beyond anything the competitors could field. But it had never been tested on people. No clinical trials. No FDA approval. And Jody couldn't predict the results.

Primate-Rhesus Four, Cleo, was a mild-mannered, soft-tempered, docile animal. She never fought, never resisted, and when testing was done, she hopped into her containment and was quiet and . . . respectful of her human masters. She had a reputation as a sweetheart among the technicians, who often quarreled with each other over which would have the privilege of working with her.

Which was why Jody was so nervous over the little event today. An event that would, under normal circumstances, have seemed totally predictable and almost benign.

One of the technicians, a young but balding man named Henry Patrickson, had gone to Cleo's cage to remove the animal and bring her out for further testing and observation. Cleo had been lying on her side, sleeping, her beige and brown-furred side rising and falling slowly. Patrickson opened the cage and reached inside to pick up the small primate. But Cleo jumped up, shrieked and then bit the man on the hand, drawing blood. She scampered to the far side of her confinement and stood there, hissing and arching her back like an infuriated cat. Patrickson closed the cage, cleaned his wound and reported Cleo's behavior to the first scientist he found outside in the hall; Jody.

Jody had assured the young man that the bite would be okay, as long as he kept the wound clean and bandaged. Cleo, like all the primates, was scanned and examined for viruses and disease every other week. She wasn't sick, at least with anything that could be passed on to a human. Patrickson had nodded and moved off to the lab to work on the rats with Franklin, and Jody had gone to check on Cleo.

Checks on blood and waste samples and blood pressure had revealed nothing out of the ordinary. P-Rh4 had been upset. But Cleo had never gotten upset like that before, and that was a fact that ate at Jody's conscience as she trudged down the corridor.

She didn't really know where she was going. She was just walking, her eyes downcast, her hands clasped behind her back.

To aid in nerve conduction time and improve reflexes genetically, they had to . . . play with the mind. And playing with the mind of any creature—rat, primate or human—could yield unexpected and often dangerous results.

Jody was a physician as well as a scientist. The ethics of her former profession dictated that she work to heal and improve the life of her patient. She couldn't *do something* to a person that could destroy him. And if something went wrong, if Cleo's sudden abhorrent behavior was an indicator of what might happen to Lloyd, then that was exactly what she had helped do. Destroy a person.

A part of her said that there was nothing to worry about, she'd done what she'd had to do, she had been forced into it. But another said she *did* have a choice, that she should have done something to stop the treatment from being used on the football player, that she was a person with free will and couldn't be forced into anything. And those feelings, coupled with her deep-rooted physician's conscience, were over-whelming her with worry and regret.

She looked up as she continued down the corridor to find herself alone. And ahead was the closed door to Dr. Angelina Moore's personal office.

The risks were just too great. Lloyd might be in danger, and even though she didn't know for sure, Jody felt that the possibility was enough. She had to take action, take respon-sibility; *do something!* Stepping forward, she knocked on the door.

"Come in." Muted, muffled.

Jody opened the door and stepped inside Angel's office. The younger woman was sitting behind her desk, her hair tied in a bun. She looked up from a notebook and smiled. "Hey, Jody. What's up?"

Jody gulped, steadied herself. "Angel, we need to talk."

"What about?" The smile was still there, too cheerful. She knew quite well *what about,* Jody realized.

A nervous sigh, and Jody forced back a rising fear. Fear! Why was she afraid of a . . . a *girl* fifteen years younger than she? And Angel looked even younger than that, anything but threatening. But the emotion surged up, and Jody had to brace herself against it.

"Julian Lloyd," Jody said, quivering. "I'm—*we're* going to bring him here and reverse both procedures. Now. If you don't agree, I'll do it myself. And I'll go to the authorities." She got the words out as fast as she could, and then waited for the reply.

"Oh, come on, Jody," Angel said, shaking her head. "Don't get cold feet. I still need you."

Jody's mouth opened, hanging. The way Angel had said that was . . . "You still *need* me? What the hell does that mean?"

"Nothing. Forget it. But just calm down and think about it. You're letting yourself get scared. You're thinking you did the wrong thing. You didn't. You did what you had to do. Don't worry about side effects and all that. If anyone is responsible for anything that happens to Lloyd, it's Nick. He backed us into a corner, Jody."

"But—"

Angel shook her head again. "No buts, Jody. You were pretty forceful in supporting the idea at first, if I remember right."

Jody swallowed a lump. "No, I was angry. I shouldn't have—"

"But you did," Angel said. "And you were right."

"No!" Jody shouted, then shut her eyes and took a deep breath. "No," she repeated. "I wasn't right. And neither were you and Dr. Franklin. We did the wrong thing, Angel, and now we need to rectify it before something horrible happens."

"Horrible?" Angel asked, raising an eyebrow in amusement. "Don't be dramatic. Nothing's going to happen."

"I think it will. But anyway, there's a huge risk. And we can't risk someone's life." Jody thought for a moment. Angel thought on a whole different wavelength, in a whole different way. She said, "If something does happen, don't you think it would be traced back to us?"

"No, I don't," Angel said. "You know better than that. There's no way they'll be able to trace it back to us. Short of a muscle biopsy. And that isn't going to happen."

"Vincent Petty—"

"Is in the same boat we are." Angel half-smiled, looking up at Jody. "Everything is taken care of, Jody. Don't worry about it."

Jody clenched her fists. Didn't this . . . this *bitch* understand the possible consequences of their actions?

"What do you want out of this, Angel?" Jody asked. "Really. What do you hope to gain?"

"A future for this company," Angel said. "You already know that."

"I don't think so," Jody said, glaring. "I think you want to set yourself up as a savior and use your clout to get rid of Dr. Nagel. And then you'll be able to set yourself up in his place. Am I right?"

Angel didn't reply. She just stared.

"I *am* right," Jody said. She turned her back and opened the door. "I'm going to the police! But first Nick needs to know—"

"Wait, Jody," Angel said, and her voice sounded desperate. Jody turned back to her, closing the door. Angel's eyes were moist, like she was upset, close to tears.

"What?" Jody said.

"You're right," Angel said. "You're absolutely right. I don't know—I just—I just needed to do something. I couldn't let the company fall apart. I mean, you know how I feel. You felt that way for a while, when Nick was going to sell out. You know what I mean."

Jody frowned. This couldn't be a genuine reversal on Angel's part. . . could it? "I did feel that way. But not anymore."

"I know," Angel said. "I know." She opened her notebook and scanned through the pages. "Look, Jody, I'm going to be busy until after hours today. Would you mind staying late? I need to discuss this with you."

"Discuss what?" The fear was gone. Jody felt a sort of hollow victory, or a sense that she had somehow won. Maybe.

"Discuss how we're going to go about fixing this thing," Angel said. "We can't just call up Julian Lloyd and tell him to come in. He won't understand. And Petty will probably sell us out if he knows. So we need to talk about it. Okay?"

Jody bit her lip, feeling apprehensive. But she nodded. What harm could come of it? "Okay, I'll be working with Cleo late, anyway."

"Fine." Angel sighed, looking away. "In that case . . ." her voice broke up a little bit, like she was holding back emotion. "I'm sorry, Jody. In that case I'll just meet you in Lab One after I'm through here."

Jody nodded. "All right. Thanks, Angel."

"No, thank you," Angel said, flipping idly through the book. "I guess you were right. You have ideals that . . . that you're willing to die for. I wish I could say the same."

She sounded sincere, but at the same time the statement

struck Jody as being a little odd. She shrugged; it was just a bunch of words, no matter what. "I appreciate that," Jody said.

"Yeah." Angel cleared her throat. She said, her voice a little stronger: "I'll see you in a while."

"Right. See you." Jody opened the door and left the room.

Outside, the sun had set and clouds obscured the stars. Thunder rumbled, reverberating through the walls of the GLI building. Jody had been finished working with Cleo—still nothing overtly wrong, except for the irritability and aggressiveness—and had gone over some earlier research while she waited for Angel. The lab was quiet. The only sound was the scratching of Jody's pen on her notepad as she scribbled down some observations.

The door opened. Jody looked up as Angel strode into the lab.

"Looks like we're going to get some rain," Angel said. She closed the door behind her and stepped over to Jody.

"I hear it," Jody said. "We need some." She put her notepad on a small waist-high table covered with a large rack of test tubes and glass containers filled with chemicals, at her side. A variety of chemicals; anaesthetics, decontaminates, even corrosive solvents. They used them all in here. Jody frowned, wondering why she had even noticed. She saw that rack every five minutes . . .

"It's been dry, I know," Angel said. She cleared her throat. "Jody, I need to ask you to reconsider."

"Reconsider?" Jody echoed, stopping short. "What do you mean?"

"Stick with me," Angel said. "Don't go to the authorities. And don't go to Lloyd. Let's see what happens."

"I don't believe this. I thought you meant what you said earlier."

"I guess I changed my mind," Angel muttered. She moved closer. "Jody, I'm . . . I'm begging you. Don't blow this. Please."

Jody laughed. Angelina Moore was hopeless. She should've gone with her first instinct. "Forget it. I wanted to talk, but that's it. I guess you've made your decision." She turned, taking one step toward the door—

And saw stars explode before her eyes as something hard and heavy slammed into the back of her head. She fell back, crashing into the table and rack and hitting the ground amid shattered glass and noxious chemicals. She groaned, willing her hands to move. She tried to get her weight beneath her, to get up, but her arms were so heavy, she couldn't move them. She forced her eyes to open—she hadn't noticed they were closed—and stared up. All she saw was the ceiling. Her head was pounding.

Jody squeezed her eyes shut against the pain. And then she smelled the chemicals, and realized she was lying in a mixing puddle of heaven-knew-what. The fumes were all around her, her head was spinning.

She moved her hands again, trying once more to find a way to get up, but that seemed like such a hard task, and she suddenly felt so tired . . . Maybe if she got some rest, a little rest, she could gather her strength and . . .

Jody felt herself drifting off. A lucid part of her mind told her to get up, that this wasn't good, but she couldn't heed that warning. Her body was no longer hers to command. The world went black, and she fell asleep.

The last thing she heard was Cleo, screaming her primeval monkey shriek and slamming her body against the cage.

Thirteen

"Check-in at nine, warmups at ten, kickoff at twelve." Davis was standing before his team on the practice field. The players knelt or stood around him, holding helmets under their arms or face masks clenched in their fingers. Julian stood a few rows of players back, his arms crossed over his chest as he listened. They weren't wearing pads—the day before a home game was free, or at the most tasked to a short walk-through. "It's the opening game of the year, men," the coach continued. "But don't make it out to be more than it is. It's just like last week. It's the same as a preseason game." He didn't add, of course, that the bullets were going to be real this time. The hits were going to be real. The plays, the scores, they all were going to count now. No more dress rehearsals.

And Julian hadn't had any dress rehearsals. He hadn't even gotten five minutes in a preseason game. He felt raw and unprepared.

"I know some of you don't feel ready. Rookies," Davis said with a little smile, and it seemed that he was looking in Julian's direction. "But once you're out on that field, and once you take that first hit—well, emotion and instinct take over. You've played this game your whole lives. So all you have to do is get out there and play some more. It's just a game." Julian frowned. For eighteen million dollars, it sure as hell had better be more than "just a game" for him.

At least, that was what the fans on the radio call-in shows said.

* * *

Detective Anthony Sutton, St. Louis County Police Department Homicide/Assault Unit, sat back in his desk chair and sipped an iced mocha, his third of the day. It was his favorite drink, with a little extra chocolate and a dash of whipped cream. It helped him relax, despite the caffeine, and was his easy ticket to calmness after a hectic day and week. He'd done nothing major, of course. Nothing exciting. Car accidents, hit-and-runs, guys falling off their roofs, stuff like that, that for some reason required a homicide detective to investigate. Probably to make sure the guy's wife hadn't *arranged* for him to fall off the roof. . . . So no, it wasn't exciting. But it did make for a lot of extra paperwork, and anyone who knew Tony Sutton knew just how much he enjoyed paperwork, and *everyone* in the West County Precinct knew him.

Sutton was thirty-four, tall and lanky, though weightlifting had added a few pounds to his frame in the last few years. His hair was dark, his skin tanned. His looks tended to give him lots of attention from the opposite sex, but he hadn't made much use of that attention. At least not since college, not since becoming a cop. He'd never found the right woman, someone compatible with him. His peers said there was no one out there capable of keeping him reeled in and under control, but the fact was, he knew but couldn't admit, there was at least one woman with that capability.

The only problem was, Cassandra Dawkins was like the sister he didn't have.

Cassie was a former New Yorker with an accent to match, tall, with fierce, intelligent brown eyes and black hair that just touched her shoulders. She was fond of black and white and sunglasses, and was wearing those colors now, with the sunglasses in her leather jacket pocket. She was walking toward him from across the crowded room, and she had *that look* on her face. Something was up.

Sutton finished his mocha and set the glass aside, out of

the way on his immaculate desk. That look. Wonderful. Probably another roof incident.

Cassie stopped in front of the desk and leaned forward, hands on the desktop. "Guess what?" she said, looking at him deadpan.

"Roof deal," Sutton said, frowning.

She shook her head. "No. It's different. Think."

"Okay, different. I like that." Sutton smiled. "Let's see . . . he fell off a *ladder?*"

Cassie rolled her eyes and pulled a slip of paper out of her pocket, placing it on the desk in front of him. "Read."

He did so, and frowned, nodding his head. "Hey, we might have one here. Finally."

"Wishing for a homicide," Cassie said, rolling her eyes. "That sucks, Tony."

Sutton shrugged, standing up and sticking the paper in his pants pocket. "It doesn't have to be a homicide. I'd settle for a shootout. Action, babe. We need action. You don't want to get old and out of shape, do you?"

She slapped his shoulder. "No. But I think the kickboxing takes care of that."

Sutton shook his head, glancing at her with mock displeasure. "Didn't I tell you not to get into that?"

"Yeah, you did. So? You got a problem?"

"Yeah, I got a problem," Sutton said. "It's too danged violent."

"Genetics Life?" Sutton asked, his eyes wide. "Sounds like a wacked life insurance company." He was driving and Cassie sat in the passenger seat beside him. The traffic was heavy, as commuters filed back into the suburbs from their jobs in the city. It was early evening, and the sun was beginning to set.

"It's a biotech company," Cassie said. "A little one. Very little."

"Obviously," Sutton said. "Has to be small for the idiots to come up with a name like that." He thought back to the report

Cassie had given to him. "Okay. So the stiff is a researcher, or a doctor or something, right?"

"Dr. Jody Kicheski, used to be a general health physician, got a doctorate in biology and joined this company back when it started," Cassie said. As always, she had researched the major players involved with this potential homicide. She was the brains behind their operation though Sutton would never admit that.

"And it happened today," he said, slowing behind a tight stream of traffic.

"Just a couple hours ago," Cassie said. "One of the other researchers found her and called 911. Parameds got there, but she was already dead. The local blue boys called the County PD for a full crime scene job." She smiled. "And you know who they got for that job."

"Of course," Sutton said. The traffic cleared a bit, and he accelerated. Ridiculous. People left the city proper to get away from this kind of thing, and ended up creating it in the suburbs. *Maybe I should move to Montana,* he thought. "We have a cause of death yet?"

"Nothing solid," Cassie replied, reading from a copy of the report she had in her hand. "Forensics should be there about the same time as us."

"So we'll make a quick sweep," Sutton said. "No problem."

Ahead, the traffic slowed to a stop.

For a potential crime scene, Genetics Life, Incorporated's main building seemed rather casual as Sutton pulled into the parking lot. A few cars were already there, but there was no police tape, no flashing lights, nothing out of the ordinary. He and Cassie left the car and entered the building. Inside, there was a small lobby waiting room. A group of people stood in a little circle, talking. Sutton recognized one of them, a tall, heavyset bald man named Ed Lankford. He was a precinct commander with the County PD. He was speaking to a nervous, disheveled fortyish man with glasses and a younger, good-looking blond woman.

Lankford looked up as Sutton and Cassie came toward him.

"Ah, Tony," he said, extending a hand. Sutton shook it. "How did I know they'd give you this one?" He smiled at Cassie. "How are you, Cassandra?"

"Great," she said, without emotion.

Lankford motioned to the two others. "Tony, Cassie, this is Dr. Nicholas Nagel"—they shook hands with the man—"and Dr. Angelina Moore"—ditto with the woman—"They're two of the head researchers here. Dr. Nagel is the chief executive officer of the company."

"Nice to meet you," Sutton said, eyeing the blonde. She seemed awfully calm . . . at least compared to her counterpart. Nagel looked like he'd just rolled out of bed, with bags under his eyes and thin hair that stuck out, like it hadn't been brushed. Moore, on the other hand . . .

"The forensics people are back there now," Lankford said, pointing down a hallway. "But it doesn't look like they'll find anything. It seems pretty cut-and-dried. Probably an unfortunate accident."

Sutton frowned, taking his eyes from Moore. "I thought—"

Lankford held up his hand. "I know what you thought. And we haven't gotten the autopsy results back yet—the coroner has the body now, but won't work on it until the morning—but it appears Dr. Kicheski fell, knocked over a tray of chemicals, hit her head and was knocked unconscious. Looks like she died from inhaling chemical fumes."

Right. "What kind of chemicals are we talking about?" Sutton said.

Lankford looked at Nagel. "Uh . . . a variety . . ." the scientist whispered. "Mainly disinfectants. Ammonia." He shook his head mournfully. "Bleach. Those two would, uh, you know . . ."

"Yeah, that would do it," Sutton said, nodding. *Unfortunately,* he added. On the surface, it did sound like an accident.

A freak accident, but an accident nonetheless. "You said she was knocked unconscious," Sutton pointed out. "Was there a head injury?"

Lankford shook his head. "Nothing major. Of course, I'm just telling you what I saw. Her head wasn't cracked open, if that's what you mean. You could tell she'd hit it. That was all."

The blonde, Moore, looked at him. "So what are you going to put in your report, Detective Sutton?"

He flashed her a smile. "We'll see." He turned to Lankford. "Can we see the cr— I mean, where she was found?"

The precinct commander nodded. "Come this way."

It was a laboratory, all right. Microscopes, test tubes, chemicals, computers. High technology stuff, which wasn't Sutton's forte, and he found the place somehow overwhelming. The actual scene of the accident was obvious. A metal rack lay on the hard white floor, broken glass all over the place. Several people hovered around that area, packing up small containers of samples and who knew what else. They would be the forensics experts.

"As you can see," Lankford said, "We've already cleaned up the chemicals. Forensics took samples. They'll have them analyzed, just to find out what exactly was in them." Sutton stepped closer to the broken glass, but Lankford stopped him. "The fumes are still pretty bad. I guess you can smell that."

Sutton nodded. It was a sharp, noxious bleach-like smell. He turned to the two scientists. "I guess one of you found her," he said, eyeing them.

The blonde opened her mouth as if to reply, but Lankford broke in. "Dr. Moore did. She was about to leave, and came in here to say good-bye to Kicheski. They were both working late."

Sutton managed not to grimace. Same old Ed Lankford. Couldn't get a word in when you were around him. Sutton looked at Moore. "What did you do when you saw her?"

"I ran to her," Moore said, looking up and making eye contact. "Checked her pulse and pulled her away from the chemicals, then called 9-1-1. After that I left it to you people. I couldn't do anything."

"Good for you," Sutton said. He couldn't get a read on this one . . . something wasn't right. Nothing on the surface, of course. But Sutton had a sense about these things, and that sense was trying to tell him something now. "That's exactly what you should do." And that was the problem, he realized. "Didn't you hear anything, though?" he asked. "A crash or a shout?"

Moore shook her head, and Lankford answered. "Nah. The way this place is built you could be standing right around the corner from that animal room and not hear a monkey scream."

Sutton looked up, nodding, and scanned the room again. There were some empty animal enclosures lining the wall across from the door. He looked at Moore. "Were there any animals in here when it happened?"

"Yes. I moved them when the paramedics got here." She looked away, eyes downcast, as if she was fighting sudden emotion. "There wasn't anything else I could do," she added.

"I guess there wasn't," Sutton said. "Ah . . . How long have you known Dr. Kike—uh—"

"Kicheski," Lankford said.

"Right," Sutton went on, shaking away his mock difficulty. "How long have you known her?"

Moore glanced at Nagel, then looked back to Sutton. "Since the start of the company. Several years."

"Years. Well. In that time, was there anyone you know of who could have wanted to kill her?"

"Oh come on, Tony," Lankford said. "Don't start with the Columbo stuff. We know what happened."

"Yeah, yeah, of course. I'm sorry." He put on an apologetic expression. "Force of habit. So, have the relatives been notified?"

"Not yet," Lankford said, giving Sutton a glare. "I believe Dr. Nagel is going to take care of that."

Nagel shut his eyes and nodded slowly. "We will, yes," he said in obvious agony. "Her kids are in college. Scholarships, both of them. Harvard." He sighed. "Her husband . . . well, she didn't even know where he is. Ran off with a twenty-two-year-old last—"

"So you're taking care of that," Sutton said, interrupting. He wasn't interested in hearing any life details.

"Yes," Nagel said. "Actually . . ." He looked at Moore. "Angel, would you mind trying to get in touch with the counselor? The number should be . . ." His voice faded. "Ah, the number should be in Jody's office."

Moore shot Nagel a dirty look, the first real expression Sutton could remember seeing from her. Perhaps she didn't feel up to the task? Or perhaps she didn't care for Kicheski. Sutton frowned at that second thought; something to consider. "Well," he said. "There's nothing more to be done here. We'll be going. Oh and Ed," he added, stabbing Lankford with a serious expression, "make sure you get the forensic analysis to me when it comes out, huh?" As opposed to a week down the line. Lankford sometimes made a habit of forgetfulness when it suited his purposes.

"Count on it," Lankford said. "Anything else?"

Sutton shook his head. "No. My deepest regrets to Genetics Life," he said, staring at Moore. She stared back. No reaction. Interesting.

"Come on, Cassie," Sutton said, and they left the lab.

"You find that blonde a little strange?" Sutton asked as he pulled the car out onto the street.

"What, the sixth sense acting up?" Cassie asked.

"Eh . . . I just found her a little strange, that's all." The traffic was lighter now, moving swiftly. Rush hour was over. "You believe the story?" he asked.

"You don't?"

Sutton squeezed the steering wheel. *Calm,* he told himself.

Stay calm. "Yes, I do. I'm just wondering about it. It's too convenient."

"For what?" Cassie shrugged. "Okay, just say for a second it was a murder. You need evidence and motive, but you've got neither. You got no sign of forced entry, nothing missing, a reasonable explanation from the only likely suspect and no evidence to say anything different. How do you stick with homicide when you got nothing to back up your suspicions?"

"I'm not sticking with homicide, I'm just saying . . ."

"Saying what?"

"Never mind," Sutton said. She was right. He had nothing to back up his . . . feeling, or whatever it was. Nothing at all. Accidents happened, sometimes freak accidents. But for some reason that Moore woman just stuck in his head. For some reason.

"Never mind," he said again, and concentrated on driving on the twilight-lit road.

Angel tried to look frustrated and upset and shocked for the rest of their meeting with Lankford, then went off at the earliest opportunity to her office with the excuse of contacting Jody's children at Harvard. She slammed her door behind her and fell into her chair. Her head was pounding, a stress headache, she guessed. Stress for obvious reasons.

She'd knocked Jody unconscious with the intention of thinking about the best course of action, the safest thing to do. Even if it meant killing her. She couldn't risk having Jody run off and tell the world about what they had done. But the way the woman had fallen, right into the chemical rack, had made the decision for her. She had left the room and waited until she was sure Jody was dead, then came back in and called 911.

Unplanned and on the spur of the moment though it was, it had worked. The cops were convinced it was an accident.

Little Angelina Moore was the only person here at the time, and she couldn't have had a reason to kill.

That detective, Sutton, had acted a little suspicious of her, but his superior had set him straight. It had only been a couple hours since the event, but Angel felt like she would get away with it. She was safe.

But now she had to call those kids . . .

The dark humor of the situation wasn't lost on her. She would call and inform the counselors, give the children her deepest regrets and all that, and she was the reason those regrets had to be offered.

But she couldn't bring herself to laugh at that fact.

She picked up the phone, dialed the number from the card she'd found in Jody's office, and got ready to *perform*.

Fourteen

"You ready, kid?"

The crowd was a distant rumble, a building vibration that permeated the walls of the locker room. Julian wrapped another layer of tape over his shoe, tossed the rest of the roll aside and looked up at Rich Mitchum. The quarterback was already wearing his helmet, chin strap fastened and mouthpiece clenched between his teeth. Julian took a deep, calming breath, at first trying to block out the ambient sounds around him, but then letting the crowd's faraway roar envelope him. He took his own helmet from its place on the bench next to him and slid it onto his head. He stood.

"I'm ready."

They joined their teammates, forty-five men crowding just in front of the exit around their coach. Jacob Davis seemed to tower above them, three-hundred-pound linemen and all.

"You all know why we're here," he said in a voice that echoed through the locker room, joining the crowd's encompassing roar. "You all know what has to be done. I'm not going to give you a speech, but I do want you to remember something: Nobody—*nobody* is going to come in here this year and leave in one piece. Even if they manage to pull out the win, I expect you to beat the hell out of them. Understood?"

"Yes sir!" The reply shattered the eerie calm and was lost with the distant roar, and then the doors were flung open and they moved out onto the field.

* * *

It all moved in slow motion. Julian followed his team in a slow jog, the men ahead of him silhouettes against the brightness at the end of the dim tunnel. They continued to move toward that brightness, and though it wasn't very far, it seemed to take forever. The crowd's rumble built into a continuous blast of thunder as seventy thousand human beings screamed at the top of their lungs. They came to a stop just before they entered the playing field. *This is a dream,* his mind told him.

This is your dream.

"Defense, special teams, backups, spread out on the field, you know the drill. We're introducing the starting offense. Go when you're called." The indicated players did as they were told, forming an aisle between them on the end zone and out to the ten yardline. The roar increased, resounding inside Julian's helmet.

The PA announcer began the introductions, and the roar quieted a bit so that he could be heard. *"At left tackle, from Texas A and M, number sixty-nine, Dave Thurmond!"* Thurmond, a big offensive lineman, left the tunnel behind, running out onto the field with his arms extended skyward. *"At left guard, from Ohio State, number seventy-one, Harold McNeill!"*

"This is the worst part," Mitchum said above the noise, his face inches from Julian's right helmet ear hole. "Once you're on the field, and all the hype's over and done, it's just a football game."

"Just a football game," Julian repeated.

"That's right. Same as the one you played when you were eight years old."

The announcer finished the offensive line and moved to the receivers.

"At tight end, from Michigan State, number eighty-six, Frank Moran!"

"You're almost up," Mitchum said.

Julian gulped down a hard lump. His stomach was being twisted in a dozen directions, and his hands were shaking. His hands were shaking! "Just a football game," he said again to himself. "Just a football game."

"At wide receiver, from the University of Miami, number eighty, Jake Riley!"

"Just a football game."

"At fullback, from Nebraska, number thirty-eight, Gabe Jenkins!"

"You're on," Mitchum said, stepping back.

"At halfback—"

"Just a football game."

"—from the University of Southern California—"

"Just a football game."

"—number thirty-two—"

"Oh, crap . . ."

"Julian LLOYD!"

He ran, almost at full speed, out of the tunnel and through the channel of his fellow Gunners, stopping a full five yards past the end of the line. The crowd had built its roar to a crescendo, louder than anything he could remember. Even those college stadiums that held ninety thousand people couldn't top this, he thought as he jogged back to stand beside the others. One of the linemen laughed, slapping his pads.

"Next time," the lineman shouted above the din, "run a little slower!"

Beneath his helmet Julian nodded, and he felt himself blush. He listened as the announcer introduced Mitchum.

Mitchum came jogging down the field, waving to some fans and giving some of his teammates high-fives. It looked like he did this every single day. The not-quite-thirty-year-old man was like an implacable sage.

"Give a round of applause for Coach Jacob Davis and the rest of YOUR Missouri Gunners!"

Davis followed, mimicking his starting quarterback's gait, minus the waving, to the end of the line of players. "Let's move, guys," he said as he passed Julian. The team, forty-five strong, followed him to the sideline.

* * *

Harris Mack sat in the network broadcast booth, high above the field of the big domed stadium, waiting for the nationally televised game's graphic introduction to end. Mack, a former player and coach in the league, was the color commentator for his network's "A-Team," the broadcast crew they sent to the designated game of the week.

Beside him, James Hunt, the play-by-play guy, sorted through a stack of statistics sheets. "Almost ready to go and I can't find the friggin' . . ." he started in his signature drawl. "Ah! Here we go." He held up another stat sheet. "Lloyd's stats from college."

"Knew you'd find it," Mack said, looking in the direction of the camera.

A producer got their attention. "Fifteen seconds!"

Hunt wet his fingers in a glass of water on the small table to his side, just out of camera range, and ran them through his thinning hair. "How do I look?" he asked Mack.

"You really wanna know?"

"Ha, ha."

"Five, four . . ."

The two men straightened up, sitting erect in their chairs overlooking the playing field. Mack made sure he had his backup papers in his hands, just in case the TelePrompter for his opening dialogue failed to function.

"And live!" The producer waved his hands and got out of the way.

"Hello, everyone," Hunt said in a cheerful, businesslike voice. "I'm James Hunt, here with my friend and partner, Harris Mack, in rainy St. Louis Missouri. Welcome to our broadcast of the week—the New York Jets versus the Missouri Gunners."

"It isn't raining here in the confines of this artificial indoor arena with a plastic field," Mack picked up, his lines working off of his reputation as a lover of old-fashioned football played in the elements. "But, hey, we can't have everything."

"You can bet that this sellout crowd of sixty-five thousand is glad *they* aren't getting wet," Hunt said. "Here in what should be an exciting game, there are a few questions that will be answered. For one: Is highly touted Gunners rookie runner Julian Lloyd back from what might have been a disastrous injury in training camp? And is he even the player he's purported to be? We have some information downstairs where our sideline reporter, Donna Marie, is waiting. Donna?"

Mack watched the small video monitor attached to the camera as it displayed the attractive brunette, standing on the Gunners' sideline.

"Thanks, guys," she said. "I spoke with Coach Davis just a moment ago, and he says that his young star, Julian Lloyd, is back and better than ever. As we all know, Lloyd injured his knee in camp, and the injury was at one point considered career-threatening. But he made an amazingly quick recovery, and was able to practice this week. Now, you'd think the young rookie would be nervous, but according to Davis, he's calm as can be." The screen cut to a clip taken yesterday, with Davis sitting alone in front of a dark backdrop.

"Julian's raring to go," the coach said, staring into the camera. "He's excited about playing, and as for the injury, it's like it never happened. He ran his fastest forty time ever in practice this week, something that put us all at ease. So no, he's not nervous at all."

The paper cup slipped out of Julian's gloved hand and splattered on the concrete floor. Julian swore and kicked it, almost slipping on the spilled Gatorade.

"Don't worry," Mitchum said, standing beside him as the team captains, receiver Jake Riley, two defensive linemen and a linebacker, took the field for the coin toss. "You know what they say; you're only nervous until that first hit."

"It's the first hit that has me nervous," Julian said.

"Nah, no problem," Mitchum assured him. "You'll do

great. 4.27 forty speed in a two-hundred-twenty-pound package, now that's scary to the other team."

The amplified voice of the referee quieted the stadium. "Visiting team, call the toss." The opposing team's captain made his call. "The call is tails." Julian looked out to midfield as the ref tossed the coin. "It is tails. Receive or kick?" He couldn't hear the answer. "The visiting team has won the toss and chooses to receive. Good luck." Boos cascaded down from the stands, and the appropriate special teams units took their places. The kicker went to the thirty-yard line, squeezing the ball between his hands as most kickers did, and placed it on the tee.

The referee waited for a few minutes until the network was ready, and blew his whistle, moving out of the line of play.

The kicker approached the ball in a trot, planted his left foot beside it, and brought his right leg forward in a rapid motion. The ball exploded off his foot and sailed seventy yards in the air before it was fielded at the goal line by the Jets' return man. He darted forward in a straight line to the fifteen, slowed and juked a tackler and accelerated between a pair of blockers to the twenty-two, where he was swarmed over.

"Betcha we hold 'em, three and out," Mitchum grinned.

Julian nodded, fighting a slight bout of nausea.

The Jets' offense and Gunners' defense met at the twenty-two yardline. The opposing quarterback shouted his signals, put a man in motion and called for the ball. He handed it to his halfback, who dashed through an opening on the left side, gaining five yards before being met shoulder-to-shoulder by a linebacker, who dragged him to the ground.

After huddling together for twenty or so seconds, they returned to the line. The quarterback took the snap, handed off to his halfback again, but this time a defensive tackle blasted his way into the backfield and dropped the runner for a loss of two yards.

Huddle. Break. Snap. The quarterback took a five-step drop, fired a dart over the middle, but his receiver bobbled the ball and took a wicked hit as he tried to gain control of it. It fell to the turf, and special teams units replaced their teammates.

"What'd I tell you, boy?" Mitchum said. "Three and *out!* Run, run, pass, punt. Nothing drives a fan crazier, you know."

"I know."

The punt sailed high, and the backup wide receiver, Nick Mills, who acted as the Gunners' return man, called for a fair catch to avoid being pancaked by three marauding defenders.

Mitchum gave Julian a thumbs-up and smiled. "Time to go," he said, and jogged into the fray.

Julian hesitated a moment, swallowing hard, but gathered his wits about him and followed the quarterback onto the field.

"This is where you see what the young guys are made of," Mack commented to a television audience of fifteen million. "I remember my first play like it was yesterday. I dropped the guy for a four-yard loss."

"The start of a great career," Hunt said. He added smugly, "And we know all the stories, so don't start."

"So funny," Mack said.

The opposing teams came to the line of scrimmage, the Gunners forty-eight-yard line.

"Teams come to the line," Hunt called. "Gunners have good field position here, let's see if they can capitalize."

"Getting good field position gives you a huge advantage over the other team," Mack said. "The difference between having to go fifty yards and having to go eighty yards is a big one."

"Mitchum takes the long count," Hunt said. "Play clock's running—here's the snap, handoff to Lloyd, running left. Stacked up at the line, no gain."

"He had a decent hole there," Mack said, "but he didn't have that burst that we saw from him in college, where you see the hole and blast through it. By the time he got there it had closed up on him."

"Perhaps he's still favoring the knee," Hunt remarked. "Gunners come back to the line. Mitchum takes the snap, five step drop, his pass over the middle complete to the tight end Moran. Six-yard gain, short of the first down. That'll bring up third and four."

"One thing about Jacob Davis," Mack said, "is that he loves to work the middle of the field. Frank Moran is a good receiving tight end, perfect for that system."

"Gunners running a no-huddle offense here early in the first quarter, perhaps trying to put this Jets defense off balance. Mitchum, five step drop, looks, pumps once—under pressure—dumps it off to Lloyd, who has blockers in front of him. Lloyd runs forward, dances around, is hit and dropped just short of the first down. That looked like the strong safety, Jordan, who collared him."

"Wasted opportunity, there," Mack said. "Julian Lloyd is a back with good size and power, but he seems to be playing timid right now. He had room to move and blockers ahead; he should have just lowered his shoulder and gone forward for the first down. Instead, he stopped, tried to use the fast feet, what I call running in place, and the safety came up and made the play."

Hunt nodded. "Both teams have gone three and out, and it seems the Gunners will punt on fourth and a short one."

"You know, Jim, you have to wonder: How long will Jacob Davis leave Lloyd in there if he doesn't perform? He has to be careful not to overuse him in his first game, especially after the injury."

"It'll be interesting to see. The punt is a high, booming effort, fielded at the thirty by the return man Jacques." They watched the return man jump back and forth, dodging tacklers but making little forward progress, before someone finally got a clean shot and leveled him at the thirty-two. "Not much of a return by the Jets, so with twelve-thirty left in the first quarter we have no score. Back in a moment."

* * *

Julian removed his helmet and took a few deep breaths. The old adage was that you were only nervous until the first hit, but he'd been hit already and the anxiety was still with him.

Davis came over to him, his eyes cold. "What the hell was that?" he demanded, glaring.

"I'm sorry, Coach," Julian said.

"You better be. I don't jump on my running backs for having a bad series, but when you've got that much room you'd sure as hell better use it. Understood?"

"Yes, sir."

"Don't play scared. It's a football game. It's *just a football game.*"

"Welcome back," Hunt told the viewers, "as the Jets offense takes the field first and ten at their own thirty-two."

"Neither team has done anything offensively yet," Mack said. "But underline *yet,* because this shouldn't be what you'd consider a defensive struggle. We have two good offenses here."

"Wilson comes under center," Hunt said, watching the quarterback through binoculars. "Long count—snap—short drop, fires a bullet to the left sideline, caught by the big receiver Roy. Tackle made by the safety, but not before Roy bowled forward for the first down. Gain of twelve on the play."

"Jay Roy used to be what you'd call a 'tweener'," Mack said. "The scouts thought he was too big to be a wideout, but too small to be a tight end. But he dropped fifteen pounds in the off-season, and got faster. He's listed at six-five, two-thirty, but he's closer to two-twenty-five."

"Back to the line, four wide receiver set. Wilson takes the snap, short drop, pass over the middle—*caught by Roy in the open field!* He's running free at the fifty—to the forty—and driven out of bounds by the corner at the thirty-eight."

"Great catch by Roy," Mack said. "He grabbed it in stride,

put it in his gut and showed some great speed as he accelerated away from the safety. I didn't know he was that fast!"

Hunt shook his head in amazement. "Neither did I, but the coaching staff had said during the preseason—when they made Roy their starting flanker—that the second-year man out of Arkansas would surprise some people this year. He's certainly done that here early in the opener."

"And the way he lowered his shoulder on that run," Mack said. "I hope Julian Lloyd's watching the replay."

"Watch that replay," Mitchum said. He stood beside Julian on the sideline, sipping water from a paper cup. "See how he lowers his shoulder? And he's a wide receiver! You know, that's what *you're* supposed to do."

"I know," Julian said. "I know. I'm just . . ."

"Nervous. You're still nervous?"

"Yes, I'm still nervous."

"Why? There's no reason to be nervous. Just keep saying what I told you: It's just a football game."

"Right. Just a football game."

Mitchum sighed and looked away, turning his gaze to the scoreboard mounted high above in the stands, the one that displayed scores from games around the league. "Hey, Julian. Niners are already up fourteen-zip over the Saints. Who woulda thunk it?"

The kicker's foot met the ball, sending it to the return man at the opposite goal line, and the game was underway.

The coverage team surged down the field, impacting with the blockers like two charging armies colliding. The return man darted through a seam up the middle, increasing the distance between himself and the kicking team. Only the kicker remained in position to make a touchdown-saving play, and he made a creditable attempt, but to no avail. His hands slipped from his target's shoulder pads and he fell to the grass.

Ryan watched the returner celebrate his score from the sideline. He was wearing street clothes—a polo shirt and khaki pants, and a team cap—sitting on the bench with the other inactive. A return for a touchdown on the very first play of the season. That couldn't be a good omen . . .

Ryan was still sitting on the bench a few moments later when the Saints return team took the field to receive the ball. He looked up just as San Francisco's kicker booted the ball down to the five-yard line, where the returner fielded it. Ryan watched as he moved forward, shaking a tackler and then shooting off to the right sideline. The crowd seemed to hold its collective breath as one last defender lunged, reaching out and grasping the runner's arm. For a long second he held on before the runner fell out of bounds at the 47. Ryan turned away, then froze when the crowd erupted. He didn't want to look, but he did, and saw a storm of activity where the return man had fallen.

"What happened?" he wondered aloud. He noticed he was alone on the bench, stood and pushed his way through coaches and players to the sideline. "What happened?" he shouted.

"Fumble," someone replied.

Par for the course.

Ryan returned to the bench, a sick feeling in the pit of his stomach; this was bad.

Despite the deafening blast coming from the crowd—60,000 strong—the Saints' sideline was as quiet as a morgue. No one spoke except the coaches and coordinators as they shouted orders into their headsets, and Ryan wasn't going to solicit a conversation. He reached for the cooler sitting on the table next to the bench, filled a paper cup with whatever was in it and took a sip while he watched the starting defense trudge out onto the field for the first time, already down 7–0.

Commercials were displayed on the big screens, but the crowd almost drowned out the sound from them. After the last one finished, one of the officials blew his whistle and the two teams met at the line of scrimmage. And the crowd fell silent in support of the home team offense.

The 49ers' quarterback handed the ball to his halfback, who tried to cut through the right side of the defensive line. A second later he was lying on his back, smashed backwards by David Falk, who met him head-on in the hole.

Not bad, Ryan thought.

It was second down now, with a full ten yards to go. This time the quarterback faked a handoff and tossed a short pass out into the right backfield to the halfback, who turned his momentum upfield. He escaped from one tackler but another—David Falk—was able to grab him low, around the knees, and jerk his feet out from under him.

Two plays, two tackles for the rookie inside linebacker. *Let's say he keeps that rate up,* Ryan thought half-seriously. *Average sixty defensive plays a game . . . sixteen games . . .* almost a thousand tackles. *Wow.* Not that that was likely, or even possible. But still, for a rookie to have this much of an impact this early in his first season was impressive.

You should've retired, bonehead.

Third down, eight yards to go. The quarterback took a long, seven step drop and launched a rainbow bomb deep down the left sideline. His receiver, a defender hanging on his back, made a desperate leap for the ball but couldn't quite reach it. Incomplete, and Ryan sighed. Then he saw the flag, a yellow marker of doom contrasting with the dark green grass, and knew why the referee had thrown it: Pass interference, on the defense. Move the ball to the spot of the foul—fifty yards downfield from the previous line of scrimmage—and throw in an automatic first down. The crowd loved it, and screamed its approval.

Ryan gulped down the rest of his drink and crumpled the cup in his fist. He had a nasty presentiment that this day was going to be very long indeed.

One play later the quarterback threw a slant over the middle that was caught by the same wide receiver who'd missed the last pass. He whipped through the secondary untouched until he reached the two yardline, where he lowered his shoulders and used his momentum to carry himself and his tackler into the end zone. Touchdown. The extra point made the score 14-0.

Ryan could do nothing but watch as his team was dismantled by an opponent whom they'd been favored to beat. The odds makers had set the line at 6½ points.

Shaking his head, he filled another paper cup with Gatorade and tried not to scream like one of those crazed fans sitting at home on the couch.

It was more difficult than he'd thought.

"Welcome back to our coverage of the New York Jets and Missouri Gunners. With nine minutes left in the first quarter, New York has taken the lead, seven to nothing." James Hunt gawked at a statistics sheet someone had stuck in front of him. He clicked off his mic. "San Fran's got the Saints down fourteen-zip just two minutes into the game."

Mack shook his head. "Bad luck."

"Looks like it." He reactivated the mic.

"Jim," Mack said, once again speaking to millions of viewers, "right now, this Gunners offense is depending on their rookie halfback. I'm not sure that Julian Lloyd's up to carrying this team, at least not yet."

"And though Rich Mitchum is a good quarterback it's doubtful he's up to the challenge of keeping the offense on track without a running game," Hunt agreed.

"That's right, Jim. We'll see if Lloyd improves on this series."

"Indeed. They come to the line in a three wideout set. Not ready to commit to the run, maybe. Mitchum, five step drop, pass over the middle complete to Moran. He's brought down just short of the first down."

"They may be trying to spread the defense out, coming in with the three and four wide receivers sets," Mack said.

"Gunners come back in the same set," Hunt said, "three receivers spread to the left of the field and Moran up on the line to the right. Mitchum takes a five step drop, passes out left, caught for a six yard gain. That'll be enough for the first down."

"This short passing West Coast type offense may work for a while," Mack said, "but the Gunners aren't geared for that. They're better off stretching the field deep with the receivers and hitting the short passes over the middle to Moran. Of course, in order to do that you need a decent running game."

"Same set," Hunt observed. "Receiver comes in motion from left to right. Snap—handoff to Lloyd running straight ahead, tackled for no gain."

"I don't want to pass judgement," Mack said, "but I just don't see any burst or desire out of this guy right now. Maybe he's still shaky from the injury, I don't know."

"They mark it second and nine at the thirty-five, so it's a one yard gain. Gunners come out in the I-formation, two receivers, two backs and Moran the tight end. Handoff, Lloyd, sweeping right. Hit and dragged down for a short gain of maybe two."

"Now that brings up a third and seven situation. You almost have to wonder why they're even running with Julian Lloyd."

Hunt nodded. "You'd expect that if they don't get some production out of him here early, he'll be benched."

Julian rolled onto his stomach and started to get to his feet, but was sent sprawling back to the ground by a blow to the back. A blast of anger took hold of him and he leapt to a standing position, turning around to see who had knocked him down. He read the number from the back of the guy's jersey: 58—the inside linebacker.

Rage boiling from deep within, from somewhere inside him that he hadn't known existed, he went to the huddle. "I want the ball," he demanded, his breaths coming in heaves. "I'm ready."

"That's good," Mitchum said, staring at him. "Because we're running a draw . . ."

* * *

"The Gunners come out in shotgun formation, Lloyd still in and standing next to Mitchum. Snap—they run the draw with Lloyd up the middle—has a hole—meets the linebacker—*whoa!* Lloyd plowed through the linebacker like he wasn't there! Still on his feet in the open field, has the first down and more, and is *finally* tackled after a gain of seventeen yards. What a run!"

"I take back anything derogatory I've said about Julian Lloyd's toughness," Mack said. "He hit the inside linebacker, Sid Freeman, number fifty-eight, and just ran him over. Freeman's almost two sixty, and Lloyd just knocked him over like a bowling pin."

"Gunners are running the no-huddle now, coming back to the line. Mitchum hands off to Lloyd, sweeping left—and that'll be a gain of seven on first down."

"It's like something just clicked in his head," Mack said. "The offensive line has been blowing open some major holes, yeah, but during that first series Lloyd wasn't taking advantage of them. Now he's hitting them right when they open and God help anybody who gets in his way."

"The ball rests at the forty-eight of the Jets, as the Gunners again take the line. Mitchum hands off again to Lloyd, who sweeps right—now cuts it back against the flow and finds a seam. Blasts through and falls forward for a gain of three and a first down."

Mack laughed. "Are you sure that's Julian Lloyd?"

"What's gotten into you?" Mitchum asked as they huddled up. He smiled. "Whatever it is, I'm likin' it."

Julian shrugged. "I don't know. I guess I'm not afraid anymore." He smiled. "It's just a football game."

Mitchum nodded. "What'd I tell you? All right. Zeke-dash right three two PA on two. *Break!*"

They lined up, Julian behind Mitchum at a distance of about five yards. Mitchum shouted the signals, took the snap and Julian stepped forward, holding his arms as if he were to receive a handoff. Instead, Mitchum snatched the ball away and rolled right while Julian jogged forward, unnoticed by the defense just a couple yards forward from the line of scrimmage. He looked back, saw the ball flying toward him over the opposing lines. He caught it, secured it and darted forward into the open. The free safety, the only person in a position to stop him, dove for his legs, but Julian pushed him away and juked, letting him land on his stomach. One of the speedy cornerbacks streaked over from the right side of the field, and Julian turned his momentum to the left. As he neared the sideline, the corner reached for him and pushed hard on his shoulder pads, trying to drive him out of bounds. Julian shifted the ball to his left arm and pushed back with his right, a hard stiff-arm move. The corner leaped onto his back; Julian carried him for another five yards before falling.

He stood, tossed the ball to an official and jogged back to join his teammates. Behind him, he heard his tackler swear, and he laughed.

Now it was getting fun.

"A nice gain on the play," Hunt said. "They're marking the ball at the eighteen, making it a twenty-yard catch and run by Julian Lloyd. I'd say he's recovered, eh?"

"That was a fine bit of running," Mack acknowledged. "Maybe he should've carried that little defensive back into the end zone, but still, the way he made the safety miss was impressive."

"You have to wonder what spurred him on," Hunt said. "He was ineffective on that first series and for the first few plays of this one."

"Running backs," Mack, the former linebacker, snorted. "They're all fruitcakes."

Mitchum dropped back five steps and Julian ran a pass pattern through the offensive line. This time a linebacker stayed close, trying to cover him and prevent a repeat of the previous play. Julian looked upfield and ran hard, noticing the safety he'd earlier made a fool of. The safety, already moving to cover Moran, slowed for a split second, torn between staying on his assigned coverage scheme and helping the linebacker keep Julian from becoming a factor.

Good.

The split second of indecision cost the safety. Julian watched Moran take the moment to accelerate past him, saw Mitchum's lob fly over the coverage and land in the tight end's hands at the four-yard line and raised his arms in celebration as Moran trotted in untouched for the score.

At that moment, a realization washed over Julian, confirming all the rhetoric he'd heard from Mitchum and Davis. This really was just football, like he'd played his whole life. The objective was the same: Get the ball over the goal line.

Julian was good at that. So good at it that it gave other players a better chance to do it as well.

You got that second chance.

Use it.

In the enemy territory that was the former Candlestick Park, New Orleans was reeling. Ahead by fourteen in the first period, San Francisco had ample time to put its opponent away early on.

Ryan stood on the sideline now, watching and shaking his head. In sixteen years of football he had rarely seen fourteen points given away in such a short time. And that was exactly what had happened; they'd been given away.

As Ryan watched, San Francisco's quarterback handed off to the halfback. The runner barely managed to dodge a surging would-be tackler in the backfield before bouncing outside and stutter-stepping through the defense for a respectable four yards on first down.

Ryan shook his head. The strategy was clear: San Francisco had jumped ahead early, and was now content to run the ball and use short dump-off passes to drive steadily down the field, draining the clock and demoralizing the defense.

They ran the ball again, this time giving it to the big full-back who followed the blocks of his interior linemen while banging his way ahead for another four yards.

The previous two plays brought up an ideal situation: Third and two. Such short yardage on third down gave the offense a plethora of options, not all of which the defense could counter at once.

Ryan looked down the sideline at the defensive coordinator as the man called his defensive scheme for the play. What was he calling? Ryan couldn't hear, but judging from the personnel who were shuttling in and out it seemed they were going with a modified nickel pass coverage scheme. Ryan frowned. Why go with the nickel, which sacrificed a linebacker for an extra defensive back, in such a short yardage situation? If it was up to him he'd go with the old Bear 46, which was featured in Gary Harrell's defense, and put pressure—

The quarterback dropped back, hesitated, then handed the ball to the halfback who squeezed through an opening for three yards and a first down. A classic short draw play. *We reacted well,* Ryan thought. But because of the nickel scheme, which had two linebackers instead of the customary three— and one of these tasked to pass coverage—the good reaction wasn't enough to stuff the play and prevent its success. The defensive backs, in man-to-man coverage, were moving to stay with the receivers and couldn't get to the line fast enough.

Bad call.

They made a few substitutions while the offense was huddled up, going back to the basic 4–3 scheme. When the opposing sides lined up, Ryan noted the positions of the linebackers and defensive tackles, placed together over the space between offensive guards and center. *Blitz package,* he thought.

The quarterback went play-action, faking a handoff and looking up to find his receiver. A defensive surge up the middle forced him to roll outside the pocket, but too late; David Falk, running hard on the blitz, grabbed him around the shoulder pads from behind and threw him down.

The sideline erupted in cheers as the team celebrated the sack, fighting in vain the boos raining down from the crowd. Falk, on the contrary, just returned to the huddle to await the next play. A sign of maturity, Ryan realized. *Been there, done that—and he* hasn't *been there!*

On second down San Francisco rammed the ball up the middle, the halfback pushing forward for five hard-earned yards before getting slammed back by Falk and two others. The kid was going to be dominant at his position, and very soon. Certainly sooner than Ryan had thought. Speed, agility, strength, awareness—he had them all and more; he had the intangibles.

Third down. From the shotgun the quarterback rolled right, outside the protection of his line. A defensive end broke free and rambled after him, lunging but missing as the quarterback ducked and whirled around, dashing back the other way. Falk bowled his way past the fullback, who had resorted to a desperate but fruitless illegal hold, and caught the quarterback in midstride, hitting and driving him hard to the ground just as he threw the ball. The ball flopped up like a duck during hunting season and bounced to the grass, bringing up a fourth down and punt for San Francisco.

Falk and the rest of the defense left the field, giving each other back slaps and smiles. Falk came over to Ryan and shook his head with a sigh.

"They never should've gotten that first down on the last series," he said. "I got caught out of position."

Ryan stared in wonder. "Well, happens to the best of us." *He blames himself for a coaching mistake?* He shrugged. "It wasn't the best scheme for that particular play."

"I guess not," Falk said. "Still, I misread it and took a bad

step. Turned away from the ball. By the time I noticed it was
a run the guy had already picked up the first."

"You made that tackle?"

"Yes. A little late."

Ryan rubbed the back of his head and took a deep breath,
in his nose, out his mouth. In just a couple defensive series,
the kid had logged at least two solo tackles, a sack and one,
maybe two quarterback hurries. That was all-pro material,
even for a veteran. For a rookie it was downright amazing.

"David," Ryan said, "if you have a few more series like that
each game for the rest of the season, you'll make rookie of
the year, easy."

"Maybe so. But what good is being rookie of the year if
you let a running back get three yards every time he needs
two? That doesn't help the team much."

Yeah, it does. David didn't realize it, Ryan observed, but
some guys gave the opponent five yards when he needed two.

"I saw you chase down the QB," Ryan said. "You run like
a wide receiver."

"I played wide receiver in high school," Falk said. "I didn't
tell you that?"

"No."

"Yeah. Coach lined me up at wide receiver, linebacker, defensive end. Heck, I even kicked if I they needed me to."

"What made the college guys put you on defense?"

Falk chuckled. "There aren't too many two hundred and
forty pound wide receivers. I did play some my freshman
year, but very limited."

"Uh-huh." They turned their attention to the field as the
49ers' punter launched a beauty of a kick. The ball arced skyward and sailed forty-five yards upfield, in the air a full 4.6
seconds before the return man took it in for a fair catch.

"Let's see if we get some offense," Falk said.

"That would be nice," Ryan agreed. He looked at David,
just stared at him for a moment, noting the rippling lines of
his sculpted frame beneath the white jersey.

The kid's played four positions. He's a physical freak with a great attitude and a brain. I'm almost forty, and only played one position in my prime. I'm getting arthritis in my knees. I'm deactivated.

What the hell was I thinking?

"Three minutes left in the first quarter," Hunt said as the commercials ended. "Tie score, seven to seven."

"Julian Lloyd's been putting on a show," Mack said. "His stats so far: Nine carries, fifty-eight yards and two catches for thirty-five yards. That's six-point-four yards per rush, and ninety-three yards of total offense. In less than a quarter."

"It appears the hype was right after all," Hunt said. The Gunners offense, having just received a New York punt, took the field. "Gunners in a three wide set his time. Lloyd back there alone again."

"They've been loving that single back three wide formation today," Mack commented.

"Mitchum hands off to Lloyd up the gut. Slams his way forward . . . give him four on the play."

"I figure at this rate," Mack said, only half-jokingly, "Julian Lloyd will put up around two-hundred-fifty yards."

"Which would be close to the rookie single-game record," Hunt said. "Don't expect that to happen."

"I know, I'm just saying—"

"Gunners come back to the line," Hunt cut him off, "Same formation. Mitchum drops back . . . throws a dart to Moran. Short gain of five."

"Now that could have been a big play for New York," Mack said. "Mitchum forced that one in there just before he was leveled by the blitz coming off the right side." He shook his head as he watched the replay. "Lloyd was supposed to hit the linebacker, pick up the blitz. He missed. Rookie mistake, but you can't let that happen too often, or your quarterback will end up a permanent part of the turf."

"Clock ticking just under two minutes left in the first now," Hunt said. "Despite the tie score the Gunners have pretty much dominated throughout behind the running of Julian Lloyd."

"The Jets are just lucky it's still early, and that it's still a tie game," Mack said. "Because if you go by the stats, they're getting the tar beat out of them."

"You see the graphic on your screen," Hunt told the audience, "indicating that New York has punted on its last three possessions. Missouri hasn't done much better, moving the ball then stalling just outside field goal range."

"But the Jets defense won't be able to take this much pressure after a while. They'll get worn down. Believe me, I know. If this keeps up, by the third quarter it'll be thirty-five to seven."

"Third and one," Hunt called the play. "Gunners come to the line, once again in that three wide set. Mitchum hands it to Lloyd, slashing through a seam and falling forward for the first down."

"There wasn't much of a push off the line," Mack said, "but Lloyd did what he had to do. He's also figured out that when you're going down you fall *forward* and not *backward.*"

"Drove you linebackers crazy, did that?" Hunt asked.

"Oh yeah. You hit the guy hard enough to rattle your own teeth, and what does he do? Slips underneath you and falls forward for an extra half-yard."

"The Gunners will likely run two more plays before the end of the quarter," Hunt said. "They're taking their time, staying in the huddle until they absolutely have to break, then running the play clock down to five or less before snapping."

"Nothing drains a defense more than a long drive powered by a running game," Mack said. "Those teams that do nothing but pass—heck, they'll put forty on the board, but the other team will put up forty-five."

"Don't let my old-school partner bother you," Hunt remarked.

"It isn't popular, but it sure is the truth," Mack defended himself.

"With just over a minute left in the first quarter, the Gunners come to the line. Mitchum takes the snap, drops back. Throws the screen out to Lloyd. Lloyd, makes a guy miss and dashes forward for about five."

Mack shook his head. "The purpose of the screen is to get the defense to attack, come after the quarterback, and then toss the ball over their heads to the 'back who has a wall of blockers in front of him. That can result in a big gain. But right there, New York played it very well. The linebacker read the play and was waiting when Lloyd got the ball."

"But he still managed to gain five," Hunt said.

"Which says all the more about this kid. Most 'backs would have lost yardage there."

"Gunners come back to the line for what should be the last play of the opening quarter. Mitchum takes a seven-step drop. He steps forward and throws down the right sideline . . . *caught* by Riley who is pulled down immediately. That'll be a thirty-six yard gain, all the way down to the eleven-yard line."

"It looked like the defense was expecting a run there, so the Gunners just went with the old fade route. Jake Riley, at six-three, was able to leap over the DB and make a heck of a catch."

"Indeed," Hunt said. "And that will end the first quarter, with the score knotted up at seven—but the Gunners are driving. Back after this."

Ryan watched Ethan Daniels drop back in the pocket, pump-fake once and then throw a bullet that sliced down the middle of the field where a receiver grabbed it and fought forward for a gain of sixteen yards.

"That's better," Ryan said. Falk nodded.

"In college, we ran a lot of the option," he said. "You wouldn't believe how tiring that offense was to defend in practice."

"But it worked."

"Yeah. It worked. Wasn't pretty."

"Doesn't have to be." Ryan pointed to San Francisco's strong safety as the two teams lined up. "Looks like a blitz."

Daniels dropped back five steps, spotted the safety's blitz and ran to the right to avoid it. The safety, unable to stop his momentum, flew past. Daniels stopped, planted his feet and heaved the ball downfield. Ryan held his breath as it began its descent—there was an open receiver—but the ball was overthrown—*no!* The receiver dove forward, stretching out his body and snagging the pass with his fingertips before sliding to the ground, the ball secure in his gut.

"Now we're talking!" Falk shouted above the cheers of his comrades around them.

"That was a good forty yards," Ryan said. "But those bombs still get me nervous."

"Why is that?"

"Call me old fashioned," Ryan said, "but I like an offense that works by running the ball, four yards at a time, six-minute drives. Keeps us defenders off the field."

"And here I was thinking you want to be *on* the field."

"Only when I have to be. It's a lot harder to score when you don't have the football, you know."

"Obviously."

The teams on the field approached the line of scrimmage, San Francisco's twenty-one-yard line. Daniels backpedaled and fired a laser shot over the middle, caught by the tight end at the six. The tight end bowled his way forward to the goal line and fell hard to the grass just inside the end zone.

Ryan gave Falk a five, amid a fresh round of cheering from the sideline—interrupted by a chorus of groans. An official's flag lay on the ground near the line of scrimmage, and that could mean but one thing.

"Holding," the referee said, "on the offense, number sixty-three. Ten yard penalty. Repeat first down."

Ryan shook his head grimly. "Did I mention penalties?"

* * *

"The Gunners have it, third and goal at the four-yard line," Hunt said. "We're tied at seven with eleven-thirty-nine left in the second quarter. Gunners come to the line, two wide, I-formation."

"Look for them to get the ball into Julian Lloyd's hands here," Mack said.

"Snap—Mitchum, play-action. Short pass over the middle caught by Lloyd—he runs it in for the touchdown! He was untouched."

"And it's as simple as that," Mack said. "You've jammed Julian Lloyd down their throats on this drive, so now they're keying on his running. They stuff eight men in the box and blitz around the tackles. So what do you do? You get the ball to Lloyd again, but this time you fake the handoff and dump it to him over the middle for the few yards needed for the score. Smart call and great execution by both Rich Mitchum and Lloyd."

"The extra point is up and good, and the Gunners have their first lead of the afternoon: Fourteen to seven."

Ethan Daniels lined up his offense and put his runningback in motion out of the backfield. Ryan nudged Falk and nodded toward San Fran's defensive backs. "Tight coverage," he said. "Ethan needs to be patient back there."

"He isn't?"

Ryan shook his head. "Sometimes in the red zone he'll get into a mode where he hurries his throws, trying to make something happen too fast."

Snap—Daniels dropped back, cocked his arm and tossed a pass toward the right front end zone pylon. The pass was a bit behind the receiver—he turned around, backing toward the pylon as he reached for the ball—

"Ah . . ." Ryan mumbled in disgust.

The cornerback dove in front of him and snatched the ball away just before it reached the outstretched hands of the receiver. He landed hard on the turf with his prize.

"I see what you mean," Falk said.

"Red zone turnovers," Ryan said, "will kill you every time." He didn't mention the thought that came to him: *This is going to be a* very *long afternoon.*

Fifteen

Hendley entered his office reading the sports section of the Monday morning *Post-Dispatch*, studying the highlights of the Gunners' 31–10 rout of the Jets. Rich Mitchum had completed sixty percent of his passes, Frank Moran had caught six balls, Jake Riley had snagged five, the defense had hounded the opposing quarterback, sacking him four times—and Julian Lloyd, after a slow start, had gashed the New York defense for 165 yards on 25 carries. 6.6 yards per rushing attempt. Staggering statistics alone, they were made all the more impressive when one considered his three receptions for 27 more yards and his two touchdowns. All that after a knee injury like the one he had suffered . . .

It was too amazing to be true. No. It was downright impossible. No human being should've been able to return to a football field so soon after such an injury. Physically, mentally, emotionally—it was impossible. Hendley's gut told him that someone, somehow, had used unapproved genetic manipulation on Lloyd. It was the only possible explanation, and Hendley, as head of APEX, knew as much about genetic manipulation as any researcher.

The problem was, Fran had found nothing useful. Nothing he could go to the FDA with. Nothing he could go public with. Just hypotheses and conjectures. Her report, compiled over a month and a half of overtime work, had named some names and thrown around some ideas. But it hadn't given him any damning information.

No proof.

But Hendley hadn't given up on that. American Physicians united against Genetic EXperiments was a large network of doctors and their staffs spread over the country. There was a plethora of information available on various biotech companies. He just had to know where to look. He had put Dan Newman, APEX's accountant, on the job. Newman had scoured the financial records of the major biotech companies, searching for the slightest unusual number. But six weeks of work had produced nothing that couldn't be verified as being legitimate. He had told Fran to check out Vincent Petty, with the theory being that Petty would have negotiated any deal involving genetic manipulation of one of his football players. But that had turned up dry as well.

Dead ends, wherever he looked. He sighed and set the paper down on his desk. He called for a cup of coffee and sat down. He just didn't know where to look.

Hendley picked up the newspaper again and flipped through it, scanning the headlines. Midway through the local section he happened upon a short story headlined FREAK ACCIDENT KILLS TOP SCIENTIST. It was an Associated Press story based out of St. Louis. Valley Park, to be exact. Interesting.

The contents of the story were even more fascinating.

Dr. Jody Kicheski, 46, a physician and respected member of the biotech research community, was killed late last week in a freak accident at her company's lab outside of St. Louis. Police say her body was found by a fellow researcher at the Genetics Life, Incorporated lab in Valley Park, Missouri. The cause of death was specified as chemical inhalation. Apparently, Dr. Kicheski fell, striking her head and breaking open several vials of disinfectants used in the lab. She lay unconscious in a pool of chemicals and . . .

Hendley stopped and scanned back up the article. *Genetics Life, Incorporated* . . .

He knew the company. It was a tiny place outside the city

here, but Hendley hadn't paid much attention to it. It was
so small; he didn't believe it would last much longer. The
last report compiled by APEX had mentioned financial
difficulties—

That's it.

Financial difficulties. Of course! Why hadn't he considered
that before? Hendley tossed the newspaper aside and grabbed
for his phone. He dialed, then pressed it to his ear.

Two rings, then: "Newman."

"Dan, it's Eric," Hendley said, forcing himself to remain
calm. "You didn't get a financial report on Genetics Life, did
you?"

"GLI?" Newman asked, his voice tinny over the phone.
"Ah . . . no, I didn't. They aren't a public company, so I'd have
had to . . . well, work a little harder to get it. And they're so
small I didn't think it would make a difference. Sorry."

"No, no problem," Hendley assured him. "I felt the same
way. But look, something has come up, and I need a report on
them, as soon as possible."

"I'll get on it," Newman said. "Give me twenty-four
hours."

"Thanks, Dan. Bye." Hendley hung up and rubbed his
hands together. He noticed someone standing before the desk
and looked up. Fran was standing there with his coffee mug.

"Sorry about that, Fran," Hendley said. "It was a little
urgent."

"It's no problem," Fran said, handing him the mug.

"Thank you," Hendley said, and took a sip. Fran stared at
him for an extra moment, and he found that somewhat unusual, but then he dismissed it as she turned and went back to
the front office. The poor girl was overworking again, and
probably hoping for a break. She was so efficient, such a
blessing to have around the office—he'd have to give her a
paid vacation or something.

She deserved it.

* * *

Lance Pollard stood before the fifteen board members of HUMINT. The table, and the people sitting around it seemed dark and dreary. Pollard, on the other hand, had a youthful exuberance and manner that excited the board, and that ability—to control their emotions—was something he used to his advantage.

"I'd like you to consider my request," Pollard said, making eye contact with each member in turn. "By opening up two new seats on the board, we will be in a better position to intercept funding that would otherwise go to our competitors—"

"Intercept funding?" Devon Delaney, a bony fifty-year-old woman with gray hair said. "Mr. Pollard, you're talking about creating more bureaucracy in this company for the sole purpose of stealing investors. And just two new seats? I doubt that will make much of a difference for our competitors."

Pollard frowned. He couldn't tell them the truth, that he had made a deal with two separate parties, both of them interested in buying onto the board of a biotech company. If he opened a seat for them, they would buy into HUMINT. And not another company . . . like Genetics Life. He had to make this work . . .

"Ms. Delaney, I assure you we can handle a little more bureaucracy," he soothed. "If I was worried about my board—you people—interfering with the day-to-day operations of the company, I'd be downsizing. But I'm not worried, because there is no such problem."

An Asian-American man with a deep scar on his forehead leaned in. Pollard didn't bother to remember his name. "I happen to agree with Mr. Pollard. Every little bit helps, as they say—"

"Oh, I don't disagree with that," Delaney said, turning to the man. "It's this crusade he's been on that bothers me. Mr. Pollard has been stealing investors away from the competition. I have no problem with that, but when it comes at the cost of board authority . . ."

"Don't make assumptions that you can't back up," Pollard

broke in, glaring at Delaney. He stepped back from the table and looked at his board as a whole. "You will lose no authority. I have not approached you with a motion to do so, and I will not. The company is running smoothly; we're trouncing the competition. We are the best. I merely wish to take a small measure that will help us remain at the top."

"Mr. Pollard," Delaney muttered, shaking her head, "I understand that. But your obsession with that . . . that minute thorn in your side, GLI—it irks me. With obsession comes incompetency, and I will not have that with this company—"

She broke off as a woman in a business suit stepped inside the room and walked over to Pollard. He leaned close to her as she whispered in his ear. "Sir, I'm sorry, but there's an urgent call for you."

Pollard shook his head. "I'm busy," he whispered back.

"The caller is Jeanette Dean," the woman added.

Pollard froze. "Uh . . . I'll be right there." The woman nodded and backed away. Pollard bit his lip and looked at the members. "I'm sorry. Continue the discussion. I'll be right back."

He stormed out of the room straight to the woman's desk, grabbing the phone from her extended hand in a huff. "You'd better have a damned good reason for this," he said into it through clenched teeth.

"I most certainly do," Jeanette lilted to him. "Dr. Hendley is about to bust the GLI case open."

Pollard felt his jaw drop. "What?" he demanded. "You told me you'd taken care of it!" He noticed the still-open door to the board room, glanced to the woman at the desk and nodded towards it. She got up and closed it.

"I did take care of it," Jeanette said. "But Hendley isn't one to take just his secretary's word on an issue he deems so important. He worked through APEX. Just this morning he ordered his accountant to dig up GLI's financial records. If he gets those, he'll find the money Vincent Petty gave to them, and he'll put two and two together."

Pollard rubbed his forehead. This was all he needed . . .

"How sure are you about this Julian Lloyd thing?" he asked. "Are you absolutely certain Hendley will find a connection?"

"Positive," Jeanette said.

"Okay. You told me Nagel has nothing to do with the deal. If not him, then who?"

"One of his partners," Jeanette said. "Why?"

Pollard frowned. "The dead one? The one who died in that accident the other day?"

"No."

"Jeanette, I'm ordering you to tell me what you know," he said, frustrated. "Don't make me—"

"Angelina Moore," Jeanette said. "It was her."

"How do you know?" Pollard held the phone tightly to his ear, as if it would help him hear her answer more clearly.

"I know her," Jeanette said. "You remember my little experiment back in graduate school?"

"Of course I do," Pollard said. He chuckled. "It's the reason I hired you."

"Right. Well, believe it or not, Angelina Moore was the brains behind that. I was just her little partner. Angel and Jean." She laughed. "Angel was a little better at manipulating people than I was. Probably because she had the looks." There was no mistaking the bitterness in Jeanette's voice.

"What happened?" Pollard asked, interested.

Jeanette snorted. "Well, when the academics caught on to what we were doing, she managed to set me up. I was the fall-girl. You understand?"

"How did she get out of it?" Pollard wondered why he'd never learned this before. It definitely explained some . . . things about Jeanette.

"Let's just say Angel knows how to use her body to get what she wants," Jeanette said.

"I see." Pollard took a breath, held it for a moment, then released it. "So. Now we need to figure out how to handle this situation. What can you do?"

"Nothing," Jeanette said. "Not without raising suspicions. As soon as Hendley gets that report, he'll contact the authorities. And he'll make them investigate. He's quite persuasive when he needs to be."

"Then make sure he never contacts the authorities," Pollard said. His eyes narrowed, and he whispered into the phone. He didn't want the secretary to hear him. "Whatever it takes."

"This could be dangerous," Jeanette said, but without the slightest bit of hesitation.

"Be creative," Pollard told her.

"I can handle that," Jeanette said. "Let me get to work."

"Yes. And be cautious," Pollard warned, and turned the phone off. He handed it to the woman at the desk, who looked at it curiously for a moment before placing it on its cradle.

"It's a rough business," Pollard said to her with a smile before returning to the board room to continue the debate.

Jacob Davis stood in the midst of his entire team on the practice field. Mondays were an open day, a day to recuperate from the rigors of the battle that was the Sunday game. But everyone got back to work on Tuesday, and it was on Tuesday that Davis always gave out his game ball.

"It's a tradition of mine to have a custom ball made for the team MVP," he said. "As many of you veterans know." He held up a new football, fresh out of the box. "This baby has our logo imprinted on it. And . . ." He rotated the ball in his hand. ". . . It's signed by Mr. Petty, Mr. Marsh and myself. It has a little message inscribed on it." His eyes went from player to player. "The coaching staff voted on the team MVP from last week's game, and this football will go to him, as will one like it after every win. Let's see if you recognize who gets this one from the stats they printed on here." He held the ball at arms' length, like a farsighted man trying to read a book. "One hundred sixty-five rushing yards, twenty-seven receiving yards, and two touchdowns. Who did that Sunday?"

"Lloyd!" the entire team shouted in unison, masculine voices in concert.

Julian smiled, trying to keep from blushing and displaying his embarrassment to his teammates. He rose from a crouch and slid between his football brethren as they patted him on the back and congratulated him for a job well done. He stopped when he got within reach of the coach and the prize he held high.

"This is for Julian Lloyd, who went through a helluva lot to even play this season," Davis said. "Much less bust open for a career day in his first game. Julian!" He held the ball out. Julian took it, caressed its leathery texture and then shook his coach's hand.

"Thanks," he said.

Davis slapped him on the back, hard, and laughed. "All right! All of you, on your feet. Enough of our feminine side. Back to work!" The group began to disperse, the men laughing and chatting among themselves. Julian hefted the ball under his arm and flowed away with his teammates. Davis covered the distance between them in a couple of steps and matched his stride. "Congratulations," he said.

"Thanks," Julian said.

"I'm serious. You don't realize how big an honor this is. I've done it ever since my first coaching job; a little two-A high school team in Virginia. It was a popular award."

"Coveted," Julian said, rolling the ball in his hand and looking each signature and inscription over.

"Yes, exactly." Davis smiled.

"I'm honored," Julian said.

Davis nodded. "You should be. And if the results are the same, I'd be happy to see you win fifteen more just like it."

Julian chuckled. "So would I."

"That was a hell of a performance," the coach said. "Worthy of the award. And the best part is that it was your first game on this level. You'll get better as you go."

"I guess that's the idea," Julian said, giving the ball a last look before turning to the coach.

"Sure is," Harrell said. "Now, go put that ball away and get your butt back out here. You don't get better if you don't work."

* * *

Ryan rolled out of bed, glanced at the clock and groaned: 9:48 A.M. He had hoped to get up bright and early, eat a nice breakfast with the family, and do some work around the house before having to check in at team headquarters at noon.

He must have been dreaming. The kids were no doubt off to school already, so seeing them was out of the question. And he remembered Vanessa telling him that she would be out from around nine until two or three, running errands, getting her hair done—female stuff.

So he was home all alone. For two hours.

He stumbled into the bathroom, leaned over the sink and looked at his reflection in the mirror. *You look like crap,* he told himself, and picked up his toothbrush.

His Rolex read 11:42 when he pulled the door open, carrying a large duffel bag, and stepped inside the team practice facility. He trudged in the direction of the locker rooms. He passed a few staffers and assistant coaches as he went, and smiled to them, saying hello and moving on. He rounded a corner and came to the big swinging doors that were the entrance to the main locker room, and reached for the door handle.

"Ryan," a voice said from behind him.

Ryan turned and nodded a greeting to Coach Harrell. "Hey, Gary."

"How was your day off?"

"Honestly?" Ryan asked with a smile.

"Sure," Harrell said, not smiling.

"I'm not sure I remember," Ryan said, and laughed. "Guess I slept late yesterday, too."

Harrell chuckled, but the reaction seemed to be forced, without humor. "Isn't as easy getting out of bed as it used to be, eh?"

Ryan nodded cautiously. "No, it's not."

"Yeah." Harrell scratched at the back of his neck. "Look, Chase called in sick. Bad cold, and he wouldn't have been of any use, so I told him to take it easy today." Chase McGuire was the linebackers coach. "Put your stuff away, and come back to my office. We'll go over some tape."

Ryan nodded. He knew what was coming, and it wasn't something to dread. "Okay, I'll be right there."

"Thanks." Harrell cracked a slight smile of gratitude and ambled down the hall.

Coaching help, Ryan thought as he opened the door and went inside the plushly carpeted locker room. The lights were muted, almost like a restaurant.

It wasn't unusual, having Harrell ask him to go over game tape, or work on some of the scheduling and drills as he would an assistant coach. For a couple years now, the coach would do that. But for the last eighteen months he would ask every few weeks, and even gave Ryan responsibilities assigned to a coordinator.

He found his locker, set the duffel on the floor beside it, hesitated a moment and walked out of the room.

"You see that?" Harrell asked, tapping the TV screen with a finger. "He has natural leverage coming around the end. We know he's got the speed—he got to there from the inside position in the first place—so I think he can be utilized outside in the nickel."

"You're talking about moving him to the roaming spot," Ryan said. "You want to turn him loose."

"Just on nickel downs, obviously."

Ryan nodded. They were poring over game tape from the loss to San Francisco, studying the defense in general—and David Falk in particular. "He can handle it," Ryan said. "He's good. Really good. He knows the game, and he's got the talent to do anything." *High school wide receiver!*

"I feel the same way," Harrell said, leaning back in his chair. "He may get caught on a bad step, or overpursue every once in a while. But that won't happen often. And we're in the nickel, what, a quarter of the game on average?" Their base defense was a three-deep zone that strived to keep the offense in front to avoid giving up the big play. The nickel was a pure pass defense that swapped a linebacker for a defensive back. The two 'backers that remained needed to be solid in pass coverage or expert pass rushers. Preferably both. And it was rare that a rookie was both.

"Give or take," Ryan said. They played it a lot more against passing teams, of course.

Harrell nodded. "Right. So, what do you think?"

"Turn him loose. He'll wreak havoc." Ryan smiled. "Like I used to do."

"You, on the other hand," Harrell said, grimacing as the latter left Ryan's mouth. "You need to turn it up a notch. We're going to need you on special teams." And that was as close to admitting a mistake as Harrell could get, Ryan realized. The special teams coverage breakdown that led to the opening kickoff touchdown return was due in part to the fact that the defensive back he had activated in Ryan's place had blown his assignment. How one could do that on kick coverage, Ryan didn't know. It was a death squad. You ran down the field and slammed into somebody. Simple.

Ryan sighed. "I'll try."

"I hope so. You're a leader, Ryan, but you aren't much of an athlete anymore."

"I know."

"You can't get by on athletic ability, so you should play smart. Pick your lanes, choose your angle carefully. Use your head."

"Even on the death squad, eh?" Ryan stretched his arms. He was still a little tired.

"Especially on the death squad," Harrell said. "I don't want another kickoff returned for a touchdown this season. You got that?"

Ryan nodded. "You bet. I'll make sure."

"A big play on special teams can make or break a game," Harrell continued. He was preaching, in his old high school coaching mode. "We played pretty well otherwise. But we got knocked off balance, and never got our footing."

"Yeah, I know."

"We'll throw a few new wrinkles into the mix this Sunday against Atlanta. We'll let David roam on passing downs, try more slants and comebacks on offense, blitz a little more. We have to knock them off balance first."

"Sounds great."

"So," Harrell finished. "Expect a whole new practice regiment for this week. More drills, more sprints, more seven-on-sevens. It'll be tougher."

"Tougher," Ryan repeated, frowning.

Harrell stood. "Yes."

Ryan did the same. "You're saying certain members of the team won't be able to take it," he said. "I don't like the meaning behind that, Gary."

Harrell stared at him. "We'll see."

Julian opened the door to his apartment and slid inside, closing it behind him. The hotel's room-like living area was dark; he made his way to the window and opened the curtains, letting in the dimming late afternoon light.

He pulled a silver compact disk, protected in a plastic sleeve, out of his pocket, sat on the sofa with a deep, soothing breath and picked up the laptop computer that lay on it next to him. He opened it, turned it on and inserted the CD. The computer hummed and whirred as it loaded. As it did, he dug the remote control out from between the sofa cushions and turned the TV to ESPN. He muted the volume, looked back to the computer screen—

Brriiing!

Julian grabbed the phone from off the hook, on the coffee table in front of the sofa, and held it to his ear. "Hello."

"Julian!"

He smiled with recognition. "Hi, Ma."

"Yes, it's your mother," her voice came, cynical. "Where have you been?"

"Very busy, Ma. I had practice today." Julian watched the

icons load on the computer desktop, and directed his pointer to the right one with the thumb pad.

"You're supposed to be off on Monday after games, though . . ." Jacklyn Lloyd said.

He frowned. "How did you know that?"

She clucked like a teacher poring over awful math scores. "Baby, I've been in on all this football stuff since way before you were even a thought."

His frown melted away. "I should've known."

"You should have, but nobody's perfect. You haven't answered the question."

Julian sighed. "Well, we're off on Mondays, but you *are* allowed to come in and work. Weights. Film. The coaches are all there."

"So you went in on your off day? You work too hard, Julian."

Julian loaded the program and waited while the computer hummed. "Nah. The guys that don't work like this are the ones who end up losing their jobs in a few years."

"I guess so. How are things? Or can you not tell your meddling mother?"

"Ma, that's the last thing you are. I'm actually glad you called. I was just about to study my playbook."

He heard a sigh combined with a laugh. "More work, huh? You should take it easy once in a while," she said.

Julian almost laughed; Jacklyn Lloyd was by far the hardest-working person he had ever known. She had to be, especially when she was forced to work outside the home to support her children after her husband's untimely death. Julian remembered, though he had been very young at the time, that her motivation had been to keep her children out of crime and drug-infested public housing projects.

"After the season," he said.

"Right. So, studying the playbook. Is it any better organized than that messy binder you used to keep all over my counter top?"

"Ma," Julian said. "You're behind the times. It's all on CD-ROM, computerized. Coach has a custom-made program that lets us see every play, every formation, every signal and even put them all up against defensive formations. It's amazing." He was looking at that program's main menu now.

"It's too high-tech for me," Jacklyn said.

"Aw, you should see it. Makes things so neat and organized. It would shock you to see how much mess it saves me from having to make."

"Only temporarily, I bet. You'll have a pile of CDs all over the floor pretty soon."

"You have so much faith in me, Ma. Makes me happy." He chuckled.

"Well, it should. Have you eaten dinner yet?" She sounded a little concerned.

"No, Mother," he assured her.

"What are you going to eat?"

He wasn't worried about that. "I don't know. I'll order something, I guess."

"You *still* haven't gotten some groceries into that little Motel Six?"

"No, I haven't, Ma. And why are you calling my apartment a Motel Six?"

"Because it isn't much more than that," she said, her voice a derogatory cluck. "And with that contract you should be living in a nice house, in style. Instead you gave me the house. What am I supposed to do with a big house?"

"I don't know," Julian chuckled. She'd been the one to pick out that big house . . . "But I could ask you the very same question."

"Anything's better than living in an apartment in the downtown area of a big city."

"It's convenient."

"Convenient, hell. Get a house."

"After the season."

In his mind's eye, he could see her frowning and shaking her head in disapproval. "You shouldn't be sarcastic with your mother."

"I'm sorry," Julian said.

"Uh-huh. Well, kid, I'm going to let you go. I know you have some *work* to do."

"I do, Ma. I'll talk to you later, okay?"

"Sure thing. Bye, Julian."

"Bye."

He hung up, yawned and turned his attention to the computer again. He finished starting up the program and clicked through the formations, in a menu on the upper-right corner of the screen. He clicked "Single-Back", then selected "2 TE" from the submenu that appeared. The screen displayed a smattering of circles, which arranged themselves into a proper football formation; two wide receivers, two tight ends, offensive line, quarterback and a single running back. Another small submenu appeared, giving him the option to select a particular play and add a defensive set, if he so desired.

He loaded a play, "Red Smash One-Five." A series of lines and arrows superimposed themselves over and around the circles, all of them white except for a single bold red arrow leading from the halfback circle up between the center and guard circles. He right-clicked, brought up a menu and selected the option "Notes and Info." A white box filled with text appeared over the formation.

> Red Smash 15. Run to halfback between C/RG. No motion unless specified. Suggested use in short yardage to primary running back, when only one or two yards need be gained for first down or touchdown. Also may be successful accompanied by play-action (Red Smash PA 15) or as a change of pace when pass has been successful.
>
> Places heavy burden on running back and interior linemen to perform. May be read by superior inside linebackers, who will be able to disrupt play from 4-3 or Nickel defense.

This thing sure beat the heck out of the piles of crumpled paperwork that he'd lugged around for eight years in high school and college. Purists sometimes complained, saying that the old-fashioned paper playbook was as much a part of football as the ball itself, but Julian disagreed. Professional football was so complicated; anything that could simplify all the new information was more than welcome to him.

Complicated, he thought, but amazing nonetheless. He clicked on another play, "Green Middle 15," a quarterback draw right up the middle of the line. He laughed to himself, trying to picture Rich Mitchum running a draw play. That was a thought, the lead-footed 230-pounder bursting through the defense for a ten yard gain. Mitchum himself often joked that the only time he could run a 4.5 forty was when the three beers he'd downed caught up with him, and the bathroom was forty yards away.

He looked up, rubbed his eyes. As he did so, he caught sight of the muted television image; the ESPN anchor was saying something, the little box over his shoulder displaying a picture of Julian himself. He turned the sound up.

"—was presented with Coach Jacob Davis's traditional award, a football imprinted with the game's achievement, today at practice. Lloyd ran for over a hundred sixty yards in his first NFL start on Sunday against the Jets. Lloyd will start once again, next Sunday versus San Francisco, though the 49ers, fresh off a dominating victory over New Orleans, may supply a greater challenge with their big run-stopping nose tackle, George Damon. Damon, as usual, had no lack of words about his next opponent." The screen cut to a huge, dark-skinned man standing close to the camera in a locker room, obviously after completing a practice.

"Julian Lloyd's a halfway decent 'back," the big man drawled, "and comin' back from that injury's made him a big story. But I can tell ya that *we* aren't falling for all that miracle bull—" *bleep!* "He's just anotha guy, and he's gonna get a real welcome this week."

The view cut back to the anchor. "George Damon," he said. "Never short on words. Turning to baseball now, the Cubs continue to chase the . . ."

Julian hit mute again.

Intimidation. Damon was a talented three-hundred-pound lineman who got his kicks from scaring the life out of his opponents before they even met on the field. Well, Julian thought, it wasn't going to work on him. He'd been intimidated before, and knew the consequences; timid play, fumbles, lost yardage, and a permanent job guarding the Gatorade cooler. He wouldn't allow it to happen again. But he thought of the huge man hitting him, landing on him—he shuddered, and turned off the TV.

Sixteen

Another day, the same routine. Outside, the sky was bright and clear, the air warm, but less humid as the afternoon wore on. Inside, Hendley's office was mild and stuffy. Sitting behind his desk, the doctor tapped the fingertips of his left hand and shifted. When Dan Newman said twenty-four hours, he meant twenty-four hours. That earnings report should be coming in any minute, he knew.

He checked his watch. His next patient was arriving. A check-up on a surgery he had performed a couple months back, a fractured elbow he had been forced to repair surgically. Hendley stood up and made his way out into the hall.

One of the technicians, a tall, pleasant heavyset woman named Kathy, came up to him from the front office entrance and gave him a folder. "File on Mrs. Dietrich," she said.

"Thanks," Hendley said, opening the folder and skimming through the papers inside. "Room Three?"

Kathy nodded.

Hendley went to that examining room, opened the door and stepped inside. A tired-looking woman in her early thirties sat on the examining table, her right arm in a sling. Her dark hair was pulled back in a messy bun, and her makeup was applied haphazardly across her face. Three rambunctious children and an incapacitating arm injury could be a killer combination for a young mother.

Hendley braced himself, then smiled at her. One thing he always remembered about Gloria Dietrich was the apparent joy she received from hearing her own voice. One had to be prepared for that when you were locked in a room with her.

"Hello, Gloria," Hendley said, stepping towards her and reaching out gently for her damaged arm. "How are things today?" And that was all he needed to say. The rest of the conversation was hers.

"Oh, pretty good," she said. "Just trying to keep up with the kids. You have any idea how hard it is to find a babysitter these days?"

Especially with a new school year underway. Hendley grunted in reply, carefully moving the woman's arm and observing it and her reactions. Not much pain; she barely flinched.

"Finally I found the girl across the street. She has a fever," Gloria Dietrich said. "But it isn't too bad. She was able to come over for a few hours. My mother would've done it, but she's on that cruise."

"Uh-huh," Hendley said.

Mrs. Dietrich went on about her mother for a while, then changed to the weather, and how little help her husband was during the football season. Hendley just added the occasional "uh-huh" and "I see" and went through the examination. He stepped back and scribbled a note in the file.

"All right, Mrs. Dietrich," he said, handing it to her. "Turn this in up front. I think we can take that off"—he nodded to the sling—"next week."

The woman smiled, exhaling her tension. "Finally," she said, hopping to her feet. "You wouldn't believe how annoying this thing has been. Chasing triplets around for two months with one arm isn't fun."

"I can imagine."

"They take advantage of it, too," Mrs. Dietrich continued. "They come up with plans. One will do something and get my attention, then start running, and ignore me, so I have to chase her and the *other* two will go and do something behind my back that they aren't supposed to do."

"Mm-hmm." Hendley reached for the door, resting his hand on the handle. She had to be close to the end by now . . .

"Don't get me wrong, they're good kids, especially for five-year-olds. But you have to keep up with them, you know. And if you can't then they walk all over you."

"Really," he said, managing not to groan.

"Yeah. I'm going to have to get them back in line now. As soon as I get rid of this cast, that is. Otherwise I just can't keep up with them."

"So you said."

"Yes. Oh, I'm sorry, I'm just rambling on here, aren't I, when you have other patients to see and a lot of work to do. And I have to get home. That girl's mother isn't going to be happy when she finds out she isn't home . . ." Gloria sighed and smiled. "Thanks, Dr. Hendley."

"Just my job," he assured her. "Have a nice day," he added as she left the office. He waited until she was back in the waiting area before stalking back out into the hall and making for his office. That fax had to be coming! Dan would be sending it to his personal, direct-office line. Not that he didn't trust his office personnel. He just felt more comfortable having that potentially sensitive information come right to him.

He opened the door to his office and looked inside. The fax machine, sitting on the table beside the right wall, was silent. Nothing had come through. Disappointed, he stepped back out and went to the front office.

One of the ladies was just finishing up with Mrs. Dietrich, and Fran was working at her computer. Hendley stopped beside her, leaned down. "Has Dan Newman tried to call?" he whispered.

Fran shook her head. "No, he hasn't. Still waiting for that fax?"

"Yes." He stood up. "Well, what's next on the list?"

Fran stopped typing again and clicked into a different program. "Hmm. I thought this was wrong."

"What?"

"Computer says the next appointment is three-fifteen, but

that one was canceled. I know for sure. Somebody forgot to update it."

A perfect example of Fran. What had he done without her?

"So that means you're free until four," Fran continued. "That's when you have to go over to the main hospital to meet Angie McDonald, who just moved here and is suspicious of doctors." She read from the computer screen. "She has a bad hip, and has been told by . . . three different specialists now that she'll need replacement."

"She can't decide on which doctor to use?"

"Nope. Give her the sales pitch."

"Sure thing. So I have an hour of free time?"

"Fifty-eight minutes." Fran pushed her glasses up on her nose. "Enjoy them."

Hendley nodded with a grin and headed back to his office. Opening the door, he stepped inside to hear the welcome sound of the fax machine humming and clicking as it printed. Finally!

He stood beside it until it finished printing, three pages covered with numbers, and gathered them up and sat at his desk to study them. He wondered if he would find something to justify his excitement.

He did.

Donation. Law firm. Johansson, Harris and . . . Petty.

Vincent Petty of the Missouri Gunners, two million dollars—no, *three* million; there was another donation lower on the list—at about the same time Lloyd had been taken out of the hospital to explore alternative treatments. . . . And APEX knew for sure that Genetics Life had no FDA testing approval.

This information alone was enough for an investigation. An APEX investigation, of course. Why go to the Food and Drug Administration—the government—when you could nail the idiots yourself, and gain the reputation and clout that came along with a "hero" status?

This was his chance, APEX's chance, to prove that playing with the human genome was unnecessary and dangerous, given to abuses caused by unholy motives. In this case, greed. And the public hated greed, hated the evil greedy corporations.

Hendley knew better. All corporations weren't evil. But if he could use that stereotype to meet his objectives, then so be it. Sometimes the end did, in fact, justify the means.

He had almost an hour of free time.

The St. Louis office of American Physicians united against genetic EXperiments was only a few minutes away by car. Hendley wasn't able to get over there that often, not like he wanted to. This was as good a reason as any.

He pulled out a marker and highlighted the pertinent information, then he left the office, informing Fran that he would be gone for only half an hour or so. He went to the parking garage, stepping out of the elevator onto the eighth level and located his black Mercedes, parked straight ahead. The garage was dim and dirty, and smelled of rotted garbage. A perfect first impression for hospital visitors. He went to the car, got inside, turned the ignition and accelerated straight, turning the wheel left to head towards the ramp. Nothing happened. The car didn't respond, and Hendley didn't even have time to take his foot off the accelerator before the car slammed into the low concrete barrier, the front tires riding up on it, and the car kept moving. A sudden surge of panic coursing through him, Hendley slammed on the brakes, but the car was already tipping forward. All he could see was the street, eighty feet below, and then the ground was flying towards him, flashing in front of his eyes, pedestrians running, cars skidding to a stop—

—a silent scream came to his lips—

And then he saw nothing.

Fran—Jeanette Dean—asked that the others handle the front office for a moment while she went back to take a break. She slipped inside Dr. Hendley's office when she was sure no one was looking and made her way over to his desk. It was cluttered, covered with papers and folders. She dug around, skimming through the stuff, but all she found were patient records, a few APEX updates on assorted companies other than Genetics Life . . . innocent things. Not what she was looking for. Frowning, she went to the fax machine. It was sitting on the little table to the side, just one sheet of paper with some copy-quality words. . . .

A fax cover sheet. From APEX headquarters, signed by Dan Newman.

The report had arrived. So where was it?

He must have taken it. Perhaps he was bringing it to the APEX offices down the road.

Fran hesitated a moment, then left the office, closing the door and walking back towards the front. She'd taken only three steps when a distraught-looking Kathy came running out of the waiting area, tears welling up in her eyes.

"Fran," she said, her voice cracking. "There's been an . . . accident."

Jeannette looked at the other woman. "An accident? What do you mean?" she asked.

Sutton was almost out the door when Cassie grabbed his shoulder and stopped him. It was late afternoon, almost time to go home after another tedious day. Sutton stood half outside, on the porch of the handsome patrol station building, and turned. Her face was blank, thoughtful, an expression he wasn't used to seeing from her. He felt a little nervous as he met her gaze.

"Something wrong?" he asked.

"Report just came over from the municipals," Cassie said. "You remember your friend Eric Hendley?"

Sutton nodded. "Yes." He remembered, although in some ways he wished he didn't. Hendley was a decent person, but it was the reason he'd been forced to meet him. . . .

Cassie sighed. "He's dead. Killed in a car wreck. Happened about an hour ago."

Sutton grimaced. He stepped back inside, letting the door close. "Damn," he said. "That's, ah . . . that's something." The look was still on Cassie's face. Sutton's grimace curled into a frown. "What else?"

"Looks like it wasn't an accident," she said. "They want you to get down to SLU hospital and check it out."

"He was murdered?" Sutton said. *Who the hell would murder a doctor like him? What did he ever do?*

"Looks that way. Steering column on his car was cut. He went out the eighth floor of a parking garage. He was DOA."

"The car is still there?" Sutton asked. He backed into the door and pushed it open again, stepping outside. Cassie followed him.

"Yeah," she said. "They want you down there now to check it out."

"Good ol' municipals," Sutton muttered. He looked at Cassie. She slipped on her dark sunglasses and looked back, giving him a little smile. "Who would kill a doc like him?" Sutton asked, shaking his head.

"That's what they want us to find out," she replied.

He looked ahead, locating his car in the lot. "Yeah," he said, and moved towards it. "Ain't that always the way?"

The St. Louis County Police Department and St. Louis Municipal Police Department were two separate entities. But they did work together for the betterment of the community, and working together sometimes meant a shared investigation. Sutton was a veteran of these investigations, a well-respected detective in his own right, never mind his status as a county cop. And Sutton had known Eric Hendley. Not personally. Not really on a first-name basis, even, but he *had* known him, known what kind of person the doctor was. And that, coupled with his reputation as one of the best homicide investigators in the state, had gotten him involved with this.

The fact that he owed Hendley his life—at least his career—made this somewhat personal. If someone had really killed the doctor, sabotaged his car, Tony Sutton was going to find him. He was determined. You just didn't get away with the murder of a good man.

He swerved in traffic, dodging a cement truck and jerking the car into the left lane, before accelerating past eighty. Cassie sat in the passenger seat, silent, her hands in her lap. Sutton whipped back into the right lane, tires screeching, as he approached an eighteen wheeler just ahead. Another trucker was pulling onto the road via the entrance ramp coming up fast, and Sutton gunned the engine again to pass it. He turned sharply back into the left lane, almost scraping against the truck's cab.

Finally, Cassie broke her silence. "You're gonna get us pulled over," she said.

"No, I'm not," Sutton said, watching the road. "Who's going to do that? We're cops."

"In an unmarked red Mustang," Cassie snorted. "Yeah, they won't even see us." She sighed. "C'mon, Tony. You didn't know the guy *that* well."

"Uh-huh. Then why did the news bother you so much?" She was right, he realized. But it was just the idea. . . .

Cassie half turned in the seat. "I know what you're thinking. It bothers me, too. But you're not the only cop he's pulled a bullet out of."

"I wouldn't be walking if it wasn't for him," Sutton said, his voice falling. He let his foot off the accelerator, and the Mustang slowed a bit.

"Yeah. I guess you're right." She straightened in the seat, looking forward. "Just don't make this personal. If we get involved, I mean. Don't make it some kind of campaign. It's the job. Got it?"

"Got it," he said, too quickly. And he knew it. Cassie was right again, as usual. Business. It was always business. He knew all too well what happened when it got personal. The only reason Cassie was here, and not with the NYPD, was because *she* had once let it get personal. She knew what she was talking about.

"Got it," he repeated. He sighed. "Let's just see what's going on. Right? Find out what happened."

Cassie smiled. "You got the idea."

"He's dead," Jeanette said. Her image was placid, her voice candid. She looked like she could be talking about her dog.

It really didn't bother her. Which was good, because it didn't bother Pollard either. Business was business, and you had to do what needed to be done. Sometimes fate didn't give you a choice in the matter.

"Is there any suspicion?" Pollard asked, leaning toward the open laptop. He was alone in his office/apartment, sitting on the couch. It was almost time to give those two new investors a tour of the place, he realized with a smile that he was sure Jeanette didn't understand.

"I don't think so," Jeanette said, shaking her head. The image cut out, the frame rate dropping and causing the motion to blur her face. It sharpened almost immediately, and Pollard made a mental note to inform his network engineers. There was no such thing as a network that didn't have an occasional minor latency spike, but it was important to strive for perfection. "I got through the first round of interviews okay. They're checking all the technicians and office personnel for possible motives."

Pollard frowned. "Where are you?"

"At my computer. In the office. Don't worry," she assured him. "There's no one here. They're outside doing interviews. The cops have cordoned off that entire area of the street."

"All right." Pollard stretched his arms. "Take care of yourself, *Fran.*" They couldn't afford to have her identified. That would be a disaster. "Stick around town. You'll have whatever resources you need. But I need you to keep an eye on things."

"I will," she said. She moved her head, looking away from the screen. The image blurred again, jumping and sticking. "I need to go. They're coming back." The words didn't match the movements of her mouth.

Pollard acknowledged, then clicked out of the program. He really needed to call those networkers. . . .

The municipal department precinct commander, Warren Schwartz, a man of average height with a graying mustache and a sagging waistline, walked over to Sutton and Cassie as they scanned the wrecked Mercedes.

The car was lying on its top, which was crushed almost flat. Debris—metal and glass—still lay on the sidewalk, but had been cleaned from the street, which was now open. Traffic was heavy as people stopped to observe the unusual wreck. The car's driver-side door was cut out, and the mangled interior was soaked in red.

"Detective Sutton," Schwartz said. He had a gravelly voice, like a smoker speaking through a mouthful of pebbles. "I've brought that last receptionist down." He stepped aside, and Sutton turned to see a small, petite, dark-haired woman with glasses step forward. Her face was lightly scarred, probably the remnants of a nasty case of acne as a teenager. "Miss Dean, this is Detective Anthony Sutton of the County Police Department," Schwartz said, motioning to Sutton. "Tony, this is Fran Dean."

"Ms. Dean," Sutton said. "I'm sorry to meet you under these circumstances." A slight nod in the direction of the wrecked car. "I'd like to ask you a few questions, if you don't mind."

"I already had an interview with the police," Fran Dean said. Her voice was soft and shy.

"I understand," Sutton said. "But I would like to ask you a few questions personally. If you don't mind."

She shook her head. "No. Go ahead."

"Thanks," Sutton said, giving her an appreciative smile, as if she'd done him a huge favor. They stepped away from the wrecked car, stopping beside the parking garage toll booth. Cassie followed but remained quiet. Silent observer, Sutton thought. "First of all," he said, making eye contact with the bespectacled woman, "I'd like to get a little history on you. How long have you worked with Dr. Hendley?"

"About eighteen months," Dean said.

Fortunately, it was pretty quiet out here besides the traffic. Otherwise he might not have been able to hear her. "And what did you do before that?" Sutton asked.

She didn't seem nervous, didn't shift her weight or look away. All good signs—or bad, depending on your perspective. She just stood there with her hands on her slim hips. "I've worked with a few companies," she said. "Doctors. Hospitals. Universities. Mostly I've done this kind of work."

"Receptionist?"

"Receptionist, secretary, yes. Whichever term you prefer."

Sutton threw a quick glance at Cassie to get her reaction, but she was just watching. Nothing interesting yet. "Did you know Dr. Hendley well?" he said.

"Just professionally. He's—I mean, he was a good person." Now she did look away, giving a little sniffle. Holding back tears. "I'm sorry. It's just . . . it's just starting to sink in . . ."

She was leaving an opening, and Sutton didn't give her a chance to cover it. "You're right about him being a good person," he said. "In fact, he was a great person. He did great work, was involved in several charities and ran a successful non-profit corporation on top of his practice and his affiliation with SLU. He was married, raised three kids, had five grandchildren and one on the way . . ." He slowed down, savoring the next words. "And he saved my neck. Literally. I wouldn't be able to walk if it wasn't for him. Whenever I spoke to him, he was down-to-earth. Totally different from how he came across during his speeches. You agree?"

It didn't seem to work, playing off any possible guilt. He'd tried the same tactic on the others and they'd broken down and cried over how tragic the whole situation was. That was why he was doing the interviews beside the wrecked car, to pry a reaction out of a guilty subconscious. Fran Dean just shook her head, sniffled again and took a deep breath. That was different . . . He gave Cassie another glance and a slight nod—*put this away for future reference*.

"Yes," Dean said finally. "It's just . . . awful."

"Sure is," Sutton said. "So, ah . . ." Intentional pause. "What do you plan to do now?"

A slight shrug. "I don't know. It's only been an hour. I just don't know."

"More work as a secretary?" he prodded.

"Probably. I don't know."

"Maybe with the hospital?" he went on.

She shifted from foot to foot. "I said I don't know," she snapped, but it seemed to come more from impatience and frustration than anger. And anger was what you would expect under these conditions. Again, not damning, but interesting, and another look to Cassie told her to catalogue this tidbit as well.

"I'm sorry," Sutton said, relieving the sudden tension. He looked away, scanning the street and wreck before returning his gaze to the woman. "I think that's all for now. Thanks again, Miss Dean."

"Anything to help," she said, turning and marching away.

Sutton turned to Cassie and smiled. "I think we'll keep an eye on her," he said.

"Suspect?" Cassie asked.

Sutton chewed at his lip. "I don't think so. Not yet, at least. We've got to get organized, and I have to find out who's in charge of this deal. They brought me in here but haven't told me what's really going on. Municipal goofs." He stalked off to find the precinct commander.

"For their sake it better not be you," Cassie muttered, following him, and Sutton allowed himself to laugh.

He approached Schwartz again, standing beside the open driver's side of the wreck. "What's the motive?" he asked, crossing his arms in front of his chest. "Anything missing?"

Schwartz shook his head. "No. All we know is the steering column was cut, and that it was too clean a job to be anything but intentional. Other than that—" He shrugged.

"Did you pull anything out of there?" Sutton asked, motioning to the bloody interior.

"Nothing interesting in particular," Schwartz said. "Of course, we'll show you everything. It's all down at headquarters with the forensics lab."

"And what is everything?" Sutton said.

Schwartz pulled at his mustache. "Some papers. Records. Ah . . . something from his organization. Like I said, nothing interesting."

"We'd like to see it," Cassie broke in, her voice loud and commanding. Schwartz flinched. "All of it," she added.

"Right," Schwartz said, nodding. "I'm pretty much done here. Follow me."

They drove a few blocks down to the station, then followed Schwartz inside. Sutton had been here before; he'd done work with the municipal department in the past, working from this building, and knew his way around. Schwartz brought them not to the forensics lab, but to a room in the back. He pulled a folder out of a file cabinet and handed it to Sutton, who leafed through it.

Patient records. Prescriptions. A couple of thank-you notes from the doctor's grandchildren. A sheet of copy paper, spotted with bloodstains and covered with numbers, arranged almost like a balance sheet. Sutton studied the latter. It was an earnings report from a company. A small company, judging from the monetary sums mentioned, but . . .

His thoughts trailed off as he read the name. He felt his body tense up, and Cassie, perceptive as always, said, "What is it?"

He turned the paper so she could see.

"How about that," she mouthed, meeting his gaze and grinning.

Sutton looked at Schwartz. "I'll be checking this out, if you don't mind." He held up the paper. "I might be able to find something."

"I don't see what," Schwartz said. "It's just an earnings report. Business stuff. See?" He tapped at the paper. "It's APEX, his organization. Looks like a routine thing to me."

"And the forensics people, too," Sutton said, nodding. "But it's also the only unusual material in the car. It's the only thing a normal doctor wouldn't have. It's also a fax. I'll bet if we call this Dan Newman"—he pointed out the name on the bottom of the page—"he'll tell us he sent this today. A little after three, if the 'time received' is right. And from talking to his technicians, he wasn't finished with patients yet. And it was after lunch. So why was he leaving his office?" Sutton went on before Schwartz could reply. "He was leaving to bring this"—he held the paper at chest level—"to someone. Doesn't APEX have an office up here?"

"Yeah," Cassie said.

"So let's say he was bringing this to his APEX office," Sutton continued. "Why?"

"Good question," Schwartz commented, frowning.

"Because he figured it was important," Sutton said. He gave Cassie a look. "I think we're going to have another little talk with the wonderful people at Genetics Life," he said in her direction. She threw him an irritated look, but gave a fractional nod.

"Genetics Life?" Schwartz asked, sounding lost. "What's that?"

Cassie slapped his shoulder. "Captain Kirk's insurance company," she told Schwartz, and turned on her heel. "Let's go, Tony." Sutton gave one last grin, then followed her.

"Ah . . . remember!" Schwartz called after them. "You're reporting back to me!"

Sutton chuckled. *I report to one man,* he thought. *Me.*

Seventeen

Angel stepped inside the restaurant, pulled off her sunglasses and scanned the dining area, looking for Nagel. It was a casual chain place, neat and clean with an attractive air, but obviously not a five-star establishment. Angel had informed the company CEO that she needed to talk to him, that it was urgent.

In the days immediately following the shocking accident that had led to the death of Jody Kicheski, work at GLI had groaned almost to a halt. Researchers and technicians did little more than feed the animals, maintain the equipment and fill out paperwork. Some of the staff had even speculated that the company would fold now that one of the primary reasons for its existence was gone. But Angel silenced those murmurings and had gotten back to work. Soon thereafter, Paul Franklin—the least affected of all the GLI employees—had done the same. The technicians had followed their lead, but Nagel had not. And it was for this reason that Angel needed to talk to him. Right now, she still needed him, especially since she no longer had access to Dr. Kicheski's talents.

Funding was still a problem as well. The operations on Lloyd had bought Genetics Life nothing but time. They still needed investors. The last few possibilities had been promising, but one had pulled out, another had grown weary of the biotech industry and a third had bought into Humanity International. Jeanette Dean's company, Angel realized. She probably made more shining Lance Pollard's shoes than Angel did as a biologist and a partner in a corporation.

But that would change. Soon enough, it would change.

She scanned the restaurant for Nagel, but couldn't find him. He was here, though; she'd seen his car in the lot when she came in. She stepped out of the way of a couple as they entered through the door and looked again, at the buffet, at the booths, at each table. She saw a pair of young women with toddlers in high chairs chatting over salads, saw a middle-aged man staring in her direction—he looked away when she met his gaze—and then caught a hand waving from behind a waitress.

That was him.

Angel walked past two college kids, slipped behind the waitress and found Nagel sitting at a small square table with two chairs on opposite sides. She hung her purse on the back of one of them, pulled it out and sat down lightly. "Hi, Nick."

"Hello." He sat with his shoulders hunched reading a menu. "You want to order now? Or talk?" His voice was sullen.

"I'll get something to drink," Angel said, maintaining a cheerful tone. "So, Nick, come on, put the menu down."

He did so, and stared at her, rubbing his forehead, then resting his chin in his palm. "What did you want to talk about?" he asked.

"You, mainly," Angel said, keeping her posture. Back straight. Show self-control. "You can't go on like this. You're acting like it's your fault."

"Angel—" He stopped as the waitress turned to them, order pad in her hand and pen primed for action.

"Are you ready?" she asked.

"Yeah. Iced tea, unsweetened," Angel said, keeping her eyes on Nagel.

He looked up at the waitress. "Um . . . give me the turkey club with a coke." The waitress scribbled on the pad, took their menus and pranced off. Nagel's eyes came back to Angel. "You're not eating anything?"

"No, I'm not hungry." She leaned in a bit, resting her arms on the table. "Back to you. Nick, you need to get your act together. Like now. You're going to end up hurting the company and yourself. You can't get all eaten up over an accident."

"That *accident* killed Jody," Nagel said. "How do you expect me to just get over something like that? She was with us from the beginning, Angel. I can't just *get over it.*"

"So you're going to take the entire company down because you're feeling upset?" Angel said. She shook her head and gave one short chuckle. "That's stupid."

"Take the company down?" Nagel echoed. "What are you talking about? We *are* down, Angel. What you did, getting help from that law firm, that was wonderful. But it isn't going to save us in the long term. We need to start thinking about the future."

Don't worry, I am. "No, Nick. *You* need to think about the future," Angel said. "We're shorthanded one genius. We need you to be running full speed if we're going to attract investors."

"It's not going to happen," Nagel said, his eyes going blank. "I've been working for months, flying around the region, begging and pleading, and I've got nothing to show for it. It just isn't going to happen."

"Yes it is," Angel said. "Be positive. Come on, Nick."

His eyes came back to her. "I just . . ." he trailed off as the waitress brought their drinks. Angel took hers and stirred in a pack of sweetener, then sipped it. "I hope you're right," Nagel whispered.

"Hey, I was right about us getting a grant, wasn't I?" Angel said.

He nodded. "Yes, I guess you were." He sighed. "So, you need old Nick Nagel back, do you?"

It took some effort for Angel to keep from rolling her eyes. "Yes, we do. Let's make Jody proud, huh?"

"I'll try," Nagel said.

"Good," Angel said. "That's the spirit. And about those investors, Nick, there have been some interesting possibilities over the last couple weeks."

"But they pulled out, all of them," Nagel said.

"They did," Angel admitted, sitting up straight again. "But we are getting closer. It's a good sign."

"I suppose." He almost smiled. "It really is," he said. "Maybe things will work out. So what time do you need to be back at work?"

"I'm going back as soon as we're done here," Angel said. "It'd be nice if you'd come, too."

Nagel nodded. "I'll stop by. I'll get back to work tomorrow. How are things with P-Rh4?"

"Cleo?" Angel shrugged. "Okay. Why?"

"I heard you were having problems with her. Behavioral problems."

Angel shook her head. "No, not anymore. Everything's fine. Her reflexes and reactions are fast. Something like eight percent higher than a normal female rhesus of that age and health level."

"So it's successful."

"So far," Angel said, and gritted her teeth. *Not quite,* was more accurate, but she couldn't tell him that right now.

"A few more successful experiments and maybe we'll be able to go after a trials approval," Nagel said. He drank from his glass. "That would be nice."

"That's thinking ahead," Angel said, trying hard to sound cheery. "Maybe we—" She was cut off by her cell phone's chirping from her pants pocket. "Oops. Sorry about this," she told Nagel, glad for the distraction. She dug the phone out of her pocket and answered it.

"Hello?"

"Angel? This is Tracy," a light female voice said. Tracy was one of the technicians. She sometimes doubled as a receptionist. "You remember that cop?"

Her heart jumped to her throat. "What cop?"

"The dark-haired guy," Tracy said. "You know, the detective. He was here that night."

Something Sutton. She remembered. "Yeah, what about him?"

"He called. He wants to be make sure you'll be here at one. He wants to talk to you."

"About?"

"He didn't say exactly," Tracy said. "Probably about Dr. Kicheski."

She couldn't react to the news, not with Nagel watching her and Tracy listening. If she said no, she made herself look guilty. If she said yes, something might happen. She'd say something, or . . . No. She wouldn't say anything. Nothing that would get her in trouble. She was always in control.

"Yeah, I'll be there," Angel said. "One o'clock."

"Yup," Tracy said. "Hey, Angel, maybe he'll ask you out. He's cute."

"I don't think so."

"Aw, come on, Angel."

"I have to go, Tracy. Bye." She turned the phone off and stuffed it in her pocket. "That detective wants to talk to me," she told Nagel.

His eyes narrowed. "About Jody?"

"I guess. A follow-up to the autopsy report, maybe," Angel suggested, and took a sip of tea.

Nagel's eyes went downcast at the reminder. "Maybe so."

Angel looked away, caught the waitress coming toward their table with Nick's sandwich. "Hey, here's your food," she said.

A change of subject just when she needed it most.

Perhaps she had fate on her side.

Angel sat behind her desk writing notes on Cleo's current status. As she did so, she heard a knock at the door.

"Come in," she said, setting her notebook and pen aside. Showtime.

The door opened, and Tracy leaned inside. "He's here," she said.

Angel sat motionless for a good ten seconds before the door opened and its frame was filled by a tall, smiling, muscular man. She recognized him. It was the annoying detective from that night . . .

"Hi, I'm Detective Tony Sutton, County PD," he said with a grin, coming toward the desk. Angel stood, smiled, shook his hand. And she glanced behind him, seeing a woman file in. Then the door closed. "That's Cassie Dawkins, my partner." Sutton waved a hand in her direction, like she was part of the scenery. An observer, Angel figured. He wasn't dismissing his partner, only attempting to put her out of Angel's consciousness. It wasn't going to work.

"Dr. Angelina Moore," she said, nodding to both of them.

She sat, motioning that they should do the same. "Well," she said. "What did you want to talk to me about? I thought you had already figured out what happened to Jody."

"We did," Sutton said, taking a casual posture in the seat. "Actually I wanted to ask you a few questions concerning another case I'm working now. You know who Dr. Eric Hendley is?"

She did. And he'd been killed yesterday in an unusual car crash. It had been all over the evening news. "Yes. He was the doctor in that accident yesterday. Why?"

"He was also an opponent of human genetic experiments," Sutton went on like he hadn't heard her. "A major opponent. Hated genetic experiments. He ran an organization called APEX. Ever heard of it?"

"Yes," Angel said, frowning at his demeanor. "Of course. If APEX has its way, we'll be out of business. It makes sense that we'd follow what they do, doesn't it?"

"Certainly," Sutton said, nodding. "Actually, what I'm asking is, why would APEX have an earnings report on Genetics Life, Incorporated?"

Angel shrugged. "To keep track of us. They do that to all the major biotech companies."

"I think your status as a major biotech company is debatable," Sutton said with a smug grin. "But that's beside the point. That earnings report I was talking about . . . The reason I bring it up is because it was in Dr. Hendley's car when he died. And it has some information on it that he apparently found interesting."

Sutton delighted in her shocked expression when he held out his hand to receive the blood-stained sheet of paper from Cassie. But she surprised him by recovering quickly and going deadpan again. Unconcerned. She was good.

He held the paper up so Moore could see the numbers. "See the highlighted area?" he said. "Those are two donations made to this company by a local law firm. I need to know why Dr. Hendley thought they were important enough to single out."

She shook her head. "I don't know. Maybe because we're so close to his headquarters."

"That doesn't seem like a valid reason," Sutton said. "And I think you do know."

Angel shrugged. "I really don't know. We don't have the resources to keep track of what APEX does. How should we know what they're up to?"

"I don't think you should," Sutton said. "I was only hoping you could shed some light on this for me." He thought for a moment. "And I wonder if the fact that Vincent Petty's law firm gave these donations had anything to do with it. Perhaps that's why Hendley noticed." He was fishing, but it seemed like as good a cast as any.

He caught a quick reaction—a sudden, sharp breath—but then she was back to normal, back in control. Another thing to log. "Dr. Nagel made a presentation to Mr. Petty's firm several months ago," she said. "At first he turned us down, but in June he changed his mind. What's wrong with that?"

"You tell me," Sutton said. "He just changed his mind? Just

like that?" He snapped his fingers once. "That seems a bit out of character for him."

"Why, do you know him?" she scoffed, then dropped her gaze. "Look, Detective Sutton, these last few days have been very difficult for all of us down here. I thought you were coming to talk about Dr. Kicheski. But all you want is to throw some crazy idea in my face, like we've done something wrong. I—"

"I didn't say you did anything wrong," Sutton interrupted.

She hesitated, looking up. "You implied it. And if this is all we're going to discuss, well, then I've got a lot of work to do . . ."

Sutton nodded rapidly. *Drop the subject.* "Right, right. I'm sorry. Perhaps you could tell me a little about this company. How it works, what you do. You know."

He felt her eyes on him. She was trying to gauge his motives. He just sat there and let her do it. She didn't have a way out, and he knew it.

"Sure," she said. "What do you want to know?"

Sutton leaned forward a little. "What do you work on, day-to-day?"

A common question, something to put her at ease. Angel hid a grimace. "We experiment on animals, actually. We work to develop and perfect genetic enhancement for medical purposes. You know. New medicines, new treatments."

"You work with humans?"

"No," she said, bracing herself. This was a dangerous topic. "We could, of course. We're at that point with our technology. But we're a small company, a very small company, and we don't really have the capability to run a large-scale clinical trials program with all the FDA requirements and such. We've actually been turned down twice. Not enough clout. Finding willing patients isn't easy, either." Unless they were athletes. Athletes came in droves to join genetic enhancement trials, whether it involved a biotech company or a university.

"So you fall under FDA jurisdiction?" Sutton asked. Leaning forward, eyes ahead, pasted to her, he looked intrigued.

She nodded. "Yes, all medical research companies in this country do. Of course."

"So tell me a little about how you're organized," Sutton said. He nodded toward the door. "Where's the funding coming from? You've got some pretty fancy toys out there, I noticed."

"Investors, at first," Angel said. "But we've been on our own since the beginning of the year. Our investors opted out. Now we operate off of a few patented techniques we've sold, and donations. We're hoping to get a new board together soon, though," she added.

"And the structure of the company . . ." he prompted.

"We're like one lab in a larger company," Angel said. There was no harm in telling him the truth on this issue. "A lab with a big budget. We had the board, but most of the decisions now are made by Dr. Nagel. He's the company executive. Dr. Franklin, Dr. Kicheski—ah, well—" she grimaced. "Dr. Franklin and I are vice presidents. And each technician holds stock. We've got fifteen of them. We all have a stake in the company. If it fails, we all fail." And that was the whole problem, she thought.

"How big are you?" Sutton asked. "Compared to the competition. They take you seriously?"

"Probably not," Angel said. "We're like a speck on the map. You know those towns in Montana with a hundred residents? That's us, competing with Los Angeles and New York."

"How do you do it?" Sutton leaned back in the chair, resuming that casual posture.

"I can't tell you exactly," Angel said. "Let's say it's through brains, not brawn. We're smaller, but smarter, than the competition. I mean, look at Dr. Kicheski. She was a physician before she became a biologist. She knew how to apply our research." Angel half-frowned, letting her eyes leave the detective. "She's going to be hard to replace."

"I'm sure she will be," Sutton said. "So, have you developed any of those applications? To sell, I mean. Or at least produce large-scale. Or whatever it is you plan to do."

"Not yet. Soon, I hope."

"And then the big bucks roll in, eh?"

"We hope so," Angel said. She smiled. "Look, Detective, I'm very busy today. We're trying to get rolling again. Things sort of skidded to a halt after Dr. Kicheski died. If you don't mind . . ."

He took his cue, jumping to his feet. "Right. I'm sorry about barging in on you like that, Dr. Moore." He offered his hand, and she shook it. The woman, Dawkins, did nothing but stand and step toward the door.

"No, I'm glad to help," Angel said. "It's just that I don't have the time right now. Perhaps I can get you a meeting with Dr. Nagel when *he* isn't so busy."

"Perhaps," Sutton said. With one last smile and a good-bye, he made his exit, his partner in tow. The door clicked shut behind them.

Angel shook her head. That one had been close. She bit her lip. Petty would want to know.

She picked up her phone and dialed his direct number.

Sutton and Cassie walked side-by-side toward his Mustang. The air was hot, but not as muggy as it had been for a long while. The sun beat down on them, and Cassie put on her sunglasses.

"What did you think?" Sutton asked her, keeping his eyes on the car ahead.

"I think you were right with that feeling," Cassie said, her tone absent of regret. "Sorry."

"Thanks," Sutton said.

"Before I give you my impression," Cassie said, to cover her apology, no doubt. "Why don't you give me yours?"

"Okay," he said. "I think she's beautiful—"

"Too beautiful," Cassie interjected.

"—intelligent—"

"Which we already knew."

"—helpful, informative, and plain old bad news," Sutton finished. They reached the car, and he dug out his keys.

"She's bad news, all right," Cassie sneered. "Be careful."

"I plan on it," he said, unlocking the passenger door and opening it for her. "Have a seat, madam," he said, accenting the last word. She gave him an amused look, one eyebrow up, but did so. Sutton went around and got in on his side.

"So what next?" Cassie asked him as he turned the ignition.

"I think we find out why Vincent Petty just up and gave them three million dollars," Sutton said.

"That isn't our turf," Cassie said. "We're working the Hendley case. Don't forget."

"I won't," he said, looking at her with a hurt expression. He backed out of the parking lot and accelerated into the street. "But doesn't it stand to reason that if we find out why Dr. Hendley was interested in that deal, we'll find out why someone would want to kill him?"

"And who it was," Cassie said. "Yeah. But we don't even know if there's something going on here. It could be legit. In which case we'll have wasted our time."

"Let the municipals handle the normal route," Sutton said. "We're here to take the back alley."

"Well, let's not get mugged," Cassie remarked.

They hit the entrance ramp, and Sutton stomped on the accelerator. The engine roared and the speedometer flew around. "We won't," Sutton said, and gave a long sigh.

At least there was the *potential* for excitement this time. He chuckled.

"What the hell are you laughing about?" Cassie said.

He shook it away, glancing at her with a smile. "Nothing. I was just thinking, you know, if we nail Petty on something, we could mess up the football season."

"What a tragedy."

"It would be," Sutton said. "That Lloyd kid is unstoppable. You didn't see what he did last Sunday, did you?"

"No," Cassie muttered. "I was kickboxing." She leered at him. "After church, of course."

"Uh-huh. Well, if he plays half as good as he did last week," Sutton said, "the Gunners are going all the way." He sighed again. "I can't wait until next Sunday."

Eighteen

The blaring music cut to a sudden stop, the crowd's roar built to a crescendo and the kicker's foot met the ball. The coverage team flew downfield; bodies collided as they slammed into opposing players.

Ryan managed to evade the first blocker as he crossed the thirty-yard line, but was swept along with five of his teammates into a wall of men trying to spring their returner for a big gain. Shouts, grunts, pushing, shoving, pulling. Suddenly a seam opened beside him and the return man exploded into it. Ryan lunged sideways. His hands made contact with the return man's shoulder pads. He dug his fingers into the guy's collar and pulled back with all his might as he was dragged forward across the twenty-five by his target's momentum. Finally, the smaller player submitted to the size and strength of his tackler and Ryan forced him down to the hard turf.

An official's whistle blew, and the impromptu battle was at a temporary end.

Ryan made his way off the field to the Saints sideline, passing defensive teammates as he went. A few of them slapped his pads, shouting, "Great play," in deep voices muffled by the presence of mouthpieces and chin straps.

As he exited the playing field, he pulled off his helmet and sat on the bench, placing it beside him. One of the assistants, the special teams coach Sam Walden, came up to him. "Nice tackle, Ryan," he said, looking up from a clipboard.

"Thanks," Ryan said. And he meant it. A nice way to start

the game. Heck, it was a nice way to start the season. Being inactive last week, sitting on the sideline, unable to do much more than shout and hope and pray—it had almost driven him mad.

"Keep it up." Walden tore a page off his clipboard and crumpled it in his fist. "Let's see . . ." His voice faded as he moved away, down to the next player. Ryan turned his attention to the field.

The referee blew his whistle, signaling the start of play. The opposing team, the gray, black and red Atlanta Falcons, sent its offense to the line of scrimmage. Ryan watched the defense line up, paying close attention to David Falk in his position a few yards back from the middle of the line.

Atlanta snapped the ball. The quarterback pitched it to the halfback, running off the right tackle on a sweep. He had blockers in front of him as he passed the line, and broke through a hole into daylight. Suddenly Falk was on top of him from behind, jerking him backwards with brute force and tackling him for five yards.

I used to do that, Ryan though. But in this business, *used to* didn't cut it. Once you were a has-been, you were a has-been. There was no going back. Very few thirty-eight-year-old players could run down a speedy halfback from behind like that. *Heck,* Ryan thought, *very few players, period, can do that.*

Atlanta broke its huddle and returned to the new line on second and five. The quarterback took the snap, dropped back five steps, looked, looked, pump-faked a pass, seemed to find a receiver—too late. One of the defensive linemen broke through and dropped him for a sack and a six yard loss, bringing up third down and eleven yards to go.

Beautiful, Ryan thought. On that play, because of the threat in the middle caused by Falk's presence, the center had surged forward after the snap in an attempt to stop or at least slow him down. One of the defensive tackles, usually double-teamed by the center and guard on his side, had found himself one-on-one with his opponent. He got low, gained leverage and drove the blocker into the backfield before breaking away and sacking the quarterback. Yet another advantage to having a linebacker like David Falk—he caused chaos even when he was taken out of the picture.

The decibel level rose as the crowd got into the game, urging their defense to stop the enemy here and now. Music exploded over the speakers. The PA crackled, and the announcer shouted, *"Thiirrrd down!"*

On third and long, everyone in the stadium knew the offense had to pass. Ryan noticed the defensive scheme, an all-out linebacker blitz. The quarterback did, too. He tried to shout, to give his team a few adjustments to compensate, but his voice was drowned out by the crowd.

"He has to take a time-out," Ryan said to no one, his own voice hard to hear.

He didn't. The play clock running down, the quarterback called for the ball. He dropped back, a deep, seven-step drop and was smashed into the turf by three defenders before he had even cocked his arm to throw.

The crowd roared even louder, filling the domed stadium. Ryan could almost feel the air vibrating around him. Fourth down, two straight sacks. An amazing display of defense to open the game.

Ryan, as a true linebacker, lacked the psychological capability to feel sorry for opposing quarterbacks. But this was as close as he would ever get; the poor guy had made a huge mistake by not calling a time-out to rearrange the blocking schemes. Because he started the play without doing so, he ended it lying on his back with three defensive players on top of him.

The punt teams took the field, with the Falcons in a tight protection scheme to prevent a disastrous block. The ball sailed back to the punter, who had to jump in order to bring it down. His powerful leg slammed into the ball, sending it arcing skyward just before a defender leaped forward with his arms outstretched to block it. Seventy thousand people groaned at the near miss.

The punt returner caught the ball on the run, made the first would-be tackler miss and ran hard down the sideline before being pushed out of bounds near the fifty.

Rout's on, Ryan thought.

"Ryan!" David Falk called, walking over to him and standing beside the bench. His helmet was off, leaving behind a messy pile of blond hair.

"Hey, David," Ryan said, looking up at him. "How's it going?"

"Great," the younger man said. "We had a pretty good series."

"Pretty good?" Ryan said. "It was awesome. I'm still not used to seeing a middle linebacker chase down running backs like you did on first down."

"They gained five yards," Falk said.

"Maybe so, but that was the best play of the series for the defense, by far. They executed perfectly and you still stopped them."

"So the sacks . . ."

"The sacks happened because they were off balance. They were reacting to us, and if an offense has to react to a defense, it's in trouble. The whole thing was set up when you caught that runner. I've been around this game a long time. I know how it works."

"Whatever you say, Coach," Falk laughed.

"What was that?" Ryan asked, stopping short.

"Coach. I called you 'Coach'."

"And why did you call me 'Coach'?"

Falk shrugged. "Why not? You have so much knowledge of the game. You're a coach on the field."

"When I get on the field, that is," Ryan mumbled.

"Funny," Falk chuckled.

"Yeah, I'm a funny guy." He slid over a little on the bench, allowing Falk to sit next to him. "Usually I'm not even trying, though."

Falk laughed again. "We're gonna win today," he said. "I can feel it."

"We haven't even scored yet."

"Neither have they," Falk said. "And we're not going to let them."

"Did you talk to Atlanta about that?" Ryan asked. "I doubt they agree."

"I'm sure they don't. But it isn't up to them."

"Oh." Ryan nodded, looking away. "I'm glad you're so confident."

The Saints offense was on the field, lined up. Ethan Daniels received the snap, dropped back three steps and threw a bullet over the middle to a wide receiver, who caught it in stride and knifed through the defense for an eighteen yard gain.

"I'm too superstitious," Ryan said. "Whatever I think, the opposite happens. I'll stick with thinking we're going to get killed. We'll end up killing them. But I didn't say that. Okay?"

"Okay."

The teams lined up again. Daniels called his signals, his voice carrying past each of his teammates and to the sidelines through a near-silent stadium. Daniels took the snap, whirled around and handed off to the halfback, who lowered his shoulders and slammed his way forward, pushing the entire line out of his way for six yards.

Thirty seconds off the clock. Line up. Hand off. Five yards; first down.

"Don't you love it?" Falk said, smiling. "Drive it down the field, put it in the end zone, hold them three and out and repeat." He threw an arm around Ryan's shoulder pads. "The recipe for success, ye olden one."

"Let's wait until we score," Ryan said. "Then you worry about stopping them."

"I'm not worried about it. I know we can do it. I'm not alone out there. The rest of the guys feel the same way."

"They do."

"Yes."

"Hmm."

Daniels dropped back five steps, scanned his receivers,

chose a target and fired another laser shot over the middle of the field. The receiver captured it in the air, running in stride, and darted forward for fifteen yards.

"Well," Ryan said. "At least we'll get a field goal out of it. Most likely."

"I'm shocked," Falk said. "I'm shocked at your pessimism, old man."

"I'm not pessimistic," Ryan said. "I have *experience.*"

"Some might call it cynicism."

A hard look. "I call it a sense of reality."

Daniels faked a hand off, rolled to his right, planted his foot and threw a deep pass down the sideline that was plucked out of the air by the receiver at the eight-yard line, a defender draped on his back. A yellow penalty flag flew onto the field as the receiver carried the cornerback over the goal line before collapsing in a heap in the end zone.

The crowd roared. On the sideline, the team cheered and shouted. Falk looked at Ryan and smiled. "Field goal, huh?"

The referee made the signal for pass interference, against the defense, and waved his arms; the penalty was declined, and the play resulted in a touchdown. 6–0 New Orleans.

"Now," Falk said. "Just so long as you boys don't let 'em run the kick back, we'll give the ball back to the offense in two minutes flat. Or less."

Ryan held his gloved hands up, palms out. "Well, I'm not going to argue anymore."

"The man has wisdom to go with his years," Falk said.

"And don't you forget it," Ryan told him.

Sutton lay back on his couch as the Saints received the opening kick of the second half. He watched the television as the return man swept through the coverage up the middle of the field to the thirty-yard line, where he was tackled by the pursuing Atlanta defenders.

Sutton's home was in Valley Park, Missouri, just outside St. Louis and not far from the Benton Street County PD patrol station. It was an average-sized place, but he kept it well-decorated and furnished, with an almost feminine touch that shocked many of his peers. He kept the place heavily cooled in the summer, heavily warmed in the winter, leading to a large monthly electric bill. Fortunately, when your deceased stockbroker father left you half the family fortune plus his market know-how, money wasn't a problem.

The Gunners didn't play until the evening, the ESPN game of the week; this was supposed to be the next-best of the day, but New Orleans had dominated up to this point. The surprised announcers had trouble voicing the depth of their disbelief at the 24–0 score going into halftime. The official betting line had been even—an advantage for neither team, and most pundits had expected a close, hard-fought brawl.

Sutton tucked his hands behind his head as a pillow and sighed. Football, silence and freedom. What a day. All he needed was some good news from the investigation front. . . .

Ethan Daniels, New Orleans' quarterback, took the snap from center and dropped back three quick steps before tossing the ball to his halfback, who wove his way through the defense for eight yards.

Sutton was getting used to watching this. The Saints' marauding defense forced a turnover, or held Atlanta three and out, and the offense moved the ball right down the field before placing it in the end zone with ease. The contest was one-sided and not what one would call entertaining, but Sutton was fascinated by the ease with which the Saints seemed to be playing. They weren't doing anything special, per se; it was almost like Atlanta was powerless to resist. Maybe it was.

Daniels handed the ball to the halfback, who pounded his way up the gut of the defense, gaining four yards and picking up a first down. How many first downs had this team compiled today? *The guys who work the chains must be worn out,* Sutton thought.

On the next play, the defense was caught off-guard when

Daniels handed the ball to the burly fullback lined up behind him. The big man slammed his body through the line and carried tacklers with him like ants riding a bowling ball for ten yards. And another first down.

Then they broke the game open.

Sutton mouthed, *uh-oh,* as the teams lined up, the Saints with four wide receivers and a visibly disoriented Atlanta defense not in position to stop them. Daniels dropped back deep into the pocket, stepped up, waited as his offensive linemen danced around him, keeping the defenders away, and heaved a bomb downfield. The camera angle followed it right into the arms of a wide receiver streaking alone down the middle of the field into the end zone, the cornerback who was supposed to cover him trailing well behind.

Wow, Sutton thought, too lazy to say it. Now *this* was a blowout.

The phone rang, close by but muffled. He rolled over, snapped up to a sitting position and dug it out from beneath the sofa cushions. He pushed "Answer" and held the phone to his ear. "Hello."

"Where the hell were you?" Cassie demanded, her harsh voice ringing in his ear.

"On the sofa, watching a game," Sutton said, reaching for the remote and muting the sound. "Did you do it?"

"Yeah," Cassie said. "I got us an appointment with him on Tuesday. It's amazing how busy he is, seeing as he doesn't even practice law anymore." They had discovered that earlier in the week, when they had first tried to get a meeting with Vincent Petty. Even Sutton, a Gunners fan, had been surprised. He'd never given that topic thought before, never thought about whether or not the old man still worked at his firm.

"Tuesday," Sutton repeated. "Excellent. What time?"

"Three o'clock. The secretary says he doesn't have much time to spare. She made it sound like she was doing us a favor. You wouldn't believe what I had to do to make her agree."

"Great, great," he condescended. "You're such a good person, Cassie . . ?"

"Shut up," she said. "I'm going to sit back and catch some *ice skating* before I have to leave for church. See you tomorrow." *Click*.

Sutton hung up, tossed the phone away—he didn't care where it landed—and looked back at the TV. Geez, Atlanta was in the process of fumbling the ball away at its own thirty-yard line. He turned up the volume.

"I guess it just isn't your day," he said to the television as the beleaguered Falcons defense returned once again to the field.

34–0. Atlanta's defense slowed the Saints offense and held them to a field goal, three points instead of seven, after their offense's fumble.

Ryan took the field, lined up in his place, jogged with the kicker toward the line and then changed gears and ran at full speed after the ball, sailing toward the arms of the returner.

He fielded it around the five, and half a dozen blockers formed a wedge, or wall, in front of him. Ryan lowered his shoulders and, with five of his teammates, rammed full-speed into that wall. Ryan drove forward like a running back for a few steps, then looked up and caught sight of the returner, dodging a tackler five yards away. He jumped away from defenders, sliding his way forward between jukes. Ryan shoved his blocker backwards and then got behind him, closing on the returner just as he jumped away from another defender. He threw his body into the returner with all his momentum at his back. They both fell to the ground, hard, and the returner rolled away, moaning. Ryan jumped to his feet, raised his arms to the cheering crowd and started walking off the field.

Falk jogged past him, chuckling. "Not bad, old man!" he said.

"Let's see you top that, kid!" Ryan shouted back, smiling. He unbuckled his chin strap and took off his helmet, trotting to the bench.

"Great job, Ryan," someone told him. He acknowledged with a little wave in the direction of the voice, filled a paper cup with water and sat down.

Atlanta had no option but to pass the ball on every play, and everyone and their mother knew it. The quarterback, clearly rattled by the roaring crowd and the sweet nothings being shouted to him by the opposing defenders, took the snap, dropped back and seemed to panic under the pass rush. He ran full speed from the pocket, evaded a sack, whirled away from the sideline and reversed his field and then heaved a pass all the way to the opposite side of the field—

That was caught by the halfback, wide open, no defensive player within ten yards. He sprinted upfield to the thirty, to the forty, past the fifty, into Saints territory before the free safety managed to close on him with an angle and pushed him out of bounds.

Atlanta's athletic young quarterback, Ryan realized, was in a wild-eyed, sandlot football mode. He was improvising, playing like a kid in his backyard. He had no other choice. But sandlot football didn't win games in the professional ranks, not when your offensive line was getting blown off the ball and losing the battle at the line of scrimmage. That was where football games were won and lost, and the Saints were winning that battle.

Atlanta was running a no-huddle offense. They came to the line. The quarterback barked his signals, amid a now-quiet crowd, took the snap and dropped back. Again his protection broke down, defensive linemen pouring into the backfield. Again the quarterback rolled away from the pressure, escaping the rush, and he dumped a short pass to his tight end running just ahead of the line. The tight end turned upfield, squared his shoulders and met David Falk head-on at the forty-five-yard line. Falk fell backwards but managed to bring the tight end down on top of him. Falk took his time getting to his feet—another veteran move when the offense was in no-huddle that most rookies didn't think of.

The offense scrambled to the line and snapped the ball.

The quarterback dropped back five steps, then tucked it away and bolted up the middle of the line, catching an obviously fooled David Falk out of position. The strong safety hit the quarterback, driving him to the ground after an eight yard gain.

"Get moving, defense," Ryan muttered, crumpling the paper cup.

The quarterback dropped back five steps but didn't have time to plant his feet before a defensive lineman was in his face. Speed. The quarterback dodged that lineman and took off, running through the hole left in his place. This time all three linebackers were out of position, and Falk seemed to trip over a teammate. The quarterback darted into the secondary, juked the strong safety and crossed the twenty-yard line before one of the cornerbacks caught him.

The defensive coordinator was screaming at someone, his scalding remarks directed toward the field. The offense was lining up, but the defense seemed to be in a state of confusion, players moving around, directing their teammates. Ryan turned toward the coordinator, taking his eye off the field, and noticed what had him—and Coach Harrell, for that matter—so mad.

He was trying to call a time-out, but the referee, standing too far from them to hear, seemed oblivious to his calls. Finally, he turned, saw the desperate signals and blew his whistle just as Atlanta snapped the ball. He waved his arms in the air to stop the clock and turned on his speaker.

"New Orleans has taken a time-out. That is their first charged time-out."

Falk ran to the sideline to Harrell. Ryan moved closer, passing other members of the team and coaching staff to do so.

"Next time, call the time-out!" Harrell screamed in Falk's face. "You almost cost us six, asshole! You screw up again like that and you'll be wearing a *hole* in that bench! If you can't handle the no-huddle then you have no place starting in my defense. Now get your ass back out there and *pay atten-*

tion!" Falk's head bobbed up and down, and ran back out onto the field. Harrell said something to the defensive coordinator, then walked over to Ryan.

"Depending on what happens here," he said, the veins in his neck still enlarged from his tirade, "we may put you in there when they run no-huddle."

"All right." Ryan frowned.

"We had all our time-outs." Harrell shook his head. "What was that kid thinking?"

"He's still a rookie," Ryan said.

"Well, if he screws up a situation like that again, he'll have plenty of time to learn from the bench." Harrell moved away.

Ryan turned back to the field just as the offense came to the line. The crowd was deathly silent, the prospect of losing the glory of a shut-out weighing down on it. The quarterback took the snap, backpedaled, stopped under good protection, set his feet, picked a target and fired a pass over the middle—

A defensive lineman slapped at the ball with an outstretched arm. It flopped up in the air like an untied balloon. Falk dove for it, arms outstretched, and snagged it, nestling it to his gut before he hit the turf.

The crowd exploded.

Ethan Daniels knelt down with the ball, and the last few seconds ticked away from the scoreboard. An almost perfect game in every respect, and one of the most dominating performances Ryan had ever had the privilege of being a part of.

It sure felt good, leaving the field as the crowd applauded the fine effort, knowing what the scoreboard read and knowing that your team had recovered from its opening-day embarrassment. With a vengeance.

The teams began to enter the tunnels. Ryan trailed behind a bit, smiling, waving to some of the fans, and gave the scoreboard one last look.

It sure felt good.

He let the satisfaction linger, then shook it away. They had won this battle, but the war was still raging. Fourteen games. Fourteen more battles. He turned and followed his team into the locker room.

Nineteen

"Whoa," Sutton said as he parked the Mustang in the Missouri Gunners training facility parking lot. "I can't believe we're actually going in there."

Cassie rolled her eyes and threw the passenger door open. "Get it straight, Tony."

"Yeah, yeah," he said, getting out and joining her as she walked toward the entrance. "But the normal fan just doesn't *get* inside the headquarters, you know. You have to be a reporter. Or you have to be buying tickets or something. But we're actually going *inside* the old man's office." He whistled. "Way cool."

"You sound like a ten-year-old," Cassie muttered.

She pulled the door open and they went inside the air-conditioned building. "Whoa," Sutton said again.

"Come on." Cassie headed down the hallway to the right. "Should be the third door," she said.

They came to the third door, and Sutton knocked. Nothing. He knocked again. He sighed, stretched his arms; time to put on the uninterested facade.

"Come in," called a faint voice through the door.

Sutton opened the door and stepped inside. Cassie followed him in silence.

"Mr. Petty," Sutton said to the trim, cultured man standing behind his desk. "It's very nice to meet you, sir." Under other circumstances, he realized he might have meant it.

Petty smiled. "The same, the same." They shook hands.

Petty motioned to the two chairs before the desk. "Please, have a seat."

"Thank you," Sutton said. "I'm Detective Tony Sutton, County PD. And the pretty lady is Cassie Dawkins. She made the appointment."

"As I was told," Petty said, sitting. "Now, I was *not* told precisely what this appointment is about." He glanced at Cassie. "I assume it is not entirely about me."

"Not entirely," Sutton said.

Petty leaned back, an expression of relaxation. "So, shall we begin?"

"This shouldn't take too long," Sutton said. "A few minutes at most." He leaned forward. "Personally," he whispered, "I think this is all a bunch of bull. But I have a job to do, sir." He sat back.

"I understand," Petty said, his expression blank.

Sutton smiled. "Great. All I need to know is, why did your law firm donate . . ." He looked away, feigning deep thought. "Ah—three point five million dollars, to a little biotech company called Genetics Life?"

Petty sighed. "Is that all?" He shook his head. "You hardly needed to waste your time meeting personally with me, Detective. That information is available at the firm itself."

"I realize that," Sutton said. "But I preferred to hear it from you." He chuckled. "It might be childish, but I wanted to get in here. The headquarters, I mean. I'm a big fan."

"I understand," Petty said, but he didn't smile. "To be blunt, our firm sets aside a sum of money every year for charitable donations, community work and the like. I was impressed with Dr. Nagel's—the company's CEO—presentation, so we gave his company a portion of the money."

The obvious answer, and one Sutton had expected. But he'd had to ask . . . "I see," he said. "Second question, about Julian Lloyd. We all heard originally that his injury was career-threatening. But now he's back on the field. Can you explain that?"

Petty shrugged. "It was just one of those things, I expect.

The injury was not as serious as first reported. And he's an amazingly tough lad."

"I'm glad he's on our side." Sutton grinned. "Two straight hundred-yard games to open the year. That's a good start."

"It is."

"Back to Genetics Life," Sutton said. Rapid subject change, a tactic designed to confuse. It didn't work on the Gunners' owner, though Sutton hadn't thought it would. "Looking at an earnings report of theirs, I found that their annual income is— gross, not net—about ten million. Give or take. And your donation, or grant, was almost half that."

Petty shrugged. "I don't see your point, Detective."

"I'm just wondering why your donation was so large," Sutton said. "I've heard of thirty thousand dollar grants, three hundred thousand dollar grants, but a *three million* dollar grant? I've never heard of *that* before."

Petty shifted in his chair. "I'll be quite honest with you, Detective, even though the truth is somewhat embarrassing."

Sutton leaned forward; this could be good. . . .

"We always set aside a certain sum per year, as I mentioned," Petty said. "Because of a few errors made by our accounting office, that money was not donated by our annual deadline. So we sought out the first company or group, and it just so happened that the company was Genetics Life. I believe their outstanding debts were in the range of two million, so it worked out quite well."

"Convenient," Sutton said.

"Very."

Sutton exchanged a fleeting glance with Cassie and stood. He extended his hand over the desk. "That's all I needed to ask. Thank you, Mr. Petty."

Petty shook his hand. "Thank you. I hope I cleared up any possible misunderstandings."

Sutton nodded. "Yes, sir. You did."

* * *

"What's the deal with that Julian Lloyd thing?" Cassie asked as Sutton pulled out of the parking lot.

"I don't know, it just came to me," Sutton said, watching the road. Traffic was light. It was lunch hour right now, and everyone was eating. Sutton frowned. He was getting hungry. "I figured it would get a reaction out of him. Why?"

"Because I just thought of something," she said. "What was the date on those donations? On the earnings report."

His frown deepened. What was she getting at?

The report was in the folder on the seat between them. Cassie opened the folder and took it out. "June twenty-fifth," she said. Sutton glanced at her. "The first donation," she explained. "The million-dollar one. It was made on June twenty-fifth."

"Okay," Sutton said. "So?"

"When was Lloyd hurt?"

There was a Burger King just ahead, the entrance to the parking lot coming up fast. Which was fortunate, because Sutton whipped the Mustang right, into the lot, barely touching the brakes, and then jerked it to a stop.

"Holy . . ." he muttered, leaning his head back and staring at the roof of the car.

"You're really gonna get me killed," Cassie remarked.

Lloyd had been injured during the second team minicamp. "June twenty-first," he said. "Damn. Cassie, I think you're on to something."

"Yeah," she said. "And when was he pulled out of the hospital?"

"Not even a week after going in," Sutton said. He looked at her, matching her sunglasses-covered eyes. "Could be co-incidence," he suggested.

Her eyebrow raised, an amused look. "You think?"

He shook his head. "No."

"You do realize this could give us suspects *and* a motive, don't you?" Cassie said. "Man, I astound myself."

"Yeah," Sutton said. "Petty and any of the people at Genetics Life. Let's say Petty had Genetics Life do some kind of

genetic deal to Lloyd. In return he gives them a large donation. Dr. Hendley, as the guy who operated on Lloyd's injury,
finds out and sniffs around. He gets close. Boom! He's dead,
and whoever did the job tried to cover it up, make it look like
a car accident." He smiled. "This I like."

"Drive-through's clear," Cassie said. "I want a Whopper."

Sutton looked at her, and frowned.

"Pure speculation," Warren Schwartz said, shaking his
head. "You have absolutely no evidence to back that up."

The man's office was hot and stuffy, his worn brown desk
cluttered, the books on the bookshelf behind him stacked haphazardly. Sutton tried not to notice the sloppiness of the place
when he looked Schwartz in the eyes.

"Why did you bring us in?" he asked, crossing his arms.

Schwartz hesitated. "You have experience in this type of
investigation," he said. "You—ah—you're . . ."

"The best," Sutton finished for him.

Schwartz looked at him. "Yes, I suppose you are," he said.
"But still, what hard evidence can you give me that says either Vince Petty or one of these scientists is a legitimate
suspect? A couple of coincidentally close events. That's it."

"And a couple of huge donations made for no apparent reason," Cassie broke in.

"I thought Petty gave you his reason."

Sutton chuckled; Schwartz frowned. "Detective Dawkins
and I did a little checking," Sutton said. "You want to know
how much Petty's law firm donated to charity last year? And
the two years before that?" He went on before Schwartz could
reply: "A grand total of two hundred thousand dollars. In
three years." Sutton gave the commander a hard look. "Now,
are you going to tell me that three million—"

"Over three million," Cassie interjected.

Sutton didn't miss a beat. "—dollars in a matter of a few
days isn't a little out of the ordinary? Do you *really* think
he got nothing in return? And is it just a *coincidence* that

Julian Lloyd was pulled out of the hospital and put into some sort of unknown advanced treatment program at approximately the same time as these donations were made to Genetics Life? And is it *another* coincidence that Dr. Hendley was interested in those donations at the same time he was killed?"

Schwartz was shaking his head in disbelief, rapping his knuckles against the desk. "You're accusing Vincent Petty of murder," he whispered.

"I didn't say it was Petty," Sutton said. He shrugged. "It could have been someone at GLI. That supposed accident—the one where that researcher was killed—never felt right to me. Maybe it wasn't an accident."

"You're speculating again," Schwartz pointed out.

"How do investigations start?" Sutton asked. "Speculation. Come on, get with the program."

The commander's face flushed pink. He pulled at his mustache. "I *am* with it," he said. "I just don't see the need to approve an off-the-wall investigation, especially one involving someone like Vincent Petty. He's—"

"Worth eight hundred million dollars," Sutton said, frowning tightly. "So he cashed in on suing tobacco companies. So? You afraid to go after him?"

"No, I'm not afraid." He leaned forward, folding his hands before him. "Look, Sutton. I'm in charge of this investigation. I will oversee its direction and scope. I don't need a couple of County PD mavericks like you to go out and try to run the show. I borrowed you. I went after you to help with this job. But I *can* send you back to your little patrol station on the corner of Benton Street. You got it?"

"I got it," Sutton nodded. "You're absolutely right, sir. You brought us here, and you can send us back. Without, I might add, even a *chance* to really get involved and screw up your investigation. I'm sure that'll cement your reputation in the County department for years to come."

"Reputation," Schwartz echoed, the pink coloring leaving his face.

"Gotta love that reputation," Cassie said, glancing at Sutton.

"Yeah," Sutton agreed. He stood, and offered his hand over the desk. "I guess I'll be going now. I'll check out the local lineups for the likely suspects. You know, the drug dealers a doctor of Eric Hendley's character and caliber would be involved with, or those serial rapists and murderers who like to hit guarded university hospitals as opposed to the thousands of women and children going about their daily lives, alone and unprotected."

"Can't forget the serial killers," Cassie agreed.

He pulled his hand back and gave her a little helpless glance. "Either that, or we could just go back to that little station on Benton Street, sit around and drink coffee and watch TV and save men from tall ladders and bicycle accidents. It isn't like you actually *need* us for anything."

Schwartz looked as though his head was swimming. He just stared through the air between them. "Fine," he muttered. "Go ahead and do your investigation. Find out how the big bad sixty-year-old lawyer killed your doctor friend." He stabbed Sutton with a glare. "I can see it's personal for you, Detective. I'd get over that. If I were you, that is. I'm sure you weren't the only officer Hendley ever operated on. I doubt he even remembered you."

"As if it makes a difference," Sutton said, meeting the commander's glare. The games were over. Now he was dead serious. "I'd like to know how a man like you came to be a precinct commander in the St. Louis Police Department," he said. "You didn't have any . . . well, *help,* did you? You know. A couple of favors for getting an annoying case or two dropped?"

Schwartz went pale. "I—I don't know what you're talking about," he said.

"I'm sure you don't," Sutton told him. He nodded to Cassie. "I guess we should be going. Places to go, you know; football owners to investigate."

"Yes."

"It's always nice talking to you," Sutton said, smiling and

extending his hand again. They shook, Schwartz's grip weak, his hand clammy.

"Let's hit it, Tony," Cassie said, and they turned and left the room.

"It's always good to have a reputation to fall back on," Sutton said with a grin as they walked toward his car. It was cooler out here than it was in Schwartz's office. It felt good. "Especially when it's someone else's."

"I wonder if it's true," Cassie said.

Sutton shrugged. "So what? It worked on him. A man with Vincent Petty's power and influence can do almost anything he wants. Especially when you're on the government's side during a large-scale lawsuit. Which Petty was."

"The investigations," Cassie said. "Could Schwartz have gotten 'em dropped?"

"He worked both cases," Sutton said. "Back in the day. You tell me."

"Guy like him?" Cassie snorted. "Oh yeah."

Sutton pulled the driver's side door open. "But like I said, it doesn't make a difference. We're on the case now. And I think we're right."

"I know we are," Cassie said. "So, who's the most likely suspect at Genetics Life?"

Sutton shrugged. "It could be anybody. You'd assume it was the head guy, Nagel, or any one of their technicians. But . . ." he broke off, drifting into thought. "Hmm."

"What?"

"The gal," Sutton said, snapping his fingers as he tried to remember her name. "The gal," he repeated, "the blond. She was there the night we went to check out that *accident*. She was the only one in the building when it happened."

"Right," Cassie said. "Moore. Angelina Moore."

"Yeah, I had a feeling about her from the beginning, you know."

"I remember," Cassie said, eyeing him.

"Yeah," Sutton said. "My partner thought I was being ridiculous." He sat down in the car and closed the door. Cassie did the same.

"Just drive, Tony," she said. "Drive."

Practices on Friday were always lighter than those on the other days. Jacob Davis liked his troops to have a little rest before they traveled to the battle zone on Saturday and then went to war on Sunday.

A dozen or so players stood around a television set, their sweaty workout clothes drying in the air conditioning of the room. The Gunners training facility lounge was occupied by coaches or staff under most circumstances, but now had been taken over by players eager to catch a particular sports show.

Julian inched closer to the TV and turned up the volume. He backed away and stood against the wall, a smile plastered on his face. Beside him, Rich Mitchum chuckled. "Enjoying this, eh?"

"Yeah," Julian nodded, keeping his eyes on the screen. The segment that was the subject of interest was about to start. "Wait until to you see the expression on the guy's face," he said.

The screen cut from a crew of arguing anchors to a football stadium, and the Missouri Gunners trotting out of the tunnel onto the artificial turf of their enclosed home stadium. "The division battle between the Gunners and Forty-Niners began as a war of words," a deep, dramatic voice said. "A one-sided war." The view cut to the image of defensive tackle George Damon. "I can tell ya that *we* aren't falling for all that miracle bull—" *bleep!* "He's just anotha guy, and he's gonna get a real welcome this week."

"If anyone got a welcome, it was Mr. Damon," the deep voice continued. Now highlights of the game were displayed—each of them a run by Julian—and Julian smiled, almost blushing at the cheering of his teammates. "Gunners rookie Julian Lloyd took the outspoken veteran to school, giving him a real lesson in the running game." On the screen, Julian's image burst through the middle of the line—through Damon's position—and slashed through the secondary into the end zone from thirty yards out. "The few times Lloyd was slowed down, quarterback Rich Mitchum"—Mitchum nodded, holding up a hand to ward off the applause—"took up the slack, passing for one hundred ninety-eight yards and a touchdown.

"Lloyd finished the game with a hundred fifty-five yards on twenty-eight carries, averaging over five yards per carry for the second week in a row. He carried his team to an easy, wordless twenty-four-to-ten victory." The screen cut to a commercial, and someone turned off the television.

A fresh round of applause burst out in the room.

Mitchum shook his head, his lips forming a mock-frown. "You really oughta try an' live up to the hype."

"Yeah, I guess I should, huh." Julian smiled back. "At least I'm earning my money now."

"Have a few more games like that," Mitchum said, jabbing a thumb in the direction of the blank TV, "and you're gonna get a steak dinner from the offensive line. Usually it's the other way around, ya know."

"Whatever works." Julian shrugged.

"It does."

Part Three

Repercussions

Twenty

St. Louis (RBPW) - The Missouri Gunners gave up a lot for rookie running back Julian Lloyd, but the move has paid off tenfold. Lloyd, the 6-1, 225-pound Heisman Trophy winner from the University of Southern California has run for 884 yards on 178 carries in eight games so far this year. He is on pace for 1768 yards, close to the NFL rookie rushing record, and his average of five yards per carry leads all but one veteran runner. Lloyd's production complements the efficient passing of quarterback Rich Mitchum. Mitchum has completed 160 of his 265 attempts for 1742 yards, ten touchdowns and only four interceptions. His passer efficiency rating is 86.1, fourth in the conference. Tight end Frank Moran leads the team with 40 receptions for 459 yards and five of Mitchum's touchdowns.

Their success, along with a good, aggressive defense, has given the team a league-best 8-0 ranking coming into their mid-season bye week. The Gunners are the only remaining undefeated team in the NFL.

Missouri comes into the second half of the season on a roll; the team has been excellent in all aspects of the game. But one thing is certain: The rest of the season will be made or broken by Julian Lloyd. If Lloyd continues to perform as he has, greatness may be within reach for the Missouri Gunners.

Sutton folded the newspaper, laid it on his desk and chomped on the last bit of his apple fritter. He swallowed it with a sip of mocha and stretched his arms above his head. He breathed in, breathed out, trying to relax. He wasn't a morning person, and as it was just after 7:30 right now, his brain was still begging for sleep. He rubbed his weary eyes with the back of his hand, closed them, opened them—

Cassie stood in front of him, as if she had materialized out of the air. Sutton jerked in his chair, pulled himself to an upright sitting position. "Yeah?" he said.

"You wanted information on Hendley's secretary," Cassie said. "I have it."

Sutton perked up. "Ah, excellent." He looked at her face, at her hands, back at her face. No folder, no notepad. "Where is it?"

Cassie didn't answer. She stood there, silent.

"You didn't find anything?" Sutton groaned. Wonderful . . . another setback.

"Well, I wouldn't say that," Cassie said, and Sutton sighed in relief. "It just wasn't enough to waste paper on."

"Great," he said. "Go ahead."

"Fran Dean," Cassie said, half-sitting on the edge of the desk. "She's thirty years old, was born in Kansas City, went to a community college and has worked as a secretary her entire adult life."

"That's it?" Sutton said. "Wonderful. Where is she now?"

Cassie shook her head. "I don't know. Nobody seems to know."

"What the hell are you talking about? *Somebody* has to know!"

"Her co-workers don't know," Cassie said. "I couldn't find any family. I even called some of her past co-workers. They either didn't know who she was, or didn't care, or didn't know where she would go. So she's gone."

"She *can't* be gone," Sutton growled, gritting his teeth. "Dammit, Cassie, she's a *suspect!*"

Six weeks of quiet work had yielded few results. They

had interviewed every Genetics Life staff member from Nicholas Nagel to the janitor, checked Vincent Petty's records over and over and over again, paid close attention to the activities of Angelina Moore in particular, on Sutton's hunch . . . but they had been unable to find *any* connection between any of them and Eric Hendley. Other than the obvious motive, there was nothing to say that any one of them had been involved in his murder. And none of them had been on the St. Louis University Hospital premises that day, as a careful, hours-long check of the hospital security tapes had shown. And Hendley had driven his car to the hospital that morning, so it was safe to say that whoever had sabotaged it *must* have done so in the garage. Unfortunately, Hendley's car was not visible on the garage videos, so *that* was another dead end. They needed to find out who at the hospital could have had a motive for killing Hendley, starting with those closest to him. All of his staff, though, seemed to love the man, and still mourned him.

Except for Fran Dean . . . and they couldn't *find* her.

Yes, it was suspicious, but what could they do about it?

"Okay," Sutton said, taking a deep breath. "Cassie, we *have* to find that woman. I don't care what we have to do."

"We could try the phone records," Cassie suggested. "See who she talked to while she worked with Hendley."

Sutton frowned. "We wouldn't know which call belonged to which staff member."

"Actually we would," Cassie said, half smiling. "If I'm not mistaken, one of the other staffers told me that each of them had a separate call-out code. Every time they made a call, they had to enter their code."

"And why did she tell you that?"

"I asked how many calls Dean made per day on average," Cassie said. "I already thought of this, Tony."

"Right," Sutton said. "So you can get the information?"

"Easy."

"Get it," he said, blinking his eyes, then closing them for a moment. His head was starting to hurt, right above his eyes. Sinuses or something. He rubbed his brow. "Maybe we'll find something."

"What are you gonna do?" Cassie asked, standing.

"Research," Sutton said. A silent moment, then he looked at her and gestured toward the door. "Go on. The sooner you get that phone list the sooner the fun starts. Get to work."

Cassie frowned, but nodded and backed away.

"How long will this take?" Sutton called after her.

"Damn, Tony," she said. "A few hours. Okay?"

"Okay." He hesitated. "Get moving. Please."

Cassie rolled her eyes.

"Makes my phone bill look like a monk's," Sutton commented, eyeing the stapled pages. Cassie had already gone through it and highlighted every call with Fran Dean's ID code. That would save a lot of time.

"Mostly patient calls," Cassie said, standing beside his chair. "But there are a couple you'll find interesting."

"Uh-huh . . ." Sutton mumbled, scanning the first page. "What's this one? Area code six-one-nine. Where is that?"

"Check. That's why you got that fancy computer."

Sutton mumbled her words as he clicked on to his Internet browser and brought up a search engine. He typed "Area Code 619" and scanned the list of results. "San Diego," he said. He looked back at the phone list. "I wonder who she was calling."

"Wanna find out?" Cassie asked.

Sutton nodded and reached for his phone. "Yes, I do." He dialed the number.

The phone rang twice. "Humanity International Corporation," a mature female voice said. "Mr. Pollard's office. May I help you?"

"Oops," Sutton said, raising the pitch of his voice a bit. "Wrong number." He hung up and turned to his computer. "Humanity International," he said to Cassie, and typed that name into the search engine.

"Sounds like a biotech company," Cassie said. "Or a pharmaceutical company."

"Well," Sutton said, reading through the results on the screen. "Either way, it appears Miss Dean called them several times. I'd like to know why." He clicked on the first entry on the list, a link to the company's Web site.

The site loaded, an elegant design, high-tech in appearance, with just the right mixture of graphics and text. A very professional job.

Welcome to HUMINT Online
Humanity International—the future of medicine
realized in the present.

Sutton scrolled through the menu bar on the left side of the page and clicked on "About HUMINT." A new page loaded, displaying information on the company's history and accomplishments, and its goals for the future.

HUMINT specializes in the research of the human genetic code—the human genome. *Click here for a history of the Human Genome Project.* HUMINT seeks to fulfill the mammoth potential of this exciting new technology, to improve medical science. In short, to one day cure the incurable. HUMINT is the industry leader in genome sequencing and research into medicinal genome enhancement, led by CEO and founder Lance Pollard.

"Mr. Pollard," Sutton said. "CEO of the company. She was calling his office. Why?"

"I've got a weird feeling about this," Cassie muttered.

"A feeling," Sutton echoed. "You mean like we're getting into something big?"

"Real big," Cassie said. *"Real* big."

Sutton pursed his lips and scrolled through the rest of the Web page. "Whatever happened to the simple domestic homicide?" he asked nobody in particular. And then he clicked on the "Print" button.

Jacob Davis stood beside the training facility's doors leading to the practice fields, and studied a readout of a new offensive play. The play was a risky double reverse, a trick deal that Davis felt his team would make good use of, if it was used at the right time in the upcoming game. When the afternoon practice started, he would hand it over to the offensive coordinator to throw into the game plan for the contest against Jacksonville—which was two weeks away because of the current midseason bye week, giving the team ample time to throw in some interesting wrinkles.

To his right, the door opened. He turned in time to see Julian Lloyd trip and stumble outside, almost falling down.

Davis turned back to his clipboard before Julian noticed he had ever looked up. "A three-hundred-pound defensive lineman can't do it," he said grimly, "but your shoelaces can."

"I think it was the doorjamb," Julian mumbled, looking down as if scolding the floor. He was wearing workout shorts and a T-shirt in team colors with the logo on the collar. He was sweating, like he'd just finished an arduous workout, but his skin looked cold and clammy.

"You look sick," Davis said, eyeing his halfback.

"Yeah, I think I'm getting the flu or something." Julian leaned against the wall and propped up his foot.

"No wonder," Davis said. "Wearing that stuff outside in fifty-degree weather, the wind blowing and you just finishing a workout. You're going to kill me, kid."

"I wasn't working out," Julian said. "I was in film with Coach Kiley."

Davis checked his watch: 1:24. "He doesn't finish until one-thirty."

"He said I should get some air. We're pretty much done, anyway."

"You look awful." Davis took a step closer. Sweat was beading around Julian's brow, soaking his face. His dark blue shirt was stained black around his armpits. "How are you feeling?"

"Like crap," Julian said.

"I want you to see the doctor. Right now. He should be in the training room. When did this start?"

Julian frowned. "I woke up feeling bad. Muscle aches. My legs . . . felt like the day after the game, only this is Thursday. I've been sweating off and on all day long. I don't have a fever, I checked."

Davis nodded. "Go tell the doc. Good thing we have a bye this week."

Julian shook his head. "I could play, Coach. No problem. I'm not that sore. It's just the sweating."

"Still, go see the doctor before practice. Or are you up to it?"

"I'm up to it."

"All right. Two-thirty. And it's open to the public, so we may end up with an audience."

"That's great."

"I think so. Fan support and all. It doesn't cost Joe Fan anything to watch a practice. Yet," he added.

"It does in a few towns," Julian said.

"I know. Sad. But hey, it's paying our salaries." He looked back down at the clipboard. "Get moving. I want to know what the problem is before two-thirty."

Julian opened the door. "Okay, Coach." He started to trot, then slowed his pace and trudged inside.

Davis looked through the tinted glass door for a moment as it closed, concerned eyes following the young halfback's dimming form as he made his way down the hall.

Julian jogged up to him an hour later on the practice field in his full uniform—helmet, jersey, pants and pads. Davis had just brought the team out of the locker room. He rubbed his neck below the back of his team cap and shivered beneath his windbreaker. The middle of the season was a *real* football time. Fall, with Thanksgiving soon on the way, the trees losing their leaves and the summer heat being replaced by a welcome chill. Today had been colder than most, almost wintry.

"The doctor shot me up with something," Julian said. "He said it doesn't look like I have the flu, and that I should be able to go full-speed."

Davis nodded. "Get with the offense."

Julian acknowledged and placed his helmet on his head. He jogged away in the direction of a small group of players fifty yards downfield.

Davis heard someone approaching from behind, grass crunching beneath three-hundred-dollar shoes. That narrowed the field of potential candidates to about two or three, since all the players were in uniform. It had to be a front-office member, and only one would be out on the field with the boldness to approach the head coach as he prepared for practice. Davis sighed, drew himself up and said, "Geoffrey."

"Jacob," the general manager said.

It was him. "What's up?" Davis asked, studying his clipboard.

A shorter, skinnier man in an expensive gray suit stepped up beside him. "How's Julian?" Geoffrey Marsh asked.

Davis shrugged. "He's fine. Doctor gave him something and said he'll be okay for practice."

"I heard he was having muscle pains. In his legs."

"More along the lines of the flu." Davis glanced at his boss. "It isn't the knee. Don't worry about it."

"I hope not. He's on a roll. And I'm not too happy about our depth at running back, which leads me to a question. What do you think about bringing in a couple of guys for workouts? Specifically Kid Maddox and Eric Hoss."

Davis looked up at the GM. "I've been wanting to take a look at Maddox since before the season," he said. "It's a miracle he's still on the market."

Marsh nodded. "I know. He's a young guy with speed and potential, and he'd come cheap. We can afford him. That type of 'back doesn't usually stay on the open market very long. I guess everyone got scared off with that thing in Kansas City during camp."

"He got a bum rap. He wasn't even driving the car."

"I know. Anyway, it's beside the point. I need you to talk to Vince and get his permission."

Davis chuckled. The point had been made. He looked back at the clipboard. "It's sad, Geoffrey, you know? There's nothing I hate more than an owner who doesn't know his place. Why do I need to ask his permission?"

Marsh looked uncomfortable. "Because I can't, Jacob."

"You mean you're afraid to."

Marsh started to shake his head, then sighed. "Yes, I'm afraid to. He said he didn't want another starting quality halfback on the roster as long as Julian's playing so well."

Davis laughed. "Thank God the kid is playing well. Otherwise . . ." He left that thread unfinished, not wanting to go where it might lead.

"I thought maybe if he heard the same concerns from you he'd reconsider," Marsh said.

"You thought wrong," Davis said. "The man doesn't give a damn what I think. All he cares about is making sure everyone knows that going after Julian was his idea, and that he's got faith in him. So much faith, in fact, that he doesn't even need a decent backup."

Marsh studied the grass for a moment before looking up. "You're right," he whispered. "We both know that. But it's something we've got to deal with."

"You deal with it," Davis snapped. "I've been fed up with him for a long time. I would have resigned a long time ago if it wasn't—"

He fell silent as two players trotted past them, nodding to their coach as they ran by. If there was one thing a player should never hear from the coach in the middle of the season, it was talk about resignation. Especially when the team was undefeated.

"But you didn't," Marsh said when the players were out of earshot.

Davis half frowned. "No, I didn't. Because I love this team and I love these guys. But I've dealt with Vincent Petty before, and I'm not going to do it again. We'll just have to make do. Either that, or you'll have to screw up the courage to get what you need yourself."

"He's fired people for disagreeing with him," Marsh said. "He wouldn't be afraid to do the same to me."

Davis shrugged. "Then we'll have to make do."

Marsh sighed. His shoulders sank, an aura of hopeless dejection clung to him. Davis could feel it. This wasn't how it was supposed to be when you were winning, playing well. "And if Julian goes down?" Marsh asked. "Neither of the other guys we have is capable of carrying the team. And you already know what happens when you have Rich throw the ball fifty times a game."

"I don't want that to happen," Davis said. "But if it does, then so be it. Pray that Julian *doesn't* go down."

"You and I will take the fall," Marsh warned. "The media will tear us apart because of *our* stupidity, and there's no way in hell Petty will say differently. He'll stoke the flames."

"Jacob!"

He turned, saw an assistant coach standing with the offense around the fifty yardline of the practice field, waving him over. He looked at Marsh with false apology. "Sorry, Geoffrey. Handle it."

"Set! Hut!"

Mitchum dropped back three steps, planted his foot and fired the ball across the field, a rifle shot that was grabbed by his tight end Frank Moran at the sideline. Moran, the ball secured in his arms, let his momentum carry him out of bounds. The offensive coordinator blew his whistle, and the players returned to the line of scrimmage.

Davis stood over the offensive coordinator's shoulder. Mark Gaddis looked up at him. "Want to run it?" he asked.

Davis nodded. "Yeah. Give them the signal. Have them do

it three times on wind, then we'll throw the defense in there and see what happens."

Gaddis cupped his hands over his mouth and shouted, "River Right Thirty-two! Run it three times." He turned to the coach. "We went over it for half an hour in the meeting earlier. They better know what they're doing."

"I don't think it'll be a problem," Davis said. "And we have a while to perfect it."

The entire offense came up to the line of scrimmage, Mitchum under center and the running backs lined up in an "I" behind him. Mitchum called a few signals, took the snap and handed the ball to Julian, who ran left, parallel to the line of scrimmage. The wide receiver on that side ran toward him at full speed. Julian held the ball out and the receiver took it, a classic reverse. That receiver handed the ball to his counterpart on the other side, who was running in the opposite direction. A double reverse. The receiver then stopped, looked, and heaved the ball downfield to Lloyd, who was now streaking down the sideline. The running back snatched the ball and jogged to a stop.

Gaddis blew his whistle. He grinned at Davis. "We'll either lose ten yards and make fools of ourselves, or we'll gain fifty and look like geniuses."

"If it makes *us* this nervous," Davis said, "just think of the defensive coordinator on the other side of the field."

Gaddis blew the whistle again, and the offense lined up in the same formation. "Keeping the ball in the backfield that long is dangerous," he said.

"I know," Davis said.

Davis looked at the field just as the wide receiver, Jake Riley, handed the ball to Julian. He watched the young halfback run, his legs pumping fast, carrying him swiftly across the grass. He didn't look sick at all. It was as if his body was more comfortable being pushed to the limit, under exertion, than it was under normal circumstances. That in itself wasn't unusual. Many running backs gained steam as the game and season wore on, outlasting their opponents and making them pay in the end. But Julian had never struck him as that type of player. He had always seemed to be more in the class of a Bo Jackson. Big, but fast and quick, the type who could lower his shoulder if necessary, but *only* if necessary. He wasn't afraid of contact, but he didn't seek it out.

But now . . .

He ran with more aggressiveness, something that was apparent even without a defense trying to stop him. He'd either changed or matured—but Julian had never been immature.

"He's looking great, eh Coach?" Gaddis asked.

"He's been great," Davis said.

"Yeah, but now he's just getting going. He's the best I've ever seen. I bet he gets close to two thousand this year."

Davis frowned at his offensive coordinator. "Don't get ahead of yourself, Mark."

"And to think," Gaddis said, as if he hadn't heard Davis, "he's doing all this after that injury."

"Get the defense in there, Mark," Davis said, turning and leaving the man behind.

A few moments later he stood alone on the sideline, watching the two sides of his team line up on the fifty-yard line. River Right 32. The defense suspected that it was coming, but they didn't know for sure. As Davis watched, Mitchum dropped back instead of handing the ball off, and threw a short pass to Moran. The tight end was wide open, uncovered as the defense moved into position to defend the bizarre reverse they thought was coming.

On the other side of the field, Gaddis blew his whistle, stopping the play.

The team lined up again, in the I-formation. Davis crossed his arms over his chest. This was it. Mitchum handed the ball to Julian, who ran left, handing the ball to the wide receiver Dean Phenix, who ran back the other way, handing the ball to Jake Riley, who stopped and threw it downfield back to Julian. Julian accelerated in the open field. A linebacker, number 51, Bobby Langham, came up in front of him to stop him, but Julian shouted something, lowered his shoulder and slammed into him. The linebacker fell backwards into the grass, hard, and Julian kept running, ignoring the frantic whistle calls by Gaddis until he reached the end zone.

What the hell was *that?*

Davis ran onto the field, intercepted Julian as he walked back to the line and grabbed his face mask. "What the hell are you thinking?" he roared. "This isn't a game, asshole!"

Through the face mask, Julian seemed almost as surprised as Davis. "I . . . don't know, Coach," he said. "I . . ." His voice trailed off. "I guess I wasn't thinking."

Davis released his face mask. "Next time, you sure as hell *better* think. You pull a stunt like that again against one of your own teammates in a *non-contact drill* and I will personally sit your butt on the bench until it gets sore. You understand?"

Julian's helmet bobbed up and down. "Yes, sir."

"Get back there and apologize to Bobby." Davis turned away from his player and trotted back to his place on the sideline. He watched Julian stop next to Langham, say something, and then pat the bigger linebacker on the back. Langham laughed, but Davis didn't find the episode funny. Not at all. You didn't *do* that in a non-contact drill!

And Julian wasn't the type of person to do something like that anyway. What had gotten into him?

He sighed and shook his head. Maybe he should talk to Petty after all.

Ryan stood next to Gary Harrell, observing the starters as they practiced for Sunday's game. The reserves had already run through their practice, and Ryan had taken off his jersey and shoulder pads. Harrell stared at his first team players, arms folded across his chest, his features arranged in a contemplative expression. "How do you think we look?" he asked, head leaning toward Ryan.

The coach laughed, asking one of his backups a question like that . . . Ryan had been on this team far longer than Harrell had coached it, but the fact that Harrell could ask a player that . . . "We look great," Ryan said. "We look ready to break even."

"There's a big difference between five-and-four and four-and-five," Harrell said. "If we win, we're in the thick of things. Lose, and we may never catch up."

Shouts rang out on the field as the quarterback Ethan Daniels threw a low pass over the middle that was intercepted by a diving David Falk. Falk secured the ball in the air, hit the ground, rolled to his feet and ran toward the end zone, dodging a few offensive players before an assistant coach stopped the play.

"With him playing like that," Ryan said, "How can we lose?"

Harrell chuckled. "It's been done."

"Yes, it has."

Harrell looked at him. "But I don't plan on doing it. Do you?"

Ryan shuddered. "No."

Julian lay on a weight bench, motionless while a trainer got a barbell ready for his bench press session. The weight room was filled with players and trainers, working with machines and barbells and dumbbells, a beehive of activity. It stank like sweat and was humid and warm, like a summer day in fall. Much warmer than it was outside.

"Okay," the trainer said, sliding one last weight onto the bar. "Two-fifty. We'll start with five reps and work our way up. Your lower body strength has been awesome—I've never seen a guy's legs blow up so fast. You just have a strong lower body. Anyway, we're at the midpoint of the season, and pretty soon your legs aren't going to be so fresh. I want tacklers to bounce off your chest if you can't quite break through them with your legs anymore." He tapped the barbells, resting in the rack above Julian's chest. "Let's get started."

Julian strained against the bar, pushed and lifted it with care from the rack. He lowered it to chest level. "Okay," he murmured.

"One," the trainer called.

Julian lifted the barbells, his arms vibrating from the effort. He extended his arms, stopped, lowered them again.

"How do you feel?" the trainer asked.

"Great."

"Good. Two."

He strained against the weight. His arms extended, retreated to his chest. "Good," he said.

"Good. Three."

The trainer watched as Julian pushed against 250 pounds of metal. The kid seemed to be getting tired by the end of the first set—he was only a running back after all—but still, 250, one set of five; that wasn't too much to ask.

"You okay, Julian?" he asked.

"I'm fine," the kid said. "Just sore."

"You want to knock it off for the day?"

Julian shook his head. "Hell, no. Don't even think about it."

"You sure?"

"Positive," Julian said. He looked annoyed.

"All right, then. Let's do a set of seven . . ."

He did the set, working with increasing vigor, it seemed, as he went on. It was as if he gained strength, increased stamina. The trainer knew that many running backs got better as the game went on, but he'd never seen it to this extent in a simple workout.

"Julian," he said when the kid finished the seventh repetition, "Let's go do some lower-body work, huh?"

Twenty-one

It was Friday, and there wasn't much to look forward to this particular weekend, as the Gunners were off. And the case was heating up. That meant a weekend of work—but for some reason, Sutton didn't mind.

He was standing in the main office of the station, letting the flow of people go around him, when Cassie came up and handed him a compilation on "Fran Dean." It was amazing what you could find with a name and social security number—which hadn't been hard to obtain from the SLU hospital.

Sutton read over the report, then shook his head and gave it back to Cassie. "So that's it," he said in disgust. "That's *all* you found. Nothing on this HUMINT connection?"

"Nothing," Cassie said. "Of course, we may not know her real name."

"I doubt we do," Sutton said. "Get me a list of alibis. I need to know what this woman goes by. And if she works for a biotech company . . . hmm." He looked up at the ceiling and bit his lip. "I wonder . . ."

"Wonder what?"

He looked at her and smiled. "I wonder if APEX would know anything about them. HUMINT, I mean." He nodded to himself. "Yeah, that's it. Cassie, you dig up her aliases. I'm going to make an appointment with APEX. All right?"

"Got it," she said, turning away. "See you back here."

"Right," Sutton said. He hesitated, then moved off to his desk and dug out a phone book.

* * *

When Sutton called and asked to meet with a representative of American Physicians united against genetic EXperiments, not only were they cooperative—they were downright amiable. The receptionist, a husky-voiced man, told him that Mr. Dan Newman was in town this week, visiting the St. Louis office, and that Mr. Newman would be more than happy to answer any questions concerning the horrible death of Dr. Hendley.

Forty minutes after hanging up with the receptionist, Sutton was walking into a downtown office building, following the signs to the sixth floor, most of which was reserved to APEX.

The offices were spacious cubicles, decorated with personal pictures and furnished with desks and computers. The man he'd spoken to over the phone took him to a large office with a window to the outside, white and neat and air-conditioned so that one didn't even notice the temperature. Dan Newman was a fiftyish man, well-built and tanned, wearing wire-frame bifocals. He introduced himself, and Sutton did likewise. Then they both took their seats, and Tony asked the first question.

"What do you know about Humanity International?" he asked, rubbing his chin.

"Quite a bit," Newman said. "They're the biggest fish in the pond, so to speak. We expend a lot of resources just watching them. We've had reason to suspect them of—how should I put it?—*questionable* business practices in the past. We just never had enough evidence to pin a single incident on them."

"Corporate warfare?" Sutton asked.

"Oh yes. In the worst way," Newman replied, nodding. He leaned forward. "Do you suspect them of being involved with Dr. Hendley's death?"

"I'm not sure yet," Sutton admitted. "We've decided that whoever sabotaged his car was in the hospital already that day. We believe the person knew him and had access to him, and was someone he trusted. So we think the murderer was a member of his office staff. We've questioned all of them, several times—except for one, a woman named Fran Dean. We haven't been able to find her."

Newman leaned back. "What does this have to do with HUMINT?"

"From the office phone records, we've found that she called the HUMINT offices, several times," Sutton said. "Just using the hospital phones. There's no telling how much she contacted them using other means. Depending on what you tell me today, we may be able to get a search warrant for the office computers and run a scan on the hard drives, to check for e-mails and such."

Newman leaned forward again, looking intrigued. "Do you know what HUMINT office she was calling?"

Sutton nodded. "Lance Pollard's."

Newman slapped his palms against the desk. His eyes went unfocused. "Damn," he said to himself. *"Damn.* I should have known that last name. Dean." He seemed to notice Sutton again. "Excuse me, Detective. Ah . . . for a while now, we've been watching one of Lance Pollard's personal aides, or assistants. These are people who report straight to him, by-passing the company board. They don't even appear on the earnings reports as staff. Just equipment, and that's how he uses them.

"Now, there's one—a woman named Jeanette Dean—that we were keeping our eye on. She was involved with a nasty incident at Cal-Tech, in graduate school. She and another student just decided one day to run a test on a person. A five-year-old child, as a matter of fact. With muscular dystrophy. Don't ask for the particulars—how they did it—but they did. Genetic enhancement. Needless to say, the child almost died from muscle complications. The parents threatened to sue. Dean and the other student, a woman named Angelina Moore, were almost expelled, but Moore managed to maneuver her way out of trouble, and somehow convinced the school that Dean was to blame. Tech settled with the parents, and that was—"

It had taken a moment for the name to process. Newman

went through the sentences with no hesitation. No time to think. But it clicked, and Sutton jerked up in the chair. "Wait a minute," he snapped. "Moore? Angelina Moore? Where is she now?"

"With a little local company," Newman said. "Genetics Life. Why?"

"GLI, right," Sutton continued. "But Hendley was interested in GLI, wasn't he? Didn't he ask you for an earnings report?"

"Yes, he did," Newman said, frowning. "But that was just routine. GLI is so small that we in the accounting department just looked over them when we made our biannual meltdown on the biotech—"

"No, it was more than routine," Sutton said, holding up a finger. "That report was in Dr. Hendley's car when he was killed. We think he was bringing it here."

"I don't understand why," Newman said.

"Maybe you would know," Sutton said. "He'd highlighted every donation made to GLI from Vincent Petty's law firm."

"Vincent Petty?"

"The owner of the Missouri Gunners," Sutton said. "The donations were made around the same time that Julian Lloyd was—"

"Oh my . . ." Newman muttered.

"Exactly," Sutton said. "Something is going on here, Mr. Newman. Something very big, bigger than a little revenge job, or an everyday homicide. Somebody was out to kill Dr. Hendley because he was getting too close to their turf."

"Perhaps someone at GLI," Newman suggested.

Sutton shook his head. "No. Remember, inside the hospital. This Jeanette Dean woman— Do you think Fran Dean is the same person?"

"Do you have a description of Fran Dean?" Newman asked.

"Little," Sutton said, holding his hand flat below his chin. "Very quiet. Dark hair—"

"Little and quiet is enough," Newman muttered. "That's her. Damn it. Right under his nose the whole time."

"Is she capable of murder?"

Newman nodded vigorously. "Oh yes. I wouldn't doubt it, not for an instant."

"But why would Humanity International want to kill Hendley?" Sutton asked. "What do they have to do with GLI?"

Newman chuckled. "It's fairly obvious, I think. Lance Pollard is a monopolist. He's always out to absorb other companies, to get them out of the way. Perhaps GLI has research he'd like to get his hands on. The best way to get it is to absorb GLI. If something were to happen to it, and it were to go out of business, that research would remain under GLI's control. Or worse, under government control. If they were in fact involved in something illegal. So he would be sure to protect them until such time as he is able to force a merger or buyout."

"So if Hendley happened upon some damning information . . ."

"The best bet would be to remove him, yes," Newman said.

"And Jeanette Dean was in perfect position to do so," Sutton said. "Quick and clean." He shook his head. "I think that's enough of a reason."

"Reason for what?"

"Reason to make Fran Dean a suspect," Sutton said. "And bring her in."

He pulled Cassie aside as she exited the forensics lab. They stepped out of the flow of traffic, beside the wall.

"Find anything?" he asked, crossing his arms over his chest. Secure with the knowledge that *he* had.

"Not much," Cassie said, frowning. "I bet you're gonna tell me *you* did though, huh?"

He nodded. "Yes. Fran Dean's real name is Jeanette. She went to graduate school with Angelina Moore at Cal-Tech, got into some trouble there, and then was hired by Humanity International. Which is a biotech company; the big fish in the pond." He smiled. "And she's the CEO's personal aide. According to the APEX guy, that makes her little more than a private assassin. Hit-man—hit-gal."

Cassie smiled at him, and for once there was no hint of sarcasm behind the expression. "Motive?"

"Try personal gain," Sutton said, his own smile widening. "The HUMINT CEO, that Pollard guy, has been after Genetics Life for a long time. He wants their technology. Dan Newman said that, in order to get it, he needs to buy them out. And to do that, he needs to drive them to the brink while at the same time keeping them from going down the hole. If GLI commits an illegal act and is caught, their research material will either be locked down, or put out on the street for anyone with a deep pocket. Dr. Hendley thought there was something going on with GLI. And obviously, *Fran* decided he was becoming a risk."

"Circumstantial," Cassie said. "But it's damn good. Now we find the babe."

"Yes," Sutton nodded. "Now we find her."

"If she's some kind of assassin deal, that might get hard," Cassie said. "I mean, we aren't gonna get much help from the municipals. They wanna keep this thing small and quiet. And a load of circumstantial talk isn't gonna convince them."

"She's been playing *secretary*," Sutton snorted. He lay his arm over Cassie's shoulders. "Come on. How hard could it be?"

Cassie shrugged. "You know, there's something else we gotta watch out for, Tony. What if somebody else turns into a threat to Genetics Life? We got no idea where this Jeanette woman is. She could . . ."

"Yeah."

Her phone rang, but Angel took her time in answering it. She finished typing the last sentence of a report on P-Rh4—Cleo was still acting up, if anything getting *worse,* despite what she had told Nagel—saved the file, copied it to a diskette, then picked up the phone.

"Genetics Life, Incorporated. Dr. Angelina Moore speaking," she said.

"Angelina," Vince Petty's voice cooed to her. "It's Vince. How are you?"

"What can I help you with?" Angel said, keeping her surprise from entering her voice. She had almost hoped she would never hear from him again; the only reason he would call would be to complain about something. She turned off her computer monitor and pressed the phone harder to her ear.

Petty said, "When we first went over this together, you mentioned possible side effects. I remembered them, and jotted them down. Flu-like symptoms, body aches, psychological effects. Correct?"

"Correct," Angel said.

"I thought so. And these psychological effects . . . what would they consist of?"

"I'm not sure. Why?"

"You're not sure," Petty clucked. "I don't like that answer. Give me an educated guess."

Butterflies flittered in her stomach. "Is there a problem, Vince?"

"I don't know," Petty said. "There may be."

"Depression, anger, even happiness," Angel said, frowning. "I don't know, because we've never seen an actual case. Why are you asking?"

The words that followed hit her like a lead weight. "I'm asking because Julian's been acting a little strange . . ."

"Strange in what way?" she asked, swallowing hard.

"Nothing too drastic," Petty said. "But I did think about what you said, about side effects, for some reason. But just by watching him during practices, and during workouts, I can tell he is a little irritable, getting into trouble, and he has had a short temper. He's always been a very patient boy; he never really gets mad. So I noticed the difference."

"Have you noticed anything else?" Angel asked. "The flu-like symptoms, maybe?"

"I know that he saw the doctor, complaining about body aches," Petty said.

Dammit, dammit, dammit! "Okay," she soothed, more for her own good than for his. "There are a few possibilities. Uh . . . First, it could be a coincidence. Maybe he's got the flu and is feeling bad, so he's been short-tempered. Second, they could be short-term side effects that will go away in time. In that case, it would be no big deal and I wouldn't worry about it. And third, it could be a sign that his body is rejecting the genetic enhancement. That's the worst-case scenario. He could sink lower and lower and the pains could get a lot worse over time."

"In that case," Petty said, his voice deadpan, "Is there any way to halt this?"

"We could reverse the modification," Angel said. "Even though it's a little early."

"Perhaps that would be best," Petty said. "Why not do it?"

"Because that would also weaken his knee," Angel said. "It's too early to let him go natural."

Petty was silent for a moment; the only sound Angel heard was his breathing. She didn't prompt him to speak.

"Which possibility is the most likely?" he asked.

"In my opinion, it's a short-term thing," Angel said. "I wouldn't worry about it. But if his condition continues to deteriorate, then you might want to consider a reversal."

"You think it's short term," Petty said.

"Yes. I do." *I hope it is . . .*

"All right. Thank you, Angelina. I appreciate it."

"You're welcome, Vince."

"Good-bye."

Angel just stared ahead, holding the phone in her hand for a moment. If Lloyd's body rejected the modification . . .

She didn't allow herself to finish that thought. The ramifications were too much for her to bear. And one of those ramifications was the discovery of the whole thing by the authorities, and the shutdown of Genetics Life. If their *illegal act* was discovered, there was no way the government would allow them to continue operations.

All they had to do was talk to Julian Lloyd. He would tell them everything that had been done to him, without even knowing what he was doing.

Evidence. There was no evidence—besides Lloyd's remarkable recovery, of course. Genetics Life had plausible deniability, because Nagel didn't know a thing about it. Even if someone decided to run tests on Lloyd to find an illegal substance there would be no problem. They wouldn't find anything. They'd have to run a muscle biopsy on him, and that wasn't going to happen in the middle of the football season.

But afterwards . . .

Angel sighed. It wasn't worth the risk. She picked up the phone again, and dialed Petty's number. When he answered, he didn't seem all that surprised to hear her voice.

"Hello, Angelina," he said.

"Vince, we have a problem," she said.

"We do."

"Yes. Is there any way you can keep Lloyd off-limits? No interviews, you know. That type of thing."

"Why?"

"Because we don't want to attract attention. We don't want the media wondering why his behavior is different. Then it'll blow over." *Maybe.*

He sighed into the phone. "Very well. I will come up with an excuse of some sort," he said. "Don't worry about it."

Angel returned his thoughtful sigh. "It could mean our freedom, Vince. I'm not going to jail over this."

"It's a line I've skirted before," Petty said. "I know what I'm doing. Just act normal. Everything is the same as it was before. Once we clamp down, this detective will lose interest, and the whole thing will blow over."

"I'm not so sure about that," Angel said. "I have a feeling about him."

"I know his type," Petty said, as if insulted.

"So do I."

"Well, I guess we'll discover which of us knows better, then."

"And when we do," Angel said, "hope that we're still sit-

ting where we are now. And not sitting in a prison cell. Good-
bye, Vince."

"Good-bye. Again."

She hung up and sank into the chair, despondent. She let her
head hang, and rubbed her aching forehead with her fingertips.

"Angel, dear," she said aloud to herself, "you've definitely
gotten yourself into it this time."

Jacob Davis was walking toward his personal office, filling
out a workout/practice schedule attached to his clipboard, when
Geoffrey Marsh approached him and matched his stride.

"Jacob," he said.

Davis grunted some semblance of a reply, and studied the
schedule.

"I need to tell you something," Marsh said.

Davis still didn't look up. "Shoot," he growled.

"It's about Julian," Marsh said. "We don't want him talking to the media. In other words, he should be off-limits."

Davis looked up from the clipboard and shook his head at
the general manager as they walked. "Petty put you up to this,
didn't he?"

"It was his suggestion, yes."

"And what was his reasoning?" Davis looked back at the
schedule. "What's his beef now?"

"I didn't ask," Marsh said.

Davis shook his head in pity for the man. "He's got you
trained now, eh? 'Don't ask why, just comply'."

"I happen to agree with him," Marsh said.

"Why?" Davis demanded. "He does well with the media.
He's well-spoken, knows the correct answers—hell, the kid
could get into politics if he wanted to. He knows how to play
the media." Yet another natural talent he possessed, that made
him a more complete football player. Off the field. Davis
chuckled. "You want to ban a player from talking to the
media? Try Rich. He's got a terminal case of foot-in-mouth
disease."

"This isn't about Rich Mitchum," Marsh said.

"It's about Julian Lloyd," Davis finished. "All right."

"You'll tell him?"

Davis smiled crookedly at his boss, a wicked half grin. "No, I won't. And I know *you* won't. There's no reason for me to do it, and one big reason *not* to do it. Because Petty wants it done."

"Jacob—"

"Tell him yourself, Geoffrey, since you just happen to agree."

Marsh looked uncomfortable, fidgety, as he always did when he was upset. "Jacob, I know how you feel—"

"Until I have a real reason to put one of my men under a gag order," Davis said, "I won't do it. That's final." He came to the door to his office. "Now, if you don't mind, I've got a football team to run." He opened the door and slid into the privacy of his office.

"Look for us to try this play and formation in third and short situations," Warren Kiley, running backs coach for the Gunners, said, standing before the team's six active and practice squad running backs. "Jay-slash twenty-three. Simple signal, simple play. It puts a heavy burden on the starting 'back, though, to pick the right time to hit the hole. Too fast, and you slam into a wall and get stuffed. Too slow and you'll get hit in the backfield. But if you get there right on time, the defensive line will be blocked and the linebackers will be out of position. That'll put you in the secondary, with the safeties to beat. Beat them and you're gone. Julian."

Julian looked up at the coach. "Yes. I was going to ask, with the linebacker Jacksonville has on the weak side—as fast as he is—what's going to stop him from getting back into position in time to stuff the hole?"

"Gabe Jenkins," Kiley said, and the big fullback, sitting three chairs away from Julian, held his arms up.

"You better believe it!" he said.

"Gabe's fast enough to get up there before you," Kiley said,

"And big enough to plug the 'backer if he's in the way. Now, this is where a decision comes in for you, Gabe." Kiley looked the fullback in the eye, the way he did only to the players under his charge. "If the linebacker is in the way, by all means take him out. But if he's caught out of position, don't go chasing him down. Instead, get upfield and clear out a safety. Do that and Julian will be in the open field with just one guy to beat. An automatic touchdown."

"Thanks to the blocking," Gabe Jenkins said, smiling. "Julian, you've got the easy part, bro."

"Yeah, maybe so," Julian whispered.

"All right, guys," Kiley said. "That's about it for now. We've got time yet before the game. We'll throw in a few more plays special for Jacksonville, and add a few more things. Maybe a trick or two that Gaddis has up his sleeve. Julian has a good arm, so Mark might be thinking option this week against those older corners."

A knock at the door interrupted him.

"Come in," Kiley said.

The door opened, and a mousy, gray-haired facility staff member peeked in. "Uh, excuse me," he said. "But the radio guy is here for a sound bite with Julian."

Julian frowned, dimly surprised at the annoyance he felt. "Right now?"

"He says he has an appointment with you," the staffer said.

"I'm busy," Julian said.

"He insists. I'm sorry."

"Damn it!" Julian said, then looked at the faces of his teammates, watching him, and he frowned again. "Sorry," he said, just above a whisper. He looked at the staffer. "I'm coming. Just . . ." He sighed. "Just give me a minute."

The staffer looked a bit unsure of himself, but nodded. "Okay," he said, and the door closed again.

"Are you okay, Julian?" Kiley asked.

"You're sweating," one of his backups said.

Julian wiped his brow with the palm of his hand. Sure enough, it came back moist and cool. A cold sweat. *More of those allergies,* he told himself. "Yeah, I'm fine," he said. "Let me get this interview over with. I'll be back."

"Julian," Kiley said, stopping him as he reached for the door handle. "Why don't you take the rest of the afternoon off? You know what you're doing."

"What?" Julian snapped. "You don't think I can work through a cold?"

"No," Kiley said, holding up his hand. "I don't mean to imply that. You just look like you need a break. It's a long season. Sometimes you can work too hard."

"I don't need a freaking break," Julian said. Something in his mind said, *What is wrong with you, bonehead?* But that thought passed through him unheeded. "I'm fine. I'll be right back."

Without another word, he left his speechless companions behind and walked down the hall to the locker room, where the radio guy was waiting for him. He entered, and the man stood from a bench and held out a hand. Julian didn't shake it.

The man let his hand drop, scratching at his head through thinning brown hair, and tried without success to hide a curious frown. "Ready, Julian?" he asked, and flicked the switch on his recorder to on.

"It might be a close one," Davis was telling the kicker, talking to the balding man in a discreet, dark corner of the locker room. "We need you to be in top condition, mentally and physically. The game could be decided by a field goal, and I want to make sure you're ready to handle that."

The kicker nodded. "I know I've been in a little slump," he said, a very distant, unrecognizable foreign accent in the background of his speech. "But I feel like I'm getting out of it. It's all a mental game. I'm finally back in it."

"That's good," Davis said, smiling. "When you're getting into it, it means the team is, in general. You're the barometer, you know that?"

"Thanks," the kicker said. "I think."

"It's a compliment," Davis told him, smiling. "Don't worry. Go take a shower."

"All right." The kicker moved off.

Davis turned and almost rounded a corner, made of the row of lockers, to exit, but stopped when he heard a voice ask: "Ready, Julian?" It sounded like one of the local sports radio reporters. Curious, he backed up to remain out of sight.

"Yeah," another voice croaked in reply. Julian, Davis realized, though he sounded strained and frustrated. Warped.

"First of all," the reporter said, "How's the knee?"

"Fine," Julian snarled. "I'm leading the league in rushing. How the hell do you think it is?"

Stunned silence. Davis himself couldn't have spoken, even if he'd wanted to.

"Um. I was just curious," the reporter said meekly. "Sorry about that. Ah . . . anyway. Second question. How has the passing game helped in your success through the first half of the season? Having a good quarterback like Rich Mitchum must take a lot of the pressure off—"

"Look," Julian cut him off. "I get the same damn questions every frigging day. I'm tired of it! Watch the news at night or listen to your own stupid show and you'll hear the answers. A thousand experts come on every night on TV and in all the magazines and tell the world how it helps me. Why don't you ask them?"

"I . . . Julian, is something bothering you?"

"Yeah!" Julian exploded. "Something's bothering me. I don't really know what the hell it is, but yeah, something's bothering me." Quiet again, and Davis got the impression that Julian was thinking it over. Finally, the young halfback said, "You know what it is, really? It's having people like *you* come over here to pick my brain and then explain my life to the whole damn world every freaking night, and to hell with what I think, as long as you get decent ratings. I'm tired of it! And not a second of *this* is going to air tonight." A startled yelp, and a smashing sound, and Davis watched a tape recorder skitter across the floor past him. "I've got to get back to work, and I don't want to talk to you people anymore! You got that?"

The reporter seemed to be searching for a reply, stuttering and stumbling over words.

Davis decided to get involved, though his own heart was pounding with shock at hearing the soft-spoken rookie rant like this. He moved out of his aisle into full view. "Julian!" he roared, in his best *pissed-off Lombardi* impression.

Julian looked right at him, brown eyes making contact and burning into him. Davis maintained his stare, and neither of them spoke until Julian finally broke eye contact. "What . . . ?" he started to say, then shook his head as if to clear it of a heavy fog, and lowered himself to the bench. The reporter slid over to the opposite end of the bench and stood up, watching wide-eyed.

Julian rubbed his eyes and forehead. "What did I just say?" he asked, not seeming to speak to any one person.

"You don't remember?" Davis asked, his voice icy calm.

Julian shook his head, then looked up. "Wait. Yes. Something . . ." He stood, turned around and looked at the reporter. "Hey . . . I'm sorry. I'm really sorry, man. I don't— I don't know what happened . . ."

The reporter inched closer to him. "No problem," he said. "I've seen worse."

Julian looked embarrassed, more than anything. "I don't know what happened," he said, his voice growing stronger with each word. "It's like . . . I don't know."

Davis patted him on a heavily muscled shoulder. "Why don't you head back over to your meeting?" he suggested quietly. "I'll finish up here."

Julian nodded, looking relieved. "I'm real sorry, sir," he told the reporter once more, and made his escape from the room.

The reporter started to walk toward the tape recorder, laying on the floor across the room. "Stop," Davis said. "None of this goes beyond this room. And the recorder is busted, besides. I saw it."

"This was an interview," the reporter protested. "I have a right to—"

"You don't have a right to do anything that I don't want you to do around here," Davis said. "And if I turn on the radio, or the TV, or open the newspaper tomorrow morning, and hear or see so much as a *syllable* about this incident, I will revoke your press license to this team. And you can forget about covering the games. I'd just as soon have your radio station dumped as a sponsor. And I'm sure you don't want to be responsible something like that. That would cause layoffs and downsizing. Probably your position, huh?"

"I don't appreciate being threatened," the reporter said.

"You test me," Davis said. "Check and see just how much of a *threat* this really is. You'll regret it, but I can't stop curiosity, can I?"

The reporter looked at him, his eyes narrowed. "It's not worth reporting, anyway," he said. "But I want my recorder."

"It's broken," Davis said. "Forget about it. I'll compensate you. Go wait for me up front. I'll be there in a minute."

The reporter frowned skeptically, but nodded and moved off. Davis watched for a moment to make sure he was gone, then went to the wall, bent over and picked up the tape recorder. He rewound it and hit PLAY.

"Yeah," Julian's voice said.

"First of all," the reporter's voice said, "How's the knee?"

"Fine. I'm leading the league in rushing. How the hell do you think it is?"

Davis pressed STOP, dropped the recorder to the floor and crushed it beneath his heel.

Then he went to find Geoffrey Marsh, to tell him that he had changed his mind.

Julian trudged down the hall to the meeting room, stopped and opened the door. He looked inside, but the room was dark and empty. The meeting was over. He'd missed the end.

Why hadn't they waited for him?

Frustrated, he stepped back and slammed the door shut.

What is wrong with you? his conscience asked him.

He didn't know. He couldn't answer. And a part of him said it was stupid to answer his own unspoken questions, anyway.

He began to accelerate, but skidded to a stop when the world began to swirl around and around, right in front of him, like he was at the center of a tornado. He felt light-headed and nauseous, and shakily placed his arms on the wall, leaning on them to steady himself. He looked at the floor, but it suddenly seemed to tilt upward and he struggled to stay upright. He closed his eyes and let his head hang, and took several deep breaths. It seemed to help. He opened his eyes again—

The entire world flipped upside down, and he fell to the cold tile floor like a half-empty sack of flour.

His eyes were open, but he couldn't see. Panic surged through him—he was blind!—but as his beleaguered mind made this recognition, his vision returned. And then went black again, and suddenly he seemed very tired. The spinning, dark, oily world around him stopped, and his body went limp, and before he could protest, his consciousness collapsed around him into oblivion.

Dark shapes hovered above him, and ghostly echoing voices spoke about him.

"He's waking up," one voice said, and it seemed to reverberate throughout the room.

"Thank God," another resounded.

Slowly the hazy images coalesced into uniform shapes, and Julian blinked his dry eyes rapidly to clear them. He tried to ask what had happened, but his mouth was too slow to react to the impulses of his brain, and he rasped, "What . . . ?"

"Don't talk," one of the men standing above him said. Julian recognized him as the team physician, Dr. Rice. "Just rest a moment."

The other man was Coach Davis. "What happened?" he

asked Julian, looking down on him in concern. Rice shot him a disapproving glance.

Julian swallowed, cleared his throat. "I don't know," he whispered. "I was . . . going to ask you the . . . same thing."

"I found you lying on the floor," Davis said, "and I got the doctor."

"How long was I out?" His voice was getting stronger, clearer.

"Not long," Rice said. "I'd say ten minutes." He checked the scribbled observations on his little notepad. "How long has this been going on, Julian?"

Julian shook his head. "It's never happened before."

"But you've been complaining of different symptoms for a while now . . ."

"Yes, but nothing like this." Julian shook his head. "I— Do you think that this—" He sighed, gathering his wits. "Do you think this has anything to do with me jumping on that guy?"

"Jumping on who?" Dr. Rice asked.

"Julian has been a little irritable," Davis said for him. "Bad temper, mood swings."

"Exactly," Julian said. "It's weird. Things that never bothered me before get me crazy now. It's like I lose control of myself." He closed his eyes.

"Well, we know you're not on drugs," the doctor said, half jokingly, holding up a chart of drug test results. He cleared his throat. "And unless you're on any medications that I don't know about . . ."

Julian shook his head.

"Supplements?"

"Just vitamins and protein shakes," Julian said.

"What brand of vitamins?"

"I don't know," Julian said. "You gave them to me."

Dr. Rice checked his charts. "Oh, right. I forgot." He shook his head, obviously perplexed. "I can't find anything wrong, Julian," he said. "There *isn't* anything wrong. I guess it's just your body reacting to the season. You've been under a heavy workload."

"I played four seasons of college football, getting the ball thirty times a game, and played three positions, three ways in high school, getting the ball on almost *every* play." Julian looked the doctor in the eye. "Nothing like this has ever happened to me before."

"It could be an aftereffect of your injury," Rice said. "That put you under a lot of stress. It wouldn't surprise me if the normal wear and tear of playing running back on the professional level, coupled with a pretty bad injury—which you returned from so soon—would cause some ill effects."

"But I'm okay . . ."

"Yes. Medically, you're healthy."

Julian exited the room a few minutes later, walking gingerly out into the hallway.

Davis looked at Rice, drawing his attention away from the charts. "What's the real story?" he asked quietly.

"You heard it," Rice said. "There's nothing medically wrong with him. No allergies. No flu. Not even a cold."

"Yet he's going crazy on a daily basis, passing out, losing his equilibrium and getting kept in bed because of muscle aches." Davis sighed. "*Something* has to be wrong."

"There isn't," Rice said. "My diagnosis is what I said: He's just taking a very heavy physical toll."

"So what do you recommend?" Davis asked. "That I bench him?"

Rice shook his head. "No. There's nothing wrong with his body. It's all up to him. If he feels he can go, then let him go."

"All right," Davis said. "So it's business as usual?"

"Yes," Rice said. "Business as usual."

Davis walked to the door, reached for the handle, twisted it and stopped. "I'm going to list him as questionable on the injury report," he said. "And I think we're going to be working overtime to work up a contingency plan. Just in case. I think Julian will be very limited this week."

He opened the door and left the room.

Twenty-two

The crowd went wild over the Gunners defense, which forced a three and out against Jacksonville on its opening series. The Jaguars were forced to punt the ball away. Nick Mills, the backup wide receiver who acted as Missouri's punt returner, caught the ball on a bounce at the twenty-two yard-line, accelerated forward, juked a defender and cut through the gut of the coverage before getting wrapped up and tackled at midfield. The offensive team began to take the field. Julian was starting to follow, snapping his chinstrap on, when Davis laid a hand on his shoulder pad and looked at him earnestly.

"You ready, Julian?" he asked, just loud enough to be heard over the crowd.

Julian nodded beneath his helmet and dark visor. "I'm ready."

"I don't want to overuse you after what happened this week," Davis said. "I need to know."

Julian unsnapped his chinstrap and pulled off his helmet. He made eye contact with his coach. "I'm ready, Coach. I'm a hundred and ten percent."

"Okay." Davis took a step back and gestured to the field, his lips forming a tight line. "Then get out there and get to work."

Julian put his helmet back on and trotted onto the field to the offensive huddle. Rich Mitchum glanced at him, concern visible on his face. The other members of the team didn't know *exactly* what had happened, but they did know *something* had happened, and a faint aura of anxiety clung to the eleven men standing here.

Mitchum cleared his throat. "Okay, boys," he said. "Jay-Slash twenty-three, on two." And his teammates joined him in saying, "Break!"

They lined up, I-formation, the fullback Gabe Jenkins standing behind Mitchum and in front of Julian. Mitchum began calling signals, and one of the receivers, Jake Riley, came in motion from left to right.

"Set! Red Sixty!" Mitchum yelled. "Hut! Hut!"

The lines slammed together, the offensive linemen driving their defensive counterparts to the left. Mitchum dropped back, spun around, handed the ball to Julian as he ran forward. Julian followed Jenkins through the hole on the right side, broke away from his lead blocker as the fullback turned to meet the middle linebacker and sped into the middle of the secondary. The strong safety closed on him, lowered his shoulder and drove it into Julian's waist, but Julian stopped his forward momentum on a cut and spun to the left, slipping out of the tackle, causing the safety to fall to the grass. He turned his momentum back upfield, squaring his shoulders and meeting the free safety head-on. He heard the *smash* of their mutual impact, heard the safety yelp in pain and surprise, felt him falling backwards and kept pumping his legs into the grass. The safety held on and pulled Julian down after being dragged forward for three more yards.

Julian hopped to his feet, looked to the sidelines at the position of the original line of scrimmage marker and then noted his current position; he had gained fourteen yards on the first play of the game.

He was in a zone. He felt it as he walked back to the huddle. He was going to dominate and control this game. And the people in the crowd felt it, too. They became deathly quiet, and seemed to settle in for what they sensed would be a long afternoon.

"Not bad," Mitchum said in the huddle, the anxiety clearing

from his expression. "Great blocking, great running. Now let's keep 'em off balance. Jay-Stroke Slam Zip One on one."

"Break!"

The formation was another I, and Jake Riley came in motion once again. This time, though, Mitchum took the snap and simply gave the ball to Julian, who followed Jenkins through the center of the line. Jenkins once again impacted with the middle linebacker, throwing him backwards and out of position, and before he could recover Julian was already dashing past him into the secondary.

There was nothing more terrifying to 190-pound defensive backs than a 220-pound running back flying into the secondary like a 747 with rocket engines. The free safety, assisted by a cornerback, met him head-on again. This time Julian drove the two smaller players backwards before one of the linebackers came to the rescue and weighed him down. Julian stayed down for just under a second. He jumped back up, lightly on his feet, and checked the distance of his run—ten yards.

They were already down to the twenty-six-yard line.

In the huddle, Mitchum said, "Jay-stroke PA Zip three on two."

I-formation once again, and once again, Jake Riley jogged into motion, from left to right. Mitchum took the snap, dropped back three steps, held the ball out for Julian to take but casually pulled it back as Julian passed him. Julian continued running as Mitchum pump-faked, gaining the belated attention of the defense. The strong safety took an errant step toward the quarterback—

And Julian flew past him, wide open down the seam of the field. He looked back, saw the ball arcing up over the line and then coming back down over his shoulder, a perfectly thrown pass. Julian caught it with ease, bringing it in just as he crossed the goal line, the strong safety uttering curses as he trailed behind.

Three plays. Three touches. Three double-digit gains. One touchdown.

Julian tossed the ball to the nearest official, the back judge, he guessed, and trotted off the field while his teammates yelled congratulations and slapped his helmet.

Davis smiled despite himself as the offense celebrated with Julian, walking off the field. Now, *that* was the kid they all knew and loved. Quiet, nondescript, unassuming. The type of kid who let his running and catching and scoring do the talking for him, even though he was well-spoken and polite. A kid who didn't lose his temper and could take a whole lot of crap from anyone without getting mad, but who was dangerous when provoked.

It's nice to have him back, Davis thought.

The Missouri defense forced a punt after a single first down on the very next series. Nick Mills fielded it and ran directly into the coverage, forcing his way forward for a respectable nine yard gain.

Julian led his offense—*his offense,* he thought, smiling beneath his plastic armor—and confidently took his position in the huddle. He touched the ball on more than forty percent of this team's offensive plays. He was responsible for almost half of the offense's total yardage.

This team was built around him. It was his offense.

Mitchum leaned forward, hands on his kneepads. "June-Sweep Forty-five Three."

"Break!" came the reply, in chorus.

They started in an I-formation, but Gabe Jenkins stood and skipped to the right a few steps before dropping back into his stance, altering the formation and making it an offset I. Julian's mouthpiece was hanging from his face mask. He had forgotten to put it in. He did so, and hurriedly got set again as Mitchum called for the snap—

The officials blew their whistles and ran toward the line,

waving the play dead as Mitchum dropped back. Mitchum chuckled and walked over to Julian, still standing in his place.

"Got a little nervous, eh?" he asked.

Julian shook his head and spit his mouthpiece out. "I guess they called me on moving. I forgot to put the mouthpiece in."

Mitchum nodded. "Oh."

They looked toward the referee, standing alone ten yards away from the action. "False start, on the offense, number thirty-two. The player moved after he was set. Five yard penalty, repeat first down."

"Well," Mitchum said. "Now it'll be a sixty-five-yard drive." The team huddled up while Mitchum received the play in his built-in headset. Then the quarterback leaned in. "Same play. June-Sweep Forty-five on three."

They lined up as before. Mitchum signaled for the play, called, "*Set! Hut! Hut! Hut!*"

He pitched the ball to Julian, running right behind Jenkins, the right guard, who had pulled in that direction, and the tight end; a solid wall of muscle leading the way. Julian ran patiently, following his blockers until they reached the outside of the field where they slammed into the defenders trying to seal off the right side. The blockers won the battle and forced the defense backwards.

And Julian kicked into high gear.

He burst through the opening and shot down the sideline. The free safety and the cornerback on that side were the only two players with a chance to stop him, but even though they both had a pursuit angle on him neither could close the distance. They ran after him, running desperately with their heads down, trying to keep up. But they couldn't. Julian was safely able to begin slowing down at the ten-yard line, and jogged into the end zone.

The crowd erupted into cheers. Julian made his signature casual toss of the football to the nearest official and left the field, once again on the receiving end of slaps and cheers.

On the sideline, he unbuttoned his chinstrap and took off

his helmet. Coach Kiley walked over to him, arms crossed over his chest and a big smile on his face.

"You're not even winded," he said.

Julian took a big, deep breath, and grinned at the running backs coach. "I'm in the zone today. I can feel it."

"And I can tell," Kiley said. "That's the fastest I've ever seen you run, in person or on tape. Including all those hours of college tape I watched. Awesome job."

"Thanks," Julian said.

"And that was an incredible job of setting up your blockers, following your blockers. The great running backs know that to be successful, you must have the ability to follow the blockers." Kiley sighed happily, like he was watching an old favorite movie for the first time in years. "I haven't seen someone like you in *years,* Julian."

"I guess that's a compliment."

Kiley chuckled. "It is. I know people like to compare you to Bo Jackson . . . but I have someone else in mind. You know I started in football as a ball boy for the old Cleveland Browns, don't you?"

"Yes," Julian said.

"We had a guy on our team by the name of Jim Brown." Kiley's smile widened. "Ever heard of him?"

"I might have." Julian almost laughed. Of course he'd heard of Jim Brown. Who *hadn't?* "You going to say I remind you of him?" Julian asked.

Kiley shook his head gravely. "No, I was going to say you're a little smaller, and a little faster, and just as powerful. I was going to say, you have the ability to be even better."

"That means a lot to me," Julian said. And he meant it. Warren Kiley didn't give away compliments like that every day. He had a reputation in the league as one of the best and most experienced position coaches around. He was almost a sage among the veteran running backs that Julian had come in contact with in his short professional career thus far. "Especially coming from you," Julian added.

"I appreciate it," Kiley said. A technician handed him a

sheet of paper, a computer printout. "Hey," Kiley said. "Want
to hear your stats?"

"Sure," Julian said.

Kiley almost laughed as he read off the paper: "Three runs
for eighty-nine yards, an average of almost thirty yards per
carry, one catch for twenty-six yards, and two touchdowns. A
hundred and fifteen yards total."

Despite himself, Julian whistled in amazement. "Wow," he
said, his voice cracking. "That's— that's, uh . . ." He laughed.
"That's pretty good."

He noticed Kiley looking up, a blank expression on his
face, as if he was concentrating. "The way I figure," he said,
looking back at Julian, "Since we're about five minutes into
the game, you're averaging around seventeen yards a minute.
The game is sixty minutes long, so if you keep up that pace
you'll get around a thousand yards." He laughed heartily.

"That's sick," Julian said.

"Thank God it's impossible," Kiley said.

"Yeah, I'll slow down."

Kiley smiled. "I doubt that."

He ran ten more times before halftime, and finished the
half with a hundred and thirteen rushing yards on thirteen
carries and fifty-five receiving yards on four catches, and
three touchdowns. Everyone, Julian thought, considered him
unstoppable today. *He* considered himself unstoppable today.
Like he'd said earlier, he was in a zone. The defenders seemed
to be moving in slow motion. They couldn't stop him, and it
came as a surprise when they tackled him. Three touchdowns.
Eighteen points for himself, twenty-one for the team. And
three for Jacksonville.

The Gunners received the second-half kickoff.

The ball was a short line drive, fielded by Nick Mills at the
fifteen. He dashed forward to the twenty-two, cut left away
from a tackler and turned back upfield, crossing the thirty-
five before taking a hit and going down at the thirty-seven.

Julian walked onto the field next to Mitchum, into the huddle. Mitchum looked at the players, his smile visible beneath his face mask.

"Okay, boys," he said. "They wanna go for the quick strike. Score now and they're dead. So we're gonna run the ole flea flicker. In complicated coach's terms, that is in our particular playbook, Jay-strike Zip Zero Bomb, on one."

"Break!"

They came out in I-formation, with three wide receivers, swapping the blocking of a tight end for the extra speed of a third wideout. The official blew his whistle, and Mitchum crouched behind the center. He took the snap and handed off to Julian, who stutter-stepped toward the line, spun around and pitched the ball back to Mitchum. The quarterback stepped up and launched a deep bomb down the middle of the field. Julian watched through the line as Jake Riley dove forward to catch the slightly overthrown ball. He did, grabbing it with the tips of his fingers and smoothly bringing it in to his gut as he fell across the goal line.

Mitchum gave Julian a five. "Rout's on," he said. "I almost feel sorry for them."

Julian frowned and shook his head. "I don't."

When the score flashed across the scoreboard in the stadium, Ryan whistled in astonishment: 28–3, Missouri over Jacksonville. Not that the Gunners winning was a surprise, but the fact that Julian Lloyd was supposed to be slowed by nagging injuries and the aftereffects of his damaged knee, coupled with the stingy run defense of their opposition, had seduced most oddsmakers to make them only a two-point favorite. A hard fought, close contest was the generally expected consensus.

28–3.

So much for that.

The close, hard-fought game was being played right here. New Orleans was leading now, in the third quarter, but by only two points, 22–20. The game had been a nerve-wracking shoot-out, with the lead changing several times due to long scoring plays.

Ryan watched as Ethan Daniels brought the Saint offense back onto the field at their own thirty-yard line with just under five minutes left in the third quarter. Pro set, two receivers. A generic formation.

They'd pass here, Ryan thought.

Daniels dropped back, pump-faked, looked, looked—and then the protection started to break down. A defensive tackle lumbered into the backfield and made a grab for him. Daniels rolled away, dashing sideways with the ball at his hip toward the right sideline, his eyes all the while scanning the field for an open receiver. Suddenly he stopped, set his feet and fired a pass downfield, just before the defensive tackle caught up with him and smashed him into the turf. The free safety managed to tip the ball as it sped toward an otherwise open receiver twenty yards downfield, and caused it to flop to the ground at the receiver's feet. The crowd groaned audibly.

Ryan frowned and turned to his right to see David Falk and the linebackers coach standing together, studying a piece of paper quite intently. He went over and stood next to Falk, leaning closer to see the paper. It was a printout of a photo, taken just before a play, with Falk's image circled.

"Next time they come out in this formation," the coach was saying, "think play-action. They're not going to run very often out of it. It'll be either a straight-out pass or a play-action."

"Right," Falk said.

"Uh . . ." Ryan said, reaching between Falk and the coach and touching a part of the photo with the tip of a gloved finger. "You may want to read the wide receiver, here. If he comes in, stops, and then they put the tight end in motion, it'll be a play-action. If the tight end doesn't move, it'll be a run toward his side."

The coach frowned at him. "I just said they won't run out of this formation—"

The pitch of the crowd's noise increased. Ryan turned his head rapidly to the field just in time to see the running back surge forward past the first down marker before getting forced out of bounds on the opposite side.

Ryan looked back at the coach. "Actually, you said they won't run out of the formation *very often*. I'm saying that they will. If you study enough game film on them you'll discover a trend; they'll play backwards, so to speak. Instead of running to set up play-action, they'll do play-action to set up the run. It's effective. It's really effective. So if they run a few successful play-action passes and then do what I said a second ago, they'll run a sweep behind the tight end."

Falk looked at him and grinned. "Thanks." He turned to the coach. "He might be after your job, Coach."

The man turned away in a huff. "Yeah, right. Ryan, mind your own business, will you?"

Ryan bit his lip to keep from smiling at the man. He was a good coach and a decent guy. But during the game, in the heat of battle, so to speak, he had a tendency to become upset with anyone who disagreed with him, as if they were out to sabotage his efforts.

The coach moved off, searching for the next linebacker under his charge, and Falk stood next to Ryan as they both observed the action.

"Thanks for the help," Falk said discreetly.

"It's my job," Ryan said, looking at the offense as it lined up. "I'm the old man veteran and you're the young kid replacement rookie. Right?"

"Right."

Ethan Daniels dropped back and quickly shot a pass over the middle to one of the wide receivers streaking across the middle. The receiver caught it in stride and took three steps before a defender slammed into him and knocked him cleanly to the turf.

"You saw the score of the Gunners game?" Ryan asked.

"Nasty," Falk said. "Julian Lloyd's run for a hundred-fifty some-odd yards already, I heard."

"And caught a few passes. And I think he's got two or three touchdowns."

Falk nodded. "He's a good 'back. He used to tear us up in college."

"That's right," Ryan said, fascinated by this fact. It wasn't something he had ever considered. "USC-Notre Dame. You guys played every year."

"We did," Falk said. "And like I said, he tore us up every time."

"Is he better now?" Ryan asked. "I mean, watching tape, do you think he's improved?"

"We haven't played them," Falk said. "So I'm not sure. But he does look faster and stronger than he was in college. It's just an impression. Maybe he's trying harder, since the competition is so much tougher."

"Maybe," Ryan said skeptically.

Daniels backpedaled five steps, looked over the line and passed over the middle again, but he threw behind his intended receiver, and the ball fell to the turf.

"Ethan's having an off-day," Ryan said.

"I noticed," Falk said.

Ryan grabbed his helmet. "Here we go," he said, and dashed out onto the field with the punt team.

The scoreboards were counting his stats, building the crowd to a frenzy as Julian neared the magic two hundred yard mark. It would be the first two hundred yard game of his career, and the rookie shuddered when he realized that most running backs never had two hundred yards in a game. Never.

The score was 38–3, with just two minutes fifty seconds left. The Gunners had the ball, and were handing it to Julian. Two first downs were all they needed to run the clock out and end this rout.

They lined up, with Julian alone in the backfield and three tight ends packed in tight. Mitchum waited until the play clock drained to one, using up every last second of time, before calling for the football and handing off to Julian, running through the right side. Julian lowered his shoulders and slammed forward, using brute force to gash the defense for five yards. As he stood up a second later, the scoreboard flashed in huge gold numbers: **182!**

In the huddle, Mitchum laughed beneath his helmet, just above the crowd's din. "You know," he said. "We might just have to slam you up there until you get those two hundred yards. Even if we have to give you the ball another eighteen times."

Julian looked at Mitchum dubiously, his eyes hidden behind his dark visor. "Yeah. Like I'd want that. I'd fake an injury first."

"Oh," Mitchum hooted. "Do that and the old man will *kill* you. And I ain't kidding."

"He's serious," one of the offensive linemen said. "I did that before."

"Call the play, damn it," a no-nonsense Jake Riley said.

"Right," Mitchum responded. "Okay. June-slam One-one, Hiss-one."

"Break!"

They lined up as before, and, as before, Julian waited in a casual stance while Mitchum let the clock run down. Finally, he took the snap and handed off to Julian, who slammed his body into a crease between center and guard. He pumped his legs and held both arms over the ball, and forced the line forward for three yards before getting weighed down. He hopped back to his feet immediately. The officials blew their whistles, and the referee announced that they had reached the two minute warning.

He watched the scoreboard blast the new stat: **185!**, and joined the huddle.

"I'm not even tired," he remarked. Some of the linemen, he noticed, had their hands on their hips and were gasping.

"Maybe we've been doin' all the work," a lineman said dryly.

Julian shook his head. "Usually I'm at least breathing

heavy by this time. Especially if I have thirty carries. I'm not tired."

"It's that physical freak stuff again," Mitchum said. He looked at Jake Riley and gave Julian a slight nod. "He's scary, man."

Riley just stared at the quarterback. "The play," he ordered.

"Whaddaya think it's gonna be?" Mitchum said. "A double reverse? June-slam One-two, Hiss-one."

"Break!"

They waited for several minutes until the referee signaled the restart of play, and again lined up in the tight single-back formation. Mitchum called for the ball and again handed it to Julian, who slashed through a hole between the guard and tackle on the left side. He met a linebacker shoulder-to-shoulder and was slowed as the defender wrapped him up. He drove his legs into the turf and pushed forward for five yards and a first down.

190!

The clocked ticked under a minute fifty seconds, but the beleaguered Jacksonville defense made no attempt to stop it, despite possessing two time-outs. Julian could see the looks in their eyes, the look of defeat. They had been beaten down and trodden on.

They repeated the sequence: Huddle, formation, clock drain. Mitchum handed off to Julian with a minute twenty seconds remaining, running straight up through a gaping hole in the center of the line. He cut through a pair of linebackers and burst into the secondary, pounding into successive defensive backs before relenting to the tacklers.

An eight yard gain.

198!

"That's it for them," Mitchum said in the huddle a moment later. "Coach's calling a kneel. It's over."

"I want the ball," Julian said. He shook his head, trying to clear it of the fog that had inexplicably materialized.

"We're kneeling on it," Mitchum said sternly.

"I want the ball," Julian repeated. "I want two hundred

yards." He looked up into the stands. *"They* want two hundred yards."

"Yeah," Mitchum said. "And it's *my* ass if I don't call the play they give me, not yours. Now. Let's go."

"Break!"

They lined up, and Mitchum took the snap and knelt down to the field. The defense barely moved, obviously anxious to get off the field.

Mitchum brought them quickly back into the huddle. "One more time," he said, "and then it's really over. Nice game, fellas."

"Let me get the two hundred yards," Julian said.

"Geez," Mitchum said, annoyed. "Shut the hell up, will you Julian?"

"Watch it, man," one of the offensive linemen said. "That ain't you. Calm down."

Julian looked at Mitchum, at the lineman, and took a deep breath. "Yeah. You're right." He breathed slowly, holding his arms at his sides as they lined up for the final time.

He glanced toward the sideline quickly, noticed some of the assistant coaches and backup players beginning to exit the field. They too knew it was over. As did the fans. His quick glance revealed thousands of empty seats as people left a bit early to beat the traffic, confident the game was well in hand.

"June, thirty-two!" Mitchum called at the line.

What?

An audible. A running play in I-formation to Julian.

"Slash three!"

Julian shuffled his formation, and looked into the stands to check the play clock. No problem; five seconds left.

The offense finished its quick reshuffling, and the defense barely reacted. The clock hit one, and Mitchum took the snap and handed off to Julian running through the right side. The defenders didn't touch him as he shot through a gaping hole in the line. He scampered into the secondary and pounded into the safety who groaned and dragged him down after ten easy yards.

The safety lay atop him for an extra second. "What the hell was that?" he growled into Julian's ear, his voice muffled by two plastic helmets.

Julian stood just as the game clock reached zero, to a round of applause and hip-hop blaring over the PA. The scoreboards displayed, **WE WIN!** and the music suddenly cut off.

"With that run," the announcer called over the PA, "Julian Lloyd has gone over two hundred yards for the game!" The crowd reacted joyfully, roaring in glee. "And your final score," the announcer said, "The Gunners thirty-eight, Jacksonville three."

Julian pulled his helmet off and followed his team off the field toward the tunnel. He looked around for Mitchum, and saw him near the entrance to the tunnel, walking with a stern-looking Jacob Davis. Both men walked with their eyes downcast, their moods completely opposite what one would expect after such a huge win.

They were ignoring the fans who were reaching down begging for autographs or at least some form of acknowledgment. They disappeared into the tunnel, and the fans turned their attention to Julian as he reached them. He smiled and took the game program and pen one fan was holding out for him.

Every coach and player on the sideline was standing near the field, watching intently, and the crowd was blasting the field with waves of sound. The Saints held a slim two point lead, 29–27, with a lone second frozen on the game clock. And Green Bay was going for the game-winning field goal from fifty-five yards out.

Ryan stood just behind the line, behind the two opposing walls that would meet and determine whether or not the kick ever got off the ground. No one on the special teams unit spoke. No words of encouragement or confidence. The crowd was too loud for that, God bless their faithful hearts. As if their sounds would cause enough vibrations in the air to effect the trajectory of a leather watermelon flying a hundred and fifty feet through the air.

The kicking team lined up. Ryan crouched into his stance and looked between linemen at the kicker. And for a moment, despite the ferocious noise being issued by the people in the stands, all was quiet. Adrenaline. Crunch-time.

Ryan thought, *David's faster. They should let* him *rush the kicker. Not me.*

When the moment came, it smashed the silence and suddenly the world went from slow motion to fast forward.

Smash! Grunts, groans, as the lines came together. Ryan dashed forward—but there was no surge up the middle, no hole to run through—he watched the kicker's foot pound the ball, heard a *pow!* and leaped upwards with his arms outstretched above his head.

The ball sailed inches above his fingers. He fell back to earth, whirled around and watched it float toward the distant goal posts, inching closer and closer.

It was going to be close . . . moving ever so slightly to the left . . .

The ball hit the left upright, midway up its height. The crowd held its collective breath.

It bounced sideways, and a little forward, just far enough to fall into the net behind the goalposts. The crowd fell completely silent. Ryan heard the kicking team celebrating, and looked around at his teammates as they slowly removed their helmets and trudged off the field.

The scoreboards changed, and now displayed the new 30–29 score. A one-point loss with a single second left.

Ryan reached the sideline before he took off his helmet and clutched it under his arm. A one-point loss with a second left.

The worst kind possible.

Part Four
The Last Play

Twenty-three

"We got a possible location," Cassie said, turning off her cell phone as she and Sutton slid into his car. "Regal Hotel on Memorial Drive, next to Jefferson."

They'd just stopped for lunch. They were already in town. The Regal was only a few minutes away, toward the Mississippi River from here.

"All right," Sutton said, restarting the engine, clapping his hands together and pulling back out onto the street. "Where are we? Tucker?"

"Yeah," Cassie said. "Take a right up here."

Sutton did so, and grimaced; he was forced to slow behind a wall of early afternoon traffic. The bad news with an unmarked detective's car: No siren. Maybe he should've gotten one of those stick-on FBI decals.

"We stay on this road until we hit a Radisson," Cassie said. "It'll be ahead. Then we head right, and the Regal'll be on the left."

"Uh-huh," Sutton said. He accelerated as the traffic cleared out. "So what's the story?"

"A woman checked in last night under the name of Jean Davison," Cassie said. "The clerk recognized her from the photo we released and called the municipal department first thing."

They had released a photo of "Fran" Dean to the local media with a brief statement informing the public that the former secretary of Dr. Eric Hendley was wanted for questioning. They had *not* released her real name. That would've started an unwelcome chain of events, Sutton figured. They couldn't alert HUMINT to the fact that they were really on to the scheme.

"The municipals there yet?" Sutton asked.

"Yeah," Cassie said. "They're waiting for us before they go in."

Sutton nodded. "Then let's hit it. If this damn traffic would let up . . ."

He led Cassie and two uniformed municipal cops to the second-floor room that was supposedly occupied by Jeanette Dean. Sutton knocked on the door once, waited a few seconds, then swished the room card key he'd gotten from the clerk downstairs through the lock. The light above it went green, and Sutton pushed the door open and stepped inside.

It was a normal hotel room. The bathroom was on the left, the moderately spacious bedroom furnished with a queen-sized bed and a television. The bed was made—it didn't even appear to have been slept in—and the lights were out, the curtains drawn. Everything was quiet.

Sutton slid farther into the room. There was a closed laptop computer next to the television, just sitting there. He reached for it.

"Detective," one of the cops said.

Sutton glanced at him. "What?"

"I think we should check for prints before we play with that, huh?"

Sutton held out his hand. Cassie slapped a pair of rubber gloves to his palm, and he slipped them on. "Better?"

The cop frowned and stepped back.

Sutton opened the computer. It was on; the drive whirred quietly when he touched the thumb pad. He opened the e-mail program and scanned through the inbox.

There wasn't much to see. A few personal messages, a few e-mailed resumes with "Fran" Dean's name. But the last message in the list—

"Tony," Cassie said.

"Yeah, I see it." He opened that message. The sender's name was POLLARD, L. The HUMINT guy. The content—

Sutton read it, then read it again and stood erect. He took a deep breath. "I think Miss Dean's getting cocky," he said, and tapped the screen.

He looked again as the two cops and Cassie leaned in to see.

Lloyd's a threat to GLI. Get rid of threat—soon! Pref. away from St. Louis to minimize suspicion.

Sutton sighed. "The plot thickens," he said, and gave a little smile.

"And how about Julian Lloyd?" a male voice said on the radio, sitting on the edge of Sutton's desk. "His team is undefeated through fifteen games, and he's run for seventeen hundred fifty yards. That includes ten—count 'em, *ten*—hundred yard rushing performances, two of which saw him go over two hundred yards."

Another, more mature, lazy voice answered. "He's met all expectations, to be sure, against pretty good competition. St. Louis's offensive line is solid but not spectacular, as is Rich Mitchum. Their defense is pretty good, but once again, not great. Lloyd is carrying that team on his back. Without him they would be a marginal playoff team at best. With him they might go undefeated, though both Seattle and New Orleans have pretty good defenses."

"Without him," the first voice said. "He's been on the injury report every week."

"That's right," the second said. "And some insiders have mentioned that he's having personal problems, though what that could be, I have no idea. It's not like he's having marital problems or is on drugs. Something about the entire situation in St. Louis seems strange to me. It's like the easiest fifteen-game winning streak in history. Not that there have been many of them."

"As a former player," the first voice said, "you know how

hard it is to win just one game. But fifteen in one season? And fifteen *straight?* How impressive is that?"

"It's very impressive," the second voice replied. "Especially considering the fact that, as I said before, the team without Lloyd is average from a talent aspect. We all know how one player can change a team's fortunes, but it's taken to an extreme here."

The radio clicked off.

Sutton looked up from his computer monitor to see Cassie standing before him. "Yeah," he said, giving her his full attention. "What's up?"

"Did you know that Petty has Julian Lloyd under a press gag?" Cassie asked. She leaned her weight on one leg and crossed her arms.

"I figured that," Sutton said. "Why?"

"No particular reason," Cassie said smugly. "Other than: Isn't it a little suspicious? Ya know . . . could help us. Especially if we can get Lloyd to tell us what happened."

Sutton frowned, not really seeing her point. "Okay . . ."

Cassie sighed. "You're slow, Tony."

He glared at her and leaned back in his chair. "Yeah, whatever."

She came closer, bending toward him and supporting herself with her hands on his desk. She was only a few inches away, her bob of dark hair framing her oval face. "Bait, Tony," she whispered; he could smell the scent of her peppermint chewing gum. "If Jeanette Dean is still in the area—maybe keeping an eye on things for HUMINT—whaddaya think she'd do if she heard that Julian Lloyd was going to be questioned by the cops? I mean, we already know she thinks he's a threat. So why not get her to act on her feelings when and where we want?"

Sutton's frown went upside down, forming a lopsided grin. "Ah-ha. Not bad, Cass. And I know exactly who could leak it for us."

* * *

"Question him for what?" Commander Schwarz said, his eyes narrowing.

They were sitting in his office. It was chilly—not warmed enough. Couldn't the guy get the thermostat right for once? Sutton wondered.

"He might have some information for us," Sutton said. "Something pertinent to the Hendley case."

"I don't see how that's possible," Schwartz said.

"I think Vince Petty could be involved," Sutton said. He managed to keep his face impassive. A smile wouldn't work well right now.

"How?" Schwartz demanded. "Huh? Vince Petty is a good man, Detective Sutton. I can vouch for his character. There is no way he could be involved with murder."

"A good man?" Sutton raised an eyebrow at that. "He's been indicted several times, on different charges. Malfeasance and financial impropriety. And his practices during the tobacco case weren't exactly clean."

"He was never convicted," Schwartz growled. "When you're the biggest fish . . ."

"I know, I know." Sutton waved the commander's words away. "I just wanted to let you know," he added. "I'm talking to Lloyd, no matter what you say. I'll be going down to New Orleans to meet him."

"You're a stubborn man, Detective Sutton," Schwartz said.

"Isn't he?" Cassie remarked.

Sutton glanced at her, a quick dirty look. Then he turned back to the commander. "I'll catch him before the game Monday."

It was Friday.

The game was in New Orleans.

This had better work. . . .

He was aching. He was always aching, except during a game or strenuous practice. It was as if his body was only working correctly when he was playing football.

Julian rustled around in his seat on the plane, trying to get comfortable. The flight was smooth and quiet, with the cabin lights dimmed, sunlight streaming in through a few uncovered windows. All around him, most of the players and coaches were sleeping or resting with their eyes closed. Julian was wearing headphones listening to the radio.

"Julian Lloyd," a voice was saying. "He's been having an awesome rookie campaign, with two incredible possibilities; one, an undefeated season for his team and two, a two thousand yard season for himself. Those possibilities go hand-in-hand. If Lloyd breaks two thousand yards rushing, expect his team to go 16–0. Get this: when Julian Lloyd runs for over a hundred yards—which has happened quite a lot this year—his team's average margin of victory is over seventeen points. The few times he's been held under a hundred yards, their average margin of victory is four points.

"The general consensus among experts," the voice continued, "is that the Gunners are a solid but not spectacular team, with a running back spectacular beyond comparison carrying them to one of the most dominating seasons in league history. Parity has been the rule for the last decade in football, but right now, for one team and one man, that rule has been broken.

"Julian Lloyd is a football machine—"

"That *bastard*," Julian muttered.

"—a machine that no one seems to be able to slow down. He's gotten better and faster as the season wears on, breaking a trend for rookie runningbacks, whose bodies normally rebel after ten or eleven games—the length of a college season. Lloyd's body hasn't rebelled. Quite the contrary, actually. Despite a horrific injury in a preseason mini-camp, he has exploded down the stretch.

"If you ask me—"

No one asked you, idiot.

"—the Saints have little chance of stopping the Gunners' rampage. There has been only one undefeated season in this league's modern era. Very soon, there will have been two.

"And we'll be back."

Julian tore off his headphones. "Sons of bitches," he said to himself aloud. "They're all a bunch of—"

"Julian," he heard Mitchum say, from the row behind him. "You awake?"

He whirled toward the quarterback as much as his seat allowed. "Yeah, I'm awake. Why?"

"Because I am, too, and I thought I heard you rambling deliriously in your sleep." Mitchum smiled. "What a nice, quiet, businesslike flight."

"Will you leave me alone, Rich?" Julian asked—demanded. "The last thing I need right now is a load of your philosophical bullcrap."

"If you ask me," Mitchum said, "my philosophical bullcrap is exactly what you need. What's gotten into you lately?"

"What are you talking about? I'm just being me. And I just can't stand all the bull I hear on the radio and on TV about *me.*"

"Well, you have two choices as far as that goes," Mitchum said. "You can get used to it, or ignore it. I got used to it. You see Gabe over there?" He motioned vaguely to the big fullback, in a light doze two rows up on the other side of the aisle. "He ignores it. It works. You need to make a decision."

Julian turned his face toward the quarterback. "You think I've been that bad, huh?"

"Darn tutin' you have."

"I don't know," Julian said softly. "It didn't bother me at first. Not much did, really. It was all just fun and games. Now *everything* bothers me."

"For the last month or so," Mitchum said. "I've noticed. We all have. You've been a different person. And you say you're not having problems . . ."

"None at all," Julian said.

"Then all I can tell you is, calm down off the field and keep it going on the field. You can handle it, man. Just calm down."

"I'll try," Julian said skeptically.

Mitchum nodded, patted Julian's shoulder, leaned his head

back on the seat and closed his eyes. Julian turned away and was reaching for his headphones when he heard Mitchum utter in a gravelly, high-pitched voice mimicking a certain Jedi Master: "Ohhh. Do, or do not. There is no try."

Julian was almost surprised when he didn't laugh. He frowned, put the headphones on and turned up the volume.

"I think we're going to have to put her down," Nagel said with a slight shake of his head in the direction of the animal enclosures. Cleo, the rhesus monkey, was, for once, sleeping soundly. Or so it seemed.

But Angel knew that should someone approach her, she would snap into full consciousness . . . and try to attack through the grill. She'd injured herself a couple times already, a light fracture in her right shoulder.

"Are you sure?" Angel said, taking off her surgical mask as they stepped toward the exit.

"She's a danger to herself and the handlers," Nagel said. "Really, we don't have much of a choice."

Angel nodded vaguely, feeling sick to her stomach. "Right. Well, you know best, Nick. I'll be in my office if you need me."

He nodded. "Oh, and have a nice vacation, Angel," he said. "You deserve it." She smiled and left, heading down the corridor to her private space, her home away from home. She closed the door behind her and went to her seat.

Now, another bit of business . . .

She picked up the phone and dialed Petty's number. He answered after two rings.

"Vincent Petty."

"Vince, it's Angel," she said, holding the phone tight to her ear and staring blankly ahead. "I saw something on the news about Julian. The police wanting to talk to him . . ."

"I'm not worried about it," Petty said. "I released that information to the press in order to put a bit of a spotlight on it. The police will not draw too much attention to this, not when the team is so successful. I believe they will wait until after the season is over before they actually move on it, and by then you will have taken care of the problem. Once you find a way to correct this . . . disorder, we will have nothing to worry about."

"We can't take that chance, Vince," she said quietly.

"I don't believe it is much of a chance, Angelina," Petty cooed. "I am not worried."

"I am," Angel said. "Lloyd's dangerous. Is he worth the risk?"

Petty's voice grew cold. "What are you saying?"

"Nothing, Vince," Angel said, staring through the wall. "Nothing."

And she hung up and rubbed her forehead. She needed a vacation, badly. But now it was ruined. Even though the plane ticket for this weekend was sitting in her desk, it was ruined.

But she had to do what she had to do, even if she didn't like it.

Ryan slowed behind the Airline Drive traffic. The practice facility was only up the street from here, beside Zephyr Stadium. It wouldn't be long now, even at a snail's pace. The sun was creeping higher in the sky in the early morning behind him, providing very little warmth. The little temperature gauge on his dashboard read 33. Freezing cold for southern Louisiana, even in December.

He turned on the radio, eager for some sort of company as he drove.

"The Saints and Gunners play Sunday," a light male voice said. "The two leading candidates for their respective rookie of the year awards, running back Julian Lloyd for Missouri and linebacker David Falk with the Saints, will meet for the first time since college. We all know what Lloyd has done, but why don't you explain just how much impact Falk has had with that Saints defense."

The inevitable guest expert chimed in with a deep, bored

voice. "Falk has a hundred and five tackles, five sacks and two interceptions this year. He's fast, smart, agile, and makes the most of all those abilities. The Saints really suffered with Ryan Walker playing inside linebacker in recent seasons, as he's well past his prime. But the situation has worked out well; Walker's been a force on special teams."

Past his prime, Ryan thought, chuckling. They were right, after all. Even he could see that.

"The Saints are 8–7 after their win last week," the first voice said. "If they can beat this undefeated Missouri team, they make the playoffs. But the oddsmakers have them as twelve-point underdogs, and not many people are giving them much of a chance. What do you think?"

"Well," the expert said, "obviously they have to stop Julian Lloyd. But no one has been able to do that, and there's no rea-son to expect his performance to drop off. Missouri has been vocal this week; they want to go undefeated, so they aren't going to rest anyone, despite the fact that they're assured of the division title and home field advantage throughout the playoffs. But even if you stop Lloyd, which isn't likely, you'll still have to deal with three other Pro Bowlers on offense; Rich Mitchum, Frank Moran and Jake Riley. They won't go down without a fight. And don't forget that Mitchum is protected by two Pro Bowl offensive linemen, and three others for whom arguments could be made that they deserved a berth as well."

"The defense is strong as well."

"Yes, it is. Once again, you've got multiple Pro Bowlers on the line and in the secondary. Their linebackers are solid, but not spectacular. They don't have a play-maker like David Falk back there. The difference in the game will be the Lloyd-Falk match-up."

Theme music began to play in the background. "And we'll be back—" the first voice started to say, but Ryan turned off the radio; he was pulling into the parking lot of Saints headquarters.

* * *

They were wearing only their pad shells. It was toward the end of the season, a time when coaches went easier on players in practice in order to save their exhausted bodies for Sunday's battles.

Julian's body *felt* exhausted as he lined up behind Mitchum and received a hand off from the quarterback. He tried to run through the hole on the left side, but could only jog. It was a non-contact drill, he knew. He could afford to slow down for a bit.

A coach blew his whistle, and they lined up again. Julian stretched his aching right leg before dropping into his stance. Mitchum took the snap and handed off to him. Julian jogged a little faster this time, through the hole and then came to a stop.

"Hey!" the middle linebacker called. "Snail man! Could you go any slower?"

They lined up. Julian stood in stance behind Mitchum, his eyes locked on the linebacker. Mitchum took the snap and handed the ball to him. He jogged again to the left, still watching the linebacker as he moved to fill the hole—

And cut back through the hole, exploding forward, lowering his shoulder and slamming into his completely unprepared teammate. The linebacker snapped backward and slammed hard into the grass, and Julian dashed forward a few more steps before trotting to a stop and returning to the line.

Julian could almost feel two burning holes in his back from Jacob Davis's acid glare. But the coach said nothing, and the practice resumed.

Ryan walked onto the edge of the practice field, wearing workout shorts and a team sweatshirt, shivered and placed his hands in the shirt's pockets. "Cold out here," he said to no one, watching the first team defense run drills through the steam coming out of his mouth.

"Sure is," a man said.

Ryan turned to see the team physician standing next to him. He nodded to the shorter, stockier man. "Haven't seen you out here in a while, Doc."

"I'm keeping an eye on a patient," Doc said.

Ryan turned to the field and watched the players run back and forth. "Who?"

"Look at David," Doc said, pointing toward the field.

It took Ryan a moment to find Falk among his teammates and the steam issuing from their mouths like a herd of buffalo. Sure enough, the linebacker was limping noticeably on his left leg as he shuttled left and right in a warm-up.

"What is it?" Ryan asked, concerned.

"Ankle sprain," Doc said. "He got it last week during the game. Didn't tell anyone about it then, or even during practice this week. But it's been getting worse, and I noticed it yesterday."

"Just a sprain?" Ryan asked. "He should be fine then. Right?"

"It's a pretty severe sprain, actually." Ryan searched Doc's face for signs of worry. He found none, but felt slight butterflies in his stomach anyway. "I think Gary's got him on the injury report this week," Doc said.

"Under what?" Ryan said. It was important to know; if Falk was out, Ryan was the obvious replacement. "Questionable? Probable?"

"Questionable," a voice said from behind them.

Ryan turned around to face the voice and saw Harrell standing there, his hands buried in his own pockets. "Gary," he said, nodding. "He's playing, huh?"

"If it's up to him," Harrell said. "He's adamant about it. Says it's just a twisted ankle, that he played through them when he was twelve, so why not now."

"The other guy didn't weigh three hundred pounds when he was twelve," Ryan said, frowning.

"I told him that. But then he said that the three-hundred-pound men haven't been able to catch him yet this year, and that they won't catch him this game, either."

Ryan chuckled. "He's starting to learn how to be a complete player," he said. "Mouth and all."

"Yeah," Harrell said coldly. "He can keep the mouth." The coach smiled despite his tone.

Ryan smiled. "Hey, he's a middle linebacker. You need to be vocal at that position."

"Right," Harrell said. "As long as you back it up on the field."

Ryan nodded. "And David has done that."

"Most definitely." Harrell walked onto the field. "Get ready for second-team drills, Ryan," he said, moving away.

Ryan nodded. "I'll see you later," he told Doc, and jogged back to the building. As he stepped inside, into warmth, he allowed his worry to overcome him.

Julian Lloyd. Seventeen hundred rushing yards. Twenty-two hundred total yards. Twenty touchdowns. Speed, strength and agility beyond compare. *Julian Lloyd against Ryan Walker.* He shivered, and went inside the locker room.

Twenty-four

Sutton carried his bag and walked through the terminal of Louis Armstrong International Airport. On either side, surrounding him beneath a canopy of world flags and amidst a flurry of bustling travelers, was a bunch of small shops. Local shops, most of them; they displayed specialty hot sauce and dried red beans, and knit blankets and rugs with images of crawfish and crabs. There was a little restaurant-style café selling those doughnuts with no holes, and some kind of coffee, but Sutton swept past all of it and went outside. He passed what looked like a passenger drop-off area, and found a small row of yellow cabs across a lane of traffic. He placed his bag on the ground and pulled his coat tighter around him. The sun was setting, and taking its warmth with it. It wasn't freezing—at least by his standards—but it was cold enough to bother him.

There weren't many taxis around here, he noticed, and wondered why. Chicago, New York—cabs covered the streets in those cities like cockroaches in the kitchen with the light turned off. Here they were sparse. He crossed the lane and came to the first taxi in line. The driver, a lanky black man who looked to be in his late forties, got out and went to the trunk, opened it.

"You can put your bag in here," he said pleasantly.

"Okay." Sutton did so, and got in the back seat.

"Where to?" the man asked, sitting down in the driver seat.

"Uh . . ." Sutton dug a slip of paper out from his coat pocket and read the name of the hotel to the driver, who nodded politely and started the car on its way.

"You ever been down here before?" the driver asked.

"To New Orleans?" Sutton said. "No. First time."

"Well," the driver said. "Welcome. Nice to have you."

"Thanks."

"Where you from?"

"St. Louis," Sutton said.

"Really," the driver said, and Sutton heard derision in the man's voice. "Here for the game?"

"Actually, yes," Sutton said. It wasn't a lie, not exactly. Lloyd was in New Orleans for the game, and Sutton was in New Orleans for Lloyd, so . . .

"Well, I won't hold that against ya." the man said. "You mind if I listen to a little radio?"

I could use some music, Sutton thought. "No problem," he said.

The driver turned the radio on to something AM, just as a show's theme music ended. "Hello, and welcome to the show," a deep-voiced host said. "Well, the big weekend is about to start. The Saints and Gunners will meet on national television Monday night. Missouri is fighting for an undefeated season, and New Orleans is fighting for a playoff berth."

The driver turned the radio volume low. "You a big Gunners fan?"

"Not huge," Sutton said. "But I do follow them."

"Well, that's okay." He laughed. "You wouldn't imagine how much bull I gotta put up with when I drive big-time fans in. All they do is talk big about that team. Pain in the butt, ya know."

"I bet."

"Yep."

Sutton thought for a moment. "The Saints are pretty big down here, it seems." He looked out at other cars, seeing a Saints team flag stuck to what looked like every other one.

The driver laughed heartily. "Considerin' their history, people get surprised when they see the love, if you know what I mean."

Sutton nodded.

"And going to the playoffs—that's big news, if it can happen." Sutton could see the man looking him over in the mirror. "You don't have any Gunners stuff, do you? Hats and shirts, I mean."

"No. Why?"

"Because you wouldn't want to wear anything like that down in the Quarter this week. You might get beat up. They got some wackos who get drunk and take it out on Gunners fans." The man winked at him in the rearview mirror.

Sutton laughed. "Thanks for the warning."

"You shoulda seen what happened when they talked about movin' the team a while back," the driver said. "The whole city—heck, the whole region—hit a stand-still. The Saints got a followin' all the way from Texas to Florida, ya know. We got scared."

"I can imagine."

The car slowed and parked beside a building. Sutton looked out the window; they were at the hotel. "Thanks for the ride," he said, pulling out his wallet and handing the driver the required amount.

"No problem," the man said. "Have a nice stay."

Sutton smiled at him, got out, went around to the trunk, which the driver popped open from inside the car. He hefted his bag, closed the trunk and stepped onto the curb. The driver waved, and drove away.

He yawned and looked up at the three flags hanging on the awning over the door: an American flag, Louisiana state flag, and New Orleans Saints team flag. He went inside the hotel, checked in at the front desk and went up to his room.

He closed the door behind him, dropped his bag, grabbed the TV remote, lay back on the bed and turned the television to ESPN.

The screen displayed an image of Julian Lloyd running through a defense; highlights from the week before, the Gunners' blowout 52–14 win over Carolina. Sutton groaned, turned the television off, tossed the remote away and closed his eyes.

* * *

He walked down the tranquil streets of the French Quarter the next morning, beneath a cloud-filled gray sky. It wasn't all that crowded, and he found himself walking slowly, admiring the museum-like architecture and little shops and restaurants. So *this* was the "European" part of New Orleans that was so famous.

Above him flew dozens of Saints flags, coupled with a few bearing the imprint of the city's NBA team—it was obvious where the loyalties of the people of this city lay. He came to a small bookstore window and stopped before it. On the display stand were the current bestsellers, as well as what looked like a few local books, one proudly displaying a fleur-de-lis and claiming to be the "single most comprehensive source of Saints information and statistics in the world."

He stepped inside the store and scanned through some of the books. Pretty good selection, he noticed, for such a small place.

"Hello, sir."

He turned to see a clerk standing beside him. "Hi."

"Can I help you?"

Sutton shook his head. "Not with the books. But is there a restaurant close by that you recommend?"

"Sure. Go right down the street, two blocks, and take a right. It's on the corner. Mesparro's. Nice place." The clerk looked at him, seeming to size him up. "And the action is on the other side of the Quarter, on Bourbon. If you're looking for it, that is."

Sutton smiled. "No thanks."

Julian picked listlessly at the food on his plate, sitting alone at the table in the hotel restaurant. Or so he thought.

"Hey, Julian," Mitchum said, setting his plate down and sitting across from his teammate. "What's up, man?"

Julian shrugged, and did not answer.

"You look like crap," Mitchum said. "So obviously some-thin's on your mind."

Julian studied his plate for a moment longer, then looked up at the quarterback. "Yeah. Something's on my mind."

Mitchum forked a bite of baked chicken into his mouth and drained it with a sip of water. "Okay. That's pretty general-ized. You need to get a little more specific before Dr. Mitchum can help."

"Maybe I don't want your help!" Julian snapped.

Mitchum frowned and set down his fork. "I think you do. Big time. Tell me what's wrong."

Julian sighed and closed his eyes. "I was talking to my mother a few minutes ago. She got on my nerves, and I got angry. And *she* hung up on me."

"What did you do?"

Julian slammed his fork down with a clang. "Why does everyone assume that *I* did something? I didn't do *anything*. I called to talk to her, and she ended up hanging up on me. And I *needed* to talk to her!"

"You can talk to me," Mitchum offered.

Julian laughed sadistically. "Yeah right, Rich. That would look really good. Put me on the couch, why don't you. All you need are the ugly glasses and the suit."

"Man to man," Mitchum said. "Like brothers."

"You're not my brother," Julian said. "And I don't want anything to do with you. Understand?"

Mitchum stood, and picked up his plate. "Yeah, I under-stand. Maybe you'd rather be alone."

Julian nodded. "Yeah. As a matter of fact, I would."

Mitchum shrugged. "No problem, man. That's fine." He turned and walked away without another word.

"Bed check!"

Davis knew he was a disciplinarian, and personal bed checks were a big part of that discipline. He walked through the hotel hallway and banged on each door with his fist until the men inside acknowledged his knocks.

He came to the room that Jimmy Haynes and Julian Lloyd were sharing, and knocked hard on it. No answer. He knocked again, and was about to do so a third time when the door was pulled open from the inside.

Haynes stood there in boxer shorts and a T-shirt, a short, powerfully built young black man. He looked at his coach tiredly. "He ain't here, Coach."

"Where is he?" Davis demanded, not entirely surprised.

"I don't know," Haynes said. "He went out about an hour and a half ago, said he would be back. He wouldn't say where he was going."

"Curfew's ten," Davis said. "He knows that."

"Yeah."

"All right, Jimmy," Davis said. He patted the shorter man's shoulder and stepped back. "Get some sleep."

Julian took a long drink from his beer bottle and set it down, staring at the television mounted on the wall above the corner of the bar. He checked the clock beside the TV— 10:05 P.M. He was past curfew.

He drained the last of the beer, slid the bottle away from him and leaned forward. "Hey," he called to the bartender. "Give me another." The bartender wordlessly set another bottle in front of him and moved away.

Julian looked around, scanning the walls on which were mounted pictures of Saints players in action, framed jerseys autographed with player names, past and present, and one general color scheme: black and gold. The people here really were obsessed with the losers, Julian thought.

He took another swallow.

There weren't that many people in here at this late hour. A man sitting alone at a table sipping a beer, a young woman who looked vaguely familiar across the room in a booth, a group of tough-looking white guys at the other end of the bar—

One of the guys was looking at him, as if recognizing someone he'd been trying to remember for some time. Julian met his gaze for an instant, and the guy tapped one of his buddies on the arm and started to move in Julian's direction.

Julian turned away and took another sip. When he looked back, the guy was standing right next to him.

"You're Julian Lloyd," he said loudly, his speech slurred. His breath stank of bad beer and old whiskey.

Julian didn't answer. He looked away and reached for his bottle—

"I *said,*" the guy repeated, taking Julian's hand in a vice grip, "you're Julian Lloyd."

Julian pushed the guy's cold hand off and stood from the barstool, feeling anger course through his veins like acid. "So what?" he demanded, right in the guy's face.

The guy laughed, and Julian wrinkled his nose at the stink of his breath. "I always knew you was jus' another nig—"

A hard right fist to the jaw shut him up and sent him spinning around, slamming into the bar where he managed to get his balance, sweeping several glasses onto the floor. Julian glared at him, rubbing his aching knuckles.

The guy wiped a trickle of blood from his lip with his jacket sleeve, got shakily to his feet and, ignoring the pleas of his comrades behind him, charged Julian with a shout.

Julian side-stepped him and sent a fist smashing down onto his back. The guy sprawled across an empty table, sliding off and dropping to the floor. He leaped back to his feet in a drunken rage and dove straight into Julian, this time connecting and pushing him back painfully into the bar. They wrestled around for a couple seconds, until the guy's buddies grabbed his shoulders and pulled him away.

Julian got back upright and jumped forward, slamming his own body into the guy and his compatriots. They all went down in a tangle of bodies, Julian punching and hitting at anyone he felt, unable to control himself, unable to care.

Suddenly he was lying on his back, and the guys were kicking his stomach and landing punches on his face. Someone pulled him to his feet and pinned his arms behind him, and the first guy pounded his face with a hard fist to the nose.

He ripped his arms free, whirled around and grabbed the guy who had been holding him, whipping him forward and sending him flying across the room into a table. He ducked another man's punch and slammed two jabs into his stomach. The man fell backwards and landed on the floor in a heap. The first guy threw a punch, missed, and Julian grabbed his arm and twisted it back against itself. The guy shouted in agony and fell to his knees—

Julian stepped back toward the door and took in the scene. Tables lay broken, glass was shattered across the floor and three men lay writhing in pain. He turned away from it all and stepped out into the night.

Sutton drank his beer, keeping an eye on Lloyd as the football player hunched over a barstool.

Even if Cassie's original plan—drawing Jeanette Dean out—didn't work, Sutton would still have the chance to question Lloyd, and depending on what Lloyd said, that conversation could provide enough of a reason to have the DA nab GLI and Vince Petty. And ruin HUMINT's—and consequentially, Jeanette Dean's—day entirely. It was a win-win—

A crash and the sound of shattered glass interrupted his thoughts. He turned just in time to see a big white man charge Lloyd at the bar. He started to get up, to try and stop the fight, but changed his mind; this wasn't the time to get involved, not when Lloyd was like this . . . Sutton stayed in his seat, trying to remain inconspicuous, and watched with intent fascination as the brawl unfolded. Lloyd took on all three of the men at once, taking a beating but dishing out a lot more than he was receiving.

Finally, with his enemies lying on the barroom floor, Lloyd staggered outside. Sutton stood, slapped the first bill he found in his wallet on the table and followed him.

Outside, the street was dark and quiet. The only person in sight was Lloyd, walking slowly away.

"Julian!" Sutton called.

Lloyd whirled around in shock, saw Sutton, turned back around and started to move quickly away from him.

Who the hell was that guy? Julian wiped blood from beneath his nose and moved at almost a run down a sidewalk toward a brightly lit parking lot that seemed all too distant. He looked back and saw the man still on his tail.

He reached the parking lot and entered it. He stopped, looked up and saw several low, wide buildings. Looked like a mall, he thought, and read the big sign on the front: *Riverwalk.*

He ran toward the entrance, up a big railed ramp, and went inside. It was a mall, all right. He moved more slowly now, to his right, toward a food court. He looked back again—

Just in time to see his pursuer come through the entrance.

He turned and went straight through the place, through another door and burst outside onto a huge concrete dock, long and wide, next to the mall and above the Mississippi River.

The air was freezing cold, and the wind whipped around his jacket, coming in off the river, making it seem even colder. His hands were numb, and his ears felt like little blocks of ice. His breath came in ragged gasps; puffs of steam hovered around his face. Across the river, the lights of the city blended with the stars in the clearing sky. Ships rumbled by, slicing through the still waters.

He walked slowly, close to the railing on the side of the dock. He looked back several times to see if he was still being pursued. He passed a dark, empty riverboat, benches and picnic tables.

He looked back again.

There he was!

The man was following him at a distance of around fifty feet, trying to blend in innocently with his surroundings but at the same time moving too quickly to do so. A female bystander got hastily out of his way and disappeared into an alley.

Julian accelerated to a run again, pumping his legs despite the pain he felt.

What the hell was he doing, trying to chase down the best running back in professional football? Was he crazy? Sutton knew he had never been known for his speed. On the department flag football team he was the quarterback, not because he had an especially strong arm, but because he was no good anywhere else.

He managed to keep Lloyd in sight, and watched him turn a sharp corner. He clenched his fists and ran that way as fast as he possibly could.

Julian slid to a stop. There was someone in the alley—someone was blocking his route—a diminutive silhouette that he couldn't identify—he whirled around, and started back the way he'd come—he heard a click, like someone cocking a gun—

Sutton rounded the corner and leaned against the wall, breathing heavily.

"Stop!" he said, gasping. "I just want to ask a few questions!"

Before he had a chance to react, Lloyd charged past him, slamming halfway into him with incredible force, knocking Sutton backwards—and then rounding the corner—

POW! Loud, piercing, like a firecracker—

Law enforcement instincts clicked in. Sutton flung himself backwards, using his momentum, and steadied his body against the side of the building.

—slow motion—

He reached under his jacket for the nine millimeter semi

strapped to his chest, whipped it out and pulled it up, aiming into the alley—

POW! POW! POW!

A sudden pressure in his left shoulder—an all too familiar pain—he dropped his left arm, but held his pistol up in his right hand, and finally got a look at the assailant, but it was too dark to make an identification—

Who cared?

The world sped into fast-forward, and Tony Sutton squeezed off six rapid shots straight into the attacker's form. The silhouette fell backwards, slamming into the slimy, trash-covered concrete ground.

Sutton slid to the ground, wincing against the burning pain in his left shoulder, beginning to feel a bout of nausea. *I hope that isn't an artery,* he thought, somewhat cynically, and concentrated on breathing for a moment. He covered the wound with his left hand and held his pistol in his right. He forced himself to get back to his feet and make his way forward, to identify the body, to make sure it was really Jeanette Dean. He knelt down beside the woman and looked close—

His breath caught in his throat. Despite the darkness, he was close enough to make out the person's features.

It was a woman all right . . . a woman with blond hair, and olive skin, and an athletic build, wearing a sweatshirt and jeans, three red holes in her chest . . .

He put his gun away, pulled out his phone, and dialed, his eyes transfixed to the lifeless, shocked expression on Dr. Angelina Moore's face.

Twenty-five

"Hello, everyone, I'm Neil Worthen, and this is my partner in crime, former pro football running back Marshall McMurry." Worthen and McMurry sat high above the artificial turf field of the Superdome in the TV press box, just beginning the coverage of the Monday night prime time game between Missouri and New Orleans. "Marshall, these are two teams with a lot to play for," Worthen said in what he always considered his *pleasant conversational tone.* "The Gunners are looking to have an extraordinary undefeated season, and the Saints are fighting for their playoff lives."

"Well," McMurry said in his deeper, more colorful voice, "I would definitely call the Gunners' accomplishment this year *extraordinary.* But one thing I wouldn't call it is unprecedented. Julian Lloyd has lived up to all the draft hype—and more. He is without a doubt the heart and soul of this football team. And as for the Saints, they have an outstanding rookie of their own. David Falk has been making plays up and down the field all year long. He's already being mentioned in the same sentences as some of the top linebackers in the league, and if you ask me, he deserves all the accolades."

"How much of a chance, though, do you give this Saints team tonight?" Worthen asked, sticking to the script.

"It's a classic case of the unstoppable force meeting the immovable object in Lloyd and Falk, respectively," Marshall said. "But the advantage will, in my opinion, lie with Lloyd if for no other reason than he's amazingly healthy for a running back this late in the year. Falk has been hobbled by that ankle sprain; it could cause him to be half a step slower tonight in some key situations. And I know better than most just how much a half a step can cost you."

Worthen nodded to the camera. "We'll return after these messages, for the coin toss."

The video feed cut off, and Worthen stretched his already tired arms, laying his microphone down on the table set up beside him. "You making a bet on the game?" he asked McMurry.

"Of course," the former running back smiled. "Fifty dollars says Julian Lloyd blows New Orleans out of the water."

"Deal," Worthen said, and shook his partner's hand.

Julian sat behind most of his teammates on the bench, waiting quietly for the coin toss. He wasn't sore right now, thank God, except for a very slight headache that came to him off and on. No problem. He could play through that easily. Anything after last night . . . whatever had happened . . .

He shook his head, trying to clear it of the cobwebs sticking to him. Sitting back here alone; it wasn't hard. It was what he wanted, to be alone, and his teammates seemed all too happy to grant him that wish in recent weeks. That was fine, perfectly fine.

He saw Mitchum standing at the other end of the long bench, the quarterback's head bent slightly downward as he drank water from an overly full paper cup, watching him out of the tops of his eyes. Then he turned away and rejoined his offensive teammates up on the edge of the sideline.

Ryan walked with Ethan Daniels and David Falk to the center of the field to meet the captains of the other team, and the referee, for the coin toss.

They all met there, and waited for a moment while the television crews caught up. Then the referee held a large coin out in the palm of his hand and displayed the two sides. "This is heads"—he flipped it over—"this is tails. Gunners will call it."

"Heads," Rich Mitchum said quietly as Ryan observed.

The referee flipped the coin up into the air and let it hit the turf. He bent over and reached for it. "It is heads," he called, and picked it up. "Kick or receive?" he asked, looking at Mitchum.

"Receive," Mitchum said.

The ref looked at Ethan Daniels, but he stepped back and allowed Ryan to answer the question. "Which will you defend?"

"This is fine," Ryan said, indicating the side on which he was currently standing.

"Missouri has won the toss," the referee said after activating his microphone, "and will receive." He clicked the mike off. "Good luck, gentlemen."

The captains shook hands, and Ryan led his teammates off the field, then returned with the special teams unit. He got into position, and sighed in an attempt to calm himself.

It was, after all, only a game.

"The referee signals the start of the game," Worthen said, "and we are underway. The opening kickoff is a nice one, down to the goal line." He watched Nick Mills vault a tackle attempt and scoot down to the thirty-five, where a shoelace grab prevented him from breaking the return open. "A nice return by Mills," Worthen said. "Tripped up at the thirty-five by Ryan Walker. First and ten for Missouri, as Rich Mitchum, Julian Lloyd and company lead their offense onto the field to meet David Falk's defense."

The Gunners lined up in I-formation. "Mitchum takes the snap . . ." Julian received the handoff, running up the middle and pushing forward for three yards. "Three yard gain by Lloyd up the middle on first down. He was met by one of the safeties. Second and seven from the thirty-two."

They lined up again, this time with the backs split behind Mitchum. "Pro formation this time," Worthen observed.

"That's Mitchum's bread and butter," McMurry said. "Look for the pass to Frank Moran here."

Mitchum dropped back and looked for a receiver. . . . "Indeed, he passes over the middle to Moran, upended close to the first down marker by David Falk."

"Falk was in coverage there," McMurry said. "It'll be interesting to see if they do that often. They really need Falk to stuff Lloyd's running."

"If at all possible," Worthen said.

"Exactly," McMurry said.

Julian lined up, this time by himself in the backfield, as Gabe Jenkins had been rotated out of the lineup in favor of a third wide receiver. Mitchum used a silent count due to the roaring crowd. He took the snap, dropped back. Julian stepped forward, hesitated next to him, and then he took the slightly extended ball from his quarterback and slashed through a gaping hole into the secondary before getting tackled up at the fifty yard-line for an eleven-yard gain on third and one.

The crowd fell silent.

Pass coverage! Ryan thought. How could they commit Jordan to pass coverage when they needed to stop Lloyd?

It wasn't his place to question the coaches, he knew, biting his tongue to keep from shouting his thoughts in the defensive coordinator's direction. *They must have a plan,* he thought.

Yeah, a sardonic interior voice told him. *They have a plan. Maybe if you let them get ahead by thirty points they'll get overconfident. You ought to try it.*

"Shut the hell up," Ryan growled to himself.

Pro formation once again, with Julian and Jenkins split behind Mitchum. The quiet crowd gave Mitchum the chance to use a long count full of decoy phrases in an attempt to draw a defender offsides. No one budged. Mitchum took the snap, dropped back five steps, and Julian moved forward and to the left.

Just in time.

A blitzing outside linebacker sped into the backfield, with his sights set on a sack. Julian got low and drove his body into the blitzing defender, stopping his progress and driving him backwards just long enough for Mitchum to fire a rocket pass into the coverage zone vacated by the linebacker. Julian released his block and watched Jake Riley catch the ball on the run and turn upfield. He passed the forty, the thirty, streaked downfield to the twenty-three before David Falk and a cornerback managed to catch him on an angle and drive him out of bounds.

No celebration. All business.

They moved up to the new line of scrimmage and formed a huddle.

For Pete's sake.

Blitz David! He's your playmaker!

Ryan chewed at the inside of his mouth, standing on the sideline with his teammates, watching as the starting defense was dissected.

Okay, he thought, trying to calm himself again. *It's early. Nothing's happened yet. We're okay.*

On the twenty-three, the Gunners broke their huddle and came to the line. The crowd tried to build up a roar, but the big play had sucked the excitement out of the Dome. Ryan could feel its absence, like the vacuum of space.

Snap—Mitchum pitched the ball to Lloyd, running right off the tackle on that side. He had a guard in front of him, who impacted with Falk, driving him away from the play. Lloyd juked another linebacker and sped down the sideline, slamming straight into a defensive back at the five yardline and pushing him backwards into the endzone.

"Touchdown, Gunners," the PA announcer said glumly.

Geez. Give David some help out there, defense!

* * *

"Clyde Brown kicks off for the Gunners," Worthen said. "They lead by seven. The ball is fielded at the three . . ." The return man got to the fifteen, where he was swarmed over by tacklers. "Gets to the fifteen and no further. So Ethan Daniels and the Saints offense will have quite a bit of work to do to stay in this game."

"Sick!" Falk said. "Absolutely sick!" He stood next to Ryan on the sideline, clutching his helmet by the face mask, holding it at his side.

"Those things happen," Ryan said. "It wasn't your fault."

"If I'd have been able to shed that block—"

"How much do you weigh?" Ryan cut him off.

"Weigh?" Falk asked, as if confused by the question. "Uh . . . about two-forty. Why?"

"Because that guard weighs three-thirty and benches six hundred pounds," Ryan said. "Once he's on you, it's over."

Falk nodded. "Then next time, he won't get on me."

"Good attitude," Ryan said. Now all they needed was for the coaches to turn the kid loose. David Falk would never blame a coach for a mistake. It was always something *he* did, something *he* messed up.

Ah, the naivete. So young and innocent.

That isn't exactly the way it works in the real world, David.

"We'll see what the Saints have up their sleeves," Worthen said. "First and ten, from the fifteen yardline."

"They've been pretty conservative on defense," McMurry said. "I'd expect the same on offense right now. Though it isn't the best plan when you're going against a monster like the Gunners."

"Daniels drops back," Worthen said. The quarterback pumped once, then launched a bomb high into the air down the left sideline, directly in front of the Saints bench. "Going deep . . ." Worthen called as the ball arced downward. "And . . . *caught!* It's caught by the receiver running free down the sideline." The crowd was suddenly alive, roaring, and the players on the sideline were jumping up and down, egging the receiver on. "To the forty! Thirty! Twenty! Changes direction, running away from a defender, turning to the right—ten, five touchdown! An eighty-five yard touchdown strike on the Saints' first play from scrimmage in this game!"

"I think," McMurry said, sounding almost disappointed, "that we may be in for a war tonight."

"I think you're right," Worthen agreed, a twinkle in his eye.

"Now we're talking!" David shouted, his voice barely audible above the crowd.

Ryan nodded his acknowledgment, not trusting his voice to get loud enough to be heard over this raucous din in a reply.

Let's just keep it up.

Nick Mills took the kickoff and made it up to the thirteen-yard line. Ryan slammed into the smaller player and smashed him to the turf. He got up, gave a scream of triumph, pumped his fists and left the field.

Rich Mitchum dropped back later on the drive, pump-faked and tossed the ball out on a five-yard route to Jake Riley. Riley juked David Falk, turned upfield and gained fifteen before the two safeties combined to bring him down.

From the goal line, Julian took a handoff and followed Gabe Jenkins into the end zone, pounding into a defender and reaching across the goal line with the ball.

On the ensuing kickoff, the Saints return man reached the fifty. Ethan Daniels threw five straight completions, the last a beauty of a catch by the tight end in the corner of the end zone for a touchdown.

Worthen said a while later: "To recap: It's been a tough, physical game thus far, accented with several big plays on both sides. We're now toward the end of the second quarter, with the Gunners holding a slim three point lead over the Saints, 20–17.

"The Saints have the ball with forty-five seconds left in the half and one time-out remaining. They have a good fifty yards before they reach field goal range."

"Ethan Daniels can make plays, though," McMurry said, not sounding all that happy about the fact. "Don't be shocked if the Saints take some shots here."

"They come to the line with four wide receivers," Worthen said. "Daniels takes the snap, drops back . . . pump fake . . . throws to the right . . . caught, and the receiver runs out of bounds to stop the clock. Ten yard gain."

"Nice play calling and execution there," McMurry said. "Make the catch, get out of bounds. That's a fifth of the yardage you need, and you only use up five seconds."

"Forty seconds left on the clock," Worthen said. "And remember; they still have a timeout. Shotgun formation now. Snap—pass over the middle caught by the receiver running the slant, and he's got the first down and more. Eighteen yard gain. The clock keeps running."

"It's down below thirty-five seconds now," McMurry said. "They may not try to stop it here."

"Doesn't look like it," Worthen agreed. "Daniels takes the snap and passes to the right—caught, and out of bounds. Eight yards."

"They're almost in field goal range with twenty-three seconds left," McMurry said. "Good clock management."

"Daniels in the shotgun again. He seems to work well out of that formation. Snap. He's under a bit of a rush, rolls away from it and now throws . . . *caught*. The receiver's brought down after a gain of fifteen! Clock continues to run. Now they come to the line and spike the ball with ten seconds remaining."

"Enough time to take a shot at the end zone," McMurry said.

"Daniels heads to the sideline to talk it over with his coach," Worthen said. "That's exactly what they're going to do. Oh, he's already heading back onto the field."

"Quick chat."

"Obviously. Shotgun formation again. Snap—they run the draw, and get a bit of a hole up the middle. That'll be a nine yard gain, and it puts them in better position for the field goal. They call the timeout with three seconds left. Why don't you try for a score there, Marshall?"

"Well," McMurry said, "When you're up against a team like the Gunners, and Julian Lloyd has gashed you for ninety-seven yards in the first half, you don't make a mistake that leaves points on the table. Here you have a chance to tie it up going into the half, and you don't want to screw that up by throwing one up for grabs."

"It'll be an attempt of thirty-eight yards," Worthen said. "Snap is back. And the kick is up and through. So the Saints tie the game at twenty as time expires in the half. Now we'll go down to our sideline reporter Allie Grogan, who is standing by with Saints coach Gary Harrell . . ."

Harrell finished speaking with the reporter just as Ryan passed him on his way to the locker room.

"How do we look?" Harrell asked, walking with him.

"You're asking me?" Ryan said.

"Yeah."

Ryan shrugged. "Pretty good. We gave up some big plays, but got some, too. Had a few penalties, but so did they. One turnover here, one turnover there. It's even so far."

Harrell nodded and started to jog away from him. "Let's keep it that way," he said over his shoulder.

"Definitely," Ryan said, and followed him.

Julian looked up at the scoreboard as Nick Mills and the punt return team took to the field: 26–20. They were *losing* 26–20 and had been shut out thus far in the second half. And he had been held to a meager twenty-seven yards, seven in the fourth quarter, while the defense had allowed a pair of field goals. This wasn't the way it was supposed to happen. Mitchum and his *idiots* had obviously lost control of the situation.

Seven minutes remained.

The punt sailed all the way to the five-yard line and bounced backwards to the ten, where it was covered by Saints defenders.

Seven minutes to journey ninety yards and score a touchdown; a field goal wouldn't do.

He slipped his helmet on and jogged toward the field. He passed the offensive coordinator as he went, and looked the man in the eye. "Give me the ball," he said, and joined the huddle.

He still wasn't very sore—of course not, his body was warmed up and active—but his head was starting to ache and his entire lower body was hurting slightly, like a mild case of the flu. Not at all like muscle fatigue.

Forget about it, he thought. *Just forget about it. Nothing's wrong.*

"It's been quite a game so far," Worthen said. "And something tells me it isn't over yet, not by any means."

"I certainly hope not," McMurry said.

"Lloyd comes out as the lone setback," Worthen said. "I expect they'll try to pass in order to conserve time for another drive, should it become necessary."

"I don't know," McMurry said. "Your best player is Julian Lloyd. I say you give it to him."

"They do give it to Lloyd on a pitch to the left side. He'll be met by Falk and tackled after squeaking through a hole and gaining five yards."

"I get the feeling we'll see a lot of him during this drive," McMurry said. "A heck of a lot."

They ran the ball with Julian on almost every play; when they didn't, he caught it or made a key block. This was *his* drive and *his* team and no one else was going to take either away from him. Certainly not the opposing defense. Not even Rich Mitchum.

He heard the PA announcer croon: "First and ten for the Gunners at the New Orleans thirty."

He checked the scoreboard time: 1:58 left, and they had two timeouts. Plenty of time. *Plenty* of time.

"David's hurting out there," Ryan said to Harrell, standing beside the coach as they watched the game unfold. The young linebacker was limping between plays, and not flying to the ball as he usually did. And that was allowing Julian Lloyd to march the Gunners down the field seemingly at will.

Harrell glanced at Ryan. "What do you want me to do?" he asked in an exasperated tone. "He's the best we've got."

Ryan didn't want to go in. He hadn't meant to imply that. But his coach's expression of a lack of faith in a veteran player of sixteen seasons . . . *It's the best choice we've got. Is David Falk at twenty-five percent better than me at a hundred percent?*

He noticed Harrell's apologetic expression. "Look, Ryan, I'm sorry—"

They turned to the field as the play began. Lloyd took a handoff and slammed up the middle of the defense, breaking a tackle at the line and juking Falk. The strong safety saved a touchdown by tackling him for a twelve yard gain. The Gunners ran a no-huddle offense, and they scrambled back to the line into formation. Snap—and another handoff, this one to Lloyd around the right side—

Julian outdistanced the defensive line to the edge and started to turn his momentum upfield, but his path was blocked by that frigging linebacker again, who had come limping—*limping,* for heaven's sake!—across the field to tackle him.

He was limping on his left ankle.

Julian ran out of sideline, and dove forward, slamming his mass into the linebacker's legs.

"Oh, *crap,*" Harrell breathed, and followed the trainers out onto the field in an almost panicked rush.

Ryan strained to get a better look, but David Falk was laying on the turf, surrounded by players and trainers. There was a lot of motion over the scene for a moment, and Ryan heard shouting—and Rich Mitchum came out of the group dragging a screaming Julian Lloyd along.

Harrell came walking back, his eyes half-closed in what looked like deep concentration. He shook his head slowly to himself.

"What is it?" Ryan asked.

"The ankle," Harrell said. "Could be broken."

"What's going on with Lloyd?" He watched as Mitchum tried to calm the rookie halfback down, without much apparent success.

"Who knows?" Harrell said. "Success has gotten to his head. He's become a psycho. I talked to the refs, but they said it was accidental, the assholes." He huffed, and put his hands on his hips. "I . . . I don't know what to do. For once, I just don't know."

Ryan turned to the coach, feeling a confidence that hadn't

resided within him for a very long time. "I can do it," he said. "I promise I can do it."

"Do what?" Harrell snapped, glaring at him. "Fill in space? Sure you can. But you need to be able to run Lloyd down from across the field. They're going to attack the perimeters. You can't do it, Ryan. I'm sorry."

Ryan lowered his eyes to Harrell's level, and stared into them. The coach looked away. "Listen to me," he said, whispering over the silent crowd. "I'm your backup inside linebacker. That's my job. And I would appreciate it very greatly if you would let me do it. You always treat me special, like a coach on the field. Well, now I don't want special treatment. I want, for one last time, to get out there and make a play. One last play. I've got it in me, Gary. You just need to allow me to let it out."

Harrell returned his stare, then let his eyes sink. "All right, Ryan. Get out there."

He needed no further encouragement. Ryan grabbed his helmet and ran onto the field, first going to check on Falk. He came to a trainer. "How is he?"

"Don't know," the trainer said. "We won't know until we do the X rays."

The crowd gave a round of applause as Falk was lifted to his feet and assisted off the field by the two trainers. He dwarfed the men, but they supported his weight with a practiced ease. The field cleared, and Ryan gathered his defense together in a huddle across the line of scrimmage.

He looked each man in the eyes, through helmets and face masks, and tried to project his aura of confidence. Confidence. Where was he getting that confidence? he wondered.

"We got our backs against the wall," Ryan said. "Another push will knock us through the other side. And that'll give them the game. That'll give the guy who hurt David the game. Well, we're not going to let that happen. Not now. Not after what David just went through. That Lloyd is a maniac. He's a machine. But machines break down. They're going to give him the ball. And it's up to us to make him break down. Now."

He looked to the sideline and got the signals from the coordinator, then called them in the huddle. "Win on three," he said. "One, two, three—"

And his teammates shouted in chorus: *"Win!"*

"Just under a minute remains," Worthen said. "You know who's going to get the ball now. Mitchum hasn't had much success through the air, and now with David Falk out, you know Jacob Davis is salivating over the prospect of smashing it in from here with Julian Lloyd."

"That's exactly right," McMurry said. "This is a running back's dream, right here. Seventy thousand people know you're going to get the ball. This is where you have to make something happen. And right now, the defense is weakest right up the middle."

"Here we go," Worthen said. "Mitchum, I-formation. Snap—hand off, Lloyd running left, dropped inbounds after a five yard gain. The clock is running, and Mitchum brings them to the line. Same formation. Now pitches it to Lloyd. Runs right, slips a tackle, slams up to the six yardline. Five more yards, and that's a first down. Hurry-up offense. Mitchum drops back to pass this time. He throws into the end zone—incomplete with thirty-three seconds left. That brings up second and goal from the six."

They were lined up in a smash-mouth I-formation again, Ryan saw. "Watch the middle!" he shouted. The building excitement in the crowd made it hard for the defense to hear him, but he tried anyway.

Mitchum ran the silent count. Ryan stared at the center. The ball snapped back. The quarterback handed it to Lloyd, running straight up the middle behind a wall of blockers—

The wall collapsed, but one of the lineman accelerated and shoved Ryan away, and Lloyd slipped through, stopped by the strong safety and weakside linebacker at the one-yard line. The clock stopped with twenty-four seconds left as Mitchum burned his last timeout.

"Mitchum goes to the sideline," Worthen said. "He has a word with Davis, and now is returning to the huddle."

"Tough situation, here," McMurry said.

"Sure is," Worthen agreed. "I-formation again. Snap— play-action this time. Mitchum throws and the pass *skips* off of Moran's hands and falls incomplete. Clock stopped with twenty seconds left, but it makes no difference. They have to score on this play, as it is now fourth down."

Davis stood on the sideline as both Mitchum and Julian came over to him. "How are you, Julian?" he asked.

"Fine," the kid rasped. He didn't look fine, Davis thought. He was covered in a cold sweat, visible through padding and uniform, and his muscles looked tight, wound like a bunch of rubber bands. Or like a spring ready to explode.

"We're going to run Red Smash Fifteen," Davis said. "Go over the top if you have to, but don't stop until that ball crosses the goal line. Got it?"

Mitchum nodded. "Yeah. Julian?"

Julian nodded, but didn't answer.

He felt like a machine. He felt coiled like a snake. He felt like he could do whatever he wanted, however he wanted, whenever he wanted. And no one could stop him.

He felt like he was about to reach a breaking point.

Julian lined up, and focused his eyes ahead.

Here it comes.

The crowd was roaring, and the atmosphere tingled with

electricity. Everything was slow, except for the noise. Seventy thousand human beings screaming at the top of their lungs. Screaming for him, Ryan Walker, and the heroic defense to make one last play.

One last play, Ryan, and you can go home. You can go home for good. Forget the game. Forget coaching. Just go home.

He looked up into the stands. Vanessa was up there, he knew. Somewhere. Up there with the kids. Nothing could've kept them away from this game. . . . The last of his apprehension melted away.

"Set!"

Somehow, despite the incomprehensibly loud crowd noise, he could still hear Rich Mitchum's signals clearly.

"Hut! Hut! Hut!"

Slow motion. The lines slammed together, pads clapping together like a whale crashing into the waves, men screaming and shouting. Mitchum handed off to Lloyd, and Lloyd ran straight toward the middle of the line. Straight toward Ryan. There was no hole to run through, but plenty of air. Lloyd leapt, flying forward, the ball clenched between his gloved hands. Ryan sprinted toward the line and flung his own body up like a ballistic missile. A missile aimed at a missile, and the stakes were life and death. He collided with Lloyd in the air and wrapped his arms around him, holding on as tightly as he could, putting *everything* into it . . .

For a single surreal moment they both hung there. Then strength turned to weakness in Ryan's arms and he felt Lloyd falling backwards, crashing to the turf, the ball still clamped between his fists. Ryan landed on top of him, and rolled to the side onto his back. He got to his feet, searching desperately for a sign that he had succeeded. He heard Lloyd moan in agony, but his cries were drowned out by the crowd, and he saw the trainers running onto the field from the Gunners sideline. He saw the officials pry the ball from Lloyd's hands and step toward the end zone with it. His eyes followed them as they bent down and placed it on the turf.

At the one-yard line.

Twenty-six

The staff at New Orleans Charity Hospital was excellent, the doctors knowledgeable about—and all too experienced with—the tending to wounds obtained during the committing of a crime.

Sutton lay back in the hospital bed, his left shoulder wrapped over and over, feeling numb. His head was swimming a bit from the painkillers, but the bullet hadn't done major damage. A few days, and he'd be able to go back to St. Louis—by car. He wouldn't be able to fly yet, but he didn't like to fly anyway, so—

He shook his head, squinting against the bright light in the room. At least it helped to stop those rambling thoughts. . . .

He saw someone enter out of the corner of his eye. He turned—black hair, black sunglasses, black jacket—Cassie strode into the room in all her glory.

"You got no idea how hard it is to get a flight down here," she said, smiling and coming up beside the bed. She bent down and kissed his forehead. "How you doing?"

He waved his hand. "Fine. You know. Nothing major. She barely got me. Lucky shot."

"Right." Cassie gave a lopsided grin. "Guess what?"

Sutton closed his eyes, savoring the moment. "You got Jeanette Dean."

"Yep," Cassie said. "We got the word out to California. They picked her up in an apartment complex out there. She even admitted to sabotaging Dr. Hendley's car. They're checking to see if that Pollard guy had something to do with it. But apparently she got what she wanted."

"Revenge."

Cassie nodded. "Yeah. Revenge. I guess Dean was still a little bitter. If GLI went down, maybe she figured she'd get back at Moore. You want the rest of the news?"

"Shoot," Sutton said. At least it was good news.

"DA is launching a full-scale investigation of Petty and GLI," Cassie said. "The NFL is already looking into the Lloyd thing; turns out he really didn't know what they were doing to him. Poor guy was a little too trusting."

"Yeah."

Cassie sighed. "The ESPN people—"

Sutton looked at her. "ESPN people? You? ESPN?"

"—are saying, Petty will lose the team, and the Gunners will probably end up having salary cap room and draft picks taken away," Cassie continued.

"Salary cap room and draft picks?" Sutton said. "Cassie? Dear? Is that you?"

She chuckled. "Yeah, I watch a little football, Tony." She shrugged. "You know."

"I didn't," he said, admiring her newfound interest.

"You do now," she told him.

"What about GLI?" Sutton asked.

"Nicholas Nagel didn't know about what was going on," Cassie said. "He's working on correcting whatever the hell his people did to Lloyd right now. He's gonna lose his company, though. And the FDA *and* the SEC are both looking into HUMINT. Lance Pollard's shit up a creek."

Sutton smiled. "You see, Cass? This is why atheism is ridiculous. Who can say there's no all-just God out there now?" He sighed, and pursed his lips. "By the way . . . there are plenty of good restaurants down here. I hear Commander's Palace is one of the best. How about we . . . you know . . ."

"Go out?" Cassie asked, her eyebrows raised.

"Well," Sutton went on rapidly, "you know, after the shoulder is healed some, and if you want to, and it doesn't have to be a date—"

Cassie smiled. "Sure. What the hell."

Tony Sutton smiled back. "Yeah. What the hell."

He woke up, as if from a deep sleep full of nightmares. Above his bed he saw several people. His mother, a doctor, and a middle-aged guy he didn't recognize, with glasses and thin brown hair.

His mom called his name, and he looked up. He noticed tears streaming down her face. She leaned close to him and kissed his cheek.

"Are you feeling okay, baby?" she asked.

He *was* feeling okay, Julian realized, as if for the first time in a long time. "Yes, Ma," he said quietly. "I'm feeling okay."

His mother straightened up and took a step back. "Everything's okay. Dr. Nagel"—she glanced at the man with glasses—"was able to correct whatever those people did to you."

"I'm glad," Julian said, a weight lifting off his chest. He let his eyes scan the ceiling, then stared into space. "I guess it's over. For me, I mean." He said it more to himself than to anyone else.

"I believe it is," Dr. Nagel said. "Your body has sustained considerable damage."

He nodded, but the expected wave of depression never came. He almost felt a sense of . . . relief? Yes, relief. It was over. A nightmare he hadn't even known he was experiencing. Thank God, it was over.

"I wonder," he said, his voice a little louder, a little stronger, than before. "I wonder what I'm going to do now."

Jacklyn Lloyd smiled. "Actually, one of the coaches at USC called me the other day," she said. "He said he wants you to call him as soon as you're ready. They want you to be an assistant running backs coach."

"Even after . . . ?"

"Yes," Jacklyn said. "Even after. It wasn't your fault."

Julian shook his head, staring at the ceiling. "Yes, it was," he said. "I should've known, Ma. It was too perfect. I trusted the wrong people. I thought that . . . I thought they were out to help me. I thought . . ."

"Then learn a lesson from it, Julian," his mother said. "Don't be so trusting next time."

He nodded, and looked at her. He felt moisture in his eyes. "Yeah. I'm sorry, Ma."

She smiled. "Don't be sorry. Now, what about that job?"

Julian laughed behind his sudden tears. "I'm going to take it," he said.

Julian Lloyd To Take USC Coaching Position

Former Missouri Gunners running back Julian Lloyd has accepted an assistant coaching position with his alma mater, the University of Southern California. Lloyd will assist the current running backs position coach with his duties, and "learn the ropes," while working his way toward a possible higher level of responsibility in the near future . . . school officials are said to be very impressed with the embattled athlete's intelligence and willingness to learn. . . .

Walker To Retire

New Orleans Saints linebacker Ryan Walker has reportedly turned down an offer by head coach Gary Harrell to take an assistant coaching job. Walker, who retired from the playing field after his team's 23–10 loss in the NFC Championship Game last season, stated that, although he loves the game of football, he "loves his family more," and wants to spend more time with his wife and children. Walker's career culminated in the heroic last play in Week 17 that gave his team a playoff berth. He did not rule out a possible future coaching position.

Genetic Modification Fiasco
Reaps Stern Response From NFL

In the aftermath of the shocking developments of the

last football season, the NFL is taking the first three rounds of the next three years' drafts from the Missouri Gunners. This comes on the heals of Vincent Petty's forced removal as owner. The team will be sold, according to League sources. In related news, authorities announced the arrest of Dr. Paul Franklin of the now-bankrupt Genetics Life, Inc. on charges of assisting in the illegal enhancement of Julian Lloyd's athletic abilities. Also, the alleged murderer of former APEX director Dr. Eric Hendley, Jeanette Dean, will be put on trial sometime next month. Sources say the prosecution is highly confident in its case.

Your Favorite Thriller Authors
Are Now Just A Phone Call Away

Get Hooked on the
Mysteries of
Jonnie Jacobs

Mischief, Murder &
Mayhem – Grab These
Kensington Mysteries